SELECTEI

SELECTED STORIES

DOVER THRIFT EDITIONS

Sherwood Anderson

DOVER PUBLICATIONS, INC.
MINEOLA, NEW YORK

DOVER THRIFT EDITIONS

GENERAL EDITOR: SUSAN L. RATTINER
EDITOR OF THIS VOLUME: MICHAEL CROLAND

Copyright

Bibliographical Note

This Dover edition, first published in 2020, is an unabridged republication of eleven stories that originally appeared in *The Triumph of the Egg: A Book of Impressions from American Life in Tales and Poems*, published in 1921, and *Horses and Men: Tales, Long and Short, from Our American Life*, published in 1923, both published by B.W. Huebsch, Inc., New York. Readers should be forewarned that the text contains racial and cultural references of the era in which it was written and may be deemed offensive by today's standards. A new introductory Note has been specially prepared for this edition.

Library of Congress Cataloging-in-Publication Data

Names: Anderson, Sherwood, 1876–1941, author.
Title: Selected stories / Sherwood Anderson.
Description: Mineola, New York : Dover Publications, Inc., 2020. | Series: Dover thrift editions | This Dover edition, first published in 2020, is an unabridged republication of eleven stories that originally appeared in The Triumph of the Egg: A Book of Impressions from American Life in Tales and Poems, published in 1921, and Horses and Men: Tales, Long and Short, from Our American Life, published in 1923, both published by B.W. Huebsch, Inc., New York. A new introductory Note has been specially prepared for this edition. | Summary: "Written in a seemingly simple narrative style, Sherwood Anderson's slice-of-life stories often explored the undercurrents of small-town life, illuminating the loneliness and frustration of that isolated world"—Provided by publisher.
Identifiers: LCCN 2019028855 | ISBN 9780486836393 (trade paperback) | ISBN 0486836398 (trade paperback)
Classification: LCC PS3501.N4 A6 2020 | DDC 813/.52—dc23
LC record available at https://lccn.loc.gov/2019028855

Manufactured in the United States by LSC Communications
83639801
www.doverpublications.com

2 4 6 8 10 9 7 5 3 1

2019

Note

SHERWOOD ANDERSON WAS born in 1876 and grew up in Clyde, Ohio, as one of seven children. He attended school on and off and labored as a newsboy, house painter, farmhand, and racetrack helper. After spending one year in a preparatory school, he dropped out at age nineteen following his mother's death.

Anderson moved to Chicago and worked as an advertising writer. In 1906, he returned to Ohio and worked as a businessman while writing fiction on the side. In 1912, he abruptly wandered away from the paint factory he owned; he showed up at a hospital four days later. After this breakdown, he left his wife and children, went back to Chicago, and devoted his life to writing.

Anderson joined Chicago's literary scene and wrote experimental verse and short fiction for *The Little Review*, *The Masses*, the *Seven Arts*, and *Poetry*. He published his first two novels, *Windy McPherson's Son* and *Marching Men*, in 1916 and 1917, respectively. In 1919, he published his best-known book, *Winesburg, Ohio*, in which a newspaper reporter narrates short stories about people in a small town.

Anderson's short stories are often regarded as his best work. His slice-of-life stories frequently explore the loneliness and frustrations of small-town life. He published several short story collections, including *The Triumph of the Egg* (1921) and *Horses and Men* (1923)—the two books that the stories in the present volume originally appeared in—as well as *Death in the Woods and Other Stories* (1933).

Anderson was prolific in numerous genres. His later novels include *Many Marriages* (1923), *Dark Laughter* (1925), and *Beyond Desire* (1932). His poetry collections are *Mid-American Chants* (1918) and *A New Testament* (1927). His autobiographical works are *A Story Teller's Story* (1924), *Tar: A Midwest Childhood* (1926), and *Memoirs*

(1942). His *Letters* came out in 1953. The latter two books were published posthumously.

Toward the end of his life, Anderson moved to Marion, Virginia. He bought and ran two local newspapers—one Democrat and one Republican—which he wrote for under the pseudonym Buck Fever. In 1941, while on vacation in Panama, he died of peritonitis when a broken toothpick got into his intestines.

Anderson was highly influential, inspiring William Faulkner, Thomas Wolfe, and Ernest Hemingway. His writing is remembered for its colloquial prose and its exploration of gender and sexuality. The writer H. L. Mencken called Anderson "America's most distinguished novelist."

Contents

Out of Nowhere into Nothing

CHAPTER I

ROSALIND WESCOTT, a tall strong looking woman of twenty-seven, was walking on the railroad track near the town of Willow Springs, Iowa. It was about four in the afternoon of a day in August, and the third day since she had come home to her native town from Chicago, where she was employed.

At that time Willow Springs was a town of about three thousand people. It has grown since. There was a public square with the town hall in the centre and about the four sides of the square and facing it were the merchandising establishments. The public square was bare and grassless, and out of it ran streets of frame houses, long straight streets that finally became country roads running away into the flat prairie country.

Although she had told everyone that she had merely come home for a short visit because she was a little homesick, and although she wanted in particular to have a talk with her mother in regard to a certain matter, Rosalind had been unable to talk with anyone. Indeed she had found it difficult to stay in the house with her mother and father and all the time, day and night, she was haunted by a desire to get out of town. As she went along the railroad tracks in the hot afternoon sunshine she kept scolding herself. "I've grown moody and no good. If I want to do it why don't I just go ahead and not make a fuss," she thought.

For two miles the railroad tracks, eastward out of Willow Springs, went through corn fields on a flat plain. Then there was a little dip in the land and a bridge over Willow Creek. The Creek was altogether dry now but trees grew along the edge of the grey streak of cracked

1

mud that in the fall, winter and spring would be the bed of the stream. Rosalind left the tracks and went to sit under one of the trees. Her cheeks were flushed and her forehead wet. When she took off her hat her hair fell down in disorder and strands of it clung to her hot wet face. She sat in what seemed a kind of great bowl on the sides of which the corn grew rank. Before her and following the bed of the stream there was a dusty path along which cows came at evening from distant pastures. A great pancake formed of cow dung lay nearby. It was covered with grey dust and over it crawled shiny black beetles. They were rolling the dung into balls in preparation for the germination of a new generation of beetles.

Rosalind had come on the visit to her home town at a time of the year when everyone wished to escape from the hot dusty place. No one had expected her and she had not written to announce her coming. One hot morning in Chicago she had got out of bed and had suddenly begun packing her bag, and on that same evening there she was in Willow Springs, in the house where she had lived until her twenty-first year, among her own people. She had come up from the station in the hotel bus and had walked into the Wescott house unannounced. Her father was at the pump by the kitchen door and her mother came into the living room to greet her wearing a soiled kitchen apron. Everything in the house was just as it always had been. "I just thought I would come home for a few days," she said, putting down her bag and kissing her mother.

Ma and Pa Wescott had been glad to see their daughter. On the evening of her arrival they were excited and a special supper was prepared. After supper Pa Wescott went up town as usual, but he stayed only a few minutes. "I just want to run to the postoffice and get the evening paper," he said apologetically. Rosalind's mother put on a clean dress and they all sat in the darkness on the front porch. There was talk, of a kind. "Is it hot in Chicago now? I'm going to do a good deal of canning this fall. I thought later I would send you a box of canned fruit. Do you live in the same place on the North Side? It must be nice in the evening to be able to walk down to the park by the lake."

Rosalind sat under the tree near the railroad bridge two miles from Willow Springs and watched the tumble bugs at work. Her whole body was hot from the walk in the sun and the thin dress she wore clung to her legs. It was being soiled by the dust on the grass under the tree.

She had run away from town and from her mother's house. All during the three days of her visit she had been doing that. She did not go from house to house to visit her old schoolgirl friends, the girls who unlike herself had stayed in Willow Springs, had got married and settled down there. When she saw one of these women on the street in the morning, pushing a baby carriage and perhaps followed by a small child, she stopped. There was a few minutes of talk. "It's hot. Do you live in the same place in Chicago? My husband and I hope to take the children and go away for a week or two. It must be nice in Chicago where you are so near the lake." Rosalind hurried away.

All the hours of her visit to her mother and to her home town had been spent in an effort to hurry away.

From what? Rosalind defended herself. There was something she had come from Chicago hoping to be able to say to her mother. Did she really want to talk with her about things? Had she thought, by again breathing the air of her home town, to get strength to face life and its difficulties?

There was no point in her taking the hot uncomfortable trip from Chicago only to spend her days walking in dusty country roads or between rows of cornfields in the stifling heat along the railroad tracks.

"I must have hoped. There is a hope that cannot be fulfilled," she thought vaguely.

Willow Springs was a rather meaningless, dreary town, one of thousands of such towns in Indiana, Illinois, Wisconsin, Kansas, Iowa, but her mind made it more dreary.

She sat under the tree by the dry bed of Willow Creek thinking of the street in town where her mother and father lived, where she had lived until she had become a woman. It was only because of a series of circumstances she did not live there now. Her one brother, ten years older than herself, had married and moved to Chicago. He had asked her to come for a visit and after she got to the city she stayed. Her brother was a traveling salesman and spent a good deal of time away from home. "Why don't you stay here with Bess and learn stenography," he asked. "If you don't want to use it you don't have to. Dad can look out for you all right. I just thought you might like to learn."

"That was six years ago," Rosalind thought wearily. "I've been a city woman for six years." Her mind hopped about. Thoughts came and went. In the city, after she became a stenographer, something

for a time awakened her. She wanted to be an actress and
went in the evening to a dramatic school. In an office where she
worked there was a young man, a clerk. They went out together, to
the theatre or to walk in the park in the evening. They kissed.

Her thoughts came sharply back to her mother and father, to her
home in Willow Springs, to the street in which she had lived until
her twenty-first year.

It was but an end of a street. From the windows at the front of
her mother's house six other houses could be seen. How well she
knew the street and the people in the houses! Did she know them?
From her eighteenth and until her twenty-first year she had stayed
at home, helping her mother with the housework, waiting for something. Other young women in town waited just as she did. They
like herself had graduated from the town highschool and their
parents had no intention of sending them away to college. There
was nothing to do but wait. Some of the young women—their
mothers and their mothers' friends still spoke of them as girls—had
young men friends who came to see them on Sunday and perhaps
also on Wednesday or Thursday evenings. Others joined the church,
went to prayer meetings, became active members of some church
organization. They fussed about.

Rosalind had done none of these things. All through those three
trying years in Willow Springs she had just waited. In the morning
there was the work to do in the house and then, in some way, the
day wore itself away. In the evening her father went up town and
she sat with her mother. Nothing much was said. After she had gone
to bed she lay awake, strangely nervous, eager for something to
happen that never would happen. The noises of the Wescott house
cut across her thoughts. What things went through her mind!

There was a procession of people always going away from her.
Sometimes she lay on her belly at the edge of a ravine. Well it was
not a ravine. It had two walls of marble and on the marble face of
the walls strange figures were carved. Broad steps led down—always
down and away. People walked along the steps, between the marble
walls, going down and away from her.

What people! Who were they? Where did they come from? Where
were they going? She was not asleep but wide awake. Her bedroom
was dark. The walls and ceiling of the room receded. She seemed to
hang suspended in space, above the ravine—the ravine with walls of
white marble over which strange beautiful lights played.

The people who went down the broad steps and away into infinite distance—they were men and women. Sometimes a young girl like herself but in some way sweeter and purer than herself, passed alone. The young girl walked with a swinging stride, going swiftly and freely like a beautiful young animal. Her legs and arms were like the slender top branches of trees swaying in a gentle wind. She also went down and away.

Others followed along the marble steps. Young boys walked alone. A dignified old man followed by a sweet faced woman passed. What a remarkable man! One felt infinite power in his old frame. There were deep wrinkles in his face and his eyes were sad. One felt he knew everything about life but had kept something very precious alive in himself. It was that precious thing that made the eyes of the woman who followed him burn with a strange fire. They also went down along the steps and away.

Down and away along the steps went others—how many others, men and women, boys and girls, single old men, old women who leaned on sticks and hobbled along.

In the bed in her father's house as she lay awake Rosalind's head grew light. She tried to clutch at something, understand something.

She couldn't. The noises of the house cut across her waking dream. Her father was at the pump by the kitchen door. He was pumping a pail of water. In a moment he would bring it into the house and put it on a box by the kitchen sink. A little of the water would slop over on the floor. There would be a sound like a child's bare foot striking the floor. Then her father would go to wind the clock. The day was done. Presently there would be the sound of his heavy feet on the floor of the bedroom above and he would get into bed to lie beside Rosalind's mother.

The night noises of her father's house had been in some way terrible to the girl in the years when she was becoming a woman. After chance had taken her to the city she never wanted to think of them again. Even in Chicago where the silence of nights was cut and slashed by a thousand noises, by automobiles whirling through the streets, by the belated footsteps of men homeward bound along the cement sidewalks after midnight, by the shouts of quarreling men drunk on summer nights, even in the great hubbub of noises there was comparative quiet. The insistent clanging noises of the city nights were not like the homely insistent noises of her father's house. Certain terrible truths about life did not abide in them, they did not cling so closely to life and did not frighten as did the noises in the one house on the quiet street in the town of Willow Springs. How often, there in the city, in the midst of the great noises she had fought to escape the little noises! Her father's feet were on the steps leading into the kitchen. Now he was putting the pail of water on the box by the kitchen sink. Upstairs her mother's body fell heavily into bed. The visions of the great marble-lined ravine down along which went the beautiful people flew away. There was the little slap of water on the kitchen floor. It was like a child's bare foot striking the floor. Rosalind wanted to cry out. Her father closed the kitchen door. Now he was winding the clock. In a moment his feet would be on the stairs—

There were six houses to be seen from the windows of the Wescott house. In the winter smoke from six brick chimneys went up into the sky. There was one house, the next one to the Wescott's place, a small frame affair, in which lived a man who was thirty-five years old when Rosalind became a woman of twenty-one and went away to the city. The man was unmarried and his mother, who had been his housekeeper, had died during the year in which Rosalind graduated from the high school. After that the man lived alone. He took his dinner and supper at the hotel, down town on the square, but he got his own breakfast, made his own bed and swept out his own house. Sometimes he walked slowly along the street past the Wescott house when Rosalind sat alone on the front porch. He raised his hat and spoke to her. Their eyes met. He had a long, hawklike nose and his hair was long and uncombed.

Rosalind thought about him sometimes. It bothered her a little that he sometimes went stealing softly, as though not to disturb her, across her daytime fancies.

As she sat that day by the dry creek bed Rosalind thought about the bachelor, who had now passed the age of forty and who lived on the street where she had lived during her girlhood. His house was separated from the Wescott house by a picket fence. Sometimes in the morning he forgot to pull his blinds and Rosalind, busy with the housework in her father's house, had seen him walking about in his underwear. It was—uh, one could not think of it.

The man's name was Melville Stoner. He had a small income and did not have to work. On some days he did not leave his house and go to the hotel for his meals but sat all day in a chair with his nose buried in a book.

There was a house on the street occupied by a widow who raised chickens. Two or three of her hens were what the people who lived on the street called "high flyers." They flew over the fence of the chicken yard and escaped and almost always they came at once into the yard of the bachelor. The neighbors laughed about it. It was significant, they felt. When the hens had come into the yard of the bachelor, Stoner, the widow with a stick in her hand ran after them. Melville Stoner came out of his house and stood on a little porch in front. The widow ran through the front gate waving her arms wildly and the hens made a great racket and flew over the fence. They ran down the street toward the widow's house. For a moment she stood by the Stoner gate. In the summer time when the windows of the Wescott house were open Rosalind could hear what the man and woman said to each other. In Willow Springs it was not thought proper for an unmarried woman to stand talking to an unmarried man near the door of his bachelor establishment. The widow wanted to observe the conventions. Still she did linger a moment, her bare arm resting on the gate post. What bright eager little eyes she had! "If those hens of mine bother you I wish you would catch them and kill them," she said fiercely. "I am always glad to see them coming along the road," Melville Stoner replied, bowing. Rosalind thought he was making fun of the widow. She liked him for that. "I'd never see you if you did not have to come here after your hens. Don't let anything happen to them," he said, bowing again.

For a moment the man and woman lingered looking into each other's eyes. From one of the windows of the Wescott house Rosalind watched the woman. Nothing more was said. There was something about the woman she had not understood—well the widow's senses were being fed. The developing woman in the house next door had hated her.

Rosalind jumped up from under the tree and climbed up the railroad embankment. She thanked the gods she had been lifted out of the life of the town of Willow Springs and that chance had set her down to live in a city. "Chicago is far from beautiful. People say it is just a big noisy dirty village and perhaps that's what it is, but there is something alive there," she thought. In Chicago, or at least during the last two or three years of her life there, Rosalind felt she had learned a little something of life. She had read books for one thing, such books as did not come to Willow Springs, books that Willow

Springs knew nothing about, she had gone to hear the Symphony Orchestra, she had begun to understand something of the possibility of line and color, had heard intelligent, understanding men speak of these things. In Chicago, in the midst of the twisting squirming millions of men and women there were voices. One occasionally saw men or at least heard of the existence of men who, like the beautiful old man who had walked away down the marble stairs in the vision of her girlhood nights, had kept some precious thing alive in themselves.

And there was something else—it was the most important thing of all. For the last two years of her life in Chicago she had spent hours, days in the presence of a man to whom she could talk. The talks had awakened her. She felt they had made her a woman, had matured her.

"I know what these people here in Willow Springs are like and what I would have been like had I stayed here," she thought. She felt relieved and almost happy. She had come home at a crisis of her own life hoping to be able to talk a little with her mother, or if talk proved impossible hoping to get some sense of sisterhood by being in her presence. She had thought there was something buried away, deep within every woman, that at a certain call would run out to other women. Now she felt that the hope, the dream, the desire she had cherished was altogether futile. Sitting in the great flat bowl in the midst of the corn lands two miles from her home town where no breath of air stirred and seeing the beetles at their work of preparing to propagate a new generation of beetles, while she thought of the town and its people, had settled something for her. Her visit to Willow Springs had come to something after all.

Rosalind's figure had still much of the spring and swing of youth in it. Her legs were strong and her shoulders broad. She went swinging along the railroad track toward town, going westward. The sun had begun to fall rapidly down the sky. Away over the tops of the corn in one of the great fields she could see in the distance to where a man was driving a motor along a dusty road. The wheels of the car kicked up dust through which the sunlight played. The floating cloud of dust became a shower of gold that settled down over the fields. "When a woman most wants what is best and truest in another woman, even in her own mother, she isn't likely to find it," she thought grimly. "There are certain things every woman has to find out for herself, there is a road she must travel alone. It may only lead to some more ugly and terrible place, but if she doesn't want death to overtake her and live within her while her body is still alive she must set out on that road."

Rosalind walked for a mile along the railroad track and then stopped. A freight train had gone eastward as she sat under the tree by the creek bed and now, there beside the tracks, in the grass was the body of a man. It lay still, the face buried in the deep burned grass. At once she concluded the man had been struck and killed by the train. The body had been thrown thus aside. All her thoughts went away and she turned and started to tiptoe away, stepping carefully along the railroad ties, making no noise. Then she stopped again. The man in the grass might not be dead, only hurt, terribly hurt. It would not do to leave him there. She imagined him mutilated but still struggling for life and herself trying to help him. She crept back along the ties. The man's legs were not twisted and beside him lay his hat. It was as though he had put it there before lying down to sleep, but a man did not sleep with his face buried in the grass in such a hot uncomfortable place. She drew nearer. "O, you Mister," she called, "O, you—are you hurt?"

The man in the grass sat up and looked at her. He laughed. It was Melville Stoner, the man of whom she had just been thinking and in thinking of whom she had come to certain settled conclusions regarding the futility of her visit to Willow Springs. He got to his feet and picked up his hat. "Well, hello, Miss Rosalind Wescott," he said heartily. He climbed a small embankment and stood beside her. "I knew you were at home on a visit but what are you doing out here?" he asked and then added, "What luck this is! Now I shall have the privilege of walking home with you. You can hardly refuse to let me walk with you after shouting at me like that."

They walked together along the tracks he with his hat in his hand. Rosalind thought he looked like a gigantic bird, an aged wise old bird, "perhaps a vulture" she thought. For a time he was silent and then he began to talk, explaining his lying with his face buried in the grass. There was a twinkle in his eyes and Rosalind wondered if he was laughing at her as she had seen him laugh at the widow who owned the hens.

He did not come directly to the point and Rosalind thought it strange that they should walk and talk together. At once his words interested her. He was so much older than herself and no doubt wiser. How vain she had been to think herself so much more knowing than all the people of Willow Springs. Here was this man and he was talking and his talk did not sound like anything she had ever expected to hear from the lips of a native of her home town. "I want to explain myself but we'll wait a little. For years I've been wanting to get at you, to talk with you, and this is my chance. You've been away now five or six years and have grown into womanhood.

"You understand it's nothing specially personal, my wanting to get at you and understand you a little," he added quickly. "I'm that way about everyone. Perhaps that's the reason I live alone, why I've never married or had personal friends. I'm too eager. It isn't comfortable to others to have me about."

Rosalind was caught up by this new view point of the man. She wondered. In the distance along the tracks the houses of the town came into sight. Melville Stoner tried to walk on one of the iron rails but after a few steps lost his balance and fell off. His long arms whirled about. A strange intensity of mood and feeling had come over Rosalind. In one moment Melville Stoner was like an old man and then he was like a boy. Being with him made her mind, that had been racing all afternoon, race faster than ever.

When he began to talk again he seemed to have forgotten the explanation he had intended making. "We've lived side by side but we've hardly spoken to each other," he said. "When I was a young man and you were a girl I used to sit in the house thinking of you. We've really been friends. What I mean is we've had the same thoughts."

He began to speak of life in the city where she had been living, condemning it. "It's dull and stupid here but in the city you have your own kind of stupidity too," he declared. "I'm glad I do not live there."

In Chicago when she had first gone there to live a thing had sometimes happened that had startled Rosalind. She knew no one but her brother and his wife and was sometimes very lonely. When she could no longer bear the eternal sameness of the talk in her brother's house she went out to a concert or to the theatre. Once or twice when she had no money to buy a theatre ticket she grew bold and walked alone in the streets, going rapidly along without looking to the right or left. As she sat in the theatre or walked in the street an odd thing sometimes happened. Someone spoke her name, a call came to her. The thing happened at a concert and she looked quickly about. All the faces in sight had that peculiar, half bored, half expectant expression one grows accustomed to seeing on the faces of people listening to music. In the entire theatre no one seemed aware of her. On the street or in the park the call had come when she was utterly alone. It seemed to come out of the air, from behind a tree in the park.

And now as she walked on the railroad tracks with Melville Stoner the call seemed to come from him. He walked along apparently absorbed with his own thoughts, the thoughts he was trying to find words to express. His legs were long and he walked with a queer loping gait. The idea of some great bird, perhaps a sea-bird stranded far inland, stayed in Rosalind's mind but the call did not come from the bird part of him. There was something else, another personality hidden away. Rosalind fancied the call came this time from a young boy, from such another clear-eyed boy as she had once seen in her waking dreams at night in her father's house, from one of the boys who walked on the marble stairway, walked down and away. A thought came that startled her. "The boy is hidden away in the body of this strange bird-like man," she told herself. The thought awoke fancies within her. It explained much in the lives of men and women. An expression, a phrase, remembered from her childhood when she had gone to Sunday School in Willow Springs, came back to her mind. "And God spoke to me out of a burning bush." She almost said the words aloud.

Melville Stoner loped along, walking on the railroad ties and talking. He seemed to have forgotten the incident of his lying with his nose buried in the grass and was explaining his life lived alone in the house in town. Rosalind tried to put her own thoughts aside and to listen to his words but did not succeed very well. "I came home here hoping to get a little closer to life, to get, for a few days, out of the company of a man so I could think about him. I fancied I could get what I wanted by being near mother, but that hasn't worked. It would be strange if I got what I am looking for by this chance meeting with another man," she thought. Her mind went on recording thoughts. She heard the spoken words of the man beside her but her own mind went on, also making words. Something within herself felt suddenly relaxed and free. Ever since she had got off the train at Willow Springs three days before there had been a great tenseness. Now it was all gone. She looked at Melville Stoner who occasionally looked at her. There was something in his eyes, a kind of laughter— a mocking kind of laughter. His eyes were grey, of a cold greyness, like the eyes of a bird.

"It has come into my mind—I have been thinking—well you see you have not married in the six years since you went to live in the city. It would be strange and a little amusing if you are like myself, if you cannot marry or come close to any other person," he was saying.

Again he spoke of the life he led in his house. "I sometimes sit in my house all day, even when the weather is fine outside," he said. "You have no doubt seen me sitting there. Sometimes I forget to eat. I read books all day, striving to forget myself and then night comes and I cannot sleep.

"If I could write or paint or make music, if I cared at all about expressing what goes on in my mind it would be different. However, I would not write as others do. I would have but little to say about what people do. What do they do? In what way does it matter? Well you see they build cities such as you live in and towns like Willow Springs, they have built this railroad track on which we are walking, they marry and raise children, commit murders, steal, do kindly acts. What does it matter? You see we are walking here in the hot sun. In five minutes more we will be in town and you will go to your house and I to mine. You will eat supper with your father and mother. Then your father will go up town and you and your mother will sit together on the front porch. There will be little said. Your mother will speak of her intention to can fruit. Then your father will come home and you will all go to bed. Your father will pump a pail of water at the pump by the kitchen door. He will carry it indoors and put it on a box by the kitchen sink. A little of the water will be spilled. It will make a soft little slap on the kitchen floor—"

"Ha!"

Melville Stoner turned and looked sharply at Rosalind who had grown a little pale. Her mind raced madly, like an engine out of control. There was a kind of power in Melville Stoner that frightened her. By the recital of a few commonplace facts he had suddenly invaded her secret places. It was almost as though he had come into the bedroom in her father's house where she lay thinking. He had in fact got into her bed. He laughed again, an unmirthful laugh. "I'll tell you what, we know little enough here in America, either in the towns or in the cities," he said rapidly. "We are all on the rush. We are all for action. I sit still and think. If I wanted to write I'd do something. I'd tell what everyone thought. It would startle people, frighten them a little, eh? I would tell you what you have been thinking this afternoon while you walked here on this railroad track with me. I would tell you what your mother has been thinking at the same time and what she would like to say to you."

Rosalind's face had grown chalky white and her hands trembled. They got off the railroad tracks and into the streets of Willow Springs. A change came over Melville Stoner. Of a sudden he seemed just a man of forty, a little embarrassed by the presence of the younger woman, a little hesitant. "I'm going to the hotel now and I must leave you here," he said. His feet made a shuffling sound on the sidewalk. "I intended to tell you why you found me lying out there with my face buried in the grass," he said. A new quality had come into his voice. It was the voice of the boy who had called to Rosalind out of the body of the man as they walked and talked on the tracks. "Sometimes I can't stand my life here," he said almost fiercely and waved his long arms about. "I'm alone too much. I grow to hate myself. I have to run out of town."

The man did not look at Rosalind but at the ground. His big feet continued shuffling nervously about. "Once in the winter time I thought I was going insane," he said. "I happened to remember an orchard, five miles from town where I had walked one day in the late fall when the pears were ripe. A notion came into my head. It was bitter cold but I walked the five miles and went into the orchard. The ground was frozen and covered with snow but I brushed the snow aside. I pushed my face into the grass. In the fall when I had walked there the ground was covered with ripe pears. A fragrance arose from them. They were covered with bees that crawled over them, drunk, filled with a kind of ecstasy. I had remembered the fragrance. That's why I went there and put my face into the frozen grass. The bees were in an ecstasy of life and I had missed life. I have always missed life. It always goes away from me. I always imagined people walking away. In the spring this year I walked on the railroad track out to the bridge over Willow Creek. Violets grew in the grass. At that time I hardly noticed them but today I remembered. The violets were like the people who walk away from me. A mad desire to run after them had take possession of me. I felt like a bird flying through space. A conviction that something had escaped me and that I must pursue it had taken possession of me."

Melville Stoner stopped talking. His face also had grown white and his hands also trembled. Rosalind had an almost irresistible desire to put out her hand and touch his hand. She wanted to shout, crying— "I am here. I am not dead. I am alive." Instead she stood in silence, staring at him, as the widow who owned the high flying hens had stared. Melville Stoner struggled to recover from the ecstasy

into which he had been thrown by his own words. He bowed and
smiled. "I hope you are in the habit of walking on railroad tracks,"
he said. "I shall in the future know what to do with my time. When
you come to town I shall camp on the railroad tracks. No doubt,
like the violets, you have left your fragrance out there." Rosalind
looked at him. He was laughing at her as he had laughed when he
talked to the widow standing at his gate. She did not mind. When
he had left her she went slowly through the streets. The phrase
that had come into her mind as they walked on the tracks came back
and she said it over and over. "And God spoke to me out of a burning bush." She kept repeating the phrase until she got back into the
Wescott house.

Rosalind sat on the front porch of the house where her girlhood had
been spent. Her father had not come home for the evening meal.
He was a dealer in coal and lumber and owned a number of unpainted
sheds facing a railroad siding west of town. There was a tiny office
with a stove and a desk in a corner by a window. The desk was piled
high with unanswered letters and with circulars from mining and
lumber companies. Over them had settled a thick layer of coal dust.
All day he sat in his office looking like an animal in a cage, but unlike
a caged animal he was apparently not discontented and did not grow
restless. He was the one coal and lumber dealer in Willow Springs.
When people wanted one of these commodities they had to come
to him. There was no other place to go. He was content. In the
morning as soon as he got to his office he read the Des Moines paper
and then if no one came to disturb him he sat all day, by the stove
in winter and by an open window through the long hot summer
days, apparently unaffected by the marching change of seasons pictured in the fields, without thought, without hope, without regret
that life was becoming an old worn out thing for him.

   In the Wescott house Rosalind's mother had already begun the
canning of which she had several times spoken. She was making
gooseberry jam. Rosalind could hear the pots boiling in the
kitchen. Her mother walked heavily. With the coming of age she
was beginning to grow fat.

   The daughter was weary from much thinking. It had been a day
of many emotions. She took off her hat and laid it on the porch
beside her. Melville Stoner's house next door had windows that were
like eyes staring at her, accusing her. "Well now, you see, you have
gone too fast," the house declared. It sneered at her. "You thought

you knew about people. After all you knew nothing." Rosalind held her head in her hands. It was true she had misunderstood. The man who lived in the house was no doubt like other people in Willow Springs. He was not, as she had smartly supposed, a dull citizen of a dreary town, one who knew nothing of life. Had he not said words that had startled her, torn her out of herself?

Rosalind had an experience not uncommon to tired nervous people. Her mind, weary of thinking, did not stop thinking but went on faster than ever. A new plane of thought was reached. Her mind was like a flying machine that leaves the ground and leaps into the air.

It took hold upon an idea expressed or implied in something Melville Stoner had said. "In every human being there are two voices, each striving to make itself heard."

A new world of thought had opened itself before her. After all human beings might be understood. It might be possible to understand her mother and her mother's life, her father, the man she loved, herself. There was the voice that said words. Words came forth from lips. They conformed, fell into a certain mold. For the most part the words had no life of their own. They had come down out of old times and many of them were no doubt once strong living words, coming out of the depth of people, out of the bellies of people. The words had escaped out of a shut-in place. They had once expressed living truth. Then they had gone on being said, over and over, by the lips of many people, endlessly, wearily.

She thought of men and women she had seen together, that she had heard talking together as they sat in the street cars or in apartments or walked in a Chicago park. Her brother, the traveling salesman, and his wife had talked half wearily through the long evenings she had spent with them in their apartment. It was with them as with the other people. A thing happened. The lips said certain words but the eyes of the people said other words. Sometimes the lips expressed affection while hatred shone out of the eyes. Sometimes it was the other way about. What a confusion!

It was clear there was something hidden away within people that could not get itself expressed except accidentally. One was startled or alarmed and then the words that fell from the lips became pregnant words, words that lived.

The vision that had sometimes visited her in her girlhood as she lay in bed at night came back. Again she saw the people on the marble stairway, going down and away, into infinity. Her own mind began to make words that struggled to get themselves expressed through her lips. She hungered for someone to whom to say the words and half arose to go to her mother, to where her mother was making gooseberry jam in the kitchen, and then sat down again. "They were going down into the hall of the hidden voices," she whispered to herself. The words excited and intoxicated her as had the words from the lips of Melville Stoner. She thought of herself as having quite suddenly grown amazingly, spiritually, even physically. She felt relaxed, young, wonderfully strong. She imagined herself as walking, as had the young girl she had seen in the vision, with swinging arms and shoulders, going down a marble stairway—down into the hidden places in people, into the hall of the little voices. "I shall understand after this, what shall I not understand?" she asked herself.

Doubt came and she trembled a little. As she walked with him on the railroad track Melville Stoner had gone down within herself. Her body was a house, through the door of which he had walked. He had known about the night noises in her father's house— her father at the well by the kitchen door, the slap of the spilled water on the floor. Even when she was a young girl and had thought herself alone in the bed in the darkness in the room upstairs in the house before which she now sat, she had not been alone. The strange bird-like man who lived in the house next door had been with her, in her room, in her bed. Years later he had remembered the terrible little noises of the house and had known how they had terrified her. There was something terrible in his knowledge too. He had spoken, given forth his knowledge, but as he did so there was laughter in his eyes, perhaps a sneer.

In the Wescott house the sounds of housekeeping went on. A man who had been at work in a distant field, who had already begun his fall plowing, was unhitching his horses from the plow. He was far away, beyond the street's end, in a field that swelled a little out of the plain. Rosalind stared. The man was hitching the horses to a wagon. She saw him as through the large end of a telescope. He would drive the horses away to a distant farmhouse and put them into a barn. Then he would go into a house where there was a woman at work. Perhaps the woman like her mother would be making gooseberry jam. He would grunt as her father did when at evening he came home from the little hot office by the railroad siding. "Hello," he would say, flatly, indifferently, stupidly. Life was like that.

Rosalind became weary of thinking. The man in the distant field had got into his wagon and was driving away. In a moment there would be nothing left of him but a thin cloud of dust that floated in the air. In the house the gooseberry jam had boiled long enough.

Her mother was preparing to put it into glass jars. The operation produced a new little side current of sounds. She thought again of Melville Stoner. For years he had been sitting, listening to sounds. There was a kind of madness in it.

She had got herself into a half frenzied condition. "I must stop it," she told herself. "I am like a stringed instrument on which the strings have been tightened too much." She put her face into her hands, wearily.

And then a thrill ran through her body. There was a reason for Melville Stoner's being what he had become. There was a locked gateway leading to the marble stairway that led down and away, into infinity, into the hall of the little voices and the key to the gateway was love. Warmth came back into Rosalind's body. "Understanding need not lead to weariness," she thought. Life might after all be a rich, a triumphant thing. She would make her visit to Willow Springs count for something significant in her life. For one thing she would really approach her mother, she would walk into her mother's life. "It will be my first trip down the marble stairway," she thought and tears came to her eyes. In a moment her father would be coming home for the evening meal but after supper he would go away. The two women would be alone together. Together they would explore a little into the mystery of life, they would find sisterhood. The thing she had wanted to talk about with another understanding woman could be talked about then. There might yet be a beautiful outcome to her visit to Willow Springs and to her mother.

CHAPTER II

THE STORY OF Rosalind's six years in Chicago is the story of thousands of unmarried women who work in offices in the city. Necessity had not driven her to work nor kept her at her task and she did not think of herself as a worker, one who would always be a worker. For a time after she came out of the stenographic school she drifted from office to office, acquiring always more skill, but with no particular interest in what she was doing. It was a way to put in the long days. Her father, who in addition to the coal and lumber yards owned three farms, sent her a hundred dollars a month. The money her work brought was spent for clothes so that she dressed better than the women she worked with.

Of one thing she was quite sure. She did not want to return to Willow Springs to live with her father and mother, and after a time she knew she could not continue living with her brother and his wife. For the first time she began seeing the city that spread itself out before her eyes. When she walked at the noon hour along Michigan Boulevard or went into a restaurant or in the evening went home in the street car she saw men and women together. It was the same when on Sunday afternoons in the summer she walked in the park or by the lake. On a street car she saw a small round-faced woman put her hand into the hand of her male companion. Before she did it she looked cautiously about. She wanted to assure herself of something. To the other women in the car, to Rosalind and the others the act said something. It was as though the woman's voice had said aloud, "He is mine. Do not draw too close to him."

There was no doubt that Rosalind was awakening out of the Willow Springs torpor in which she had lived out her young womanhood. The city had at least done that for her. The city was wide. It flung itself out. One had but to let his feet go thump, thump upon the pavements to get into strange streets, see always new faces.

On Saturday afternoon and all day Sunday one did not work. In the summer it was a time to go to places—to the park, to walk among the strange colorful crowds in Halsted Street, with a half dozen young people from the office, to spend a day on the sand dunes at the foot of Lake Michigan. One got excited and was hungry, hungry, always hungry—for companionship. That was it. One wanted to possess something—a man—to take him along on jaunts, be sure of him, yes—own him.

She read books—always written by men or by manlike women. There was an essential mistake in the viewpoint of life set forth in the books. The mistake was always being made. In Rosalind's time it grew more pronounced. Someone had got hold of a key with which the door to the secret chamber of life could be unlocked. Others took the key and rushed in. The secret chamber of life was filled with a noisy vulgar crowd. All the books that dealt with life at all dealt with it through the lips of the crowd that had newly come into the sacred place. The writer had hold of the key. It was his time to be heard. "Sex," he cried. "It is by understanding sex I will untangle the mystery."

It was all very well and sometimes interesting but one grew tired of the subject.

She lay abed in her room at her brother's house on a Sunday night in the summer. During the afternoon she had gone for a walk and on a street on the Northwest Side had come upon a religious procession. The Virgin was being carried through the streets. The houses were decorated and women leaned out at the windows of houses. Old priests dressed in white gowns waddled along. Strong young men carried the platform on which the Virgin rested. The procession stopped. Someone started a chant in a loud clear voice. Other voices took it up. Children ran about gathering in money. All the time there was a loud hum of ordinary conversation going on. Women shouted across the street to other women. Young girls walked on the sidewalks and laughed softly as the young men in white, clustered about the Virgin, turned to stare at them. On every street corner merchants sold candies, nuts, cool drinks—

In her bed at night Rosalind put down the book she had been reading. "The worship of the Virgin is a form of sex expression," she read.

"Well what of it? If it be true what does it matter?"

She got out of bed and took off her nightgown. She was herself a virgin. What did that matter? She turned herself slowly about, looking at her strong young woman's body. It was a thing in which sex lived. It was a thing upon which sex in others might express itself. What did it matter?

There was her brother sleeping with his wife in another room near at hand. In Willow Springs, Iowa, her father was at just this moment pumping a pail of water at the well by the kitchen door. In a moment he would carry it into the kitchen to set it on the box by the kitchen sink.

Rosalind's cheeks were flushed. She made an odd and lovely figure standing nude before the glass in her room there in Chicago. She was so much alive and yet not alive. Her eyes shone with excitement. She continued to turn slowly round and round twisting her head to look at her naked back. "Perhaps I am learning to think," she decided. There was some sort of essential mistake in people's conception of life. There was something she knew and it was of as much importance as the things the wise men knew and put into books. She also had found out something about life. Her body was still the body of what was called a virgin. What of it? "If the sex impulse within it had been gratified in what way would my problem be solved? I am lonely now. It is evident that after that had happened I would still be lonely."

CHAPTER III

ROSALIND'S LIFE IN Chicago had been like a stream that apparently turns back toward its source. It ran forward, then stopped, turned, twisted. At just the time when her awakening became a half realized thing she went to work at a new place, a piano factory on the Northwest Side facing a branch of the Chicago River. She became secretary to a man who was treasurer of the company. He was a slender, rather small man of thirty-eight with thin white restless hands and with gray eyes that were clouded and troubled. For the first time she became really interested in the work that ate up her days. Her employer was charged with the responsibility of passing upon the credit of the firm's customers and was unfitted for the task. He was not shrewd and within a short time had made two costly mistakes by which the company had lost money. "I have too much to do. My time is too much taken up with details. I need help here," he had explained, evidently irritated, and Rosalind had been engaged to relieve him of details.

Her new employer, named Walter Sayers, was the only son of a man who in his time had been well known in Chicago's social and club life. Everyone had thought him wealthy and he had tried to live up to people's estimate of his fortune. His son Walter had wanted to be a singer and had expected to inherit a comfortable fortune. At thirty he had married and three years later when his father died he was already the father of two children.

And then suddenly he had found himself quite penniless. He could sing but his voice was not large. It wasn't an instrument with which one could make money in any dignified way. Fortunately his wife had some money of her own. It was her money, invested in the piano manufacturing business, that had secured him the position as treasurer of the company. With his wife he withdrew from social life and they went to live in a comfortable house in a suburb.

Walter Sayers gave up music, apparently surrendered even his interest in it. Many men and women from his suburb went to hear the orchestra on Friday afternoons but he did not go. "What's the use of torturing myself and thinking of a life I cannot lead?" he said to himself. To his wife he pretended a growing interest in his work at the factory. "It's really fascinating. It's a game, like moving men back and forth on a chess board. I shall grow to love it," he said.

He had tried to build up interest in his work but had not been successful. Certain things would not get into his consciousness.

Although he tried hard he could not make the fact that profit or loss to the company depended upon his judgment seem important to himself. It was a matter of money lost or gained and money meant nothing to him. "It's father's fault," he thought. "While he lived money never meant anything to me. I was brought up wrong. I am ill prepared for the battle of life." He became too timid and lost business that should have come to the company quite naturally. Then he became too bold in the extension of credit and other losses followed.

His wife was quite happy and satisfied with her life. There were four or five acres of land about the suburban house and she became absorbed in the work of raising flowers and vegetables. For the sake of the children she kept a cow. With a young negro gardener she puttered about all day, digging in the earth, spreading manure about the roots of bushes and shrubs, planting and transplanting. In the evening when he had come home from his office in his car she took him by the arm and led him eagerly about. The two children trotted at their heels. She talked glowingly. They stood at a low spot at the foot of the garden and she spoke of the necessity of putting in tile. The prospect seemed to excite her. "It will be the best land on the place when it's drained," she said. She stooped and with a trowel turned over the soft black soil. An odor arose. "See! Just see how rich and black it is!" she exclaimed eagerly. "It's a little sour now because water has stood on it." She seemed to be apologizing as for a wayward child. "When it's drained I shall use lime to sweeten it," she added. She was like a mother leaning over the cradle of a sleeping babe. Her enthusiasm irritated him.

When Rosalind came to take the position in his office the slow fires of hatred that had been burning beneath the surface of Walter Sayers' life had already eaten away much of his vigor and energy. His body sagged in the office chair and there were heavy sagging lines at the corners of his mouth. Outwardly he remained always kindly and cheerful but back of the clouded, troubled eyes the fires of hatred burned slowly, persistently. It was as though he was trying to awaken from a troubled dream that gripped him, a dream that frightened a little, that was unending. He had contracted little physical habits. A sharp paper cutter lay on his desk. As he read a letter from one of the firm's customers he took it up and jabbed little holes in the leather cover of his desk. When he had several letters to sign he took up his pen and jabbed it almost viciously into the inkwell. Then before signing he jabbed it in again. Sometimes he did the thing a dozen times in succession.

Sometimes the things that went on beneath the surface of Walter Sayers frightened him. In order to do what he called "putting in his Saturday afternoons and Sundays" he had taken up photography. The camera took him away from his own house and the sight of the garden where his wife and the negro were busy digging, and into the fields and into stretches of woodland at the edge of the suburban village. Also it took him away from his wife's talk, from her eternal planning for the garden's future. Here by the house tulip bulbs were to be put in in the fall. Later there would be a hedge of lilac bushes shutting off the house from the road. The men who lived in the other houses along the suburban street spent their Saturday afternoons and Sunday mornings tinkering with motor cars. On Sunday afternoons they took their families driving, sitting up very straight and silent at the driving wheel. They consumed the afternoon in a swift dash over country roads. The car ate up the hours. Monday morning and the work in the city was there, at the end of the road. They ran madly toward it.

For a time the use of the camera made Walter Sayers almost happy. The study of light, playing on the trunk of a tree or over the grass in a field appealed to some instinct within. It was an uncertain delicate business. He fixed himself a dark room upstairs in the house and spent his evenings there. One dipped the films into the developing liquid, held them to the light and then dipped them again. The little nerves that controlled the eyes were aroused. One felt oneself being enriched, a little—

One Sunday afternoon he went to walk in a strip of woodland and came out upon the slope of a low hill. He had read somewhere that the low hill country southwest of Chicago, in which his suburb lay, had once been the shore of Lake Michigan. The low hills sprang out of the flat land and were covered with forests. Beyond them the flat lands began again. The prairies went on indefinitely, into infinity. People's lives went on so. Life was too long. It was to be spent in the endless doing over and over of an unsatisfactory task. He sat on the slope and looked out across the land.

He thought of his wife. She was back there, in the suburb in the hills, in her garden making things grow. It was a noble sort of thing to be doing. One shouldn't be irritated.

Well he had married her expecting to have money of his own. Then he would have worked at something else. Money would not have been involved in the matter and success would not have been a thing one must seek. He had expected his own life would be motivated. No matter how much or how hard he worked he would not have been a great singer. What did that matter? There was a way to live—a way of life in which such things did not matter. The delicate shades of things might be sought after. Before his eyes, there on the grass covered flat lands, the afternoon light was playing. It was like a breath, a vapor of color blown suddenly from between red lips out over the grey dead burned grass. Song might be like that. The beauty might come out of himself, out of his own body.

Again he thought of his wife and the sleeping light in his eyes flared up, it became a flame. He felt himself being mean, unfair. It didn't matter. Where did the truth lie? Was his wife, digging in her garden, having always a succession of small triumphs, marching forward with the seasons—well, was she becoming a little old, lean and sharp, a little vulgarized?

It seemed so to him. There was something smug in the way in which she managed to fling green growing flowering things over the black land. It was obvious the thing could be done and that there was satisfaction in doing it. It was a little like running a business and making money by it. There was a deep seated vulgarity involved in the whole matter. His wife put her hands into the black ground. They felt about, caressed the roots of the growing things. She laid hold of the slender trunk of a young tree in a certain way—as though she possessed it.

One could not deny that the destruction of beautiful things was involved. Weeds grew in the garden, delicate shapely things. She plucked them out without thought. He had seen her do it.

As for himself, he also had been pulled out of something. Had he not surrendered to the fact of a wife and growing children? Did he not spend his days doing work he detested? The anger within him burned bright. The fire came into his conscious self. Why should a weed that is to be destroyed pretend to a vegetable existence? As for puttering about with a camera—was it not a form of cheating? He did not want to be a photographer. He had once wanted to be a singer.

He arose and walked along the hillside, still watching the shadows play over the plains below. At night—in bed with his wife—well, was she not sometimes with him as she was in the garden? Something was plucked out of him and another thing grew in its place—something she wanted to have grow. Their love making was like his puttering with a camera—to make the weekends pass. She came at him a little too determinedly—sure. She was plucking delicate weeds in order that things she had determined upon—"vegetables," he exclaimed in disgust—in order that vegetables might grow. Love was a fragrance, the shading of a tone over the lips, out of the throat. It was like the afternoon light on the burned grass. Keeping a garden and making flowers grow had nothing to do with it.

Walter Sayers' fingers twitched. The camera hung by a strap over his shoulder. He took hold of the strap and walked to a tree. He swung the box above his head and brought it down with a thump against the tree trunk. The sharp breaking sound—the delicate parts of the machine being broken—was sweet to his ears. It was as though a song had come suddenly from between his lips. Again he swung the box and again brought it down against the tree trunk.

CHAPTER IV

ROSALIND AT WORK in Walter Sayers' office was from the beginning something different, apart from the young woman from Iowa who had been drifting from office to office, moving from rooming house to rooming house on Chicago's North Side, striving feebly to find out something about life by reading books, going to the theatre and walking alone in the streets. In the new place her life at once began to have point and purpose, but at the same time the perplexity that was later to send her running to Willow Springs and to the presence of her mother began to grow in her.

Walter Sayers' office was a rather large room on the third floor of the factory whose walls went straight up from the river's edge. In the morning Rosalind arrived at eight and went into the office and closed the door. In a large room across a narrow hallway and shut off from her retreat by two thick, clouded-glass partitions was the company's general office. It contained the desks of salesmen, several clerks, a bookkeeper and two stenographers. Rosalind avoided becoming acquainted with these people. She was in a mood to be alone, to spend as many hours as possible alone with her own thoughts.

She got to the office at eight and her employer did not arrive until nine-thirty or ten. For an hour or two in the morning and in the late afternoon she had the place to herself. Immediately she shut the door into the hallway and was alone, she felt at home. Even in her father's house it had never been so. She took off her wraps and walked about the room touching things, putting things to rights. During the night a negro woman had scrubbed the floor and wiped the dust off her employer's desk but she got a cloth and wiped the desk again. Then she opened the letters that had come in and after reading arranged them in little piles. She wanted to spend a part of her wages for flowers and imagined clusters of flowers arranged in small hanging baskets along the grey walls. "I'll do that later, perhaps," she thought.

The walls of the room enclosed her. "What makes me so happy here?" she asked herself. As for her employer—she felt she scarcely knew him. He was a shy man, rather small—

She went to a window and stood looking out. Near the factory a bridge crossed the river and over it went a stream of heavily loaded wagons and motor trucks. The sky was grey with smoke. In the afternoon, after her employer had gone for the day, she would stand again by the window. As she stood thus she faced westward and in the afternoon saw the sun fall down the sky. It was glorious to be there alone during the late hours of the afternoon. What a tremendous thing this city in which she had come to live! For some reason after she went to work for Walter Sayers the city seemed, like the room in which she worked, to have accepted her, taken her into itself. In the late afternoon the rays of the departing sun fell across great banks of clouds. The whole city seemed to reach upwards. It left the ground and ascended into the air. There was an illusion produced. Stark grim factory chimneys, that all day were stiff cold formal things sticking up into the air and belching forth black smoke, were now slender upreaching pencils of light and wavering color. The tall chimneys detached themselves from the buildings and sprang into the air. The factory in which Rosalind stood had such a chimney. It also was leaping upward. She felt herself being lifted, an odd floating sensation was achieved. With what a stately tread the day went away, over the city! The city, like the factory chimneys yearned after it, hungered for it.

In the morning gulls came in from Lake Michigan to feed on the sewage floating in the river below. The river was the color of chrysoprase. The gulls floated above it as sometimes in the evening the whole city seemed to float before her eyes. They were graceful, living, free things. They were triumphant. The getting of food, even the eating of sewage was done thus gracefully, beautifully. The gulls turned and twisted in the air. They wheeled and floated and then fell downward to the river in a long curve, just touching, caressing the surface of the water and then rising again.

Rosalind raised herself on her toes. At her back beyond the two glass partitions were other men and women, but there, in that room, she was alone. She belonged there. What an odd feeling she had. She also belonged to her employer, Walter Sayers. She scarcely knew the man and yet she belonged to him. She threw her arms above her head, trying awkwardly to imitate some movement of the birds.

Her awkwardness shamed her a little and she turned and walked about the room. "I'm twenty-five years old and it's a little late to begin trying to be a bird, to be graceful," she thought. She resented the slow stupid heavy movements of her father and mother, the movements she had imitated as a child. "Why was I not taught to be graceful and beautiful in mind and body, why in the place I came from did no one think it worth while to try to be graceful and beautiful?" she whispered to herself.

How conscious of her own body Rosalind was becoming! She walked across the room, trying to go lightly and gracefully. In the office beyond the glass partitions someone spoke suddenly and she was startled. She laughed foolishly. For a long time after she went to work in the office of Walter Sayers she thought the desire in herself to be physically more graceful and beautiful and to rise also out of the mental stupidity and sloth of her young womanhood was due to the fact that the factory windows faced the river and the western sky, and that in the morning she saw the gulls feeding and in the afternoon the sun going down through the smoke clouds in a riot of colors.

CHAPTER V

ON THE AUGUST evening as Rosalind sat on the porch before her father's house in Willow Springs, Walter Sayers came home from the factory by the river and to his wife's suburban garden. When the family had dined he came out to walk in the paths with the two children, boys, but they soon tired of his silence and went to join their mother. The young negro came along a path by the kitchen door and joined the party. Walter went to sit on a garden seat that was concealed behind bushes. He lighted a cigarette but did not smoke. The smoke curled quietly up through his fingers as it burned itself out.

Closing his eyes Walter sat perfectly still and tried not to think. The soft evening shadows began presently to close down and around him. For a long time he sat thus motionless, like a carved figure placed on the garden bench. He rested. He lived and did not live. The intense body, usually so active and alert, had become a passive thing. It was thrown aside, on to the bench, under the bush, to sit there, waiting to be reinhabited.

This hanging suspended between consciousness and unconsciousness was a thing that did not happen often. There was something to be settled between himself and a woman and the woman had gone away. His whole plan of life had been disturbed. Now he wanted to rest. The details of his life were forgotten. As for the woman he did not think of her, did not want to think of her. It was ridiculous that he needed her so much. He wondered if he had ever felt that way about Cora, his wife. Perhaps he had. Now she was near him, but a few yards away. It was almost dark but she with the negro remained at work, digging in the ground—somewhere near—caressing the soil, making things grow.

When his mind was undisturbed by thoughts and lay like a lake in the hills on a quiet summer evening little thoughts did come. "I want you as a lover—far away. Keep yourself far away." The words trailed through his mind as the smoke from the cigarette trailed slowly upwards through his fingers. Did the words refer to Rosalind Wescott? She had been gone from him three days. Did he hope she would never come back or did the words refer to his wife?

His wife's voice spoke sharply. One of the children in playing about, had stepped on a plant. "If you are not careful I shall have to make you stay out of the garden altogether." She raised her voice and called, "Marian!" A maid came from the house and took the children away. They went along the path toward the house protesting. Then they ran back to kiss their mother. There was a struggle and then acceptance. The kiss was acceptance of their fate—to obey. "O, Walter," the mother's voice called, but the man on the bench did not answer. Tree toads began to cry. "The kiss is acceptance. Any physical contact with another is acceptance," he reflected.

The little voices within Walter Sayers were talking away at a great rate. Suddenly he wanted to sing. He had been told that his voice was small, not of much account, that he would never be a singer. It was quite true no doubt but here, in the garden on the quiet summer night, was a place and a time for a small voice. It would be like the voice within himself that whispered sometimes when he was quiet, relaxed. One evening when he had been with the woman, Rosalind, when he had taken her into the country in his car, he had suddenly felt as he did now. They sat together in the car that he had run into a field. For a long time they had remained silent. Some cattle came and stood nearby, their figures soft in the night. Suddenly he had felt like a new man in a new world and had begun to sing. He sang one song over and over, then sat in silence for a time and after that drove out of the field and through a gate into the road. He took the woman back to her place in the city.

In the quiet of the garden on the summer evening he opened his lips to sing the same song. He would sing with the tree toad hidden away in the fork of a tree somewhere. He would lift his voice up from the earth, up into the branches, of trees, away from the ground in which people were digging, his wife and the young negro.

The song did not come. His wife began speaking and the sound of her voice took away the desire to sing. Why had she not, like the other woman, remained silent?

He began playing a game. Sometimes, when he was alone the thing happened to him that had now happened. His body became like a tree or a plant. Life ran through it unobstructed. He had dreamed of being a singer but at such a moment he wanted also to be a dancer. That would have been sweetest of all things—to sway like the tops of young trees when a wind blew, to give himself as grey weeds in a sunburned field gave themself to the influence of passing shadows, changing color constantly, becoming every moment something new, to live in life and in death too, always to live, to be unafraid of life, to let it flow through his body, to let the blood flow through his body, not to struggle, to offer no resistance, to dance.

Walter Sayers' children had gone into the house with the nurse girl Marian. It had become too dark for his wife to dig in the garden. It was August and the fruitful time of the year for farms and gardens had come, but his wife had forgotten fruitfulness. She was making plans for another year. She came along the garden path followed by the negro. "We will set out strawberry plants there," she was saying. The soft voice of the young negro murmured his assent. It was evident the young man lived in her conception of the garden. His mind sought out her desire and gave itself.

The children Walter Sayers had brought into life through the body of his wife Cora had gone into the house and to bed. They bound him to life, to his wife, to the garden where he sat, to the office by the riverside in the city.

They were not his children. Suddenly he knew that quite clearly. His own children were quite different things. "Men have children just as women do. The children come out of their bodies. They play about," he thought. It seemed to him that children, born of his fancy, were at that very moment playing about the bench where he sat. Living things that dwelt within him and that had at the same time the power to depart out of him were now running along paths, swinging from the branches of trees, dancing in the soft light.

His mind sought out the figure of Rosalind Wescott. She had gone away, to her own people in Iowa. There had been a note at the office saying she might be gone for several days. Between himself and Rosalind the conventional relationship of employer and employee had long since been swept quite away. It needed something in a man he did not possess to maintain that relationship with either men or women.

At the moment he wanted to forget Rosalind. In her there was a struggle going on. The two people had wanted to be lovers and he had fought against that. They had talked about it. "Well," he said, "it will not work out. We will bring unnecessary unhappiness upon ourselves."

He had been honest enough in fighting off the intensification of their relationship. "If she were here now, in this garden with me, it wouldn't matter. We could be lovers and then forget about being lovers," he told himself.

His wife came along the path and stopped nearby. She continued talking in a low voice, making plans for another year of gardening. The negro stood near her, his figure making a dark wavering mass against the foliage of a low growing bush. His wife wore a white dress. He could see her figure quite plainly. In the uncertain light it looked girlish and young. She put her hand up and took hold of the body of a young tree. The hand became detached from her body. The pressure of her leaning body made the young tree sway a little. The white hand moved slowly back and forth in space.

Rosalind Wescott had gone home to tell her mother of her love. In her note she had said nothing of that but Walter Sayers knew that was the object of her visit to the Iowa town. It was an odd sort of thing to try to do—to tell people of love, to try to explain it to others.

The night was a thing apart from Walter Sayers, the male being sitting in silence in the garden. Only the children of his fancy understood it. The night was a living thing. It advanced upon him, enfolded him. "Night is the sweet little brother of Death," he thought.

His wife stood very near. Her voice was soft and low and the voice of the negro when he answered her comments on the future of the garden was soft and low. There was music in the negro's voice, perhaps a dance in it. Walter remembered about him.

The young negro had been in trouble before he came to the Sayers. He had been an ambitious young black and had listened to the voices of people, to the voices that filled the air of America, rang through the houses of America. He had wanted to get on in life and had tried to educate himself. The black had wanted to be a lawyer.

How far away he had got from his own people, from the blacks of the African forests! He had wanted to be a lawyer in a city in America. What a notion!

Well he had got into trouble. He had managed to get through college and had opened a law office. Then one evening he went out to walk and chance led him into a street where a woman, a white woman, had been murdered an hour before. The body of the woman was found and then he was found walking in the street. Mrs. Sayers' brother, a lawyer, had saved him from being punished as a murderer and after the trial, and the young negro's acquittal, had induced his sister to take him as gardener. His chances as a professional man in the city were no good. "He has had a terrible experience and has just escaped by a fluke" the brother had said. Cora Sayers had taken the young man. She had bound him to herself, to her garden.

It was evident the two people were bound together. One cannot bind another without being bound. His wife had no more to say to the negro who went away along the path that led to the kitchen door. He had a room in a little house at the foot of the garden. In the room he had books and a piano. Sometimes in the evening he sang. He was going now to his place. By educating himself he had cut himself off from his own people.

Cora Sayers went into the house and Walter sat alone. After a time the young negro came silently down the path. He stopped by the tree where a moment before the white woman had stood talking to him. He put his hand on the trunk of the young tree where her hand had been and then went softly away. His feet made no sound on the garden path.

An hour passed. In his little house at the foot of the garden the negro began to sing softly. He did that sometimes in the middle of the night. What a life he had led too! He had come away from his black people, from the warm brown girls with the golden colors playing through the blue black of their skins and had worked his way through a Northern college, had accepted the patronage of impertinent people who wanted to uplift the black race, had listened to them, had bound himself to them, had tried to follow the way of life they had suggested.

Now he was in the little house at the foot of the Sayers' garden. Walter remembered little things his wife had told him about the man. The experience in the court room had frightened him horribly and he did not want to go off the Sayers' place. Education, books had done something to him. He could not go back to his own people. In Chicago, for the most part, the blacks lived crowded into a few streets on the South Side. "I want to be a slave," he had said to Cora Sayers. "You may pay me money if it makes you feel better but I shall have no use for it. I want to be your slave. I would be happy if I knew I would never have to go off your place."

The black sang a low voiced song. It ran like a little wind on the surface of a pond. It had no words. He had remembered the song from his father who had got it from his father. In the South, in Alabama and Mississippi the blacks sang it when they rolled cotton bales onto the steamers in the rivers. They had got it from other rollers of cotton bales long since dead. Long before there were any cotton bales to roll black men in boats on rivers in Africa had sung it. Young blacks in boats floated down rivers and came to a town they intended to attack at dawn. There was bravado in singing the song then. It was addressed to the women in the town to be attacked and contained both a caress and a threat. "In the morning your husbands and brothers and sweethearts we shall kill. Then we shall come into your town to you. We shall hold you close. We shall make you forget. With our hot love and our strength we shall make you forget." That was the old significance of the song.

Walter Sayers remembered many things. On other nights when the negro sang and when he lay in his room upstairs in the house, his wife came to him. There were two beds in their room. She sat upright in her bed. "Do you hear, Walter?" she asked. She came to sit on his bed, sometimes she crept into his arms. In the African villages long ago when the song floated up from the river men arose and prepared for battle. The song was a defiance, a taunt. That was all gone now. The young negro's house was at the foot of the garden and Walter with his wife lay upstairs in the larger house situated on high ground. It was a sad song, filled with race sadness. There was something in the ground that wanted to grow, buried deep in the ground. Cora Sayers understood that. It touched something instinctive in her.

Her hand went out and touched, caressed her husband's face, his body. The song made her want to hold him tight, possess him.

The night was advancing and it grew a little cold in the garden. The negro stopped singing. Walter Sayers arose and went along the path toward the house but did not enter. Instead he went through a gate into the road and along the suburban streets until he got into the open country. There was no moon but the stars shone brightly. For a time he hurried along looking back as though afraid of being followed, but when he got out into a broad flat meadow he went more slowly. For an hour he walked and then stopped and sat on a tuft of dry grass. For some reason he knew he could not return to his house in the suburb that night. In the morning he would go to the office and wait there until Rosalind came. Then? He did not know what he would do then. "I shall have to make up some story. In the morning I shall have to telephone Cora and make up some silly story," he thought. It was an absurd thing that he, a grown man, could not spend a night abroad, in the fields without the necessity of explanations. The thought irritated him and he arose and walked again. Under the stars in the soft night and on the wide flat plains the irritation soon went away and he began to sing softly, but the song he sang was not the one he had repeated over and over on that other night when he sat with Rosalind in the car and the cattle came. It was the song the negro sang, the river song of the young black warriors that slavery had softened and colored with sadness. On the lips of Walter Sayers the song had lost much of its sadness. He walked almost gaily along and in the song that flowed from his lips there was a taunt, a kind of challenge.

CHAPTER VI

AT THE END of the short street on which the Wescotts lived in Willow Springs there was a cornfield. When Rosalind was a child it was a meadow and beyond was an orchard.

On summer afternoons the child often went there to sit alone on the banks of a tiny stream that wandered away eastward toward Willow Creek, draining the farmer's fields on the way. The creek had made a slight depression in the level contour of the land and she sat with her back against an old apple tree and with her bare feet almost touching the water. Her mother did not permit her to run bare footed through the streets but when she got into the orchard she took her shoes off. It gave her a delightful naked feeling.

Overhead and through the branches the child could see the great sky. Masses of white clouds broke into fragments and then the fragments came together again. The sun ran in behind one of the cloud masses and grey shadows slid silently over the face of distant fields. The world of her child life, the Wescott household, Melville Stoner sitting in his house, the cries of other children who lived in her street, all the life she knew went far away. To be there in that silent place was like lying awake in bed at night only in some way sweeter and better. There were no dull household sounds and the air she breathed was sweeter, cleaner. The child played a little game. All the apple trees in the orchard were old and gnarled and she had given all the trees names. There was one fancy that frightened her a little but was delicious too. She fancied that at night when she had gone to bed and was asleep and when all the town of Willow Springs had gone to sleep the trees came out of the ground and walked about. The grasses beneath the trees, the bushes that grew beside the fence— all came out of the ground and ran madly here and there. They danced wildly. The old trees, like stately old men, put their heads together and talked. As they talked their bodies swayed slightly—back and forth, back and forth. The bushes and flowering weeds ran in great circles among the little grasses. The grasses hopped straight up and down.

Sometimes when she sat with her back against the tree on warm bright afternoons the child Rosalind had played the game of dancing-life until she grew afraid and had to give it up. Nearby in the fields men were cultivating corn. The breasts of the horses and their wide strong shoulders pushed the young corn aside and made a low rustling sound. Now and then a man's voice was raised in a shout. "Hi, there you Joe! Get in there Frank!" The widow of the hens owned a little woolly dog that occasionally broke into a spasm of barking, apparently without cause, senseless, eager, barking. Rosalind shut all the sounds out. She closed her eyes and struggled, trying to get into the place beyond human sounds. After a time her desire was accomplished. There was a low sweet sound like the murmuring of voices far away. Now the thing was happening. With a kind of tearing sound the trees came up to stand on top of the ground. They moved with stately tread toward each other. Now the mad bushes and the flowering weeds came running, dancing madly, now the joyful grasses hopped. Rosalind could not stay long in her world of fancy. It was too mad, too joyful. She opened her eyes and jumped to her feet. Everything was all right. The trees stood solidly rooted in the ground, the weeds and bushes had gone back to their places by the fence, the grasses lay asleep on the ground. She felt that her father and mother, her brother, everyone she knew would not approve of her being there among them. The world of dancing life was a lovely but a wicked world. She knew. Sometimes she was a little mad herself and then she was whipped or scolded. The mad world of her fancy had to be put away. It frightened her a little. Once after the thing appeared she cried, went down to the fence crying. A man who was cultivating corn came along and stopped his horses. "What's the matter?" he asked sharply. She couldn't tell him so she told a lie. "A bee stung me," she said. The man laughed. "It'll get well. Better put on your shoes," he advised.

The time of the marching trees and the dancing grasses was in Rosalind's childhood. Later when she had graduated from the Willow Springs High School and had the three years of waiting about the Wescott house before she went to the city she had other experiences in the orchard. Then she had been reading novels and had talked with other young women. She knew many things that after all she did not know. In the attic of her mother's house there was a cradle in which she and her brother had slept when they were babies. One day she went up there and found it. Bedding for the cradle was packed away in a trunk and she took it out. She arranged the cradle for the reception of a child. Then after she did it she was ashamed. Her mother might come up the attic stairs and see it. She put the bedding quickly back into the trunk and went down stairs, her cheeks burning with shame.

What a confusion! One day she went to the house of a schoolgirl friend who was about to be married. Several other girls came and they were all taken into a bedroom where the bride's trousseau was laid out on a bed. What soft lovely things! All the girls went forward and stood over them, Rosalind among them. Some of the girls were shy, others bold. There was one, a thin girl who had no breasts. Her body was flat like a door and she had a thin sharp voice and a thin sharp face. She began to cry out strangely. "How sweet, how sweet, how sweet," she cried over and over. The voice was not like a human voice. It was like something being hurt, an animal in the forest, far away somewhere by itself, being hurt. Then the girl dropped to her knees beside the bed and began to weep bitterly. She declared she could not bear the thought of her schoolgirl friend being married. "Don't do it! O, Mary don't do it!" she pleaded. The other girls laughed but Rosalind couldn't stand it. She hurried out of the house.

That was one thing that had happened to Rosalind and there were other things. Once she saw a young man on the street. He clerked in a store and Rosalind did not know him. However her fancy played with the thought that she had married him. Her own thoughts made her ashamed.

Everything shamed her. When she went into the orchard on summer afternoons she sat with her back against the apple tree and took off her shoes and stockings just as she had when she was a child, but the world of her childhood fancy was gone, nothing could bring it back.

Rosalind's body was soft but all her flesh was firm and strong. She moved away from the tree and lay on the ground. She pressed her body down into the grass, into the firm hard ground. It seemed to her that her mind, her fancy, all the life within her, except just her physical life, went away. The earth pressed upwards against her body. Her body was pressed against the earth. There was darkness. She was imprisoned. She pressed against the walls of her prison. Everything was dark and there was in all the earth silence. Her fingers clutched a handful of the grasses, played in the grasses.

Then she grew very still but did not sleep. There was something that had nothing to do with the ground beneath her or the trees or the clouds in the sky, that seemed to want to come to her, come into her, a kind of white wonder of life.

The thing couldn't happen. She opened her eyes and there was the sky overhead and the trees standing silently about. She went again to sit with her back against one of the trees. She thought with dread of the evening coming on and the necessity of going out of the orchard and to the Wescott house. She was weary. It was the weariness that made her appear to others a rather dull stupid young woman. Where was the wonder of life? It was not within herself, not in the ground. It must be in the sky overhead. Presently it would be night and the stars would come out. Perhaps the wonder did not really exist in life. It had something to do with God. She wanted to ascend upwards, to go at once up into God's house, to be there among the light strong men and women who had died and left dullness and heaviness behind them on the earth. Thinking of them took some of her weariness away and sometimes she went out of the orchard in the late afternoon walking almost lightly. Something like grace seemed to have come into her tall strong body.

Rosalind had gone away from the Wescott house and from Willow Springs, Iowa, feeling that life was essentially ugly. In a way she hated life and people. In Chicago sometimes it was unbelievable how ugly the world had become. She tried to shake off the feeling but it clung to her. She walked through the crowded streets and the buildings were ugly. A sea of faces floated up to her. They were the faces of dead people. The dull death that was in them was in her also. They too could not break through the walls of themselves to the white wonder of life. After all perhaps there was no such thing as the white wonder of life. It might be just a thing of the mind. There was something essentially dirty about life. The dirt was on her and in her. Once as she walked at evening over the Rush Street bridge to her room on the North Side she looked up suddenly and saw the chrysoprase river running inland from the lake. Near at hand stood a soap factory. The men of the city had turned the river about, made it flow inland from the lake. Someone had erected a great soap factory there near the river's entrance to the city, to the land of men. Rosalind stopped and stood looking along the river toward the lake. Men and women, wagons, automobiles rushed past her. They were dirty. She was dirty. "The water of an entire sea and millions of cakes of soap will not wash me clean," she thought. The dirtiness of life seemed a part of her very being and an almost overwhelming desire to climb upon the railing of the bridge and leap down into the chrysoprase river swept over her. Her body trembled violently and putting down her head and staring at the flooring of the bridge she hurried away.

And now Rosalind, a grown woman, was in the Wescott house at the supper table with her father and mother. None of the three people ate. They fussed about with the food Ma Wescott had prepared. Rosalind looked at her mother and thought of what Melville Stoner had said.

"If I wanted to write I'd do something. I'd tell what everyone thought. It would startle people, frighten them a little, eh? I would tell what you have been thinking this afternoon while you walked here on this railroad track with me. I would tell what your mother has been thinking at the same time and what she would like to say to you."

What had Rosalind's mother been thinking all through the three days since her daughter had so unexpectedly come home from Chicago? What did mothers think in regard to the lives led by their daughters? Had mothers something of importance to say to daughters and if they did when did the time come when they were ready to say it?

She looked at her mother sharply. The older woman's face was heavy and sagging. She had grey eyes like Rosalind's but they were dull like the eyes of a fish lying on a slab of ice in the window of a city meat market. The daughter was a little frightened by what she saw in her mother's face and something caught in her throat. There was an embarrassing moment. A strange sort of tenseness came into the air of the room and all three people suddenly got up from the table.

Rosalind went to help her mother with the dishes and her father sat in a chair by a window and read a paper. The daughter avoided looking again into her mother's face. "I must gather myself together if I am to do what I want to do," she thought. It was strange—in fancy she saw the lean bird-like face of Melville Stoner and the eager tired face of Walter Sayers floating above the head of her mother who leaned over the kitchen sink, washing the dishes. Both of the men's faces sneered at her. "You think you can but you can't. You are a young fool," the men's lips seemed to be saying.

Rosalind's father wondered how long his daughter's visit was to last. After the evening meal he wanted to clear out of the house, go up town, and he had a guilty feeling that in doing so he was being discourteous to his daughter. While the two women washed the dishes he put on his hat and going into the back yard began chopping wood. Rosalind went to sit on the front porch. The dishes were all washed and dried but for a half hour her mother would putter about in the kitchen. She always did that. She would arrange and rearrange. Pick up dishes and put them down again. She clung to the kitchen. It was as though she dreaded the hours that must pass before she could go upstairs and to bed and asleep, to fall into the oblivion of sleep.

When Henry Wescott came around the corner of the house and confronted his daughter he was a little startled. He did not know what was the matter but he felt uncomfortable. For a moment he stopped and looked at her. Life radiated from her figure. A fire burned in her eyes, in her grey intense eyes. Her hair was yellow like corn-silk. She was, at the moment, a complete, a lovely daughter of the cornlands, a being to be loved passionately, completely by some son of the cornlands—had there been in the land a son as alive as this daughter it had thrown aside. The father had hoped to escape from the house unnoticed. "I'm going up town a little while," he said hesitatingly. Still he lingered a moment. Some old sleeping thing awoke in him, was awakened in him by the startling beauty of his daughter. A little fire flared up among the charred rafters of the old house that was his body. "You look pretty, girly," he said sheepishly and then turned his back to her and went along the path to the gate and the street.

Rosalind followed her father to the gate and stood looking as he went slowly along the short street and around a corner. The mood induced in her by her talk with Melville Stoner had returned. Was it possible that her father also felt as Melville Stoner sometimes did? Did loneliness drive him to the door of insanity and did he also run through the night seeking some lost, some hidden and half forgotten loveliness?

When her father had disappeared around the corner she went through the gate and into the street. "I'll go sit by the tree in the orchard until mother has finished puttering about the kitchen," she thought.

Henry Wescott went along the streets until he came to the square about the court house and then went into Emanuel Wilson's Hardware Store. Two or three other men presently joined him there. Every evening he sat among these men of his town saying nothing. It was an escape from his own house and his wife. The other men came for the same reason. A faint perverted kind of male fellowship was achieved. One of the men of the party, a little old man who followed the house-painters trade, was unmarried and lived with his mother. He was himself nearing the age of sixty but his mother was still alive. It was a thing to be wondered about. When in the evening the house painter was a trifle late at the rendezvous a mild flurry of speculation arose, floated in the air for a moment and then settled like dust in an empty house. Did the old house painter do the house-work in his own house, did he wash the dishes, cook the food, sweep and make the beds or did his feeble old mother do these things? Emanuel Wilson told a story he had often told before. In a town in Ohio where he had lived as a young man he had once heard a tale. There was an old man like the house painter whose mother was also still alive and lived with him. They were very poor and in the winter had not enough bedclothes to keep them both warm. They crawled into a bed together. It was an innocent enough matter, just like a mother taking her child into her bed.

Henry Wescott sat in the store listening to the tale Emanuel Wilson told for the twentieth time and thought about his daughter. Her beauty made him feel a little proud, a little above the men who were his companions. He had never before thought of his daughter as a beautiful woman. Why had he never before noticed her beauty? Why had she come from Chicago, there by the lake, to Willow Springs, in the hot month of August? Had she come home from Chicago because she really wanted to see her father and mother? For a moment he was ashamed of his own heavy body, of his shabby clothes and his unshaven face and then the tiny flame that had flared up within him burned itself out. The house painter came in and the faint flavor of male companionship to which he clung so tenaciously was reestablished.

In the orchard Rosalind sat with her back against the tree in the same spot where her fancy had created the dancing life of her child-hood and where as a young woman graduate of the Willow Springs High School she had come to try to break through the wall that separated her from life. The sun had disappeared and the grey shadows of night were creeping over the grass, lengthening the shadows cast by the trees. The orchard had long been neglected and many of the trees were dead and without foliage. The shadows of the dead branches were like long lean arms that reached out, felt their way forward over the grey grass. Long lean fingers reached and clutched. There was no wind and the night would be dark and without a moon, a hot dark starlit night of the plains.

In a moment more it would be black night. Already the creeping shadows on the grass were barely discernible. Rosalind felt death all about her, in the orchard, in the town. Something Walter Sayers had once said to her came sharply back into her mind. "When you are in the country alone at night sometime try giving yourself to the night, to the darkness, to the shadows cast by trees. The experience, if you really give yourself to it, will tell you a startling story. You will find that, although the white men have owned the land for several generations now and although they have built towns every-where, dug coal out of the ground, covered the land with railroads, towns and cities, they do not own an inch of the land in the whole continent. It still belongs to a race who in their physical life are now dead. The red men, although they are practically all gone still own the American continent. Their fancy has peopled it with ghosts, with gods and devils. It is because in their time they loved the land. The proof of what I say is to be seen everywhere. We have given our towns no beautiful names of our own because we have not built the towns beautifully. When an American town has a beautiful name it was stolen from another race, from a race that still owns the land in which we live. We are all strangers here. When you are alone at night in the country, anywhere in America, try giving yourself to the night. You will find that death only resides in the conquering whites and that life remains in the red men who are gone."

The spirits of the two men, Walter Sayers and Melville Stoner, dominated the mind of Rosalind. She felt that. It was as though they were beside her, sitting beside her on the grass in the orchard. She was quite certain that Melville Stoner had come back to his house and was now sitting within sound of her voice, did she raise her voice to call. What did they want of her? Had she suddenly begun to love two men, both older than herself? The shadows of the branches of trees made a carpet on the floor of the orchard, a soft carpet spun of some delicate material on which the footsteps of men could make no sound. The two men were coming toward her, advancing over the carpet. Melville Stoner was near at hand and Walter Sayers was coming from far away, out of the distance. The spirit of him was creeping toward her. The two men were in accord. They came bearing some male knowledge of life, something they wanted to give her.

She arose and stood by the tree, trembling. Into what a state she had got herself! How long would it endure? Into what knowledge of life and death was she being led? She had come home on a simple mission. She loved Walter Sayers, wanted to offer herself to him but before doing so had felt the call to come home to her mother. She had thought she would be bold and would tell her mother the story of her love. She would tell her and then take what the older woman offered. If her mother understood and sympathized, well that would be a beautiful thing to have happen. If her mother did not understand—at any rate she would have paid some old debt, would have been true to some old, unexpressed obligation.

The two men—what did they want of her? What had Melville Stoner to do with the matter? She put the figure of him out of her mind. In the figure of the other man, Walter Sayers, there was something less aggressive, less assertive. She clung to that.

She put her arm about the trunk of the old apple tree and laid her cheek against its rough bark. Within herself she was so intense, so excited that she wanted to rub her cheeks against the bark of the tree until the blood came, until physical pain came to counteract the tenseness within that had become pain.

Since the meadow between the orchard and the street end had been planted to corn she would have to reach the street by going along a lane, crawling under a wire fence and crossing the yard of the widowed chicken raiser. A profound silence reigned over the orchard and when she had crawled under the fence and reached the widow's back yard she had to feel her way through a narrow opening between a chicken house and a barn by running her fingers forward over the rough boards.

Her mother sat on the porch waiting and on the narrow porch before his house next door sat Melville Stoner. She saw him as she hurried past and shivered slightly. "What a dark vulture-like thing he is! He lives off the dead, off dead glimpses of beauty, off dead old sounds heard at night," she thought. When she got to the Wescott house she threw herself down on the porch and lay on her back with her arms stretched above her head. Her mother sat on a rocking chair beside her. There was a street lamp at the corner at the end of the street and a little light came through the branches of trees and lighted her mother's face. How white and still and death-like it was. When she had looked Rosalind closed her eyes. "I mustn't. I shall lose courage," she thought.

There was no hurry about delivering the message she had come to deliver. It would be two hours before her father came home. The silence of the village street was broken by a hubbub that arose in the house across the street. Two boys playing some game ran from room to room through the house, slamming doors, shouting. A baby began to cry and then a woman's voice protested. "Quit it! Quit it!" the voice called. "Don't you see you have wakened the baby? Now I shall have a time getting him to sleep again."

Rosalind's fingers closed and her hands remained clenched. "I came home to tell you something. I have fallen in love with a man and can't marry him. He is a good many years older than myself and is already married. He has two children. I love him and I think he loves me—I know he does. I want him to have me too. I wanted to come home and tell you before it happened," she said speaking in a low clear voice. She wondered if Melville Stoner could hear her declaration.

Nothing happened. The chair in which Rosalind's mother sat had been rocking slowly back and forth and making a slight creaking sound. The sound continued. In the house across the street the baby stopped crying. The words Rosalind had come from Chicago to say to her mother were said and she felt relieved and almost happy. The silence between the two women went on and on. Rosalind's mind wandered away. Presently there would be some sort of reaction from her mother. She would be condemned. Perhaps her mother would say nothing until her father came home and would then tell him. She would be condemned as a wicked woman, ordered to leave the house. It did not matter.

Rosalind waited. Like Walter Sayers, sitting in his garden, her mind seemed to float away, out of her body. It ran away from her mother to the man she loved.

One evening, on just such another quiet summer evening as this one, she had gone into the country with Walter Sayers. Before that he had talked to her, at her, on many other evenings and during long hours in the office. He had found in her someone to whom he could talk, to whom he wanted to talk. What doors of life he had opened for her! The talk had gone on and on. In her presence the man was relieved, he relaxed out of the tenseness that had become the habit of his body. He had told her of how he had wanted to be a singer and had given up the notion. "It isn't my wife's fault nor the children's fault," he had said. "They could have lived without me. The trouble is I could not have lived without them. I am a defeated man, was intended from the first to be a defeated man and I needed something to cling to, something with which to justify my defeat. I realize that now. I am a dependent. I shall never try to sing now because I am one who has at least one merit. I know defeat. I can accept defeat."

That is what Walter Sayers had said and then on the summer evening in the country as she sat beside him in his car he had suddenly begun to sing. He had opened a farm gate and had driven the car silently along a grass covered lane and into a meadow. The lights had been put out and the car crept along. When it stopped some cattle came and stood nearby.

Then he began to sing, softly at first and with increasing boldness as he repeated the song over and over. Rosalind was so happy she had wanted to cry out. "It is because of myself he can sing now," she had thought proudly. How intensely, at the moment she loved the man, and yet perhaps the thing she felt was not love after all.

There was pride in it. It was for her a moment of triumph. He had crept up to her out of a dark place, out of the dark cave of defeat. It had been her hand reached down that had given him courage.

She lay on her back, at her mother's feet, on the porch of the Wescott house trying to think, striving to get her own impulses clear in her mind. She had just told her mother that she wanted to give herself to the man, Walter Sayers. Having made the statement she already wondered if it could be quite true. She was a woman and her mother was a woman. What would her mother have to say to her? What did mothers say to daughters? The male element in life—what did it want? Her own desires and impulses were not clearly realized within herself. Perhaps what she wanted in life could be got in some sort of communion with another woman, with her mother. What a strange and beautiful thing it would be if mothers could suddenly begin to sing to their daughters, if out of the darkness and silence of old women song could come.

Men confused Rosalind, they had always confused her. On that very evening her father for the first time in years had really looked at her. He had stopped before her as she sat on the porch and there had been something in his eyes. A fire had burned in his old eyes as it had sometimes burned in the eyes of Walter. Was the fire intended to consume her quite? Was it the fate of women to be consumed by men and of men to be consumed by women?

In the orchard, an hour before she had distinctly felt the two men, Melville Stoner and Walter Sayers coming toward her, walking silently on the soft carpet made of the dark shadows of trees.

They were again coming toward her. In their thoughts they approached nearer and nearer to her, to the inner truth of her. The street and the town of Willow Springs were covered with a mantle of silence. Was it the silence of death? Had her mother died? Did her mother sit there now a dead thing in the chair beside her?

The soft creaking of the rocking chair went on and on. Of the two men whose spirits seemed hovering about one, Melville Stoner, was bold and cunning. He was too close to her, knew too much of her. He was unafraid. The spirit of Walter Sayers was merciful. He was gentle, a man of understanding. She grew afraid of Melville Stoner. He was too close to her, knew too much of the dark, stupid side of her life. She turned on her side and stared into the darkness toward the Stoner house remembering her girlhood. The man was too physically close. The faint light from the distant street lamp that had lighted her mother's face crept between branches of trees and over the tops of bushes and she could see dimly the figure of Melville Stoner sitting before his house. She wished it were possible with a thought to destroy him, wipe him out, cause him to cease to exist. He was waiting. When her mother had gone to bed and when she had gone upstairs to her own room to lie awake he would invade her privacy. Her father would come home, walking with dragging foot-steps along the sidewalk. He would come into the Wescott house and through to the back door. He would pump the pail of water at the pump and bring it into the house to put it on the box by the kitchen sink. Then he would wind the clock. He would—

Rosalind stirred uneasily. Life in the figure of Melville Stoner had her, it gripped her tightly. She could not escape. He would come into her bedroom and invade her secret thoughts. There was no escape for her. She imagined his mocking laughter ringing through the silent house, the sound rising above the dreadful commonplace sounds of everyday life there. She did not want that to happen. The sudden death of Melville Stoner would bring sweet silence. She wished it possible with a thought to destroy him, to destroy all men. She wanted her mother to draw close to her. That would save her from the men. Surely, before the evening had passed her mother would have something to say, something living and true.

Rosalind forced the figure of Melville Stoner out of her mind. It was as though she had got out of her bed in the room upstairs and had taken the man by the arm to lead him to the door. She had put him out of the room and had closed the door.

Her mind played her a trick. Melville Stoner had no sooner gone out of her mind than Walter Sayers came in. In imagination she was with Walter in the car on the summer evening in the pasture and he was singing. The cattle with their soft broad noses and the sweet grass-flavored breaths were crowding in close.

There was sweetness in Rosalind's thoughts now. She rested and waited, waited for her mother to speak. In her presence Walter Sayers had broken his long silence and soon the old silence between mother and daughter would also be broken.

The singer who would not sing had begun to sing because of her presence. Song was the true note of life, it was the triumph of life over death.

What sweet solace had come to her that time when Walter Sayers sang! How life had coursed through her body! How alive she had suddenly become! It was at that moment she had decided definitely, finally, that she wanted to come closer to the man, that she wanted with him the ultimate physical closeness—to find in physical expression through him what in his song he was finding through her.

It was in expressing physically her love of the man she would find the white wonder of life, the wonder of which, as a clumsy and crude girl, she had dreamed as she lay on the grass in the orchard. Through the body of the singer she would approach, touch the white wonder of life. "I shall willingly sacrifice everything else on the chance that may happen," she thought.

How peaceful and quiet the summer night had become! How clearly now she understood life! The song Walter Sayers had sung in the field, in the presence of the cattle was in a tongue she had not understood, but now she understood everything, even the meaning of the strange foreign words.

The song was about life and death. What else was there to sing about? The sudden knowledge of the content of the song had not come out of her own mind. The spirit of Walter was coming toward her. It had pushed the mocking spirit of Melville Stoner aside. What things had not the mind of Walter Sayers already done to her mind, to the awakening woman within her. Now it was telling her the story of the song. The words of the song itself seemed to float down the silent street of the Iowa town. They described the sun going down in the smoke clouds of a city and the gulls coming from a lake to float over the city.

Now the gulls floated over a river. The river was the color of chrysoprase. She, Rosalind Wescott, stood on a bridge in the heart of the city and she had become entirely convinced of the filth and ugliness of life. She was about to throw herself into the river, to destroy herself in an effort to make herself clean.

It did not matter. Strange sharp cries came from the birds. The cries of the birds were like the voice of Melville Stoner. They whirled and turned in the air overhead. In a moment more she would throw herself into the river and then the birds would fall straight down in a long graceful line. The body of her would be gone, swept away by the stream, carried away to decay but what was really alive in herself would arise with the birds, in the long graceful upward line of the flight of the birds.

Rosalind lay tense and still on the porch at her mother's feet. In the air above the hot sleeping town, buried deep in the ground beneath all towns and cities, life went on singing, it persistently sang. The song of life was in the humming of bees, in the calling of tree toads, in the throats of negroes rolling cotton bales on a boat in a river.

The song was a command. It told over and over the story of life and of death, life forever defeated by death, death forever defeated by life.

The long silence of Rosalind's mother was broken and Rosalind tried to tear herself away from the spirit of the song that had begun to sing itself within her—

> The sun sank down into the western sky over a city—
>> Life defeated by death,
>> Death defeated by life.
> The factory chimneys had become pencils of light—
>> Life defeated by death,
>> Death defeated by life.

The rocking chair in which Rosalind's mother sat kept creaking. Words came haltingly from between her white lips. The test of Ma Wescott's life had come. Always she had been defeated. Now she must triumph in the person of Rosalind, the daughter who had come out of her body. To her she must make clear the fate of all women. Young girls grew up dreaming, hoping, believing. There was a conspiracy. Men made words, they wrote books and sang songs about a thing called love. Young girls believed. They married or entered into close relationships with men without marriage. On the marriage night there was a brutal assault and after that the woman had to try to save herself as best as she could. She withdrew within herself, further and further within herself. Ma Wescott had stayed all her life hidden away within her own house, in the kitchen of her house. As the years passed and after the children came her man had demanded less and less of her. Now this new trouble had come. Her daughter was to have the same experience, to go through the experience that had spoiled life for her.

How proud she had been of Rosalind, going out into the world, making her own way. Her daughter dressed with a certain air, walked with a certain air. She was a proud, upstanding, triumphant thing. She did not need a man.

"God, Rosalind, don't do it, don't do it," she muttered over and over.

How much she had wanted Rosalind to keep clear and clean! Once she also had been a young woman, proud, upstanding. Could anyone think she had ever wanted to become Ma Wescott, fat, heavy and old? All through her married life she had stayed in her own house, in the kitchen of her own house, but in her own way she had watched, she had seen how things went with women. Her man had known how to make money, he had always housed her comfortably. He was a slow, silent man but in his own way he was as good as any of the men of Willow Springs. Men worked for money, they ate heavily and then at night they came home to the woman they had married.

Before she married, Ma Wescott had been a farmer's daughter. She had seen things among the beasts, how the male pursued the female. There was a certain hard insistence, cruelty. Life perpetuated itself that way. The time of her own marriage was a dim, terrible time. Why had she wanted to marry? She tried to tell Rosalind about it. "I saw him on the Main Street of town here, one Saturday evening when I had come to town with father, and two weeks after that I met him again at a dance out in the country," she said. She spoke like one who has been running a long distance and who has some important, some immediate message to deliver. "He wanted me to marry him and I did it. He wanted me to marry him and I did it."

She could not get beyond the fact of her marriage. Did her daughter think she had no vital thing to say concerning the relationship of men and women? All through her married life she had stayed in her husband's house, working as a beast might work, washing dirty clothes, dirty dishes, cooking food.

She had been thinking, all through the years she had been thinking. There was a dreadful lie in life, the whole fact of life was a lie.

She had thought it all out. There was a world somewhere unlike the world in which she lived. It was a heavenly place in which there was no marrying or giving in marriage, a sexless quiet windless place where mankind lived in a state of bliss. For some unknown reason mankind had been thrown out of that place, had been thrown down upon the earth. It was a punishment for an unforgivable sin, the sin of sex.

The sin had been in her as well as in the man she had married. She had wanted to marry. Why else did she do it? Men and women were condemned to commit the sin that destroyed them. Except for a few rare sacred beings no man or woman escaped.

What thinking she had done! When she had just married and after her man had taken what he wanted of her he slept heavily but she did not sleep. She crept out of bed and going to a window looked at the stars. The stars were quiet. With what a slow stately tread the moon moved across the sky. The stars did not sin. They did not touch one another. Each star was a thing apart from all other stars, a sacred inviolate thing. On the earth, under the stars everything was corrupt, the trees, flowers, grasses, the beasts of the field, men and women. They were all corrupt. They lived for a moment and then fell into decay. She herself was falling into decay. Life was a lie. Life perpetuated itself by the lie called love. The truth was that life itself came out of sin, perpetuated itself only by sin.

"There is no such thing as love. The word is a lie. The man you are telling me about wants you for the purpose of sin," she said and getting heavily up went into the house.

Rosalind heard her moving about in the darkness. She came to the screen door and stood looking at her daughter lying tense and waiting on the porch. The passion of denial was so strong in her that she felt choked. To the daughter it seemed that her mother standing in the darkness behind her had become a great spider, striving to lead her down into some web of darkness. "Men only hurt women," she said, "they can't help wanting to hurt women. They are made that way. The thing they call love doesn't exist. It's a lie."

"Life is dirty. Letting a man touch her dirties a woman." Ma Wescott fairly screamed forth the words. They seemed torn from her, from some deep inner part of her being. Having said them she moved off into the darkness and Rosalind heard her going slowly toward the stairway that led to the bedroom above. She was weeping in the peculiar half choked way in which old fat women weep. The heavy feet that had begun to mount the stair stopped and there was silence. Ma Wescott had said nothing of what was in her mind. She had thought it all out, what she wanted to say to her daughter. Why would the words not come? The passion for denial within her was not satisfied. "There is no love. Life is a lie. It leads to sin, to death and decay," she called into the darkness.

A strange, almost uncanny thing happened to Rosalind. The figure of her mother went out of her mind and she was in fancy again a young girl and had gone with other young girls to visit a friend about to be married. With the others she stood in a room where white dresses lay on a bed. One of her companions, a thin, flat breasted girl fell on her knees beside the bed. A cry arose. Did it come from the girl or from the old tired defeated woman within the Wescott house? "Don't do it. O, Rosalind don't do it," pleaded a voice broken with sobs.

The Wescott house had become silent like the street outside and like the sky sprinkled with stars into which Rosalind gazed. The tenseness within her relaxed and she tried again to think. There was a thing that balanced, that swung backward and forward. Was it merely her heart beating? Her mind cleared.

The song that had come from the lips of Walter Sayers was still singing within her—

> Life the conqueror over death,
> Death the conqueror over life.

She sat up and put her head into her hands. "I came here to Willow Springs to put myself to a test. Is it the test of life and death?" she asked herself. Her mother had gone up the stairway, into the darkness of the bedroom above.

The song singing within Rosalind went on—

> Life the conquerer over death,
> Death the conquerer over life.

Was the song a male thing, the call of the male to the female, a lie, as her mother had said? It did not sound like a lie. The song had come from the lips of the man Walter and she had left him and had come to her mother. Then Melville Stoner, another male, had come to her. In him also was singing the song of life and death. When the song stopped singing within one did death come? Was death but denial? The song was singing within herself. What a confusion!

After her last outcry Ma Wescott had gone weeping up the stairs and to her own room and to bed. After a time Rosalind followed. She threw herself onto her own bed without undressing. Both women lay waiting. Outside in the darkness before his house sat Melville Stoner, the male, the man who knew of all that had passed between mother and daughter. Rosalind thought of the bridge over the river near the factory in the city and of the gulls floating in the air high above the river. She wished herself there, standing on the bridge. "It would be sweet now to throw my body down into the river,"

she thought. She imagined herself falling swiftly and the swifter fall
of the birds down out of the sky. They were swooping down to pick
up the life she was ready to drop, sweeping swiftly and beautifully
down. That was what the song Walter had sung was about.

Henry Wescott came home from his evening at Emanuel Wilson's
store. He went heavily through the house to the back door and the
pump. There was the slow creaking sound of the pump working and
then he came into the house and put the pail of water on the box
by the kitchen sink. A little of the water spilled. There was a soft
little slap—like a child's bare feet striking the floor—

Rosalind arose. The dead cold weariness that had settled down
upon her went away. Cold dead hands had been gripping her.
Now they were swept aside. Her bag was in a closet but she had
forgotten it. Quickly she took off her shoes and holding them in
her hands went out into the hall in her stockinged feet. Her father
came heavily up the stairs past her as she stood breathless with her
body pressed against the wall in the hallway.

How quick and alert her mind had become! There was a train
Eastward bound toward Chicago that passed through Willow Springs
at two in the morning. She would not wait for it. She would walk
the eight miles to the next town to the east. That would get her out
of town. It would give her something to do. "I need to be moving
now," she thought as she ran down the stairs and went silently out
of the house.

She walked on the grass beside the sidewalk to the gate before
Melville Stoner's house and he came down to the gate to meet her.
He laughed mockingly. "I fancied I might have another chance to
walk with you before the night was gone," he said bowing. Rosalind
did not know how much of the conversation between herself and
her mother he had heard. It did not matter. He knew all Ma Wescott
had said, all she could say and all Rosalind could say or understand.
The thought was infinitely sweet to Rosalind. It was Melville Stoner
who lifted the town of Willow Springs up out of the shadow of
death. Words were unnecessary. With him she had established the
thing beyond words, beyond passion—the fellowship in living,
the fellowship in life.

They walked in silence to the town's edge and then Melville
Stoner put out his hand. "You'll come with me?" she asked, but
he shook his head and laughed. "No," he said, "I'll stay here. My

time for going passed long ago. I'll stay here until I die. I'll stay here with my thoughts."

He turned and walked away into the darkness beyond the round circle of light cast by the last street lamp on the street that now became a country road leading to the next town to the east. Rosalind stood to watch him go and something in his long loping gait again suggested to her mind the figure of a gigantic bird. "He is like the gulls that float above the river in Chicago," she thought. "His spirit floats above the town of Willow Springs. When the death in life comes to the people here he swoops down, with his mind, plucking out the beauty of them."

She walked at first slowly along the road between corn fields. The night was a vast quiet place into which she could walk in peace. A little breeze rustled the corn blades but there were no dreadful significant human sounds, the sounds made by those who lived physically but who in spirit were dead, had accepted death, believed only in death. The corn blades rubbed against each other and there was a low sweet sound as though something was being born, old dead physical life was being torn away, cast aside. Perhaps new life was coming into the land.

Rosalind began to run. She had thrown off the town and her father and mother as a runner might throw off a heavy and unnecessary garment. She wished also to throw off the garments that stood between her body and nudity. She wanted to be naked, new born. Two miles out of town a bridge crossed Willow Creek. It was now empty and dry but in the darkness she imagined it filled with water, swift running water, water the color of chrysoprase. She had been running swiftly and now she stopped and stood on the bridge her breath coming in quick little gasps.

After a time she went on again, walking until she had regained her breath and then running again. Her body tingled with life. She did not ask herself what she was going to do, how she was to meet the problem she had come to Willow Springs half hoping to have solved by a word from her mother. She ran. Before her eyes the dusty road kept coming up to her out of darkness. She ran forward, always forward into a faint streak of light. The darkness unfolded before her. There was joy in the running and with every step she took she achieved a new sense of escape. A delicious notion came into her mind. As she ran she thought the light under her feet became more distinct. It was, she thought, as though the darkness had grown afraid in her presence and sprang aside, out of her path. There was a sensation of boldness. She had herself become something that within itself contained light. She was a creator of light. At her approach darkness grew afraid and fled away into the distance. When that thought came she found herself able to run without stopping to rest and half wished she might run on forever, through the land, through towns and cities, driving darkness away with her presence.

The Egg

My FATHER WAS, I am sure, intended by nature to be a cheerful, kindly man. Until he was thirty-four years old he worked as a farm-hand for a man named Thomas Butterworth whose place lay near the town of Bidwell, Ohio. He had then a horse of his own and on Saturday evenings drove into town to spend a few hours in social intercourse with other farm-hands. In town he drank several glasses of beer and stood about in Ben Head's saloon—crowded on Saturday evenings with visiting farm-hands. Songs were sung and glasses thumped on the bar. At ten o'clock father drove home along a lonely country road, made his horse comfortable for the night and himself went to bed, quite happy in his position in life. He had at that time no notion of trying to rise in the world.

It was in the spring of his thirty-fifth year that father married my mother, then a country school-teacher, and in the following spring I came wriggling and crying into the world. Something happened to the two people. They became ambitious. The American passion for getting up in the world took possession of them.

It may have been that mother was responsible. Being a school-teacher she had no doubt read books and magazines. She had, I presume, read of how Garfield, Lincoln, and other Americans rose from poverty to fame and greatness and as I lay beside her—in the days of her lying-in—she may have dreamed that I would some day rule men and cities. At any rate she induced father to give up his place as a farm-hand, sell his horse and embark on an independent enterprise of his own. She was a tall silent woman with a long nose and troubled grey eyes. For herself she wanted nothing. For father and myself she was incurably ambitious.

The first venture into which the two people went turned out badly. They rented ten acres of poor stony land on Griggs's Road, eight miles from Bidwell, and launched into chicken raising. I grew into boyhood on the place and got my first impressions of life there. From the beginning they were impressions of disaster and if, in my turn, I am a gloomy man inclined to see the darker side of life, I attribute it to the fact that what should have been for me the happy joyous days of childhood were spent on a chicken farm.

One unversed in such matters can have no notion of the many and tragic things that can happen to a chicken. It is born out of an egg, lives for a few weeks as a tiny fluffy thing such as you will see pictured on Easter cards, then becomes hideously naked, eats quantities of corn and meal bought by the sweat of your father's brow, gets diseases called pip, cholera, and other names, stands looking with stupid eyes at the sun, becomes sick and dies. A few hens and now and then a rooster, intended to serve God's mysterious ends, struggle through to maturity. The hens lay eggs out of which come other chickens and the dreadful cycle is thus made complete. It is all unbelievably complex. Most philosophers must have been raised on chicken farms. One hopes for so much from a chicken and is so dreadfully disillusioned. Small chickens, just setting out on the journey of life, look so bright and alert and they are in fact so dreadfully stupid. They are so much like people they mix one up in one's judgments of life. If disease does not kill them they wait until your expectations are thoroughly aroused and then walk under the wheels of a wagon—to go squashed and dead back to their maker. Vermin infest their youth, and fortunes must be spent for curative powders. In later life I have seen how a literature has been built up on the subject of fortunes to be made out of the raising of chickens. It is intended to be read by the gods who have just eaten of the tree of the knowledge of good and evil. It is a hopeful literature and declares that much may be done by simple ambitious people who own a few hens. Do not be led astray by it. It was not written for you. Go hunt for gold on the frozen hills of Alaska, put your faith in the honesty of a politician, believe if you will that the world is daily growing better and that good will triumph over evil, but do not read and believe the literature that is written concerning the hen. It was not written for you.

I, however, digress. My tale does not primarily concern itself with the hen. If correctly told it will centre on the egg. For ten years my father and mother struggled to make our chicken farm pay and then they gave up that struggle and began another. They moved into the town of Bidwell, Ohio and embarked in the restaurant business. After ten years of worry with incubators that did not hatch, and with tiny—and in their own way lovely—balls of fluff that passed on into semi-naked pullethood and from that into dead henhood, we threw all aside and packing our belongings on a wagon drove down Griggs's Road toward Bidwell, a tiny caravan of hope looking for a new place from which to start on our upward journey through life.

We must have been a sad looking lot, not, I fancy, unlike refugees fleeing from a battlefield. Mother and I walked in the road. The wagon that contained our goods had been borrowed for the day from Mr. Albert Griggs, a neighbor. Out of its sides stuck the legs of cheap chairs and at the back of the pile of beds, tables, and boxes filled with kitchen utensils was a crate of live chickens, and on top of that the baby carriage in which I had been wheeled about in my infancy. Why we stuck to the baby carriage I don't know. It was unlikely other children would be born and the wheels were broken. People who have few possessions cling tightly to those they have. That is one of the facts that make life so discouraging.

Father rode on top of the wagon. He was then a bald-headed man of forty-five, a little fat and from long association with mother and the chickens he had become habitually silent and discouraged. All during our ten years on the chicken farm he had worked as a laborer on neighboring farms and most of the money he had earned had been spent for remedies to cure chicken diseases, on Wilmer's White Wonder Cholera Cure or Professor Bidlow's Egg Producer or some other preparations that mother found advertised in the poultry papers. There were two little patches of hair on father's head just above his ears. I remember that as a child I used to sit looking at him when he had gone to sleep in a chair before the stove on Sunday afternoons in the winter. I had at that time already begun to read books and have notions of my own and the bald path that led over the top of his head was, I fancied, something like a broad road, such a road as Caesar might have made on which to lead his legions out of Rome and into the wonders of an unknown world. The tufts of hair that grew above father's ears were, I thought, like forests. I fell into a half-sleeping, half-waking state and dreamed I was a tiny thing going along the road into a far beautiful place where there were no chicken farms and where life was a happy eggless affair.

One might write a book concerning our flight from the chicken farm into town. Mother and I walked the entire eight miles—she to be sure that nothing fell from the wagon and I to see the wonders of the world. On the seat of the wagon beside father was his greatest treasure. I will tell you of that.

On a chicken farm where hundreds and even thousands of chickens come out of eggs surprising things sometimes happen. Grotesques are born out of eggs as out of people. The accident does not often occur—perhaps once in a thousand births. A chicken is, you see, born that has four legs, two pairs of wings, two heads or what not. The things do not live. They go quickly back to the hand of their maker that has for a moment trembled. The fact that the poor little things could not live was one of the tragedies of life to father. He had some sort of notion that if he could but bring into henhood or rooster-hood a five-legged hen or a two-headed rooster his fortune would be made. He dreamed of taking the wonder about to county fairs and of growing rich by exhibiting it to other farmhands.

At any rate he saved all the little monstrous things that had been born on our chicken farm. They were preserved in alcohol and put each in its own glass bottle. These he had carefully put into a box and on our journey into town it was carried on the wagon seat beside him. He drove the horses with one hand and with the other clung to the box. When we got to our destination the box was taken down at once and the bottles removed. All during our days as keepers of a restaurant in the town of Bidwell, Ohio, the grotesques in their little glass bottles sat on a shelf back of the counter. Mother sometimes protested but father was a rock on the subject of his treasure. The grotesques were, he declared, valuable. People, he said, liked to look at strange and wonderful things.

Did I say that we embarked in the restaurant business in the town of Bidwell, Ohio? I exaggerated a little. The town itself lay at the foot of a low hill and on the shore of a small river. The railroad did not run through the town and the station was a mile away to the north at a place called Pickleville. There had been a cider mill and pickle factory at the station, but before the time of our coming they had both gone out of business. In the morning and in the evening busses came down to the station along a road called Turner's Pike from the hotel on the main street of Bidwell. Our going to the out of the way place to embark in the restaurant business was mother's idea. She talked of it for a year and then one day went off and rented an empty store building opposite the railroad station. It was her idea that the restaurant would be profitable. Travelling men, she said, would be always waiting around to take trains out of town and town people would come to the station to await incoming trains. They would come to the restaurant to buy pieces of pie and drink coffee. Now that I am older I know that she had another motive in going. She was ambitious for me. She wanted me to rise in the world, to get into a town school and become a man of the towns.

At Pickleville father and mother worked hard as they always had done. At first there was the necessity of putting our place into shape to be a restaurant. That took a month. Father built a shelf on which he put tins of vegetables. He painted a sign on which he put his name in large red letters. Below his name was the sharp command—"EAT HERE"—that was so seldom obeyed. A show case was bought and filled with cigars and tobacco. Mother scrubbed the floor and the walls of the room. I went to school in the town and was glad to be away from the farm and from the presence of the discouraged, sad-looking chickens. Still I was not very joyous. In the evening I walked home from school along Turner's Pike and remembered the children I had seen playing in the town school yard. A troop of little girls had gone hopping about and singing. I tried that. Down along the frozen road I went hopping solemnly on one leg. "Hippity Hop To The Barber Shop," I sang shrilly. Then I stopped and looked doubtfully about. I was afraid of being seen in my gay mood. It must have seemed to me that I was doing a thing that should not be done by one who, like myself, had been raised on a chicken farm where death was a daily visitor.

Mother decided that our restaurant should remain open at night. At ten in the evening a passenger train went north past our door followed by a local freight. The freight crew had switching to do in Pickleville and when the work was done they came to our restaurant for hot coffee and food. Sometimes one of them ordered a fried egg. In the morning at four they returned north-bound and again visited us. A little trade began to grow up. Mother slept at night and during the day tended the restaurant and fed our boarders while father slept. He slept in the same bed mother had occupied during the night and I went off to the town of Bidwell and to school. During the long nights, while mother and I slept, father cooked meats that were to go into sandwiches for the lunch baskets of our boarders. Then an idea in regard to getting up in the world came into his head. The American spirit took hold of him. He also became ambitious.

In the long nights when there was little to do father had time to think. That was his undoing. He decided that he had in the past been an unsuccessful man because he had not been cheerful enough and that in the future he would adopt a cheerful outlook on life. In the early morning he came upstairs and got into bed with mother. She woke and the two talked. From my bed in the corner I listened.

It was father's idea that both he and mother should try to entertain the people who came to eat at our restaurant. I cannot now remember his words, but he gave the impression of one about to become in some obscure way a kind of public entertainer. When people, particularly young people from the town of Bidwell, came into our place, as on very rare occasions they did, bright entertaining conversation was to be made. From father's words I gathered that something of the jolly innkeeper effect was to be sought. Mother must have been doubtful from the first, but she said nothing discouraging. It was father's notion that a passion for the company of himself and mother would spring up in the breasts of the younger people of the town of Bidwell. In the evening bright happy groups would come singing down Turner's Pike. They would troop shouting with joy and laughter into our place. There would be song and festivity. I do not mean to give the impression that father spoke so elaborately of the matter. He was as I have said an uncommunicative man. "They want some place to go. I tell you they want some place to go," he said over and over. That was as far as he got. My own imagination has filled in the blanks.

For two or three weeks this notion of father's invaded our house. We did not talk much, but in our daily lives tried earnestly to make smiles take the place of glum looks. Mother smiled at the boarders and I, catching the infection, smiled at our cat. Father became a little feverish in his anxiety to please. There was no doubt, lurking somewhere in him, a touch of the spirit of the showman. He did not waste much of his ammunition on the railroad men he served at night but seemed to be waiting for a young man or woman from Bidwell to come in to show what he could do. On the counter in the restaurant there was a wire basket kept always filled with eggs, and it must have been before his eyes when the idea of being entertaining was born in his brain. There was something pre-natal about the way eggs kept themselves connected with the development of his idea. At any rate an egg ruined his new impulse in life. Late one night I was awakened by a roar of anger coming from father's throat. Both mother and I sat upright in our beds. With trembling hands she lighted a lamp that stood on a table by her head. Downstairs the front door of our restaurant went shut with a bang and in a few minutes father tramped up the stairs. He held an egg in his hand and his hand trembled as though he were having a chill. There was a half insane light in his eyes. As he stood glaring at us I was sure he intended throwing the egg at either mother or me. Then he laid it gently on the table beside the lamp and dropped on his knees beside mother's bed. He began to cry like a boy and I, carried away by his grief, cried with him. The two of us filled the little upstairs room with our wailing voices. It is ridiculous, but of the picture we made I can remember only the fact that mother's hand continually stroked the bald path that ran across the top of his head. I have forgotten what mother said to him and how she induced him to tell her of what had happened downstairs. His explanation also has gone out of my mind. I remember only my own grief and fright and the shiny path over father's head glowing in the lamp light as he knelt by the bed.

As to what happened downstairs. For some unexplainable reason I know the story as well as though I had been a witness to my father's discomfiture. One in time gets to know many unexplainable things. On that evening young Joe Kane, son of a merchant of Bidwell, came to Pickleville to meet his father, who was expected on the ten o'clock evening train from the South. The train was three hours late and Joe came into our place to loaf about and to wait for its arrival. The local freight train came in and the freight crew were fed. Joe was left alone in the restaurant with father.

From the moment he came into our place the Bidwell young man must have been puzzled by my father's actions. It was his notion that father was angry at him for hanging around. He noticed that the restaurant keeper was apparently disturbed by his presence and he thought of going out. However, it began to rain and he did not fancy the long walk to town and back. He bought a five-cent cigar and ordered a cup of coffee. He had a newspaper in his pocket and took it out and began to read. "I'm waiting for the evening train. It's late," he said apologetically.

For a long time father, whom Joe Kane had never seen before, remained silently gazing at his visitor. He was no doubt suffering from an attack of stage fright. As so often happens in life he had thought so much and so often of the situation that now confronted him that he was somewhat nervous in its presence.

For one thing, he did not know what to do with his hands. He thrust one of them nervously over the counter and shook hands with Joe Kane. "How-de-do," he said. Joe Kane put his newspaper down and stared at him. Father's eye lighted on the basket of eggs that sat on the counter and he began to talk. "Well," he began hesitatingly, "well, you have heard of Christopher Columbus, eh?" He seemed to be angry. "That Christopher Columbus was a cheat," he declared emphatically. "He talked of making an egg stand on its end. He talked, he did, and then he went and broke the end of the egg."

My father seemed to his visitor to be beside himself at the duplicity of Christopher Columbus. He muttered and swore. He declared it was wrong to teach children that Christopher Columbus was a great man when, after all, he cheated at the critical moment. He had declared he would make an egg stand on end and then when his bluff had been called he had done a trick. Still grumbling at Columbus, father took an egg from the basket on the counter and began to walk up and down. He rolled the egg between the palms of his hands. He smiled genially. He began to mumble words regarding the effect to be produced on an egg by the electricity that comes out of the human body. He declared that without breaking its shell and by virtue of rolling it back and forth in his hands he could stand the egg on its end. He explained that the warmth of his hands and the gentle rolling movement he gave the egg created a new centre of gravity, and Joe Kane was mildly interested. "I have handled thousands of eggs," Father said. "No one knows more about eggs than I do."

He stood the egg on the counter and it fell on its side. He tried the trick again and again, each time rolling the egg between the palms of his hands and saying the words regarding the wonders of electricity and the laws of gravity. When after a half hour's effort he did succeed in making the egg stand for a moment he looked up to find that his visitor was no longer watching. By the time he had succeeded in calling Joe Kane's attention to the success of his effort the egg had again rolled over and lay on its side.

Afire with the showman's passion and at the same time a good deal disconcerted by the failure of his first effort, father now took the bottles containing the poultry monstrosities down from their place on the shelf and began to show them to his visitor. "How would you like to have seven legs and two heads like this fellow?" he asked, exhibiting the most remarkable of his treasures. A cheerful smile played over his face. He reached over the counter and tried to slap Joe Kane on the shoulder as he had seen men do in Ben Head's saloon when he was a young farm-hand and drove to town on Saturday evenings. His visitor was made a little ill by the sight of the body of the terribly deformed bird floating in the alcohol in the bottle and got up to go. Coming from behind the counter father took hold of the young man's arm and led him back to his seat. He grew a little angry and for a moment had to turn his face away and force himself to smile. Then he put the bottles back on the shelf. In a outburst of generosity he fairly compelled Joe Kane to have a fresh cup of coffee and another cigar at his expense. Then he took a pan and filling it with vinegar, taken from a jug that sat beneath the counter, he declared himself about to do a new trick. "I will heat this egg in this pan of vinegar," he said. "Then I will put it through the neck of a bottle without breaking the shell. When the egg is inside the bottle it will resume its normal shape and the shell will become hard again. Then I will give the bottle with the egg in it to you. You can take it about with you wherever you go. People will want to know how you got the egg in the bottle. Don't tell them. Keep them guessing. That is the way to have fun with this trick."

Father grinned and winked at his visitor. Joe Kane decided that the man who confronted him was mildly insane but harmless. He drank the cup of coffee that had been given him and began to read his paper again. When the egg had been heated in vinegar father carried it on a spoon to the counter and going into a back room got an empty bottle. He was angry because his visitor did not watch him as he began to do his trick, but nevertheless went cheerfully to work. For a long time he struggled, trying to get the egg to go through the neck of the bottle. He put the pan of vinegar back on the stove, intending to reheat the egg, then picked it up and burned his fingers. After a second bath in the hot vinegar the shell of the egg had been softened a little but not enough for his purpose. He worked and worked and a spirit of desperate determination took possession of him. When he thought that at last the trick was about to be consummated the delayed train came in at the station and Joe Kane started to go nonchalantly out at the door. Father made a last desperate effort to conquer the egg and make it do the thing that would establish his reputation as one who knew how to entertain guests who came into his restaurant. He worried the egg. He attempted to be somewhat rough with it. He swore and the sweat stood out on his forehead. The egg broke under his hand. When the contents spurted over his clothes, Joe Kane, who had stopped at the door, turned and laughed.

A roar of anger rose from my father's throat. He danced and shouted a string of inarticulate words. Grabbing another egg from the basket on the counter, he threw it, just missing the head of the young man as he dodged through the door and escaped.

Father came upstairs to mother and me with an egg in his hand. I do not know what he intended to do. I imagine he had some idea of destroying it, of destroying all eggs, and that he intended to let mother and me see him begin. When, however, he got into the presence of mother something happened to him. He laid the egg gently on the table and dropped on his knees by the bed as I have already explained. He later decided to close the restaurant for the night and to come upstairs and get into bed. When he did so he blew out the light and after much muttered conversation both he and mother went to sleep. I suppose I went to sleep also, but my sleep was troubled. I awoke at dawn and for a long time looked at the egg that lay on the table. I wondered why eggs had to be and why from the egg came the hen who again laid the egg. The question got into my blood. It has stayed there, I imagine, because I am the son of my father. At any rate, the problem remains unsolved in my mind. And that, I conclude, is but another evidence of the complete and final triumph of the egg—at least as far as my family is concerned.

The Other Woman

"I AM IN love with my wife," he said—a superfluous remark, as I had not questioned his attachment to the woman he had married. We walked for ten minutes and then he said it again. I turned to look at him. He began to talk and told me the tale I am now about to set down.

The thing he had on his mind happened during what must have been the most eventful week of his life. He was to be married on Friday afternoon. On Friday of the week before he got a telegram announcing his appointment to a government position. Something else happened that made him very proud and glad. In secret he was in the habit of writing verses and during the year before several of them had been printed in poetry magazines. One of the societies that give prizes for what they think the best poems published during the year put his name at the head of its list. The story of his triumph was printed in the newspapers of his home city and one of them also printed his picture.

As might have been expected he was excited and in a rather highly strung nervous state all during that week. Almost every evening he went to call on his fiancée, the daughter of a judge. When he got there the house was filled with people and many letters, telegrams and packages were being received. He stood a little to one side and men and women kept coming up to speak to him. They congratulated him upon his success in getting the government position and on his achievement as a poet. Everyone seemed to be praising him and when he went home and to bed he could not sleep. On Wednesday evening he went to the theatre and it seemed to him that people all over the house recognized him. Everyone nodded and smiled. After the first act five or six men and two women left their seats to gather about him. A little group was formed. Strangers sitting along the same row of seats stretched their necks and looked. He had never received so much attention before, and now a fever of expectancy took possession of him.

As he explained when he told me of his experience, it was for him an altogether abnormal time. He felt like one floating in air. When he got into bed after seeing so many people and hearing so many words of praise his head whirled round and round. When he closed his eyes a crowd of people invaded his room. It seemed as though the minds of all the people of his city were centred on himself. The most absurd fancies took possession of him. He imagined himself riding in a carriage through the streets of a city. Windows were thrown open and people ran out at the doors of houses. "There he is. That's him," they shouted, and at the words a glad cry arose. The carriage drove into a street blocked with people. A hundred thousand pairs of eyes looked up at him. "There you are! What a fellow you have managed to make of yourself!" the eyes seemed to be saying.

My friend could not explain whether the excitement of the people was due to the fact that he had written a new poem or whether, in his new government position, he had performed some notable act. The apartment where he lived at that time was on a street perched along the top of a cliff far out at the edge of his city, and from his bedroom window he could look down over trees and factory roofs to a river. As he could not sleep and as the fancies that kept crowding in upon him only made him more excited, he got out of bed and tried to think.

As would be natural under such circumstances, he tried to control his thoughts, but when he sat by the window and was wide awake a most unexpected and humiliating thing happened. The night was clear and fine. There was a moon. He wanted to dream of the woman who was to be his wife, to think out lines for noble poems or make plans that would affect his career. Much to his surprise his mind refused to do anything of the sort.

At a corner of the street where he lived there was a small cigar store and newspaper stand run by a fat man of forty and his wife, a small active woman with bright grey eyes. In the morning he stopped there to buy a paper before going down to the city. Sometimes he saw only the fat man, but often the man had disappeared and the woman waited on him. She was, as he assured me at least twenty times in telling me his tale, a very ordinary person with nothing special or notable about her, but for some reason he could not explain, being in her presence stirred him profoundly. During that week in the midst of his distraction she was the only person he knew who stood out clear and distinct in his mind. When he wanted so much to think noble thoughts he could think only of her. Before he knew what was happening his imagination had taken hold of the notion of having a love affair with the woman.

"I could not understand myself," he declared, in telling me the story. "At night, when the city was quiet and when I should have been asleep, I thought about her all the time. After two or three days of that sort of thing the consciousness of her got into my daytime thoughts. I was terribly muddled. When I went to see the woman who is now my wife I found that my love for her was in no way affected by my vagrant thoughts. There was but one woman in the world I wanted to live with and to be my comrade in undertaking to improve my own character and my position in the world, but for the moment, you see, I wanted this other woman to be in my arms. She had worked her way into my being. On all sides people were saying I was a big man who would do big things, and there I was. That evening when I went to the theatre I walked home because I knew I would be unable to sleep, and to satisfy the annoying impulse in myself I went and stood on the sidewalk before the tobacco shop. It was a two story building, and I knew the woman lived upstairs with her husband. For a long time I stood in the darkness with my body pressed against the wall of the building, and then I thought of the two of them up there and no doubt in bed together. That made me furious.

"Then I grew more furious with myself. I went home and got into bed, shaken with anger. There are certain books of verse and some prose writings that have always moved me deeply, and so I put several books on a table by my bed.

"The voices in the books were like the voices of the dead. I did not hear them. The printed words would not penetrate into my consciousness. I tried to think of the woman I loved, but her figure had also become something far away, something with which I for the moment seemed to have nothing to do. I rolled and tumbled about in the bed. It was a miserable experience.

"On Thursday morning I went into the store. There stood the woman alone. I think she knew how I felt. Perhaps she had been thinking of me as I had been thinking of her. A doubtful hesitating smile played about the corners of her mouth. She had on a dress made of cheap cloth and there was a tear on the shoulder. She must have been ten years older than myself. When I tried to put my pennies on the glass counter, behind which she stood, my hand trembled so that the pennies made a sharp rattling noise. When I spoke the voice that came out of my throat did not sound like anything that had ever belonged to me. It barely arose above a thick whisper. 'I want you,' I said. 'I want you very much. Can't you run away from your husband? Come to me at my apartment at seven tonight.'

"The woman did come to my apartment at seven. That morning she didn't say anything at all. For a minute perhaps we stood looking at each other. I had forgotten everything in the world but just her. Then she nodded her head and I went away. Now that I think of it I cannot remember a word I ever heard her say. She came to my apartment at seven and it was dark. You must understand this was in the month of October. I had not lighted a light and I had sent my servant away.

"During that day I was no good at all. Several men came to see me at my office, but I got all muddled up in trying to talk with them. They attributed my rattle-headedness to my approaching marriage and went away laughing.

"It was on that morning, just the day before my marriage, that I got a long and very beautiful letter from my fiancée. During the night before she also had been unable to sleep and had got out of bed to write the letter. Everything she said in it was very sharp and real, but she herself, as a living thing, seemed to have receded into the distance. It seemed to me that she was like a bird, flying far away in distant skies, and that I was like a perplexed bare-footed boy standing in the dusty road before a farm house and looking at her receding figure. I wonder if you will understand what I mean?

"In regard to the letter. In it she, the awakening woman, poured out her heart. She of course knew nothing of life, but she was a woman. She lay, I suppose, in her bed feeling nervous and wrought up as I had been doing. She realized that a great change was about to take place in her life and was glad and afraid too. There she lay thinking of it all. Then she got out of bed and began talking to me on the bit of paper. She told me how afraid she was and how glad too. Like most young women she had heard things whispered. In the letter she was very sweet and fine. 'For a long time, after we are married, we will forget we are a man and woman,' she wrote. 'We will be human beings. You must remember that I am ignorant and often I will be very stupid. You must love me and be very patient and kind. When I know more, when after a long time you have taught me the way of life, I will try to repay you. I will love you tenderly and passionately. The possibility of that is in me or I would not want to marry at all. I am afraid but I am also happy. O, I am so glad our marriage time is near at hand!'

"Now you see clearly enough what a mess I was in. In my office, after I had read my fiancée's letter, I became at once very resolute and strong. I remember that I got out of my chair and walked about, proud of the fact that I was to be the husband of so noble a woman. Right away I felt concerning her as I had been feeling about myself before I found out what a weak thing I was. To be sure I took a strong resolution that I would not be weak. At nine that evening I had planned to run in to see my fiancée. 'I'm all right now,' I said to myself. 'The beauty of her character has saved me from myself. I will go home now and send the other woman away.' In the morning I had telephoned to my servant and told him that I did not want him to be at the apartment that evening and I now picked up the telephone to tell him to stay at home.

"Then a thought came to me. 'I will not want him there in any event,' I told myself. 'What will he think when he sees a woman coming in my place on the evening before the day I am to be married?' I put the telephone down and prepared to go home. 'If I want my servant out of the apartment it is because I do not want him to hear me talk with the woman. I cannot be rude to her. I will have to make some kind of an explanation,' I said to myself.

"The woman came at seven o'clock, and, as you may have guessed, I let her in and forgot the resolution I had made. It is likely I never had any intention of doing anything else. There was a bell on my door, but she did not ring, but knocked very softly. It seems to me that everything she did that evening was soft and quiet, but very determined and quick. Do I make myself clear? When she came I was standing just within the door where I had been standing and waiting for a half hour. My hands were trembling as they had trembled in the morning when her eyes looked at me and when I tried to put the pennies on the counter in the store. When I opened the door she stepped quickly in and I took her into my arms. We stood together in the darkness. My hands no longer trembled. I felt very happy and strong.

"Although I have tried to make everything clear I have not told you what the woman I married is like. I have emphasized, you see, the other woman. I make the blind statement that I love my wife, and to a man of your shrewdness that means nothing at all. To tell the truth, had I not started to speak of this matter I would feel more comfortable. It is inevitable that I give you the impression that I am in love with the tobacconist's wife. That's not true. To be sure I was very conscious of her all during the week before my marriage, but after she had come to me at my apartment she went entirely out of my mind.

"Am I telling the truth? I am trying very hard to tell what happened to me. I am saying that I have not since that evening thought of the woman who came to my apartment. Now, to tell the facts of the case, that is not true. On that evening I went to my fiancée at nine, as she had asked me to do in her letter. In a kind of way I cannot explain the other woman went with me. This is what I mean—you see I had been thinking that if anything happened between me and the tobacconist's wife I would not be able to go through with my marriage. 'It is one thing or the other with me,' I had said to myself.

"As a matter of fact I went to see my beloved on that evening filled with a new faith in the outcome of our life together. I am afraid I muddle this matter in trying to tell it. A moment ago I said the other woman, the tobacconist's wife, went with me. I do not mean she went in fact. What I am trying to say is that something of her faith in her own desires and her courage in seeing things through went with me. Is that clear to you? When I got to my fiancée's house there was a crowd of people standing about. Some were relatives from distant places I had not seen before. She looked up quickly when I came into the room. My face must have been radiant. I never saw her so moved. She thought her letter had affected me deeply, and of course it had. Up she jumped and ran to meet me. She was like a glad child. Right before the people who turned and looked inquiringly at us, she said the thing that was in her mind. 'O, I am so happy,' she cried. 'You have understood. We will be two human beings. We will not have to be husband and wife.'

"As you may suppose everyone laughed, but I did not laugh. The tears came into my eyes. I was so happy I wanted to shout. Perhaps you understand what I mean. In the office that day when I read the letter my fiancée had written I had said to myself, 'I will take care of the dear little woman.' There was something smug, you see, about that. In her house when she cried out in that way, and when everyone laughed, what I said to myself was something like this: 'We will take care of ourselves.' I whispered something of the sort into her ears. To tell you the truth I had come down off my perch. The spirit of the other woman did that to me. Before all the people gathered about I held my fiancée close and we kissed. They thought it very sweet of us to be so affected at the sight of each other. What they would have thought had they known the truth about me God only knows!

"Twice now I have said that after that evening I never thought of the other woman at all. That is partially true but, sometimes in the evening when I am walking alone in the street or in the park as we are walking now, and when evening comes softly and quickly as it has come to-night, the feeling of her comes sharply into my body and mind. After that one meeting I never saw her again. On the next day I was married and I have never gone back into her street. Often however as I am walking along as I am doing now, a quick sharp earthy feeling takes possession of me. It is as though I were a seed in the ground and the warm rains of the spring had come. It is as though I were not a man but a tree.

"And now you see I am married and everything is all right. My marriage is to me a very beautiful fact. If you were to say that my marriage is not a happy one I could call you a liar and be speaking the absolute truth. I have tried to tell you about this other woman. There is a kind of relief in speaking of her. I have never done it before. I wonder why I was so silly as to be afraid that I would give you the impression I am not in love with my wife. If I did not instinctively trust your understanding I would not have spoken. As the matter stands I have a little stirred myself up. To-night I shall think of the other woman. That sometimes occurs. It will happen after I have gone to bed. My wife sleeps in the next room to mine and the door is always left open. There will be a moon to-night, and when there is a moon long streaks of light fall on her bed. I shall awake at midnight to-night. She will be lying asleep with one arm thrown over her head.

"What is it that I am now talking about? A man does not speak of his wife lying in bed. What I am trying to say is that, because of this talk, I shall think of the other woman to-night. My thoughts will not take the form they did during the week before I was married. I will wonder what has become of the woman. For a moment I will again feel myself holding her close. I will think that for an hour I was closer to her than I have ever been to anyone else. Then I will think of the time when I will be as close as that to my wife. She is still, you see, an awakening woman. For a moment I will close my eyes and the quick, shrewd, determined eyes of that other woman will look into mine. My head will swim and then I will quickly open my eyes and see again the dear woman with whom I have undertaken to live out my life. Then I will sleep and when I awake in the morning it will be as it was that evening when I walked out of my dark apartment after having had the most notable experience of my life. What I mean to say, you understand is that, for me, when I awake, the other woman will be utterly gone."

I Want to Know Why

WE GOT UP at four in the morning, that first day in the east. On the evening before we had climbed off a freight train at the edge of town, and with the true instinct of Kentucky boys had found our way across town and to the race track and the stables at once. Then we knew we were all right. Hanley Turner right away found a nigger we knew. It was Bildad Johnson who in the winter works at Ed Becker's livery barn in our home town, Beckersville. Bildad is a good cook as almost all our niggers are and of course he, like everyone in our part of Kentucky who is anyone at all, likes the horses. In the spring Bildad begins to scratch around. A nigger from our country can flatter and wheedle anyone into letting him do most anything he wants. Bildad wheedles the stable men and the trainers from the horse farms in our country around Lexington. The trainers come into town in the evening to stand around and talk and maybe get into a poker game. Bildad gets in with them. He is always doing little favors and telling about things to eat, chicken browned in a pan, and how is the best way to cook sweet potatoes and corn bread. It makes your mouth water to hear him.

When the racing season comes on and the horses go to the races and there is all the talk on the streets in the evenings about the new colts, and everyone says when they are going to Lexington or to the spring meeting at Churchill Downs or to Latonia, and the horsemen that have been down to New Orleans or maybe at the winter meeting at Havana in Cuba come home to spend a week before they start out again, at such a time when everything talked about in Beckersville is just horses and nothing else and the outfits start out and horse racing is in every breath of air you breathe, Bildad

71

shows up with a job as cook for some outfit. Often when I think about it, his always going all season to the races and working in the livery barn in the winter where horses are and where men like to come and talk about horses, I wish I was a nigger. It's a foolish thing to say, but that's the way I am about being around horses, just crazy. I can't help it.

Well, I must tell you about what we did and let you in on what I'm talking about. Four of us boys from Beckersville, all whites and sons of men who live in Beckersville regular, made up our minds we were going to the races, not just to Lexington or Louisville, I don't mean, but to the big eastern track we were always hearing our Beckersville men talk about, to Saratoga. We were all pretty young then. I was just turned fifteen and I was the oldest of the four. It was my scheme. I admit that and I talked the others into trying it. There was Hanley Turner and Henry Rieback and Tom Tumberton and myself. I had thirty-seven dollars I had earned during the winter working nights and Saturdays in Enoch Myer's grocery. Henry Rieback had eleven dollars and the others, Hanley and Tom had only a dollar or two each. We fixed it all up and laid low until the Kentucky spring meetings were over and some of our men, the sportiest ones, the ones we envied the most, had cut out—then we cut out too.

I won't tell you the trouble we had beating our way on freights and all. We went through Cleveland and Buffalo and other cities and saw Niagara Falls. We bought things there, souvenirs and spoons and cards and shells with pictures of the falls on them for our sisters and mothers, but thought we had better not send any of the things home. We didn't want to put the folks on our trail and maybe be nabbed.

We got into Saratoga as I said at night and went to the track. Bildad fed us up. He showed us a place to sleep in hay over a shed and promised to keep still. Niggers are all right about things like that. They won't squeal on you. Often a white man you might meet, when you had run away from home like that, might appear to be all right and give you a quarter or a half dollar or something, and then go right and give you away. White men will do that, but not a nigger. You can trust them. They are squarer with kids. I don't know why.

At the Saratoga meeting that year there were a lot of men from home. Dave Williams and Arthur Mulford and Jerry Myers and others. Then there was a lot from Louisville and Lexington Henry

Rieback knew but I didn't. They were professional gamblers and Henry Rieback's father is one too. He is what is called a sheet writer and goes away most of the year to tracks. In the winter when he is home in Beckersville he don't stay there much but goes away to cities and deals faro. He is a nice man and generous, is always sending Henry presents, a bicycle and a gold watch and a boy scout suit of clothes and things like that.

My own father is a lawyer. He's all right, but don't make much money and can't buy me things and anyway I'm getting so old now I don't expect it. He never said nothing to me against Henry, but Hanley Turner and Tom Tumberton's fathers did. They said to their boys that money so come by is no good and they didn't want their boys brought up to hear gamblers' talk and be thinking about such things and maybe embrace them.

That's all right and I guess the men know what they are talking about, but I don't see what it's got to do with Henry or with horses either. That's what I'm writing this story about. I'm puzzled. I'm getting to be a man and want to think straight and be O. K., and there's something I saw at the race meeting at the eastern track I can't figure out.

I can't help it, I'm crazy about thoroughbred horses. I've always been that way. When I was ten years old and saw I was growing to be big and couldn't be a rider I was so sorry I nearly died. Harry Hellinfinger in Beckersville, whose father is Postmaster, is grown up and too lazy to work, but likes to stand around in the street and get up jokes on boys like sending them to a hardware store for a gimlet to bore square holes and other jokes like that. He played one on me. He told me that if I would eat a half a cigar I would be stunted and not grow any more and maybe could be a rider. I did it. When father wasn't looking I took a cigar out of his pocket and gagged it down some way. It made me awful sick and the doctor had to be sent for, and then it did no good. I kept right on growing. It was a joke. When I told what I had done and why most fathers would have whipped me but mine didn't.

Well, I didn't get stunted and didn't die. It serves Harry Hellinfinger right. Then I made up my mind I would like to be a stable boy, but had to give that up too. Mostly niggers do that work and I knew father wouldn't let me go into it. No use to ask him.

If you've never been crazy about thoroughbreds it's because you've never been around where they are much and don't know any better. They're beautiful. There isn't anything so lovely and clean and full of spunk and honest and everything as some race horses. On the big horse farms that are all around our town Beckersville there are tracks and the horses run in the early morning. More than a thousand times I've got out of bed before daylight and walked two or three miles to the tracks. Mother wouldn't of let me go but father always says, "Let him alone," so I got some bread out of the bread box and some butter and jam, gobbled it and lit out.

At the tracks you sit on the fence with men, whites and niggers, and they chew tobacco and talk, and then the colts are brought out. It's early and the grass is covered with shiny dew and in another field a man is plowing and they are frying things in a shed where the track niggers sleep, and you know how a nigger can giggle and laugh and say things that make you laugh. A white man can't do it and some niggers can't but a track nigger can every time.

And so the colts are brought out and some are just galloped by stable boys, but almost every morning on a big track owned by a rich man who lives maybe in New York, there are always, nearly every morning, a few colts and some of the old race horses and geldings and mares that are cut loose.

It brings a lump up into my throat when a horse runs. I don't mean all horses but some. I can pick them nearly every time. It's in my blood like in the blood of race track niggers and trainers. Even when they just go slop-jogging along with a little nigger on their backs I can tell a winner. If my throat hurts and it's hard for me to swallow, that's him. He'll run like Sam Hill when you let him out. If he don't win every time it'll be a wonder and because they've got him in a pocket behind another or he was pulled or got off bad at the post or something. If I wanted to be a gambler like Henry Rieback's father I could get rich. I know I could and Henry says so too. All I would have to do is to wait 'til that hurt comes when I see a horse and then bet every cent. That's what I would do if I wanted to be a gambler, but I don't.

When you're at the tracks in the morning—not the race tracks but the training tracks around Beckersville—you don't see a horse, the kind I've been talking about, very often, but it's nice anyway. Any thoroughbred, that is sired right and out of a good mare and trained by a man that knows how, can run. If he couldn't what would he be there for and not pulling a plow?

Well, out of the stables they come and the boys are on their backs and it's lovely to be there. You hunch down on top of the fence and itch inside you. Over in the sheds the niggers giggle and sing. Bacon is being fried and coffee made. Everything smells lovely. Nothing smells better than coffee and manure and horses and niggers and bacon frying and pipes being smoked out of doors on a morning like that. It just gets you, that's what it does.

But about Saratoga. We was there six days and not a soul from home seen us and everything came off just as we wanted it to, fine weather and horses and races and all. We beat our way home and Bildad gave us a basket with fried chicken and bread and other eatables in, and I had eighteen dollars when we got back to Beckersville. Mother jawed and cried but Pop didn't say much. I told everything we done except one thing. I did and saw that alone. That's what I'm writing about. It got me upset. I think about it at night. Here it is.

At Saratoga we laid up nights in the hay in the shed Bildad had showed us and ate with the niggers early and at night when the race people had all gone away. The men from home stayed mostly in the grandstand and betting field, and didn't come out around the places where the horses are kept except to the paddocks just before a race when the horses are saddled. At Saratoga they don't have paddocks under an open shed as at Lexington and Churchill Downs and other tracks down in our country, but saddle the horses right out in an open place under trees on a lawn as smooth and nice as Banker Bohon's front yard here in Beckersville. It's lovely. The horses are sweaty and nervous and shine and the men come out and smoke cigars and look at them and the trainers are there and the owners, and your heart thumps so you can hardly breathe.

Then the bugle blows for post and the boys that ride come running out with their silk clothes on and you run to get a place by the fence with the niggers.

I always am wanting to be a trainer or owner, and at the risk of being seen and caught and sent home I went to the paddocks before every race. The other boys didn't but I did.

We got to Saratoga on a Friday and on Wednesday the next week the big Mullford Handicap was to be run. Middlestride was in it and Sunstreak. The weather was fine and the track fast. I couldn't sleep the night before.

What had happened was that both these horses are the kind it makes my throat hurt to see. Middlestride is long and looks awkward and is a gelding. He belongs to Joe Thompson, a little owner from home who only has a half dozen horses. The Mullford Handicap is for a mile and Middlestride can't untrack fast. He goes away slow and is always way back at the half, then he begins to run and if the race is a mile and a quarter he'll just eat up everything and get there.

Sunstreak is different. He is a stallion and nervous and belongs on the biggest farm we've got in our country, the Van Riddle place that belongs to Mr. Van Riddle of New York. Sunstreak is like a girl you think about sometimes but never see. He is hard all over and lovely too. When you look at his head you want to kiss him. He is trained by Jerry Tillford who knows me and has been good to me lots of times, lets me walk into a horse's stall to look at him close and other things. There isn't anything as sweet as that horse. He stands at the post quiet and not letting on, but he is just burning up inside. Then when the barrier goes up he is off like his name, Sunstreak. It makes you ache to see him. It hurts you. He just lays down and runs like a bird dog. There can't be anything I ever see run like him except Middlestride when he gets untracked and stretches himself.

Gee! I ached to see that race and those two horses run, ached and dreaded it too. I didn't want to see either of our horses beaten. We had never sent a pair like that to the races before. Old men in Beckersville said so and the niggers said so. It was a fact.

Before the race I went over to the paddocks to see. I looked a last look at Middlestride, who isn't such a much standing in a paddock that way, then I went to see Sunstreak.

It was his day. I knew when I see him. I forgot all about being seen myself and walked right up. All the men from Beckersville were there and no one noticed me except Jerry Tillford. He saw me and something happened. I'll tell you about that.

I was standing looking at that horse and aching. In some way, I can't tell how, I knew just how Sunstreak felt inside. He was quiet and letting the niggers rub his legs and Mr. Van Riddle himself put the saddle on, but he was just a raging torrent inside. He was like the water in the river at Niagara Falls just before it goes plunk down. That horse wasn't thinking about running. He don't have to think about that. He was just thinking about holding himself back 'til the time for the running came. I knew that. I could just in a way see right inside him. He was going to do some awful running and I knew it. He wasn't bragging or letting on much or prancing or making a fuss, but just waiting. I knew it and Jerry Tillford his trainer knew. I looked up and then that man and I looked into each other's eyes. Something happened to me. I guess I loved the man as much as I did the horse because he knew what I knew. Seemed to me there wasn't anything in the world but that man and the horse and me.

I cried and Jerry Tillford had a shine in his eyes. Then I came away to the fence to wait for the race. The horse was better than me, more steadier, and now I know better than Jerry. He was the quietest and he had to do the running.

Sunstreak ran first of course and he busted the world's record for a mile. I've seen that if I never see anything more. Everything came out just as I expected. Middlestride got left at the post and was way back and closed up to be second, just as I knew he would. He'll get a world's record too some day. They can't skin the Beckersville country on horses.

I watched the race calm because I knew what would happen. I was sure. Hanley Turner and Henry Rieback and Tom Tumberton were all more excited than me.

A funny thing had happened to me. I was thinking about Jerry Tillford the trainer and how happy he was all through the race. I liked him that afternoon even more than I ever liked my own father. I almost forgot the horses thinking that way about him. It was because of what I had seen in his eyes as he stood in the paddocks beside Sunstreak before the race started. I knew he had been watching and working with Sunstreak since the horse was a baby colt, had taught him to run and be patient and when to let himself out and not to quit, never. I knew that for him it was like a mother seeing her child do something brave or wonderful. It was the first time I ever felt for a man like that.

After the race that night I cut out from Tom and Hanley and Henry. I wanted to be by myself and I wanted to be near Jerry Tillford if I could work it. Here is what happened.

The track in Saratoga is near the edge of town. It is all polished up and trees around, the evergreen kind, and grass and everything painted and nice. If you go past the track you get to a hard road made of asphalt for automobiles, and if you go along this for a few miles there is a road turns off to a little rummy-looking farm house set in a yard.

That night after the race I went along that road because I had seen Jerry and some other men go that way in an automobile. I didn't expect to find them. I walked for a ways and then sat down by a fence to think. It was the direction they went in. I wanted to be as near Jerry as I could. I felt close to him. Pretty soon I went up the side road—I don't know why—and came to the rummy farm house. I was just lonesome to see Jerry, like wanting to see your father at night when you are a young kid. Just then an automobile came along

and turned in. Jerry was in it and Henry Rieback's father, and Arthur
Bedford from home, and Dave Williams and two other men I didn't
know. They got out of the car and went into the house, all but Henry
Rieback's father who quarreled with them and said he wouldn't go.
It was only about nine o'clock, but they were all drunk and the
rummy looking farm house was a place for bad women to stay in.
That's what it was. I crept up along a fence and looked through a
window and saw.

It's what give me the fantods. I can't make it out. The women in
the house were all ugly mean-looking women, not nice to look at
or be near. They were homely too, except one who was tall and
looked a little like the gelding Middlestride, but not clean like him,
but with a hard ugly mouth. She had red hair. I saw everything plain.
I got up by an old rose bush by an open window and looked. The
women had on loose dresses and sat around in chairs. The men came
in and some sat on the women's laps. The place smelled rotten and
there was rotten talk, the kind a kid hears around a livery stable in
a town like Beckersville in the winter but don't ever expect to
hear talked when there are women around. It was rotten. A nigger
wouldn't go into such a place.

I looked at Jerry Tillford. I've told you how I had been feeling
about him on account of his knowing what was going on inside of
Sunstreak in the minute before he went to the post for the race in
which he made a world's record.

Jerry bragged in that bad woman house as I know Sunstreak
wouldn't never have bragged. He said that he made that horse,
that it was him that won the race and made the record. He lied
and bragged like a fool. I never heard such silly talk.

And then, what do you suppose he did! He looked at the woman
in there, the one that was lean and hard-mouthed and looked a little
like the gelding Middlestride, but not clean like him, and his eyes
began to shine just as they did when he looked at me and at Sunstreak
in the paddocks at the track in the afternoon. I stood there by the
window—gee!—but I wished I hadn't gone away from the tracks,
but had stayed with the boys and the niggers and the horses. The tall
rotten looking woman was between us just as Sunstreak was in the
paddocks in the afternoon.

Then, all of a sudden, I began to hate that man. I wanted to scream
and rush in the room and kill him. I never had such a feeling before.
I was so mad clean through that I cried and my fists were doubled
up so my finger nails cut my hands.

And Jerry's eyes kept shining and he waved back and forth, and then he went and kissed that woman and I crept away and went back to the tracks and to bed and didn't sleep hardly any, and then next day I got the other kids to start home with me and never told them anything I seen.

I been thinking about it ever since. I can't make it out. Spring has come again and I'm nearly sixteen and go to the tracks mornings same as always, and I see Sunstreak and Middlestride and a new colt named Strident I'll bet will lay them all out, but no one thinks so but me and two or three niggers.

But things are different. At the tracks the air don't taste as good or smell as good. It's because a man like Jerry Tillford, who knows what he does, could see a horse like Sunstreak run, and kiss a woman like that the same day. I can't make it out. Darn him, what did he want to do like that for? I keep thinking about it and it spoils looking at horses and smelling things and hearing niggers laugh and everything. Sometimes I'm so mad about it I want to fight someone. It gives me the fantods. What did he do it for? I want to know why.

Brothers

I AM AT my house in the country and it is late October. It rains. Back of my house is a forest and in front there is a road and beyond that open fields. The country is one of low hills, flattening suddenly into plains. Some twenty miles away, across the flat country, lies the huge city Chicago.

On this rainy day the leaves of the trees that line the road before my window are falling like rain, the yellow, red and golden leaves fall straight down heavily. The rain beats them brutally down. They are denied a last golden flash across the sky. In October leaves should be carried away, out over the plains, in a wind. They should go dancing away.

Yesterday morning I arose at daybreak and went for a walk. There was a heavy fog and I lost myself in it. I went down into the plains and returned to the hills, and everywhere the fog was as a wall before me. Out of it trees sprang suddenly, grotesquely, as in a city street late at night people come suddenly out of the darkness into the circle of light under a street lamp. Above there was the light of day forcing itself slowly into the fog. The fog moved slowly. The tops of trees moved slowly. Under the trees the fog was dense, purple. It was like smoke lying in the streets of a factory town.

An old man came up to me in the fog. I know him well. The people here call him insane. "He is a little cracked," they say. He lives alone in a little house buried deep in the forest and has a small dog he carries always in his arms. On many mornings I have met him walking on the road and he has told me of men and women who are his brothers and sisters, his cousins, aunts, uncles, brothers-in-law. It is confusing. He cannot draw close to people near at hand so he gets hold of a name out of a newspaper and his mind plays with it. On one morning he told me he was a cousin to the man named Cox who at the time when I write is a candidate for the presidency. On another morning he told me that Caruso the singer had married a woman who was his sister-in-law. "She is my wife's sister," he said, holding the little dog close. His grey watery eyes looked appealing up to me. He wanted me to believe. "My wife was a sweet slim girl," he declared. "We lived together in a big house and in the morning walked about arm in arm. Now her sister has married Caruso the singer. He is of my family now."

As someone had told me the old man had never married, I went away wondering. One morning in early September I came upon him sitting under a tree beside a path near his house. The dog barked at me and then ran and crept into his arms. At that time the Chicago newspapers were filled with the story of a millionaire who had got into trouble with his wife because of an intimacy with an actress. The old man told me that the actress was his sister. He is sixty years old and the actress whose story appeared in the newspapers is twenty but he spoke of their childhood together. "You would not realize it to see us now but we were poor then," he said. "It's true. We lived in a little house on the side of a hill. Once when there was a storm, the wind nearly swept our house away. How the wind blew! Our father was a carpenter and he built strong houses for other people but our own house he did not build very strong!" He shook his head sorrowfully. "My sister the actress has got into trouble. Our house is not built very strongly," he said as I went away along the path.

For a month, two months, the Chicago newspapers, that are delivered every morning in our village, have been filled with the story of a murder. A man there has murdered his wife and there seems no reason for the deed. The tale runs something like this—

The man, who is now on trial in the courts and will no doubt be hanged, worked in a bicycle factory where he was a foreman and lived with his wife and his wife's mother in an apartment in Thirty-second Street. He loved a girl who worked in the office of the factory where he was employed. She came from a town in Iowa and when she first came to the city lived with her aunt who has since died. To the foreman, a heavy stolid looking man with grey eyes, she seemed the most beautiful woman in the world. Her desk was by a window at an angle of the factory, a sort of wing of the building, and the foreman, down in the shop had a desk by another window.

He sat at his desk making out sheets containing the record of the work done by each man in his department. When he looked up he could see the girl sitting at work at her desk. The notion got into his head that she was peculiarly lovely. He did not think of trying to draw close to her or of winning her love. He looked at her as one might look at a star or across a country of low hills in October when the leaves of the trees are all red and yellow gold. "She is a pure, virginal thing," he thought vaguely. "What can she be thinking about as she sits there by the window at work."

In fancy the foreman took the girl from Iowa home with him to his apartment in Thirty-second Street and into the presence of his wife and his mother-in-law. All day in the shop and during the evening at home he carried her figure about with him in his mind. As he stood by a window in his apartment and looked out toward the Illinois Central railroad tracks and beyond the tracks to the lake, the girl was there beside him. Down below women walked in the street and in every woman he saw there was something of the Iowa girl. One woman walked as she did, another made a gesture with her hand that reminded of her. All the women he saw except his wife and his mother-in-law were like the girl he had taken inside himself.

The two women in his own house puzzled and confused him. They became suddenly unlovely and commonplace. His wife in particular was like some strange unlovely growth that had attached itself to his body.

In the evening after the day at the factory he went home to his own place and had dinner. He had always been a silent man and when he did not talk no one minded. After dinner he with his wife went to a picture show. There were two children and his wife expected another. They came into the apartment and sat down. The climb up two flights of stairs had wearied his wife. She sat in a chair beside her mother groaning with weariness.

The mother-in-law was the soul of goodness. She took the place of a servant in the home and got no pay. When her daughter wanted to go to a picture show she waved her hand and smiled. "Go on," she said. "I don't want to go. I'd rather sit here." She got a book and sat reading. The little boy of nine awoke and cried. He wanted to sit on the po-po. The mother-in-law attended to that.

After the man and his wife came home the three people sat in silence for an hour or two before bed time. The man pretended to read a newspaper. He looked at his hands. Although he had washed them carefully grease from the bicycle frames left dark stains under the nails. He thought of the Iowa girl and of her white quick hands playing over the keys of a typewriter. He felt dirty and uncomfortable.

The girl at the factory knew the foreman had fallen in love with her and the thought excited her a little. Since her aunt's death she had gone to live in a rooming house and had nothing to do in the evening. Although the foreman meant nothing to her she could in a way use him. To her he became a symbol. Sometimes he came into the office and stood for a moment by the door. His large hands were covered with black grease. She looked at him without seeing. In his place in her imagination stood a tall slender young man. Of the foreman she saw only the grey eyes that began to burn with a strange fire. The eyes expressed eagerness, a humble and devout eagerness. In the presence of a man with such eyes she felt she need not be afraid.

She wanted a lover who would come to her with such a look in his eyes. Occasionally, perhaps once in two weeks, she stayed a little late at the office, pretending to have work that must be finished. Through the window she could see the foreman waiting. When everyone had gone she closed her desk and went into the street. At the same moment the foreman came out at the factory door.

They walked together along the street a half dozen blocks to where she got aboard her car. The factory was in a place called South Chicago and as they went along evening was coming on. The streets were lined with small unpainted frame houses and dirty faced children ran screaming in the dusty roadway. They crossed over a bridge. Two abandoned coal barges lay rotting in the stream.

He went by her side walking heavily and striving to conceal his hands. He had scrubbed them carefully before leaving the factory but they seemed to him like heavy dirty pieces of waste matter hanging at his side. Their walking together happened but a few times and during one summer. "It's hot," he said. He never spoke to her of anything but the weather. "It's hot," he said. "I think it may rain."

She dreamed of the lover who would some time come, a tall fair young man, a rich man owning houses and lands. The workingman who walked beside her had nothing to do with her conception of love. She walked with him, stayed at the office until the others had gone to walk unobserved with him because of his eyes, because of

the eager thing in his eyes that was at the same time humble, that
bowed down to her. In his presence there was no danger, could be
no danger. He would never attempt to approach too closely, to touch
her with his hands. She was safe with him.

In his apartment in the evening the man sat under the electric
light with his wife and his mother-in-law. In the next room his
two children were asleep. In a short time his wife would have
another child. He had been with her to a picture show and in a
short time they would get into bed together.

He would lie awake thinking, would hear the creaking of the
springs of a bed where, in another room, his mother-in-law was
crawling between the sheets. Life was too intimate. He would lie
awake eager, expectant—expecting, what?

Nothing. Presently one of the children would cry. It wanted to
get out of bed and sit on the po-po. Nothing strange or unusual or
lovely would or could happen. Life was too close, intimate. Nothing
that could happen in the apartment could in any way stir him; the
things his wife might say, her occasional half-hearted outbursts of
passion, the goodness of his mother-in-law who did the work of a
servant without pay—

He sat in the apartment under the electric light pretending to read
a newspaper—thinking. He looked at his hands. They were large,
shapeless, a workingman's hands.

The figure of the girl from Iowa walked about the room. With
her he went out of the apartment and walked in silence through
miles of streets. It was not necessary to say words. He walked with her
by a sea, along the crest of a mountain. The night was clear and
silent and the stars shone. She also was a star. It was not necessary to
say words.

Her eyes were like stars and her lips were like soft hills rising out
of dim, star lit plains. "She is unattainable, she is far off like the stars,"
he thought. "She is unattainable like the stars but unlike the stars she
breathes, she lives, like myself she has being."

One evening, some six weeks ago, the man who worked as
foreman in the bicycle factory killed his wife and he is now in the
courts being tried for murder. Every day the newspapers are filled
with the story. On the evening of the murder he had taken his wife
as usual to a picture show and they started home at nine. In Thirty-
second Street, at a corner near their apartment building, the figure
of a man darted suddenly out of an alleyway and then darted back

again. The incident may have put the idea of killing his wife into the man's head.

They got to the entrance to the apartment building and stepped into a dark hallway. Then quite suddenly and apparently without thought the man took a knife out of his pocket. "Suppose that man who darted into the alleyway had intended to kill us," he thought. Opening the knife he whirled about and struck at his wife. He struck twice, a dozen times—madly. There was a scream and his wife's body fell.

The janitor had neglected to light the gas in the lower hallway. Afterwards, the foreman decided, that was the reason he did it, that and the fact that the dark slinking figure of a man darted out of an alleyway and then darted back again. "Surely," he told himself, "I could never have done it had the gas been lighted."

He stood in the hallway thinking. His wife was dead and with her had died her unborn child. There was a sound of doors opening in the apartments above. For several minutes nothing happened. His wife and her unborn child were dead—that was all.

He ran upstairs thinking quickly. In the darkness on the lower stairway he had put the knife back into his pocket and, as it turned out later, there was no blood on his hands or on his clothes. The knife he later washed carefully in the bathroom, when the excitement had died down a little. He told everyone the same story. "There has been a holdup," he explained. "A man came slinking out of an alleyway and followed me and my wife home. He followed us into the hallway of the building and there was no light. The janitor has neglected to light the gas." Well—there had been a struggle and in the darkness his wife had been killed. He could not tell how it had happened. "There was no light. The janitor has neglected to light the gas," he kept saying.

For a day or two they did not question him specially and he had time to get rid of the knife. He took a long walk and threw it away into the river in South Chicago where the two abandoned coal barges lay rotting under the bridge, the bridge he had crossed when on the summer evenings he walked to the street car with the girl who was virginal and pure, who was far off and unattainable, like a star and yet not like a star.

And then he was arrested and right away he confessed—told everything. He said he did not know why he killed his wife and was careful to say nothing of the girl at the office. The newspapers tried to discover the motive for the crime. They are still trying. Someone had seen him on the few evenings when he walked with the girl and she was dragged into the affair and had her picture printed in the papers. That has been annoying for her as of course she has been able to prove she had nothing to do with the man.

Yesterday morning a heavy fog lay over our village here at the edge of the city and I went for a long walk in the early morning. As I returned out of the lowlands into our hill country I met the old man whose family has so many and such strange ramifications. For a time he walked beside me holding the little dog in his arms. It was cold and the dog whined and shivered. In the fog the old man's face was indistinct. It moved slowly back and forth with the fog banks of the upper air and with the tops of trees. He spoke of the man who has killed his wife and whose name is being shouted in the pages of the city newspapers that come to our village each morning. As he walked beside me he launched into a long tale concerning a life he and his brother, who has now become a murderer, once lived together. "He is my brother," he said over and over, shaking his head. He seemed afraid I would not believe. There was a fact that must be established. "We were boys together that man and I," he began again. "You see we played together in a barn back of our father's house. Our father went away to sea in a ship. That is the way our names became confused. You understand that. We have different names, but we are brothers. We had the same father. We played together in a barn back of our father's house. For hours we lay together in the hay in the barn and it was warm there."

In the fog the slender body of the old man became like a little gnarled tree. Then it became a thing suspended in air. It swung back and forth like a body hanging on the gallows. The face beseeched me to believe the story the lips were trying to tell. In my mind everything concerning the relationship of men and women became confused, a muddle. The spirit of the man who had killed his wife came into the body of the little old man there by the roadside. It was striving to tell me the story it would never be able to tell in the court room in the city, in the presence of the judge. The whole story of mankind's loneliness, of the effort to reach out to unattainable beauty tried to get itself expressed from the lips of a mumbling old man, crazed with loneliness, who stood by the side of a country road on a foggy morning holding a little dog in his arms.

The arms of the old man held the dog so closely that it began to whine with pain. A sort of convulsion shook his body. The soul seemed striving to wrench itself out of the body, to fly away through the fog, down across the plain to the city, to the singer, the politician, the millionaire, the murderer, to its brothers, cousins, sisters, down in the city. The intensity of the old man's desire was terrible and in sympathy my body began to tremble. His arms tightened about the body of the little dog so that it cried with pain. I stepped forward and tore the arms away and the dog fell to the ground and lay whining. No doubt it had been injured. Perhaps ribs had been crushed. The old man stared at the dog lying at his feet as in the hallway of the apartment building the worker from the bicycle factory had stared at his dead wife. "We are brothers," he said again. "We have different names but we are brothers. Our father you understand went off to sea."

I am sitting in my house in the country and it rains. Before my eyes the hills fall suddenly away and there are the flat plains and beyond the plains the city. An hour ago the old man of the house in the forest went past my door and the little dog was not with him. It may be that as we talked in the fog he crushed the life out of his companion. It may be that the dog like the workman's wife and her unborn child is now dead. The leaves of the trees that line the road before my window are falling like rain—the yellow, red and golden leaves fall straight down, heavily. The rain beat them brutally down. They are denied a last golden flash across the sky. In October leaves should be carried away, out over the plains, in a wind. They should be dancing away.

The New Englander

HER NAME WAS Elsie Leander and her girlhood was spent on her father's farm in Vermont. For several generations the Leanders had all lived on the same farm and had all married thin women, and so she was thin. The farm lay in the shadow of a mountain and the soil was not very rich. From the beginning and for several generations there had been a great many sons and few daughters in the family. The sons had gone west or to New York City and the daughters had stayed at home and thought such thoughts as come to New England women who see the sons of their fathers' neighbors slipping away, one by one, into the West.

Her father's house was a small white frame affair and when you went out at the back door, past a small barn and chicken house, you got into a path that ran up the side of a hill and into an orchard. The trees were all old and gnarled. At the back of the orchard the hill dropped away and bare rocks showed.

Inside the fence a large grey rock stuck high up out of the ground. As Elsie sat with her back to the rock, with a mangled hillside at her feet, she could see several large mountains, apparently but a short distance away, and between herself and the mountains lay many tiny fields surrounded by neatly built stone walls. Everywhere rocks appeared. Large ones, too heavy to be moved, stuck out of the ground in the centre of the fields. The fields were like cups filled with a green liquid that turned grey in the fall and white in the winter. The mountains, far off but apparently near at hand, were like giants ready at any moment to reach out their hands and take the cups one by one and drink off the green liquid. The large rocks in the fields were like the thumbs of the giants.

Elsie had three brothers, born before her, but they had all gone away. Two of them had gone to live with her uncle in the West and her oldest brother had gone to New York City where he had married and prospered. All through his youth and manhood her father had worked hard and had lived a hard life, but his son in New York City had begun to send money home, and after that things went better. He still worked every day about the barn or in the fields but he did not worry about the future. Elsie's mother did house work in the mornings and in the afternoons sat in a rocking chair in her tiny living room and thought of her sons while she crocheted table covers and tidies for the backs of chairs. She was a silent woman, very thin and with very thin bony hands. She did not case herself into a rocking chair but sat down and got up suddenly, and when she crocheted her back was as straight as the back of a drill sergeant.

The mother rarely spoke to the daughter. Sometimes in the afternoons as the younger woman went up the hillside to her place by the rock at the back of the orchard, her father came out of the barn and stopped her. He put a hand on her shoulder and asked her where she was going. "To the rock," she said and her father laughed. His laughter was like the creaking of a rusty barn door hinge and the hand he had laid on her shoulders was thin like her own hands and like her mother's hands. The father went into the barn shaking his head. "She's like her mother. She is herself like a rock," he thought. At the head of the path that led from the house to the orchard there was a great cluster of bayberry bushes. The New England farmer came out of his barn to watch his daughter go along the path, but she had disappeared behind the bushes. He looked away past his house to the fields and to the mountains in the distance. He also saw the green cup-like fields and the grim mountains. There was an almost imperceptible tightening of the muscles of his half worn-out old body. For a long time he stood in silence and then, knowing from long experience the danger of having thoughts, he went back into the barn and busied himself with the mending of an agricultural tool that had been mended many times before.

The son of the Leanders who went to live in New York City was the father of one son, a thin sensitive boy who looked like Elsie. The son died when he was twenty-three years old and some years later the father died and left his money to the old people on the New England farm. The two Leanders who had gone west had lived there with their father's brother, a farmer, until they grew into manhood. Then Will, the younger, got a job on a railroad. He was killed one

winter morning. It was a cold snowy day and when the freight train
he was in charge of as conductor left the city of Des Moines, he
started to run over the tops of the cars. His feet slipped and he shot
down into space. That was the end of him.

Of the new generation there was only Elsie and her brother Tom,
whom she had never seen, left alive. Her father and mother talked
of going west to Tom for two years before they came to a decision.
Then it took another year to dispose of the farm and make preparations. During the whole time Elsie did not think much about the
change about to take place in her life.

The trip west on the railroad train jolted Elsie out of herself. In
spite of her detached attitude toward life she became excited. Her
mother sat up very straight and stiff in the seat in the sleeping car
and her father walked up and down in the aisle. After a night when
the younger of the two women did not sleep but lay awake with red
burning cheeks and with her thin fingers incessantly picking at the
bed clothes in her berth while the train went through towns and
cities, crawled up the sides of hills and fell down into forest-clad
valleys, she got up and dressed to sit all day looking at a new kind of
land. The train ran for a day and through another sleepless night in
a flat land where every field was as large as a farm in her own country. Towns appeared and disappeared in a continual procession. The
whole land was so unlike anything she had ever known that she
began to feel unlike herself. In the valley where she had been
born and where she had lived all her days everything had an air of
finality. Nothing could be changed. The tiny fields were chained to
the earth. They were fixed in their places and surrounded by aged
stone walls. The fields like the mountains that looked down at them
were as unchangeable as the passing days. She had a feeling they had
always been so, would always be so.

Elsie sat like her mother, upright in the car seat and with a back
like the back of a drill sergeant. The train ran swiftly along through
Ohio and Indiana. Her thin hands like her mother's hands were
crossed and locked. One passing casually through the car might have
thought both women prisoners handcuffed and bound to their seats.
Night came on and she again got into her berth. Again she lay awake
and her thin cheeks became flushed, but she thought new thoughts.
Her hands were no longer gripped together and she did not pick at
the bed clothes. Twice during the night she stretched herself and
yawned, a thing she had never in her life done before. The train

stopped at a town on the prairies, and as there was something the matter with one of the wheels of the car in which she lay the trainsmen came with flaming torches to tinker with it. There was a great pounding and shouting. When the train went on its way she wanted to get out of her berth and run up and down in the aisle of the car. The fancy had come to her that the men tinkering with the car wheel were new men out of the new land who with strong hammers had broken away the doors of her prison. They had destroyed forever the programme she had made for her life.

Elsie was filled with joy at the thought that the train was still going on into the West. She wanted to go on forever in a straight line into the unknown. She fancied herself no longer on a train and imagined she had become a winged thing flying through space. Her long years of sitting alone by the rock on the New England farm had got her into the habit of expressing her thoughts aloud. Her thin voice broke the silence that lay over the sleeping car and her father and mother, both also lying awake, sat up in their berth to listen.

Tom Leander, the only living male representative of the new generation of Leanders, was a loosely built man of forty inclined to corpulency. At twenty he had married the daughter of a neighboring farmer, and when his wife inherited some money she and Tom moved into the town of Apple Junction in Iowa where Tom opened a grocery. The venture prospered as did Tom's matrimonial venture. When his brother died in New York City and his father, mother, and sister decided to come west Tom was already the father of a daughter and four sons.

On the prairies north of town and in the midst of a vast level stretch of cornfields, there was a partly completed brick house that had belonged to a rich farmer named Russell who had begun to build the house intending to make it the most magnificent place in the county, but when it was almost completed he had found himself without money and heavily in debt. The farm, consisting of several hundred acres of corn land, had been split into three farms and sold. No one had wanted the huge unfinished brick house. For years it had stood vacant, its windows staring out over the fields that had been planted almost up to the door.

In buying the Russell house Tom was moved by two motives. He had a notion that in New England the Leanders had been rather magnificent people. His memory of his father's place in the Vermont valley was shadowy, but in speaking of it to his wife he became very definite. "We had good blood in us, we Leanders," he said, straightening his shoulders. "We lived in a big house. We were important people."

Wanting his father and mother to feel at home in the new place, Tom had also another motive. He was not a very energetic man and, although he had done well enough as keeper of a grocery, his success was largely due to the boundless energy of his wife. She did not pay much attention to her household and her children, like little animals, had to take care of themselves, but in any matter concerning the store her word was law.

To have his father the owner of the Russell place Tom felt would establish him as a man of consequence in the eyes of his neighbors. "I can tell you what, they're used to a big house," he said to his wife. "I tell you what, my people are used to living in style."

The exaltation that had come over Elsie on the train wore away in the presence of the grey empty Iowa fields, but something of the effect of it remained with her for months. In the big brick house life went on much as it had in the tiny New England house where she had always lived. The Leanders installed themselves in three or four rooms on the ground floor. After a few weeks the furniture that had been shipped by freight arrived and was hauled out from town in one of Tom's grocery wagons. There were three or four acres of ground covered with great piles of boards the unsuccessful farmer had intended to use in the building of stables. Tom sent men to haul the boards away and Elsie's father prepared to plant a garden. They had come west in April and as soon as they were installed in the house ploughing and planting began in the fields nearby. The habit of a lifetime returned to the daughter of the house. In the new place there was no gnarled orchard surrounded by a half-ruined stone fence. All of the fences in all of the fields that stretched away out of sight to the north, south, east, and west were made of wire and looked like spider webs against the blackness of the ground when it had been freshly ploughed.

There was however the house itself. It was like an island rising out of the sea. In an odd way the house, although it was less than ten years old, was very old. Its unnecessary bigness represented an old impulse in men. Elsie felt that. At the east side there was a door leading to a stairway that ran into the upper part of the house that was kept locked. Two or three stone steps led up to it. Elsie could sit on the top step with her back against the door and gaze into the distance without being disturbed. Almost at her feet began the fields that seemed to go on and on forever. The fields were like the waters of a sea. Men came to plough and plant. Giant horses moved in a procession across the prairies. A young man who drove six horses came directly toward her. She was fascinated. The breasts of the horses as they came forward with bowed heads seemed like the breasts of giants. The soft spring air that lay over the fields was also like a sea. The horses were giants walking on the floor of a sea. With their breasts they pushed the waters of the sea before them. They were pushing the waters out of the basin of the sea. The young man who drove them also was a giant.

Elsie pressed her body against the closed door at the top of the steps. In the garden back of the house she could hear her father at work. He was raking dry masses of weeds off the ground preparatory to spading it for a family garden. He had always worked in a tiny confined place and would do the same thing here. In this vast open place he would work with small tools, doing little things with infinite care, raising little vegetables. In the house her mother would crochet little tidies. She herself would be small. She would press her body against the door of the house, try to get herself out of sight. Only the feeling that sometimes took possession of her, and that did not form itself into a thought would be large.

The six horses turned at the fence and the outside horse got entangled in the traces. The driver swore vigorously. Then he turned and started at the pale New Englander and with another oath pulled the heads of the horses about and drove away into the distance. The field in which he was ploughing contained two hundred acres. Elsie did not wait for him to return but went into the house and sat with folded arms in a room. The house she thought was a ship floating in a sea on the floor of which giants went up and down.

May came and then June. In the great fields work was always going on and Elsie became somewhat used to the sight of the young man in the field that came down to the steps. Sometimes when he drove his horses down to the wire fence he smiled and nodded.

In the month of August, when it is very hot, the corn in Iowa fields grows until the corn stalks resemble young trees. The corn fields become forests. The time for the cultivating of the corn has passed and weeds grow thick between the corn rows. The men with their giant horses have gone away. Over the immense fields silence broods.

When the time of the laying-by of the crop came that first summer after Elsie's arrival in the West her mind, partially awakened by the strangeness of the railroad trip, awakened again. She did not feel like a staid thin woman with a back like the back of a drill sergeant, but like something new and as strange as the new land into which she had come to live. For a time she did not know what was the matter. In the field the corn had grown so high that she could not see into the distance. The corn was like a wall and the little bare spot of land on which her father's house stood was like a house built behind the walls of a prison. For a time she was depressed, thinking that she had come west into a wide open country, only to find herself locked up more closely than ever.

An impulse came to her. She arose and going down three or four steps seated herself almost on a level with the ground.

Immediately she got a sense of release. She could not see over the corn but she could see under it. The corn had long wide leaves that met over the rows. The rows became long tunnels running away into infinity. Out of the black ground grew weeds that made a soft carpet of green. From above light sifted down. The corn rows were mysteriously beautiful. They were warm passageways running out into life. She got up from the steps and, walking timidly to the wire fence that separated her from the field, put her hand between the wires and took hold of one of the corn stalks. For some reason after she had touched the strong young stalk and had held it for a moment firmly in her hand she grew afraid. Running quickly back to the step she sat down and covered her face with her hands. Her body trembled. She tried to imagine herself crawling through the fence and wandering along one of the passageways. The thought of trying the experiment fascinated but at the same time terrified. She got quickly up and went into the house.

One Saturday night in August Elsie found herself unable to sleep. Thoughts, more definite than any she had ever known before, came into her mind. It was a quiet hot night and her bed stood near a window. Her room was the only one the Leanders occupied on the second floor of the house. At midnight a little breeze came up from the south and when she sat up in bed the floor of corn tassels lying below her line of sight looked in the moonlight like the face of a sea just stirred by a gentle breeze.

A murmuring began in the corn and murmuring thoughts and memories awoke in her mind. The long wide succulent leaves had begun to dry in the intense heat of the August days and as the wind stirred the corn they rubbed against each other. A call, far away, as of a thousand voices arose. She imagined the voices were like the voices of children. They were not like her brother Tom's children, noisy boisterous little animals, but something quite different, tiny little things with large eyes and thin sensitive hands. One after another they crept into her arms. She became so excited over the fancy that she sat up in bed and taking a pillow into her arms held it against her breast. The figure of her cousin, the pale sensitive young Leander who had lived with his father in New York City and who had died at the age of twenty-three, came into her mind. It was as though the young man had come suddenly into the room. She dropped the pillow and sat waiting, intense, expectant.

Young Harry Leander had come to visit his cousin on the New England farm during the late summer of the year before he died. He had stayed there for a month and almost every afternoon had gone with Elsie to sit by the rock at the back of the orchard. One afternoon when they had both been for a long time silent he began to talk. "I want to go live in the West," he said. "I want to go live in the West. I want to grow strong and be a man," he repeated. Tears came into his eyes.

They got up to return to the house, Elsie walking in silence beside the young man. The moment marked a high spot in her life. A strange trembling eagerness for something she had not realized in her experience of life had taken possession of her. They went in silence through the orchard but when they came to the bayberry bush her cousin stopped in the path and turned to face her. "I want you to kiss me," he said eagerly, stepping toward her.

A fluttering uncertainty had taken possession of Elsie and had been transmitted to her cousin. After he had made the sudden and unexpected demand and had stepped so close to her that his breath could be felt on her cheek, his own cheeks became scarlet and his hand that had taken her hand trembled. "Well, I wish I were strong. I only wish I were strong," he said hesitatingly and turning walked away along the path toward the house.

And in the strange new house, set like an island in its sea of corn, Harry Leander's voice seemed to arise again above the fancied voices of the children that had been coming out of the fields. Elsie got out of bed and walked up and down in the dim light coming through the window. Her body trembled violently. "I want you to kiss me," the voice said again and to quiet it and to quiet also the answering voice in herself she went to kneel by the bed and taking the pillow again into her arms pressed it against her face.

Tom Leander came with his wife and family to visit his father and mother on Sundays. The family appeared at about ten o'clock in the morning. When the wagon turned out of the road that ran past the Russell place Tom shouted. There was a field between the house and the road and the wagon could not be seen as it came along the narrow way through the corn. After Tom had shouted, his daughter Elizabeth, a tall girl of sixteen, jumped out of the wagon. All five children came tearing toward the house through the corn. A series of wild shouts arose on the still morning air.

The groceryman had brought food from the store. When the horse had been unhitched and put into a shed he and his wife began to carry packages into the house. The four Leander boys, accompanied by their sister, disappeared into the near-by fields. Three dogs that had trotted out from town under the wagon accompanied the children. Two or three children and occasionally a young man from a neighboring farm had come to join in the fun. Elsie's sister-in-law dismissed them all with a wave of her hand. With a wave of her hand she also brushed Elsie aside. Fires were lighted and the house reeked with the smell of cooking. Elsie went to sit on the step at the side of the house. The corn fields that had been so quiet rang with shouts and with the barking of dogs.

Tom Leander's oldest child, Elizabeth, was like her mother, full of energy. She was thin and tall like the women of her father's house but very strong and alive. In secret she wanted to be a lady but when she tried her brothers, led by her father and mother, made fun of her. "Don't put on airs," they said. When she got into the country with no one but her brothers and two or three neighboring farm boys she herself became a boy. With the boys she went tearing through the fields, following the dogs in pursuit of rabbits. Sometimes a young man came with the children from a near-by farm. Then she did not know what to do with herself. She wanted to walk demurely along the rows through the corn but was afraid her brothers would laugh and in desperation outdid the boys in roughness and noisiness. She screamed and shouted and running wildly tore her dress on the wire fences as she scrambled over in pursuit of the dogs. When a rabbit was caught and killed she rushed in and tore it out of the grasp of the dogs. The blood of the little dying animal dripped on her clothes. She swung it over her head and shouted.

The farm hand who had worked all summer in the field within sight of Elsie became enamoured of the young woman from town. When the groceryman's family appeared on Sunday mornings he also appeared but did not come to the house. When the boys and dogs came tearing through the fields he joined them. He also was self-conscious and did not want the boys to know the purpose of his coming and when he and Elizabeth found themselves alone together he became embarrassed. For a moment they walked together in silence. In a wide circle about them, in the forest of the corn, ran the boys and dogs. The young man had something he wanted to say, but when he tried to find words his tongue became thick and his lips felt hot and dry. "Well," he began, "let's you and me—"

Words failed him and Elizabeth turned and ran after her brothers and for the rest of the day he could not manage to get her out of their sight. When he went to join them she became the noisiest member of the party. A frenzy of activity took possession of her. With hair hanging down her back, with clothes torn and with cheeks and hands scratched and bleeding she led her brothers in the endless wild pursuit of the rabbits.

The Sunday in August that followed Elsie Leander's sleepless night was hot and cloudy. In the morning she was half ill and as soon as the visitors from town arrived she crept away to sit on the step at the side of the house. The children ran away into the fields. An almost overpowering desire to run with them, shouting and playing along the corn rows took possession of her. She arose and went to the back of the house. Her father was at work in the garden, pulling weeds from between rows of vegetables. Inside the house she could hear her sister-in-law moving about. On the front porch her brother Tom was asleep with his mother beside him. Elsie went back to the step and then arose and went to where the corn came down to the fence. She climbed awkwardly over and went a little way along one of the rows. Putting out her hand she touched the firm stalks and then, becoming afraid, dropped to her knees on the carpet of weeds that covered the ground. For a long time she stayed thus listening to the voices of the children in the distance.

An hour slipped away. Presently it was time for dinner and her sister-in-law came to the back door and shouted. There was an answering whoop from the distance and the children came running through the fields. They climbed over the fence and ran shouting across her father's garden. Elsie also arose. She was about to attempt to climb back over the fence unobserved when she heard a rustling in the corn. Young Elizabeth Leander appeared. Beside her walked the ploughman who but a few months earlier had planted the corn in the field where Elsie now stood. She could see the two people coming slowly along the rows. An understanding had been established between them. The man reached through between the corn stalks and touched the hand of the girl who laughed awkwardly and running to the fence climbed quickly over. In her hand she held the limp body of a rabbit the dogs had killed.

The farm hand went away and when Elizabeth had gone into the house Elsie climbed over the fence. Her niece stood just within the kitchen door holding the dead rabbit by one leg. The other leg had been torn away by the dogs. At sight of the New England woman, who seemed to look at her with hard unsympathetic eyes, she was ashamed and went quickly into the house. She threw the rabbit upon a table in the parlor and then ran out of the room. Its blood ran out on the delicate flowers of a white crocheted table cover that had been made by Elsie's mother.

The Sunday dinner with all the living Leanders gathered about the table was gone through in a heavy lumbering silence. When the dinner was over and Tom and his wife had washed the dishes they went to sit with the older people on the front porch. Presently they were both asleep. Elsie returned to the step at the side of the house but when the desire to go again into the cornfields came sweeping over her she got up and went indoors.

The woman of thirty-five tip-toed about the big house like a frightened child. The dead rabbit that lay on the table in the parlour had become cold and stiff. Its blood had dried on the white table cover. She went upstairs but did not go to her own room. A spirit of adventure had hold of her. In the upper part of the house there were many rooms and in some of them no glass had been put into the windows. The windows had been boarded up and narrow streaks of light crept in through the cracks between the boards.

Elsie tip-toed up the flight of stairs past the room in which she slept and opening doors went into other rooms. Dust lay thick on the floors. In the silence she could hear her brother snoring as he slept in the chair on the front porch. From what seemed a far away place there came the shrill cries of the children. The cries became soft. They were like the cries of unborn children that had called to her out of the fields on the night before.

Into her mind came the intense silent figure of her mother sitting on the porch beside her son and waiting for the day to wear itself out into night. The thought brought a lump into her throat. She wanted something and did not know what it was. Her own mood frightened her. In a windowless room at the back of the house one of the boards over a window had been broken and a bird had flown in and become imprisoned.

The presence of the woman frightened the bird. It flew wildly about. Its beating wings stirred up dust that danced in the air. Elsie stood perfectly still, also frightened, not by the presence of the bird but by the presence of life. Like the bird she was a prisoner. The thought gripped her. She wanted to go outdoors where her niece Elizabeth walked with the young ploughman through the corn, but was like the bird in the room—a prisoner. She moved restlessly about. The bird flew back and forth across the room. It alighted on the window sill near the place where the board was broken away. She stared into the frightened eyes of the bird that in turn stared into her eyes. Then the bird flew away, out through the window, and Elsie turned and ran nervously downstairs and out into the yard. She climbed over the wire fence and ran with stooped shoulders along one of the tunnels.

Elsie ran into the vastness of the cornfields filled with but one desire. She wanted to get out of her life and into some new and sweeter life she felt must be hidden away somewhere in the fields. After she had run a long way she came to a wire fence and crawled over. Her hair became unloosed and fell down over her shoulders. Her cheeks became flushed and for the moment she looked like a young girl. When she climbed over the fence she tore a great hole in the front of her dress. For a moment her tiny breasts were exposed and then her hand clutched and held nervously the sides of the tear. In the distance she could hear the voices of the boys and the barking of the dogs. A summer storm had been threatening for days and now black clouds had begun to spread themselves over the sky. As she ran nervously forward, stopping to listen and then running on again, the dry corn blades brushed against her shoulders and a fine shower of yellow dust from the corn tassels fell on her hair. A continued crackling noise accompanied her progress. The dust made a golden crown about her head. From the sky overhead a low rumbling sound, like the growling of giant dogs, came to her ears.

The thought that having at last ventured into the corn she would never escape became fixed in the mind of the running woman. Sharp pains shot through her body. Presently she was compelled to stop and sit on the ground. For a long time she sat with closed eyes. Her dress became soiled. Little insects that live in the ground under the corn came out of their holes and crawled over her legs.

Following some obscure impulse the tired woman threw herself on her back and lay still with closed eyes. Her fright passed. It was warm and close in the room-like tunnels. The pain in her side went away. She opened her eyes and between the wide green corn blades could see patches of a black threatening sky. She did not want to be alarmed and so closed her eyes again. Her thin hand no longer gripped the tear in her dress and her little breasts were exposed. They expanded and contracted in spasmodic jerks. She threw her hands back over her head and lay still.

It seemed to Elsie that hours passed as she lay thus, quiet and passive under the corn. Deep within her there was a feeling that something was about to happen, something that would lift her out of herself, that would tear her away from her past and the past of her people. Her thoughts were not definite. She lay still and waited as she had waited for days and months by the rock at the back of the orchard on the Vermont farm when she was a girl. A deep grumbling noise went on in the sky overhead but the sky and everything she had ever known seemed very far away, no part of herself.

After a long silence, when it seemed to her that she had gone out of herself as in a dream, Elsie heard a man's voice calling. "Aho, aho, aho," shouted the voice and after another period of silence there arose answering voices and then the sound of bodies crashing through the corn and the excited chatter of children. A dog came running along the row where she lay and stood beside her. His cold nose touched her face and she sat up. The dog ran away. The Leander boys passed. She could see their bare legs flashing in and out across one of the tunnels. Her brother had become alarmed by the rapid approach of the thunder storm and wanted to get his family to town. His voice kept calling from the house and the voices of the children answered from the fields.

Elsie sat on the ground with her hands pressed together. An odd feeling of disappointment had possession of her. She arose and walked slowly along in the general direction taken by the children. She came to a fence and crawled over, tearing her dress in a new place. One of her stockings had become unloosed and had slipped down over her shoe top. The long sharp weeds had scratched her leg so that it was criss-crossed with red lines, but she was not conscious of any pain.

The distraught woman followed the children until she came within sight of her father's house and then stopped and again sat on the ground. There was another loud crash of thunder and Tom Leander's voice called again, this time half angrily. The name of the girl Elizabeth was shouted in loud masculine tones that rolled and echoed like the thunder along the aisles under the corn.

And then Elizabeth came into sight accompanied by the young ploughman. They stopped near Elsie and the man took the girl into his arms. At the sound of their approach Elsie had thrown herself face downward on the ground and had twisted herself into a position where she could see without being seen. When their lips met her tense hands grasped one of the corn stalks. Her lips pressed themselves into the dust. When they had gone on their way she raised her head. A dusty powder covered her lips.

What seemed another long period of silence fell over the fields. The murmuring voices of unborn children, her imagination had created in the whispering fields, became a vast shout. The wind blew harder and harder. The corn stalks were twisted and bent. Elizabeth went thoughtfully out of the field and climbing the fence confronted her father. "Where you been? What you been a doing?" he asked. "Don't you think we got to get out of here?"

When Elizabeth went toward the house Elsie followed, creeping on her hands and knees like a little animal, and when she had come within sight of the fence surrounding the house she sat on the ground and put her hands over her face. Something within herself was being twisted and whirled about as the tops of the corn stalks were now being twisted and whirled by the wind. She sat so that she did not look toward the house and when she opened her eyes she could again see along the long mysterious aisles.

Her brother with his wife and children went away. By turning her head Elsie could see them driving at a trot out of the yard back of her father's house. With the going of the younger woman the farm house in the midst of the cornfield rocked by the winds seemed the most desolate place in the world.

Her mother came out at the back door of the house. She ran to the steps where she knew her daughter was in the habit of sitting and then in alarm began to call. It did not occur to Elsie to answer. The voice of the older woman did not seem to have anything to do with herself. It was a thin voice and was quickly lost in the wind and in the crashing sound that arose out of the fields. With her head turned toward the house Elsie stared at her mother who ran wildly around the house and then went indoors. The back door of the house went shut with a bang.

The storm that had been threatening broke with a roar. Broad sheets of water swept over the cornfields. Sheets of water swept over the woman's body. The storm that had for years been gathering in her also broke. Sobs arose out of her throat. She abandoned herself to a storm of grief that was only partially grief. Tears ran out of her eyes and made little furrows through the dust on her face. In the lulls that occasionally came in the storm she raised her head and heard, through the tangled mass of wet hair that covered her ears and above the sound of millions of rain-drops that alighted on the earthen floor inside the house of the corn, the thin voices of her mother and father calling to her out of the Leander house.

Unlighted Lamps

MARY COCHRAN WENT out of the rooms where she lived with her father, Doctor Lester Cochran, at seven o'clock on a Sunday evening. It was June of the year nineteen hundred and eight and Mary was eighteen years old. She walked along Tremont to Main Street and across the railroad tracks to Upper Main, lined with small shops and shoddy houses, a rather quiet cheerless place on Sundays when there were few people about. She had told her father she was going to church but did not intend doing anything of the kind. She did not know what she wanted to do. "I'll get off by myself and think," she told herself as she walked slowly along. The night she thought promised to be too fine to be spent sitting in a stuffy church and hearing a man talk of things that had apparently nothing to do with her own problem. Her own affairs were approaching a crisis and it was time for her to begin thinking seriously of her future.

The thoughtful serious state of mind in which Mary found herself had been induced in her by a conversation had with her father on the evening before. Without any preliminary talk and quite suddenly and abruptly he had told her that he was a victim of heart disease and might die at any moment. He had made the announcement as they stood together in the Doctor's office, back of which were the rooms in which the father and daughter lived.

It was growing dark outside when she came into the office and found him sitting alone. The office and living rooms were on the second floor of an old frame building in the town of Huntersburg, Illinois, and as the Doctor talked he stood beside his daughter near one of the windows that looked down into Tremont Street. The hushed murmur of the town's Saturday night life went on in Main

Street just around a corner, and the evening train, bound to Chicago fifty miles to the east, had just passed. The hotel bus came rattling out of Lincoln Street and went through Tremont toward the hotel on Lower Main. A cloud of dust kicked up by the horses' hoofs floated on the quiet air. A straggling group of people followed the bus and the row of hitching posts on Tremont Street was already lined with buggies in which farmers and their wives had driven into town for the evening of shopping and gossip.

After the station bus had passed three or four more buggies were driven into the street. From one of them a young man helped his sweetheart to alight. He took hold of her arm with a certain air of tenderness, and a hunger to be touched thus tenderly by a man's hand, that had come to Mary many times before, returned at almost the same moment her father made the announcement of his approaching death.

As the Doctor began to speak Barney Smithfield, who owned a livery barn that opened into Tremont Street directly opposite the building in which the Cochrans lived, came back to his place of business from his evening meal. He stopped to tell a story to a group of men gathered before the barn door and a shout of laughter arose. One of the loungers in the street, a strongly built young man in a checkered suit, stepped away from the others and stood before the liveryman. Having seen Mary he was trying to attract her attention. He also began to tell a story and as he talked he gesticulated, waved his arms and from time to time looked over his shoulder to see if the girl still stood by the window and if she were watching.

Doctor Cochran had told his daughter of his approaching death in a cold quiet voice. To the girl it had seemed that everything concerning her father must be cold and quiet. "I have a disease of the heart," he said flatly, "have long suspected there was something of the sort the matter with me and on Thursday when I went into Chicago I had myself examined. The truth is I may die at any moment. I would not tell you but for one reason—I will leave little money and you must be making plans for the future."

The Doctor stepped nearer the window where his daughter stood with her hand on the frame. The announcement had made her a little pale and her hand trembled. In spite of his apparent coldness he was touched and wanted to reassure her. "There now," he said hesitatingly, "it'll likely be all right after all. Don't worry. I haven't been a doctor for thirty years without knowing there's a great deal of nonsense about these pronouncements on the part of experts. In a matter like this, that is to say when a man has a disease of the heart, he may putter about for years." He laughed uncomfortably. "I've even heard it said that the best way to insure a long life is to contract a disease of the heart."

With these words the Doctor had turned and walked out of his office, going down a wooden stairway to the street. He had wanted to put his arm about his daughter's shoulder as he talked to her, but never having shown any feeling in his relations with her could not sufficiently release some tight thing in himself.

Mary had stood for a long time looking down into the street. The young man in the checkered suit, whose name was Duke Yetter, had finished telling his tale and a shout of laughter arose. She turned to look toward the door through which her father had passed and dread took possession of her. In all her life there had never been anything warm and close. She shivered although the night was warm and with a quick girlish gesture passed her hand over her eyes.

The gesture was but an expression of a desire to brush away the cloud of fear that had settled down upon her but it was misinterpreted by Duke Yetter who now stood a little apart from the other men before the livery barn. When he saw Mary's hand go up he smiled and turning quickly to be sure he was unobserved began jerking his head and making motions with his hand as a sign that he wished her to come down into the street where he would have an opportunity to join her.

On the Sunday evening Mary, having walked through Upper Main, turned into Wilmott, a street of workmen's houses. During that year the first sign of the march of factories westward from Chicago into the prairie towns had come to Huntersburg. A Chicago manufacturer of furniture had built a plant in the sleepy little farming town, hoping thus to escape the labor organizations that had begun to give him trouble in the city. At the upper end of town, in Wilmott, Swift, Harrison and Chestnut Streets and in cheap, badly-constructed frame houses, most of the factory workers lived. On the warm summer evening they were gathered on the porches at the front of the houses and a mob of children played in the dusty streets. Red-faced men in white shirts and without collars and coats slept in chairs or lay sprawled on strips of grass or on the hard earth before the doors of the houses.

The laborers' wives had gathered in groups and stood gossiping by the fences that separated the yards. Occasionally the voice of one of the women arose sharp and distinct above the steady flow of voices that ran like a murmuring river through the hot little streets.

In the roadway two children had got into a fight. A thick-shouldered red-haired boy struck another boy who had a pale sharp-featured face, a blow on the shoulder. Other children came running. The mother of the red-haired boy brought the promised fight to an end. "Stop it Johnny, I tell you to stop it. I'll break your neck if you don't," the woman screamed.

The pale boy turned and walked away from his antagonist. As he went slinking along the sidewalk past Mary Cochran his sharp little eyes, burning with hatred, looked up at her.

Mary went quickly along. The strange new part of her native town with the hubbub of life always stirring and asserting itself had a strong fascination for her. There was something dark and resentful in her own nature that made her feel at home in the crowded place where life carried itself off darkly, with a blow and an oath. The habitual silence of her father and the mystery concerning the unhappy married life of her father and mother, that had affected the attitude toward her of the people of the town, had made her own life a lonely one and had encouraged in her a rather dogged determination to in some way think her own way through the things of life she could not understand.

And back of Mary's thinking there was an intense curiosity and a courageous determination toward adventure. She was like a little animal of the forest that has been robbed of its mother by the gun of a sportsman and has been driven by hunger to go forth and seek food. Twenty times during the year she had walked alone at evening in the new and fast growing factory district of her town. She was eighteen and had begun to look like a woman, and she felt that other girls of the town of her own age would not have dared to walk in such a place alone. The feeling made her somewhat proud and as she went along she looked boldly about.

Among the workers in Wilmott Street, men and women who had been brought to town by the furniture manufacturer, were many who spoke in foreign tongues. Mary walked among them and liked the sound of the strange voices. To be in the street made her feel that she had gone out of her town and on a voyage into a strange land. In Lower Main Street or in the residence streets in the eastern part of town where lived the young men and women she had always known and where lived also the merchants, the clerks, the lawyers and the more well-to-do American workmen of Huntersburg, she felt always a secret antagonism to herself. The antagonism was not due to anything in her own character. She was sure of that. She had kept so much to herself that she was in fact but little known. "It is because I am the daughter of my mother," she told herself and did not walk often in the part of town where other girls of her class lived.

Mary had been so often in Wilmott Street that many of the people had begun to feel acquainted with her. "She is the daughter of some farmer and has got into the habit of walking into town," they said. A red-haired, broad-hipped woman who came out at the front door of one of the houses nodded to her. On a narrow strip of grass beside another house sat a young man with his back against a tree. He was smoking a pipe, but when he looked up and saw her he took the pipe from his mouth. She decided he must be an Italian, his hair and eyes were so black. "Ne bella! si fai un onore a passare di qua," he called waving his hand and smiling.

Mary went to the end of Wilmott Street and came out upon a country road. It seemed to her that a long time must have passed since she left her father's presence although the walk had in fact occupied but a few minutes. By the side of the road and on top of a small hill there was a ruined barn, and before the barn a great hole filled with the charred timbers of what had once been a farmhouse. A pile of stones lay beside the hole and these were covered with creeping vines. Between the site of the house and the barn there was an old orchard in which grew a mass of tangled weeds.

Pushing her way in among the weeds, many of which were covered with blossoms, Mary found herself a seat on a rock that had been rolled against the trunk of an old apple tree. The weeds half concealed her and from the road only her head was visible. Buried away thus in the weeds she looked like a quail that runs in the tall grass and that on hearing some unusual sound, stops, throws up its head and looks sharply about.

The doctor's daughter had been to the decayed old orchard many times before. At the foot of the hill on which it stood the streets of the town began, and as she sat on the rock she could hear faint shouts and cries coming out of Wilmott Street. A hedge separated the orchard from the fields on the hillside. Mary intended to sit by the tree until darkness came creeping over the land and to try to think out some plan regarding her future. The notion that her father was soon to die seemed both true and untrue, but her mind was unable to take hold of the thought of him as physically dead. For the moment death in relation to her father did not take the form of a cold inanimate body that was to be buried in the ground, instead it seemed to her that her father was not to die but to go away somewhere on a journey. Long ago her mother had done that. There was a strange hesitating sense of relief in the thought. "Well," she told herself, "when the time comes I also shall be setting out, I shall get out of here and into the world." On several occasions Mary had gone to spend a day with her father in Chicago and she was fascinated by the thought that soon she might be going there to live. Before her mind's eye floated a vision of long streets filled with thousands of people all strangers to herself. To go into such streets and to live her life among strangers would be like coming out of a waterless desert and into a cool forest carpeted with tender young grass.

In Huntersburg she had always lived under a cloud and now she was becoming a woman and the close stuffy atmosphere she had always breathed was becoming constantly more and more oppressive. It was true no direct question had ever been raised touching her own standing in the community life, but she felt that a kind of prejudice against her existed. While she was still a baby there had been a scandal involving her father and mother. The town of Huntersburg had rocked with it and when she was a child people had sometimes looked at her with mocking sympathetic eyes. "Poor child! It's too bad," they said. Once, on a cloudy summer evening when her father had driven off to the country and she sat alone in the darkness by his office window, she heard a man and woman in the street mention her name. The couple stumbled along in the darkness on the sidewalk below the office window. "That daughter of Doc Cochran's is a nice girl," said the man. The woman laughed. "She's growing up and attracting men's attention now. Better keep your eyes in your head. She'll turn out bad. Like mother, like daughter," the woman replied.

For ten or fifteen minutes Mary sat on the stone beneath the tree in the orchard and thought of the attitude of the town toward herself and her father. "It should have drawn us together," she told herself, and wondered if the approach of death would do what the cloud that had for years hung over them had not done. It did not at the moment seem to her cruel that the figure of death was soon to visit her father. In a way Death had become for her and for the time a lovely and gracious figure intent upon good. The hand of death was to open the door out of her father's house and into life. With the cruelty of youth she thought first of the adventurous possibilities of the new life.

Mary sat very still. In the long weeds the insects that had been disturbed in their evening song began to sing again. A robin flew into the tree beneath which she sat and struck a clear sharp note of alarm. The voices of people in the town's new factory district came softly up the hillside. They were like bells of distant cathedrals calling people to worship. Something within the girl's breast seemed to break and putting her head into her hands she rocked slowly back and forth. Tears came accompanied by a warm tender impulse toward the living men and women of Huntersburg.

And then from the road came a call. "Hello there kid," shouted a voice, and Mary sprang quickly to her feet. Her mellow mood passed like a puff of wind and in its place hot anger came.

In the road stood Duke Yetter who from his loafing place before the livery barn had seen her set out for the Sunday evening walk and had followed. When she went through Upper Main Street and into the new factory district he was sure of his conquest. "She doesn't want to be seen walking with me," he had told himself, "that's all right. She knows well enough I'll follow but doesn't want me to put in an appearance until she is well out of sight of her friends. She's a little stuck up and needs to be brought down a peg, but what do I care? She's gone out of her way to give me this chance and maybe she's only afraid of her dad."

Duke climbed the little incline out of the road and came into the orchard, but when he reached the pile of stones covered by vines he stumbled and fell. He arose and laughed. Mary had not waited for him to reach her but had started toward him, and when his laugh broke the silence that lay over the orchard she sprang forward and with her open hand struck him a sharp blow on the cheek. Then she turned and as he stood with his feet tangled in the vines ran out to the road. "If you follow or speak to me I'll get someone to kill you," she shouted.

Mary walked along the road and down the hill toward Wilmott Street. Broken bits of the story concerning her mother that had for years circulated in town had reached her ears. Her mother, it was said, had disappeared on a summer night long ago and a young town rough, who had been in the habit of loitering before Barney Smithfield's Livery Barn, had gone away with her. Now another young rough was trying to make up to her. The thought made her furious.

Her mind groped about striving to lay hold of some weapon with which she could strike a more telling blow at Duke Yetter. In desperation it lit upon the figure of her father already broken in health and now about to die. "My father just wants the chance to kill some such fellow as you," she shouted, turning to face the young man, who having got clear of the mass of vines in the orchard, had followed her into the road. "My father just wants to kill someone because of the lies that have been told in this town about mother."

Having given way to the impulse to threaten Duke Yetter Mary was instantly ashamed of her outburst and walked rapidly along, the tears running from her eyes. With hanging head Duke walked at her heels. "I didn't mean no harm, Miss Cochran," he pleaded. "I didn't mean no harm. Don't tell your father. I was only funning with you. I tell you I didn't mean no harm."

The light of the summer evening had begun to fall and the faces of the people made soft little ovals of light as they stood grouped under the dark porches or by the fences in Wilmott Street. The voices of the children had become subdued and they also stood in groups. They became silent as Mary passed and stood with upturned faces and staring eyes. "The lady doesn't live very far. She must be almost a neighbor," she heard a woman's voice saying in English. When she turned her head she saw only a crowd of dark-skinned men standing before a house. From within the house came the sound of a woman's voice singing a child to sleep.

The young Italian, who had called to her earlier in the evening and who was now apparently setting out of his own Sunday evening's adventures, came along the sidewalk and walked quickly away into the darkness. He had dressed himself in his Sunday clothes and had put on a black derby hat and a stiff white collar, set off by a red necktie. The shining whiteness of the collar made his brown skin look almost black. He smiled boyishly and raised his hat awkwardly but did not speak.

Mary kept looking back along the street to be sure Duke Yetter had not followed but in the dim light could see nothing of him. Her angry excited mood went away.

She did not want to go home and decided it was too late to go to church. From Upper Main Street there was a short street that ran eastward and fell rather sharply down a hillside to a creek and a bridge that marked the end of the town's growth in that direction. She went down along the street to the bridge and stood in the failing light watching two boys who were fishing in the creek.

A broad-shouldered man dressed in rough clothes came down along the street and stopping on the bridge spoke to her. It was the first time she had ever heard a citizen of her home town speak with feeling of her father. "You are Doctor Cochran's daughter?" he asked hesitatingly. "I guess you don't know who I am but your father does." He pointed toward the two boys who sat with fishpoles in their hands on the weed-grown bank of the creek. "Those are my boys and I have four other children," he explained. "There is another boy and I have three girls. One of my daughters has a job in a store. She is as old as yourself." The man explained his relations with Doctor Cochran. He had been a farm laborer, he said, and had but recently moved to town to work in the furniture factory. During the previous winter he had been ill for a long time and had no money. While he lay in bed one of his boys fell out of a barn loft and there was a terrible cut in his head.

"Your father came every day to see us and he sewed up my Tom's head." The laborer turned away from Mary and stood with his cap in his hand looking toward the boys. "I was down and out and your father not only took care of me and the boys but he gave my old woman money to buy the things we had to have from the stores in town here, groceries and medicines." The man spoke in such low tones that Mary had to lean forward to hear his words. Her face almost touched the laborer's shoulder. "Your father is a good man and I don't think he is very happy," he went on. "The boy and I got well and I got work here in town but he wouldn't take any money from me. 'You know how to live with your children and with your wife. You know how to make them happy. Keep your money and spend it on them,' that's what he said to me."

The laborer went on across the bridge and along the creek bank toward the spot where his two sons sat fishing and Mary leaned on the railing of the bridge and looked at the slow moving water. It was almost black in the shadows under the bridge and she thought that it was thus her father's life had been lived. "It has been like a stream running always in shadows and never coming out into the sunlight," she thought, and fear that her own life would run on in darkness gripped her. A great new love for her father swept over her and in fancy she felt his arms about her. As a child she had continually dreamed of caresses received at her father's hands and now the dream came back. For a long time she stood looking at the stream and she resolved that the night should not pass without an effort on her part to make the old dream come true. When she again looked up the laborer had built a little fire of sticks at the edge of the stream. "We catch bullheads here," he called. "The light of the fire draws them close to the shore. If you want to come and try your hand at fishing the boys will lend you one of the poles."

"O, I thank you, I won't do it tonight," Mary said, and then fearing she might suddenly begin weeping and that if the man spoke to her again she would find herself unable to answer, she hurried away. "Good bye!" shouted the man and the two boys. The words came quite spontaneously out of the three throats and created a sharp trumpet-like effect that rang like a glad cry across the heaviness of her mood.

When his daughter Mary went out for her evening walk Doctor Cochran sat for an hour alone in his office. It began to grow dark and the men who all afternoon had been sitting on chairs and boxes before the livery barn across the street went home for the evening meal. The noise of voices grew faint and sometimes for five or ten minutes there was silence. Then from some distant street came a child's cry. Presently church bells began to ring.

The Doctor was not a very neat man and sometimes for several days he forgot to shave. With a long lean hand he stroked his half grown beard. His illness had struck deeper than he had admitted even to himself and his mind had an inclination to float out of his body. Often when he sat thus his hands lay in his lap and he looked at them with a child's absorption. It seemed to him they must belong to someone else. He grew philosophic. "It's an odd thing about my body. Here I've lived in it all these years and how little use I have had of it. Now it's going to die and decay never having been used. I wonder why it did not get another tenant." He smiled sadly over this fancy but went on with it. "Well I've had thoughts enough concerning people and I've had the use of these lips and a tongue but I've let them lie idle. When my Ellen was here living with me I let her think me cold and unfeeling while something within me was straining and straining trying to tear itself loose."

He remembered how often, as a young man, he had sat in the evening in silence beside his wife in this same office and how his hands had ached to reach across the narrow space that separated them and touch her hands, her face, her hair.

Well, everyone in town had predicted his marriage would turn out badly! His wife had been an actress with a company that came to Huntersburg and got stranded there. At the same time the girl became ill and had no money to pay for her room at the hotel. The young doctor had attended to that and when the girl was convalescent took her to ride about the country in his buggy. Her life had been a hard one and the notion of leading a quiet existence in the little town appealed to her.

And then after the marriage and after the child was born she had suddenly found herself unable to go on living with the silent cold man. There had been a story of her having run away with a young sport, the son of a saloon keeper who had disappeared from town at the same time, but the story was untrue. Lester Cochran had himself taken her to Chicago where she got work with a company going into the far western states. Then he had taken her to the door of her hotel, had put money into her hands and in silence and without even a farewell kiss had turned and walked away.

The Doctor sat in his office living over that moment and other intense moments when he had been deeply stirred and had been on the surface so cool and quiet. He wondered if the woman had known. How many times he had asked himself that question. After he left her that night at the hotel door she never wrote. "Perhaps she is dead," he thought for the thousandth time.

A thing happened that had been happening at odd moments for more than a year. In Doctor Cochran's mind the remembered figure of his wife became confused with the figure of his daughter. When at such moments he tried to separate the two figures, to make them stand out distinct from each other, he was unsuccessful. Turning his head slightly he imagined he saw a white girlish figure coming through a door out of the rooms in which he and his daughter lived. The door was painted white and swung slowly in a light breeze that came in at an open window. The wind ran softly and quietly through the room and played over some papers lying on a desk in a corner. There was a soft swishing sound as of a woman's skirts. The doctor arose and stood trembling. "Which is it? Is it you Mary or is it Ellen?" he asked huskily.

On the stairway leading up from the street there was the sound of heavy feet and the outer door opened. The doctor's weak heart fluttered and he dropped heavily back into his chair.

A man came into the room. He was a farmer, one of the doctor's patients, and coming to the centre of the room he struck a match, held it above his head and shouted. "Hello!" he called. When the doctor arose from his chair and answered he was so startled that the match fell from his hand and lay burning faintly at his feet.

The young farmer had sturdy legs that were like two pillars of stone supporting a heavy building, and the little flame of the match that burned and fluttered in the light breeze on the floor between his feet threw dancing shadows along the walls of the room. The doctor's confused mind refused to clear itself of his fancies that now began to feed upon this new situation.

He forgot the presence of the farmer and his mind raced back over his life as a married man. The flickering light on the wall recalled another dancing light. One afternoon in the summer during the first year after his marriage his wife Ellen had driven with him into the country. They were then furnishing their rooms and at a farmer's house Ellen had seen an old mirror, no longer in use, standing against a wall in a shed. Because of something quaint in the design the mirror had taken her fancy and the farmer's wife had given it to her. On the drive home the young wife had told her husband of her pregnancy and the doctor had been stirred as never before. He sat holding the mirror on his knees while his wife drove and when she announced the coming of the child she looked away across the fields.

How deeply etched, that scene in the sick man's mind! The sun was going down over young corn and oat fields beside the road. The prairie land was black and occasionally the road ran through short lanes of trees that also looked black in the waning light.

The mirror on his knees caught the rays of the departing sun and sent a great ball of golden light dancing across the fields and among the branches of trees. Now as he stood in the presence of the farmer and as the little light from the burning match on the floor recalled that other evening of dancing lights, he thought he understood the failure of his marriage and of his life. On that evening long ago when Ellen had told him of the coming of the great adventure of their marriage he had remained silent because he had thought no words he could utter would express what he felt. There had been a defense for himself built up. "I told myself she should have understood without words and I've all my life been telling myself the same thing about Mary. I've been a fool and a coward. I've always been silent because I've been afraid of expressing myself—like a blundering fool. I've been a proud man and a coward.

"Tonight I'll do it. If it kills me I'll make myself talk to the girl," he said aloud, his mind coming back to the figure of his daughter.

"Hey! What's that?" asked the farmer who stood with his hat in his hand waiting to tell of his mission.

The doctor got his horse from Barney Smithfield's livery and drove off to the country to attend the farmer's wife who was about to give birth to her first child. She was a slender narrow-hipped woman and the child was large, but the doctor was feverishly strong. He worked desperately and the woman, who was frightened, groaned and struggled. Her husband kept coming in and going out of the room and two neighbor women appeared and stood silently about waiting to be of service. It was past ten o'clock when everything was done and the doctor was ready to depart for town.

The farmer hitched his horse and brought it to the door and the doctor drove off feeling strangely weak and at the same time strong. How simple now seemed the thing he had yet to do. Perhaps when he got home his daughter would have gone to bed but he would ask her to get up and come into the office. Then he would tell the whole story of his marriage and its failure sparing himself no humiliation. "There was something very dear and beautiful in my Ellen and I must make Mary understand that. It will help her to be a beautiful woman," he thought, full of confidence in the strength of his resolution.

He got to the door of the livery barn at eleven o'clock and Barney Smithfield with young Duke Yetter and two other men sat talking there. The liveryman took his horse away into the darkness of the barn and the doctor stood for a moment leaning against the wall of the building. The town's night watchman stood with the group by the barn door and a quarrel broke out between him and Duke Yetter, but the doctor did not hear the hot words that flew back and forth or Duke's loud laughter at the night watchman's anger. A queer hesitating mood had taken possession of him. There was something he passionately desired to do but could not remember. Did it have to do with his wife Ellen or Mary his daughter? The figures of the two women were again confused in his mind and to add to the confusion there was a third figure, that of the woman he had just assisted through child birth. Everything was confusion. He started across the street toward the entrance of the stairway leading to his office and then stopped in the road and stared about. Barney Smithfield having returned from putting his horse in the stall shut the door of the barn and a hanging lantern over the door swung back and forth. It threw grotesque dancing shadows down over the faces and forms of the men standing and quarreling beside the wall of the barn.

Mary sat by a window in the doctor's office awaiting his return. So absorbed was she in her own thoughts that she was unconscious of the voice of Duke Yetter talking with the men in the street.

When Duke had come into the street the hot anger of the early part of the evening had returned and she again saw him advancing toward her in the orchard with the look of arrogant male confidence in his eyes but presently she forgot him and thought only of her father. An incident of her childhood returned to haunt her. One afternoon in the month of May when she was fifteen her father had asked her to accompany him on an evening drive into the country. The doctor went to visit a sick woman at a farmhouse five miles from town and as there had been a great deal of rain the roads were heavy. It was dark when they reached the farmer's house and they went into the kitchen and ate cold food off a kitchen table. For some reason her father had, on that evening, appeared boyish and almost gay. On the road he had talked a little. Even at that early age Mary had grown tall and her figure was becoming womanly. After the cold supper in the farm kitchen he walked with her around the house and she sat on a narrow porch. For a moment her father stood before her. He put his hands into his trouser pockets and throwing back his head laughed almost heartily. "It seems strange to think you will soon be a woman," he said. "When you do become a woman what do you suppose is going to happen, eh? What kind of a life will you lead? What will happen to you?"

The doctor sat on the porch beside the child and for a moment she had thought he was about to put his arm around her. Then he jumped up and went into the house leaving her to sit alone in the darkness.

As she remembered the incident Mary remembered also that on that evening of her childhood she had met her father's advances in silence. It seemed to her that she, not her father, was to blame for the life they had led together. The farm laborer she had met on the bridge had not felt her father's coldness. That was because he had himself been warm and generous in his attitude toward the man who had cared for him in his hour of sickness and misfortune. Her father had said that the laborer knew how to be a father and Mary remembered with what warmth the two boys fishing by the creek had called to her as she went away into the darkness. "Their father has known how to be a father because his children have known how to give themselves," she thought guiltily. She also would give herself. Before the night had passed she would do that. On that evening long ago and as she rode home beside her father he had made another unsuccessful effort to break through the wall that separated them. The heavy rains had swollen the streams they had to cross and when they had almost reached town he had stopped the horse on a wooden bridge. The horse danced nervously about and her father held the reins firmly and occasionally spoke to him. Beneath the bridge the swollen stream made a great roaring sound and beside the road in a long flat field there was a lake of flood water. At that moment the moon had come out from behind clouds and the wind that blew across the water made little waves. The lake of flood water was covered with dancing lights. "I'm going to tell you about your mother and myself," her father said huskily, but at that moment the timbers of the bridge began to crack dangerously and the horse plunged forward. When her father had regained control of the frightened beast they were in the streets of the town and his diffident silent nature had reasserted itself.

Mary sat in the darkness by the office window and saw her father drive into the street. When his horse had been put away he did not, as was his custom, come at once up the stairway to the office but lingered in the darkness before the barn door. Once he started to cross the street and then returned into the darkness.

Among the men who for two hours had been sitting and talking quietly a quarrel broke out. Jack Fisher the town nightwatchman had been telling the others the story of a battle in which he had fought during the Civil War and Duke Yetter had begun bantering him. The nightwatchman grew angry. Grasping his nightstick he limped up and down. The loud voice of Duke Yetter cut across the shrill angry voice of the victim of his wit. "You ought to a flanked the fellow, I tell you Jack. Yes sir 'ee, you ought to a flanked that reb and then when you got him flanked you ought to a knocked the stuffings out of the cuss. That's what I would a done," Duke shouted, laughing boisterously. "You would a raised hell, you would," the night watchman answered, filled with ineffectual wrath.

The old soldier went off along the street followed by the laughter of Duke and his companions and Barney Smithfield, having put the doctor's horse away, came out and closed the barn door. A lantern hanging above the door swung back and forth. Doctor Cochran again started across the street and when he had reached the foot of the stairway turned and shouted to the men. "Good night," he called cheerfully. A strand of hair was blown by the light summer breeze across Mary's cheek and she jumped to her feet as though she had been touched by a hand reached out to her from the darkness. A hundred times she had seen her father return from drives in the evening but never before had he said anything at all to the loiterers by the barn door. She became half convinced that not her father but some other man was now coming up the stairway.

The heavy dragging footsteps rang loudly on the wooden stairs and Mary heard her father set down the little square medicine case he always carried. The strange cheerful hearty mood of the man continued but his mind was in a confused riot. Mary imagined she could see his dark form in the doorway. "The woman has had a baby," said the hearty voice from the landing outside the door. "Who did that happen to? Was it Ellen or that other woman or my little Mary?"

A stream of words, a protest came from the man's lips. "Who's been having a baby? I want to know. Who's been having a baby? Life doesn't work out. Why are babies always being born?" he asked.

A laugh broke from the doctor's lips and his daughter leaned forward and gripped the arms of her chair. "A babe has been born," he said again. "It's strange eh, that my hands should have helped a baby be born while all the time death stood at my elbow?"

Doctor Cochran stamped upon the floor of the landing. "My feet are cold and numb from waiting for life to come out of life," he said heavily. "The woman struggled and now I must struggle."

Silence followed the stamping of feet and the tired heavy declaration from the sick man's lips. From the street below came another loud shout of laughter from Duke Yetter.

And then Doctor Cochran fell backward down the narrow stairs to the street. There was no cry from him, just the clatter of his shoes upon the stairs and the terrible subdued sound of the body falling.

Mary did not move from her chair. With closed eyes she waited. Her heart pounded. A weakness complete and overmastering had possession of her and from feet to head ran little waves of feeling as though tiny creatures with soft hair-like feet were playing upon her body.

It was Duke Yetter who carried the dead man up the stairs and laid him on a bed in one of the rooms back of the office. One of the men who had been sitting with him before the door of the barn followed lifting his hands and dropping them nervously. Between his fingers he held a forgotten cigarette the light from which danced up and down in the darkness.

"Unused"

A TALE OF LIFE IN OHIO

"Unused," that was one of the words the Doctor used that day in speaking of her. He, the doctor, was an extraordinarily large and immaculately clean man, by whom I was at that time employed. I swept out his office, mowed the lawn before his residence, took care of the two horses in his stable and did odd jobs about the yard and kitchen—such as bringing in firewood, putting water in a tub in the sun behind a grape arbor for the doctor's bath and even sometimes, during his bath, scrubbing for him those parts of his broad back he himself could not reach.

The doctor had a passion in life with which he early infected me. He loved fishing and as he knew all of the good places in the river, several miles west of town, and in Sandusky Bay, some nineteen or twenty miles to the north, we often went off for long delightful days together.

It was late in the afternoon of such a fishing day in the late June, when the doctor and I were together in a boat on the bay, that a farmer came running to the shore, waving his arms and calling to the doctor. Little May Edgley's body had been found floating near a river's mouth half a mile away, and, as she had been dead for several days, as the doctor had just had a good bite, and as there was nothing he could do anyway, it was all nonsense, his being called. I remembered how he growled and grumbled. He did not then know what had happened but the fish were just beginning to bite splendidly, I had just landed a fine bass and the good evening's fishing was all ahead of us. Well, you know how it is—a doctor is always at everyone's beck and call.

119

"Dang it all! That's the way it always goes! Here we are—as good a fishing evening as we'll find this summer—wind just right and the sky clouding over—and will you look at my dang luck? A doctor in the neighborhood and that farmer knows it and so, just to accommodate me, he goes and stubs his toe, like as not, or his boy falls out of a barn loft, or his old woman gets the toothache. Like as not it's one of his women folks. I know 'em! His wife's got an unmarried sister living with her. Dang sentimental old maid! She's got a nervous complaint—gets all worked up and thinks she's going to die. Die nothing! I know that kind. Lots of 'em like to have a doctor fooling around. Let a doctor come near, so they can get him alone in a room, and they'll spend hours talking about themselves—if he'll let 'em."

The doctor was reeling in his line, grumbling and complaining as he did so and then, suddenly, with the characteristic cheerfulness that I had seen carry him with a smile on his lips through whole days and nights of work and night driving over rough frozen earth roads in the winter, he picked up the oars and rowed vigorously ashore. When I offered to take the oars he shook his head. "No kid, it's good for the figure," he said, looking down at his huge paunch. He smiled. "I got to keep my figure. If I don't I'll be losing some of my practice among the unmarried women."

As for the business ashore—there was May Edgley, of our town, drowned in that out of the way place, and her body had been in the water several days. It had been found among some willows that grew near the mouth of a deep creek that emptied into the bay, had lodged in among the roots of the willows, and when we got ashore the farmer, his son and the hired man, had got it out and had laid it on some boards near a barn that faced the bay.

That was my own first sight of death and I shall not forget the moment when I followed the doctor in among the little group of silent people standing about and saw the dead, discolored and bloated body of the woman lying there.

The doctor was used to that sort of thing, but to me it was all new and terrifying. I remember that I looked once and then ran away. Dashing into the barn I went to lean against the feedbox of a stall, where an old farm-horse was eating hay. The warm day outside had suddenly seemed cold and chill but in the barn it was warm again. Oh, what a lovely thing to a boy is a barn, with the rich warm comforting smell of the cured hay and the animal life, lying like a soft bed over it all. At the doctor's house, while I lived and worked there, the doctor's wife used to put on my bed, on winter nights, a kind of soft warm bed cover called a "comfortable." That's what it was like to me that day in the barn when we had just found May Edgley's body.

As for the body—well, May Edgley had been a small woman with small firm hands and in one of her hands, tightly gripped, when they had found her, was a woman's hat—a great broad-brimmed gaudy thing it must have been, and there had been a huge ostrich feather sticking out of the top, such an ostrich feather as you see sometimes sticking out of the hat of a kind of big flashy woman at the horse races or at second-rate summer resorts near cities.

It stayed in my mind, that bedraggled ostrich feather, little May Edgley's hand had gripped so determinedly when death came, and as I stood shivering in the barn I could see it again, as I had so often seen it perched on the head of big bold Lil Edgley, May Edgley's sister, as she went, half-defiantly always, through the streets of our town, Bidwell, Ohio.

And then as I stood shivering with boyish dread of death in that old barn, the farm-horse put his head through an opening at the front of the stall and rubbed his soft warm nose against my cheek. The farmer, on whose place we were, must have been one who was kind to his animals. The old horse rubbed his nose up and down my cheek. "You are a long ways from death, my lad, and when the time comes for you you won't shiver so much. I am old and I know. Death is a kind comforting thing to those who are through with their lives."

Something of that sort the old farmhorse seemed to be saying and at any rate he quieted me, took the fear and the chill all out of me.

It was when the doctor and I were driving home together that evening in the dusk, and after all arrangements for sending May Edgley's body back to town and to her people had been made, that he spoke of her and used the word I am now using as the title for her story. The doctor said a great many things that evening that I cannot now remember and I only remember how the night came softly on and how the grey road faded out of sight, and then how the moon came out and the road that had been grey became silvery white, with patches of inky blackness where the shadows of trees fell across it. The doctor was one sane enough not to talk down to a boy. How often he spoke intimately to me of his impressions of men and events! There were many things in the fat old doctor's mind of which his patients knew nothing, but of which his stable boy knew.

The doctor's old bay horse went steadily along, doing his work as cheerfully as the doctor did his and the doctor smoked a cigar. He spoke of the dead woman, May Edgley, and of what a bright girl she had been.

As for her story—he did not tell it completely. I was myself much alive that evening—that is to say the imaginative side of myself was much alive—and the doctor was as a sower, sowing seed in a fertile soil. He was as one who goes through a wide long field, newly plowed by the hand of Death, the plowman, and as he went along he flung wide the seeds of May Edgley's story, wide, far over the land, over the rich fertile land of a boy's awakening imagination.

CHAPTER I

THERE WERE THREE boys and as many girls in the Edgley family of Bidwell, Ohio, and of the girls Lillian and Kate were known in a dozen towns along the railroad that ran between Cleveland and Toledo. The fame of Lillian, the eldest, went far. On the streets of the neighboring towns of Clyde, Norwalk, Fremont, Tiffin, and even in Toledo and Cleveland, she was well known. On summer evenings she went up and down our main street wearing a huge hat with a white ostrich feather that fell down almost to her shoulder. She, like her sister Kate, who never succeeded in attaining to a position of prominence in the town's life, was a blonde with cold staring blue eyes. On almost any Friday evening she might have been seen setting forth on some adventure, from which she did not return until the following Monday or Tuesday. It was evident the adventures were profitable, as the Edgley family were working folk and it is certain her brothers did not purchase for her the endless number of new dresses in which she arrayed herself.

It was a Friday evening in the summer and Lillian appeared on the upper main street of Bidwell. Two dozen men and boys loafed by the station platform, awaiting the arrival of the New York Central train, eastward bound. They stared at Lillian who stared back at them. In the west, from which direction the train was presently to come, the sun went down over young corn fields. A dusky golden splendor lit the skies and the loafers were awed into silence, hushed, both by the beauty of the evening and by the challenge in Lillian's eyes.

Then the train arrived and the spell of silence was broken. The conductor and brakeman jumped to the station platform and waved their hands at Lillian and the engineer put his head out of the cab.

Aboard the train Lillian found a seat by herself and as soon as the train had started and the fares were collected the conductor came to sit with her. When the train arrived at the next town and the conductor was compelled to attend to his affairs, the brakeman came to lean over her seat. The men talked in undertones and occasionally the silence in the car was broken by outbursts of laughter. Other women from Bidwell, going to visit relatives in distant towns, were embarrassed. They turned their heads to look out at car windows and their cheeks grew red.

On the station platform at Bidwell, where darkness was settling down over the scene, the men and boys still lingered about speaking of Lillian and her adventures. "She can ride anywhere she pleases and never has to pay a cent of fare," declared a tall bearded man who leaned against the station door. He was a buyer of pigs and cattle and was compelled to go to the Cleveland market once every week. The thought of Lillian, the light o' love traveling free over the railroads filled his heart with envy and anger.

The entire Edgley family bore a shaky reputation in Bidwell but with the exception of May, the youngest of the girls, they were people who knew how to take care of themselves. For years Jake, the eldest of the boys, tended bar for Charley Shuter in a saloon in lower Main Street and then, to everyone's surprise, he bought out the place. "Either Lillian gave him the money or he stole it from Charley," the men said, but nevertheless, and throwing moral standards aside, they went into the bar to buy drinks. In Bidwell vice, while openly condemned, was in secret looked upon as a mark of virility in young manhood.

Frank and Will Edgley were teamsters and draymen like their father John and were hard working men. They owned their own teams and asked favors of no man and when they were not at work did not seek the society of others. Late on Saturday afternoons, when the week's work was done and the horses cleaned, fed and bedded down for the night they dressed themselves in black suits, put on white collars and black derby hats and went into our main street to drink themselves drunk. By ten o'clock they had succeeded and went reeling homeward. When in the darkness under the maple trees on Vine or Walnut Streets they met a Bidwell citizen, also homeward bound, a row started. "Damn you, get out of our way. Get off the sidewalk," Frank Edgley shouted and the two men rushed forward intent on a fight.

One evening in the month of June, when there was a moon and when insects sang loudly in the long grass between the sidewalks and the road, the Edgley brothers met Ed Pesch, a young German farmer, out for an evening's walk with Caroline Dupee, daughter of a Bidwell drygoods merchant, and the fight the Edgley boys had long been looking for took place. Frank Edgley shouted and he and his brother plunged forward but Ed Pesch did not run into the road and leave them to go triumphantly homeward. He fought and the brothers were badly beaten, and on Monday morning appeared driving their team and with faces disfigured and eyes blackened. For a week they went up and down alleyways and along residence streets, delivering ice and coal to houses and merchandise to the stores without lifting their eyes or speaking. The town was delighted and clerks ran from store to store making comments, they longed to repeat within hearing of one of the brothers. "Have you seen the Edgley boys?" they asked one another. "They got what was coming to them. Ed Pesch gave them what for." The more excitable and imaginative of the clerks spoke of the fight in the darkness as though they had been on hand and had seen every blow struck. "They are bullies and can be beaten by any man who stands up for his rights," declared Walter Wills, a slender, nervous young man who worked for Albert Twist, the grocer. The clerk hungered to be such another fighter as Ed Pesch had proven himself. At night he went home from the store in the soft darkness and imagined himself as meeting the Edgleys. "I'll show you—you big bullies," he muttered and his fists shot out, striking at nothingness. An eager strained feeling ran along the muscles of his back and arms but his night time courage did not abide with him through the day. On Wednesday when Will Edgley came to the back door of the store, his wagon loaded with salt in barrels, Walter went into the alleyway to enjoy the sight of the cut lips and blackened eyes. Will stood with hands in pockets looking at the ground. An uncomfortable silence ensued and in the end it was broken by the voice of the clerk. "There's no one here and those barrels are heavy," he said heartily. "I might as well make myself useful and help you unload." Taking off his coat Walter Wills voluntarily helped at the task that belonged to Will Edgley, the drayman.

If May Edgley, during her girlhood, rose higher than any of the others of the Edgley family she also fell lower. "She had her chance and threw it away," was the word that went round and surely no one else in that family ever had so completely the town's sympathy.

Lillian Edgley was outside the pale of the town's life, and Kate was but a lesser edition of her sister. She waited on table at the Fownsby House, and on almost any evening might have been seen walking out with some traveling man. She also took the evening train to neighboring towns but returned to Bidwell later on the same night or at daylight the next morning. She did not prosper as Lillian did and grew tired of the dullness of small town life. At twenty-two she went to live in Cleveland where she got a job as cloak model in a large store. Later she went on the road as an actress, in a burlesque show, and Bidwell heard no more of her.

As for May Edgley, all through her childhood and until her seventeenth year she was a model of good behavior. Everyone spoke of it. She was, unlike the other Edgleys, small and dark, and unlike her sisters dressed herself in plain neat-fitting clothes. As a young girl in the public school she began to attract attention because of her proficiency in the classes. Both Lillian and Kate Edgley had been slovenly students, who spent their time ogling boys and the men teachers but May looked at no one and as soon as school was dismissed in the afternoon went home to her mother, a tall tired-looking woman who seldom went out of her own house.

In Bidwell, Tom Means, who later became a soldier and who has recently won high rank in the army because of his proficiency in training recruits for the World War, was the prize pupil in the schools. Tom was working for his appointment to West Point, and did not spend his evenings loafing on the streets, as did other young men. He stayed in his own house, intent on his studies. Tom's father was a lawyer and his mother was third cousin to a Kentucky woman who had married an English baronet. The son aspired to be a soldier and a gentleman and to live on the intellectual plane, and had a good deal of contempt for the mental capacities of his fellow students, and when one of the Edgley family set up as his rival he was angry and embarrassed and the schoolroom was delighted. Day after day and year after year the contest between him and May Edgley went on and in a sense the whole town of Bidwell got back of the girl. In all such things as history and English literature Tom swept all before him but in spelling, arithmetic, and geography May defeated him without effort. At her desk she sat like a little terrier in the presence of a trap filled with rats. A question was asked or a problem in arithmetic put on the blackboard and like a terrier she jumped. Her hand went up and her sensitive mouth quivered. Fingers were snapped vigorously. "I know," she said, and the entire class knew she did. When she had answered the question or had gone to the blackboard to solve the problem the half-grown children along the rows of benches laughed and Tom Means stared out through a window. May returned to her seat, half triumphant, half ashamed of her victory.

The country lying west of Bidwell, like all the Ohio country down that way, is given to small fruit and berry raising, and in June and after school has been dismissed for the year all the younger men, boys, and girls, with most of the women of the town go to work in the fruit harvest. To the fields immediately after breakfast the citizens go trooping away. Lunches are carried in baskets and until the sun goes down everyone stays in the fields.

And in the berry fields as in the schoolroom May was a notable figure. She did not walk or ride to the work with the other young girls, or join the parties at lunch at the noon hour, but everyone understood that that was because of her family. "I know how she feels, if I came from a family like that I wouldn't ask or want other people's attention," said one of the women, the wife of a carpenter, who trudged along with the others in the dust of the road.

In a berry field, belonging to a farmer named Peter Short, some thirty women, young men and tall awkward boys crawled over the ground, picking the red fragrant berries. Ahead of them, in a row by herself, went May, the exclusive, the woman who walked by herself. Her hands flitted in and out of the berry vines as the tail of a squirrel disappears among the leaves of a tree when one walks in a wood. The other pickers went slowly, stopping occasionally to eat berries and talk and when one had crawled a little ahead of the others he stopped and waited, sitting on his haunches. The pickers were paid in proportion to the number of quarts picked during the day but, as they often said, "pay was not everything." The berry picking was in a way a social function, and who were the pickers, wives, sons and daughters of prosperous artisans, to kill themselves for a few paltry dollars?

With May Edgley they understood it was different. Everyone knew that she and her mother got practically no money from John Edgley, the father—from the boys, Jake, Frank and Will—or from the girls, Lilian and Kate, who spent their takings on clothes for themselves. If she were to be decently dressed, she had to earn the money for the purpose during the vacation time when she could stay out of school. Later it was understood she planned to be a school teacher herself, and to attain to that position it was necessary that she keep herself well dressed and show herself industrious and alert in affairs.

Tirelessly, therefore, May worked and the boxes of berries, filled by her ever alert fingers, grew into mountains. Peter Short with his son came walking down the rows to gather the filled crates and put them aboard a wagon to be hauled to town. He looked at May with pride in his eyes and the other pickers lumbering slowly along became the target for his scorn. "Ah, you talking women and you big lazy boys, you're not much good," he cried. "Ain't you ashamed of yourselves? Look at you there, Sylvester and Al—letting yourself be beat, twice over, by a girl so little you could almost carry her home in your pocket."

It was in the summer of her seventeenth year that May fell down from her high place in the life of the town of Bidwell. Two vital and dramatic events had happened to her that year. Her mother died in April and she graduated from the high school in June, second only in honors to Tom Means. As Tom's father had been on the school board for years the town shook its head over the decision that placed him ahead of May and in everyone's eyes May had really walked off with the prize. When she went into the fields, and when they remembered the fact of her mother's recent death, even the women were ready to forget and forgive the fact of her being a member of the Edgley family. As for May, it seemed to her at that moment that nothing that could happen to her could very much matter.

And then the unexpected. As more than one Bidwell wife said afterwards to her husband. "It was then that blood showed itself."

A man named Jerome Hadley first found out about May. He went that year to Peter Short's field, as he himself said, "just for fun," and he found it. Jerome was pitcher for the Bidwell baseball nine and worked as mail clerk on the railroad. After he had returned from a run he had several days' rest and went to the berry field because the town was deserted. When he saw May working off by herself he winked at the other young men and going to her got down on his knees and began picking at a speed almost as great as her own. "Come on here, little woman," he said, "I'm a mail clerk and have got my hand in, sorting letters. My fingers can go pretty fast. Come on now, let's see if you can keep up with me."

For an hour Jerome and May went up and down in the rows and then the thing happened that set the town by the ears. The girl, who had never talked to others, began talking to Jerome and the other pickers turned to look and wonder. She no longer picked at lightning speed but loitered along, stopping to rest and put choice berries into her mouth. "Eat that," she said boldly passing a great red berry across the row to the man. She put a handful of berries into his box. "You won't make as much as seventy-five cents all day if you don't get a move on you," she said, smiling shyly.

At the noon hour the other pickers found out the truth. The tired workers had gone to the pump by Peter Short's house and then to a near-by orchard to sit under the trees and rest after the eating of lunches.

There was no doubt something had happened to May. Everyone felt it. It was later understood that she had, during that noon hour in June and quite calmly and deliberately, decided to become like her two sisters and go on the town.

The berry pickers as usual ate their lunches in groups, the women and girls sitting under one tree and the young men and boys under another. Peter Short's wife brought hot coffee and tin cups were filled. Jokes went back and forth and the girls giggled.

In spite of the unexpectedness of May's attitude toward Jerome, a bachelor and quite legitimate game for the unmarried women, no one suspected anything serious would happen. Flirtations were always going on in the berry fields. They came, played themselves out, and passed like the clouds in the June sky. In the evening, when the young men had washed the dirt of the fields away and had put on their Sunday clothes, things were different. Then a girl must look out for herself. When she went to walk in the evening with a young man under the trees or out into country lanes—then anything might happen.

But in the fields, with all the older women about—to have thought anything at all of a young man and a girl working together and blushing and laughing, would have been to misunderstand the whole spirit of the berry picking season.

And it was evident May had misunderstood. Later no one blamed Jerome, at least none of the young fellows did. As the pickers ate lunch May sat a little apart from the others. That was her custom and Jerry lay in the long grass at the edge of the orchard also a little apart. A sudden tenseness crept into the groups under the trees. May had not gone to the pump with the others when she came in from the field but sat with her back braced against a tree and the hand that held the sandwich was black with the soil of her morning labors. It trembled and once the sandwich fell out of her hand.

Suddenly she got to her feet and put her lunch basket into the fork of a tree, and then, with a look of defiance in her eyes, she climbed over a fence and started along a lane past Peter Short's barn. The lane ran down to a meadow, crossed a bridge and went on beside a waving wheatfield to a wood.

May went a little way along the lane and then stopped to look back and the other pickers stared at her, wondering what was the matter. Then Jerome Hadley got to his feet. He was ashamed and climbed awkwardly over the fence and walked away without looking back.

Everyone was quite sure it had all been arranged. As the girls and women got to their feet and stood watching, May and Jerome went out of the lane and into the wood. The older women shook their heads. "Well, well," they exclaimed while the boys and young men began slapping each other on the back and prancing grotesquely about.

It was unbelievable. Before they had got out of sight of the others under the tree Jerome had put his arm about May's waist and she had put her head down on his shoulder. It was as though May Edgley who, as all the older women agreed, had been treated almost as an equal by all of the others had wanted to throw something ugly right in their faces.

Jerome and May stayed for two hours in the wood and then came back together to the field where the others were at work. May's cheeks were pale and she looked as though she had been crying. She picked alone as before and after a few moments of awkward silence Jerome put on his coat and went off along a road toward town. May made a little mountain of filled berry boxes during that afternoon but two or three times filled boxes dropped out of her hands. The spilled fruit lay red and shining against the brown and black of the soil.

No one saw May in the berry fields after that, and Jerome Hadley had something of which to boast. In the evening when he came among the young fellows he spoke of his adventure at length.

"You couldn't blame me for taking the chance when I had it," he said laughing. He explained in detail what had occurred in the wood, while other young men stood about filled with envy. As he talked he grew both proud and a little ashamed of the public attention his adventure was attaining. "It was easy," he said. "That May Edgley's the easiest thing that ever lived in this town. A fellow don't have to ask to get what he wants. That's how easy it is."

CHAPTER II

In BIDWELL, AND after she had fairly flung herself against the wall of
village convention by going into the wood with Jerome, May lived
at home, doing the work her mother had formerly done in the Edgley
household. She washed the clothes, cooked the food and made the
beds. There was, for the time, something sweet to her in the thoughts
of doing lowly tasks and she washed and ironed the dresses in which
Lillian and Kate were to array themselves and the heavy overalls worn
by her father and brothers with a kind of satisfaction in the task. "It
makes me tired and I can sleep and won't be thinking," she told
herself. As she worked over the washtubs, among the beds soiled by
the heavy slumbers of her brothers who on the evening before had
perhaps come home drunk, or stood over the hot stove in the kitchen,
she kept thinking of her dead mother. "I wonder what she would
think," she asked herself and then added, "If she hadn't died it wouldn't
have happened. If I had someone, I could go to and talk with, things
would be different."

During the day when the men of the household were gone with
their teams and when Lillian was away from town May had the
house to herself. It was a two-storied frame building, standing at
the edge of a field near the town's edge, and had once been painted
yellow. Now, water washing from the roofs had discolored the paint,
and the side walls of the old building were all mottled and streaked.
The house stood on a little hill and the land fell sharply away from
the kitchen door. There was a creek under the hill and beyond the
creek a field that at certain times during the year became a swamp.
At the creek's edge willows and elders grew and often in the afternoon, when there was no one about, May went softly out at the
kitchen door, looking to be sure there was no one in the road that
ran past the front of the house, and if the coast was clear went down
the hill and crept in among the fragrant elders and willows. "I am
lost here and no one can see me or find me," she thought, and the
thought gave her intense satisfaction. Her cheeks grew flushed and
hot and she pressed the cool green leaves of the willows against them.
When a wagon passed in the road or someone walked along the
board sidewalk at the roadside she drew herself into a little lump and
closed her eyes. The passing sounds seemed far away and to herself
it seemed that she had in some way escaped from life. How warm
and close it was there, buried amid the dark green shadows of the
willows. The gnarled twisted limbs of the trees were like arms but

unlike the arms of the man with whom she had lain in the wood they did not grasp her with terrifying convulsive strength. For hours she lay still in the shadows and nothing came to frighten her and her lacerated spirit began to heal a little. "I have made myself an outlaw among people but I am not an outlaw here," she told herself.

Having heard of the incident with Jerome Hadley, in the berry field, Lillian and Kate Edgley were irritated and angry and one evening when they were both at the house and May was at work in the kitchen they spoke about it. Lillian was very angry and had decided to give May what she spoke of as "a piece of her mind." "What'd she want to go in the cheap for?" she asked. "It makes me sick when I think of it—a fellow like that Jerome Hadley! If she was going to cut loose what made her want to go on the cheap?"

In the Edgley family it had always been understood that May was of a different clay and old John Edgley and the boys had always paid her a kind of crude respect. They did not swear at her as they sometimes did at Lillian and Kate, and in secret they thought of her as a link between themselves and the more respectable life of the town. Ma Edgley was respectable enough but she was old and tired and never went out of the house and it was in May the family held up its head. The two brothers were proud of their sister because of her record in the town school. They themselves were working men and never expected to be anything else but, they thought, "that sister of ours has shown the town that an Edgley can beat them at their own game. She is smarter than any of them. See how she has forced the town to pay attention to her."

As for Lillian—before the incident with Jerome Hadley, she continually talked of her sister. In Norwalk, Fremont, Clyde and the other towns she visited she had many friends. Men liked her because, as they often said, she was a woman to be trusted. One could talk to her, say anything, and she would keep her mouth shut and in her presence one felt comfortably free and easy. Among her secret associates were members of churches, lawyers, owners of prosperous businesses, heads of respectable families. To be sure they saw Lillian in secret but she seemed to understand and respect their desire for secrecy. "You don't need to make no bones about it with me. I know you got to be careful," she said.

On a summer evening, in one of the towns she was in the habit of visiting, an arrangement was made. The man with whom she was to spend the evening waited until darkness had come and then, hiring a horse at a livery stable, drove to an appointed place. Side curtains were put on the buggy and the pair set forth into the darkness and loneliness of country roads. As the evening advanced and the more ardent mood of the occasion passed, a sudden sense of freedom swept over the man. "It is better not to fool around with a young girl or with some other man's wife. With Lillian one does not get found out and get into trouble," he thought.

The horse went slowly, along out of the way roads—bars were let down and the couple drove into a field. For hours they sat in the buggy and talked. The men talked to Lillian as they could talk to no other woman they had ever known. She was shrewd and in her own way capable and often the men spoke of their affairs, asking her advice. "Now what do you think, Lil'—if you were me would you buy or sell?" one of them asked.

Other and more intimate things crept into the conversations. "Well, Lil', my wife and I are all right. We get along well enough, but we ain't what you might speak of as lovers," Lillian's temporary intimate said. "She jaws me a lot when I smoke too much or when I don't want to go to church. And then, you see, we're worried about the kids. My oldest girl is running around a lot with young Harry Garvner and I keep asking myself, 'Is he any good?' I can't make up my mind. You've seen him around, Lil', what do you think?"

Having taken part in many such conversations Lillian had come to depend on her sister May to furnish her with a topic of conversation. "I know how you feel. I feel that way about May," she said. More than a hundred times she had explained that May was different from the rest of the Edgleys. "She's smart," she explained. "I tell you what, she's the smartest girl that ever went to the high school in Bidwell."

Having so often used May as an example of what an Edgley could be Lillian was shocked when she heard of the affair in the berry field. For several weeks she said nothing and then one evening in July when the two were alone in the house together she spoke. She had intended to be motherly, direct and kind—if firm, but when the words came her voice trembled and she grew angry. "I hear, May, you been fooling with a man," she began as they sat together on the front porch of the house. It was a hot evening and dark and a thunder storm threatened and for a long time after Lillian had spoken there was silence and then May put her head into her hands and leaning forward began to cry softly. Her body rocked back and forth and occasionally a dry broken sob broke the silence. "Well," Lillian added sharply, being determined to terminate her remarks before she also broke into tears, "well, May, you've made a darn fool of yourself. I didn't think it of you. I didn't think you'd turn out a fool."

In the attempt to control her own unhappiness and to conceal it, Lillian became more and more angry. Her voice continued to tremble and to regain control of it she got up and went inside the house. When she came out again May still sat in the chair at the edge of the porch with her head held in her hands. Lillian was moved to pity. "Well, don't break your heart about it, kid. I'm only an old fool after all. Don't pay too much attention to me. I guess Kate and I haven't set you such a good example," she said softly.

Lillian sat on the edge of the porch and put her hand on May's knee and when she felt the trembling of the younger woman's body a sharp mother feeling awakened within her. "I say, kid," she began again, "a girl gets notions into her head. I've had them myself. A girl thinks she'll find a man that's all right. She kinda dreams of a man that doesn't exist. She wants to be good and at the same time she wants to be something else. I guess I know how you felt but, believe me, kid, it's bunk. Take it from me, kid, I know what I'm talking about. I been with men enough. I ought to know something."

Intent now on giving advice and having for the first time definitely accepted her sister as a comrade Lillian did not realize that what she now had to say would hurt May more than her anger. "I've often wondered about mother," she said reminiscently. "She was always so glum and silent. When Kate and I went on the turf she never had nothing to say and even when I was a kid and began running around with men evenings, she kept still. I remember the first time I went over to Fremont with a man and stayed out all night. I was ashamed to come home. 'I'll catch hell,' I thought but she never said nothing at all and it was the same way with Kate. She never said nothing to her. I guess Kate and I thought she was like the rest of the family— she was banking on you."

"To Ballyhack with Dad and the boys," Lillian added sharply. "They're men and don't care about anything but getting filled up with booze and when they're tired sleeping like dogs. They're like all the other men only not so much stuck on themselves."

Lillian became angry again. "I was pretty proud of you, May, and now I don't know what to think," she said. "I've bragged about you a thousand times and I suppose Kate has. It makes me sore to think of it, you an Edgley and being as smart as you are, to fall for a cheap one like that Jerome Hadley. I bet he didn't even give you any money or promise to marry you either."

May arose from her chair, her whole body trembling as with a chill, and Lillian arose and stood beside her. The older woman got down to the kernel of what she wanted to say. "You ain't that way are you, sis—you ain't going to have a kid?" she asked. May stood by the door, leaning against the door jamb and the rain that had been threatening began to fall. "No, Lillian," she said. Like a child begging for mercy she held out her hand. Her face was white and in a flash of lightning Lillian could see it plainly. It seemed to leap out of the darkness toward her. "Don't talk about it any more, Lillian, please don't. I won't ever do it again," she pleaded.

Lillian was determined. When May went indoors and up the stairway to her room above she followed to the foot of the stairs and finished what she felt she had to say. "I don't want you to do it, May," she said, "I don't want you to do it. I want to see there be one Edgley that goes straight but if you intend to go crooked don't be a fool. Don't take up with a cheap one, like Jerome Hadley, who just give you soft talk. If you are going to do it anyway you just come to me. I'll get you in with men who have money and I'll fix it so you don't have no trouble. If you're going to go on the turf, like Kate and I did, don't be a fool. You just come to me."

In all her life May had never achieved a friendship with another woman, although often she had dreamed of such a possibility. When she was still a school girl she saw other girls going homeward in the evening. They loitered along, their arms linked, and how much they had to say to each other. When they came to a corner, where their ways parted, they could not bear to leave each other. "You go a piece with me to-night and to-morrow night I'll go a piece with you," one of them said.

May hurried homeward alone, her heart filled with envy, and after she had finished her time in the school and, more than ever after the incident in the berry field—always spoken of by Lillian as the time of her troubles—the dream of a possible friendship with some other woman grew more intense.

During the summer of that last year of her life in Bidwell a young woman from another town moved into a house on her street. Her father had a job on the Nickel Plate Railroad and Bidwell was at the end of a section of that road. The railroad man was seldom at home, his wife had died a few months before and his daughter, whose name was Maud, was not well and did not go about town with the other young women. Every afternoon and evening she sat on the front porch of her father's house, and May, who was sometimes compelled to go to one of the stores, often saw her sitting there. The newcomer in Bidwell was tall and slender and looked like an invalid. Her cheeks were pale and she looked tired. During the year before she had been operated upon and some part of her internal machinery had been taken away and her paleness and the look of weariness on her face, touched May's heart. "She looks as though she might be wanting company," she thought hopefully.

After his wife's death an unmarried sister had become the railroad man's housekeeper. She was a short strongly built woman with hard grey eyes and a determined jaw and sometimes she sat with the new girl. Then May hurried past without looking, but, when Maud sat alone, she went slowly, looking slyly at the pale face and drooped figure in the rocking chair. One day she smiled and the smile was returned. May lingered a moment. "It's hot," she said leaning over the fence, but before a conversation could be started she grew alarmed and hurried away.

When the evening's work was done on that evening and when the Edgley men had gone up town, May went into the street. Lillian was away from home and the sidewalk further up the street was deserted. The Edgley house was the last one on the street, and in the direction of town and on the same side of the street, there was—first a vacant lot, then a shed that had once been used as a blacksmith shop but that was now deserted, and after that the house where the new girl had come to live.

When the soft darkness of the summer evening came May went a little way along the street and stopped by the deserted shed. The girl in the rocking chair on the porch saw her there, and seemed to understand May's fear of her aunt. Arising she opened the door and peered into the house to be sure she was unobserved and then came down a brick walk to the gate and along the street to May, occasionally looking back to be sure she had escaped unnoticed. A large stone lay at the edge of the sidewalk before the shed and May urged the new girl to sit down beside her and rest herself.

May was flushed with excitement. "I wonder if she knows? I wonder if she knows about me?" she thought.

"I saw you wanted to be friendly and I thought I'd come and talk," the new girl said. She was filled with a vague curiosity. "I heard something about you but I know it ain't true," she said.

May's heart jumped and her hands trembled. "I've let myself in for something," she thought. The impulse to jump to her feet and run away along the sidewalk, to escape at once from the situation her hunger for companionship had created, almost overcame her and she half arose from the stone and then sat down again. She became suddenly angry and when she spoke her voice was firm, filled with indignation. "I know what you mean," she said sharply, "you mean the fool story about me and Jerome Hadley in the woods?" The new girl nodded. "I don't believe it," she said. "My aunt heard it from a woman."

Now that Maud had boldly mentioned the affair, that had, May knew, made her an outlaw in the town's life May felt suddenly free, bold, capable of meeting any situation that might arise and was lost in wonder at her own display of courage. Well, she had wanted to love the new girl, take her as a friend, but now that impulse was lost in another passion that swept through her. She wanted to conquer, to come out of a bad situation with flying colors. With the boldness of another Lillian she began to speak, to tell lies. "It just shows what happens," she said quickly. A re-creation of the incident in the wood with Jerome had come to her swiftly, like a flash of sunlight on a dark day. "I went into the woods with Jerome Hadley—why? You won't believe it when I tell you, maybe," she added.

May began laying the foundation of her lie. "He said he was in trouble and wanted to speak with me, off somewhere where no one could hear, in some secret place," she explained. "I said, 'If you're in trouble let's go over into the woods at noon.' It was my idea, our going off together that way. When he told me he was in trouble his eyes looked so hurt I never thought of reputation or nothing. I just said I'd go and I been paid for it. A girl always has to pay if she's good to a man I suppose."

May tried to look and talk like a wise woman, as she imagined Lillian would have talked under the circumstances. "I've got a notion to tell what that Jerome Hadley talked to me about all the time when we were in there—in the woods—but I won't," she declared. "He lied about me afterwards because I wouldn't do what he wanted me to, but I'll keep my word. I won't tell you any names but I'll tell you this much—I know enough to have Jerome Hadley sent to jail if I wanted to do it."

May watched her companion. To Maud, whose life had always been a dull affair, the evening was like going to a theatre. It was better than that. It was like going to the theatre where the star is your friend, where you sit among strangers and have the sense of superiority that comes with knowing, as a person much like yourself, the hero in the velvet gown with the sword clanking at his side. "Oh, do tell me all you dare. I want to know," she said.

"It was about a woman he was in trouble," May answered. "One of these days maybe the whole town will find out what I alone know." She leaned forward and touched Maud's arm. The lie she was telling made her fell glad and free. As on a dark day, when the sun suddenly breaks through clouds, everything in life now seemed bright and glowing and her imagination took a great leap forward. She had been inventing a tale to save herself but went on for the joy of seeing what she could do with the story that had come suddenly, unexpectedly, to her lips. As when she was a girl in school her mind worked swiftly, eagerly. "Listen," she said impressively, "and don't you never tell no one. Jerome Hadley wanted to kill a man here in this town, because he was in love with the man's woman. He had got poison and intended to give it to the woman. She is married and rich too. Her husband is a big man here in Bidwell. Jerome was to give the poison to the woman and she was to put it in her husband's coffee and, when the man died, the woman was to marry Jerome. I put a stop to it. I prevented the murder. Now do you understand why I went into the woods with that man?"

The fever of excitement that had taken possession of May was transmitted to her companion. It drew them closer together and now Maud put her arm about May's waist. "The nerve of him," May said boldly, "he wanted me to take the stuff to the woman's house and he offered me money too. He said the rich woman would give me a thousand dollars, but I laughed at him. 'If anything happens to that man I'll tell and you'll get hung for murder,' that's what I said to him."

May described the scene that had taken place there in the deep dark forest with the man, intent upon murder. They fought, she said, for more than two hours and the man tried to kill her. She would have had him arrested at once, she explained, but to do so involved telling the story of the poison plot and she had given her word to save him, and if he reformed, she would not tell. After a long time, when the man saw she was not to be moved and would neither take part in the plot or allow it to be carried out, he grew quieter. Then, as they were coming out of the woods, he sprang upon her again and tried to choke her. Some berry pickers in a field, among whom she had been working during the morning, saw the struggle.

"They went and told lies about me," May said emphatically. "They saw us struggling and they went and said he was making love to me. A girl there, who was in love with Jerome herself and was jealous when she saw us together, started the story. It spread all over town and now I'm so ashamed I hardly dare to show my face."

With an air of helpless annoyance May arose. "Well," she said, "I promised him I wouldn't tell the name of the man he was going to murder or nothing about it and I won't. I've told you too much as it is but you gave me your word you wouldn't tell. It's got to be a secret between us." She started off along the sidewalk toward the Edgley house and then turned and ran back to the new girl, who had got almost to her own gate. "You keep still," May whispered dramatically. "If you go talking now remember you may get a man hung."

CHAPTER III

A NEW LIFE began to unfold itself to May Edgley. After the affair in the berry field, and until the time of the conversation with Maud Welliver, she had felt as one dead. As she went about in the Edgley household, doing the daily work, she sometimes stopped and stood still, on the stairs or in the kitchen by the stove. A whirlwind seemed to be going on around her while she stood thus, becalmed—fear made her body tremble. It had happened even in the moments when she was hidden under the elders by the creek. At such times the trunks of the willow trees and the fragrance of the elders comforted but did not comfort enough. There was something wanting. They were too impersonal, too sure of themselves.

To herself, at such moments, May was like one sealed up in a vessel of glass. The light of days came to her and from all sides came the sound of life going on but she herself did not live. She but breathed, ate food, slept and awakened but what she wanted out of life seemed far away, lost to her. In a way, and ever since she had been conscious of herself, it had been so.

She remembered faces she had seen, expressions that had come suddenly to peoples' faces as she passed them on the streets. In particular old men had always been kind to her. They stopped to speak to her. "Hello, little girl," they said. For her benefit eyes had been lifted, lips had smiled, kindly words had been spoken, and at such moments it had seemed to her that some tiny sluiceway out of the great stream of human life had been opened to her. The stream flowed on somewhere, in the distance, on the further side of a wall, behind a mountain of iron—just out of sight, out of hearing—but a few drops of the living waters of life had reached her, had bathed her. Understanding of the secret thing that went on within herself was not impossible. It could exist.

In the days after the talk with Lillian the puzzled woman in the yellow house thought much about life. Her mind, naturally a busy active one, could not remain passive and for the time she dared not think much of herself and of her own future. She thought abstractly.

She had done a thing and how natural and yet how strange the doing of it had been. There she was at work in a berry field—it was morning, the sun shone, boys, young girls, and mature women laughed and talked in the rows behind her. Her fingers were very busy but she listened while a woman's voice talked of canning fruit. "Cherries take so much sugar," the voice said. A young girl's voice talked endlessly of some boy and girl affair. There was a tale of a ride into the country on a hay wagon, and an involved recital of "he saids" and "I saids."

And then the man had come along the rows and had got down on his knees to work beside herself—May Edgley. He was a man out of the town's life, and had come thus, suddenly, unexpectedly. No one had ever come to her in that way. Oh, people had been kind. They had smiled and nodded, and had gone their own ways.

May had not seen the sly winks Jerome Hadley had bestowed on the other berry pickers and had taken his impulse to come to her as a simple and lovely fact in life. Perhaps he was lonely like herself. For a time the two had worked together in silence and then a bantering conversation began. May had found herself able to carry her end of a conversation, to give and take with the man. She laughed at him because, although his fingers were skilled, he could not fill the berry boxes as fast as herself.

And then, quite suddenly, the tone of the conversation had changed. The man became bold and his boldness had excited May. What words he had said. "I'd like to hold you in my arms. I'd like to have you alone where I could kiss you. I'd like to be alone with you in the woods or somewhere." The others working, now far away along the rows, young girls and women, too, must also have heard just such words from the lips of men. It was the fact that they had heard such words and responded to them in kind that differentiated them from herself. It was by responding to such words that a woman got herself a lover, got married, connected herself with the stream of life. She heard such words and something within herself stirred, as it was stirring now in herself. Like a flower she opened to receive life. Strange beautiful things happened and her experience became the experience of all life, of trees, of flowers, of grasses and most of all of other women. Something arose within her and then broke. The wall of life was broken down. She became a living thing, receiving life, giving it forth, one with all life.

In the berry field that morning May had gone on working after the words were said. Her fingers automatically picked berries and put them in the boxes slowly, hesitatingly. She turned to the man and laughed. How wonderful that she could control herself so.

Her mind had raced. What a thing her mind was. It was always doing that—racing, running madly, a little out of control. Her fingers moved more slowly. She picked berries and put them in the man's box, and now and then gave him large fine round berries to eat and was conscious that the others in the field were looking in her direction. They were listening, wondering, and she grew resentful. "What did they want? What did all this have to do with them?"

Her mind took a new turn. "What would it be like to be held in the arms of a man, to have a man's lips pressed down upon her lips. It was an experience all women, who had lived, had known. It had come to her own mother, to the married women, working with her in the field, to young girls, too, to many much younger than herself." She imagined arms soft and yet firm, strong arms, holding her closely, and sank into a dim, splendid world of emotion. The stream of life in which she had always wanted to float had picked her up—it carried her along. All life became colorful. The red berries in the boxes—how red they were, the green of the vines, what a living green! The colors merged—they ran together, the stream of life was flowing over them, over her.

What a terrible day that had been for May. Later she could not focus her mind upon it, dared not do so. The actual experience with the man in the forest had been quite brutal—an assault had been made upon her. She had consented—yes—but not to what happened. Why had she gone into the woods with him? Well, she had gone, and by her manner she had invited, urged him to follow, but she had not expected anything really to happen.

It had been her own fault, everything had been her own fault. She had got up from among the berry pickers, angry at them—resentful. They knew too much and not enough and she had hated their knowledge, their smartness. She had got up and walked away from them, looking back, expecting him.

What had she expected? What she had expected could not get itself put into words. She knew nothing of poets and their efforts, of the things they live to try to do, of things men try to paint into canvasses, translate into song. She was an Ohio woman, an Edgley, the daughter of a teamster, the sister of Lillian Edgley who had gone on the turf. May expected to walk into a new world, into life—she expected to bathe herself in the living waters of life. There was to be something warm, close, comforting, secure. Hands were to arise out of darkness and grasp her hands, her hands covered with the stain of red berries and the yellow dust of fields. She was to be held closely in the warm place and then like a flower she was to break open, throw herself, her fragrance into the air.

What had been the matter with her, with her notion of life? May had asked herself that question a thousand times, had asked it until she was weary of asking, could not ask any more. She had known her mother—thought she had known her—if she had not, no Edgley had. Had none of the others cared? Her mother had met a man and had been held in his arms, she had become the mother of sons and daughters, and the sons and daughters had gone their own way, lived brutally. They had gone after what they thought they wanted from life, directly, brutally—like animals. And her mother had stood aside. How long ago she must have died, really. It was then only flesh and blood that went on living, working, making beds, cooking, lying with a husband.

It was plain that was true of her mother—it must have been true. If it were not true why had she not spoken, why had no words come to her lips. Day after day May had worked with her mother. Well, then she was a virgin, young, tender and her mother had not kissed her, had not held her closely. No word had been said. It was not true, as Lillian had said, that her mother had counted on her. It was because of death that she was silent, when Lillian and then Kate went on the turf. The dead did not care! The dead are dead!

May wondered if she herself had passed out of life, if she had died. "It may be," she thought, "I may never have lived and my thinking I was alive may only have been a trick of mind."

"I'm smart," May thought. Lillian had said that, her brothers had said it, the whole town had said it. How she hated her own smartness.

The others had been proud of it, glad of it. The whole town had been proud of her, had hailed her. It was because she was smart, because she thought quicker and faster than others, it was because of that the women schoolteachers had smiled at her, because of that old men spoke to her on the streets.

Once an old man had met her on the sidewalk in front of one of the stores and taking her by the hand had led her inside and had bought her a bag of candy. The man was a merchant in Bidwell and had a daughter who was a teacher in the schools, but May had never seen him before, had heard nothing of him, knew nothing about him. He came up to her out of nothingness, out of the stream of life. He had heard about May, of her quick active mind, that always defeated the other children in the school room, that in every test came out ahead. Her imagination played about his figure.

At that time May went every Sunday morning to the Presbyterian Sunday School, as there was a tradition in the Edgley family that Ma Edgley had once been a Presbyterian. None of the other children had ever gone, but for a time she did and they all seemed to want her to go. She remembered the men, the Sunday School teachers were always talking about. There was a gigantic strong old man named Abraham who walked in God's footsteps. He must have been huge, strong, and good, too. His children were like the sands of the seas for numbers, and was that not a sign of strength. How many children! All the children in the world could not be more than that! The man who had taken hold of her hand and had led her into the store to buy the candy for her was, she imagined just such another. He also must own lands and be the father of innumerable children and no doubt he could ride all day on a fast horse and never get off his own possessions. It was possible he thought her one of his innumerable children.

There was no doubt he was a mighty man. He looked like one and he had admired her. "I'm giving you this candy because my daughter says you are the smartest girl in school," he said. She remembered that another man stood in the store and that, as she ran away with the bag of candy gripped in her small fingers, the old man, the mighty one, turned to him. He said something to the man. "They are all cattle except her, just cattle," he had said. Later she had thought out what he meant. He meant her family, the Edgleys.

How many things she had thought out as she went back and forth to school, always alone. There was always plenty of time for thinking things out—in the late afternoons as she helped her mother with the housework and in the long winter evenings when she went to bed early and for a long time did not go to sleep. The old man in the store had admired her quick brain—for that he had forgiven her being an Edgley, one of the cattle. Her thoughts went round and round in circles. Even as a child she had always felt shut in, walled in from life. She struggled to escape out of herself, out into life.

And now she was a woman who had experienced life, tested it, and she stood, silent and attentive on the stairway of the Edgley house or by the stove in the kitchen and with an effort forced herself to quit thinking. On another street, in another house, a door banged. Her sense of hearing was extraordinarily acute, and it seemed to her she could hear every sound made by every man, woman, and child in town. The circle of thoughts began again and again she fought to think, to feel her way out of herself. On another street, in another house a woman was doing housework, just as she had been doing—making beds, washing dishes, cooking food. The woman had just passed from one room of her house to another and a door had shut with a bang. "Well," May thought, "she is a human being, she feels things as I do, she thinks, eats food, sleeps, dreams, walks about her house."

It didn't matter who the woman was. Being or not being an Edgley made no difference. Any woman would do for the purposes of May's thoughts. All people who lived, lived! Men walked about too, and had thoughts, young girls laughed. She had heard a girl in school, when no one was speaking to her—paying any attention to her—burst suddenly into loud laughter. What was she laughing about?

How cruelly the town had patronized May, setting her apart from the others, calling her smart. They had cared about her because of her smartness. She was smart. Her mind was quick, it reached out. And she was one of the Edgleys—"cattle," the bearded man in the store had said.

And what of that—what was an Edgley—why were they cattle? An Edgley also slept, ate food, had dreams, walked about. Lillian had said that an Edgley man was like all other men, only less stuck on himself.

May's mind fought to realize herself in the world of people, she wanted to be a part of all life, to function in life—did not want to be a special thing—smart—patted on the head—smiled at because she was smart.

What was smartness? She could work out problems in school quickly, swiftly, but as each problem was solved she forgot it. It meant nothing to her. A merchant in Egypt wanted to transport goods across the desert and had 370 pounds of tea and such another number of pounds of dried fruits and spices. There was a problem concerning the matter. Camels were to be loaded. How far away? The result of all her quick thinking was some number like twelve or eighteen, arrived at before the others. There was a little trick. It consisted in throwing everything else out of the mind and concentrating on the one thing—and that was smartness.

But what did it matter to her about the loading of camels? It might have meant something could she have seen into the mind, the soul of the man who owned all that merchandise and who was to carry it so far, if she could have understood him, if she could have understood anyone, if anyone could have understood her.

May stood in the kitchen of the Edgley house, quiet, attentive—for ten minutes, a half hour. Once a dish she held in her hand fell to the floor and broke, awakening her suddenly and to awaken was like coming back to the Edgley house after a long journey, during which she had traveled far, over mountains, rivers, seas—it was like coming back to a place she wanted to leave for good.

"And all the time," she told herself, "life swept on, other people lived, laughed, achieved life."

And then, through the lie she had told Maud Welliver, May stepped into a new world, a world of boundless release. Through the lie and the telling of it she found out that, if she could not live in the life about her, she could create a life. If she was walled in, shut off from participation in the life of the Ohio town—hated, feared by the town—she could come out of the town. The people would not really look at her, try to understand her and they would not let her look down into themselves.

The lie she had told was the foundation stone, the first of the foundation stones. A tower was to be built, a tall tower on which she could stand, from the ramparts of which she could look down into a world created by herself, by her own mind. If her mind was really what Lillian, the teachers in the school, all the others, had said, she would use it, it would become the tool which in her hands, would force stone after stone into its place in her tower.

In the Edgley house May had a room of her own, a tiny room at the back of the house and there was one window looking down into the field, that every spring and fall became a swamp. In the winter sometimes it was covered with ice and boys came there to skate. On the evening she had told Maud Welliver the great lie—recreated the incident in the wood with Jerome Hadley—she hurried home and went up to her room and, pulling a chair to the window, sat down. What a thing she had done! The encounter with Jerome Hadley in the wood had been terrible—she had been unable to think about it, did not dare to think about it, and trying not to think had almost upset her reason.

And now it was gone. The whole thing had really never happened. What had happened was this other thing, or something like that, something no one knew about. There had really been an attempt at murder. May sat by the window and smiled sadly. "I stretched it a little," she thought. "Of course I stretched it, but what was the use trying to tell what happened. I couldn't make it understood. I can't understand it myself."

All through the weeks that had passed since that day in the wood May had been obsessed by the notion that she was unclean, physically unclean. Doing the housework she wore calico dresses—she had several of them and two or three times a day she changed her dress and the soiled dress she could not leave hanging in a closet until washday but washed the dress at once and hung it on a line in the back yard. The wind blowing through it gave her a comforting feeling.

The Edgleys had no bathroom or bathtub. Few people in towns in her day owned any such luxurious appendages to life. And a washtub was kept in the woodshed by the kitchen door and what baths were taken were taken in the tub. It was a ceremony that did not often occur in the family, and when it did occur the tub was filled from the cistern and set in the sun to warm. Then it was carried into the shed. The candidate for cleanliness went into the shed and closed the door. In the winter the ceremony took place in the kitchen and Ma Edgley came at the last moment and poured a kettle of boiling water into the cold water in the tub. In the summer in the shed that was not necessary. The bather undressed and put his clothes about, on the piles of wood, and there was a great splashing.

During that summer May took a bath every afternoon, but did not bother to put the water out in the sun. How good it felt to have it cold! Often when there was no one about, she filled the tub and got into it again before going to bed. Her small body, dark and strong, sank into the cold water and she took strong soap and scrubbed her legs, her breasts, her neck where Jerome Hadley's kisses had alighted. Her neck and breasts she wished she could scrub quite away.

Her body was strong and wiry. All the Edgleys, even Ma Edgley, had been strong. They were all, except May, large people and in her the family strength seemed to have concentrated. She was never physically weary and after the time of her intensive thinking began, and when she often slept little at night her body seemed to grow constantly stronger. Her breasts grew larger and her figure changed slightly. It grew less boyish. She was becoming a woman.

After the telling of the lie, May's body became for a time no more than a tree growing in a forest through which she walked. It was something through which life made itself manifest; it was a house within which she lived, a house, in which, and in spite of the enmity of the town, life went on. "I'm not dead like those who die while their bodies are still alive," May thought, and there was intense comfort in the thought.

She sat by the window of her room in the darkness thinking. Jerome Hadley had tried to commit a murder and how often such attempts must have been made in the history of other men and women—and how often they must have succeeded. The spirit within was killed. Boys and girls grew up full of notions, brave notions too. In Bidwell, as in other towns, they went to schools and Sunday schools. Words were said—they heard many brave words—but within themselves, within their own tiny houses, all life was uncertain, hesitating. They looked abroad and saw men and women, bearded men, kind strong women. How many were dead! How many of the houses were but empty haunted places! Their town was not the town they had thought it and some day they would have to find that out. It was not a place of warm friendly closeness. Feeling instinctively the uncertainty of life, the difficulty of arriving at truth the people did not draw together. They were not humble in the face of the great mystery. The mystery was to be solved with lies, with truth put away. A great noise must be made. Everything was to be covered up. There must be a great noise and bustle, the firing of cannons, the roll of drums, the shouting of many words. The spirit within must be killed. "What liars people are," May thought breathlessly. It seemed to her that all the people of her town stood before her, were in a way being judged by her, and her own lie, told to defeat a universal lie, now seemed a small, a white innocent thing.

There was a very tender delicate thing within her, many people had wanted to kill—that was certain. To kill the delicate thing within was a passion that obsessed mankind. All men and women tried to do it. First the man or woman killed the thing within himself, and then tried to kill it in others. Men and women were afraid to let the thing live.

May sat in the darkness in her room in the Edgley house having such thoughts as had never come to her before and the night seemed alive as no other night of her life had been. For her gods walked abroad in the land. The Edgley house was but a poor little affair of boards—of thin walls—and she looked out, in the dim wavering light of the night, into a field, that at times during the year became a bog where cattle sank in black mud to their knees. Her town was but a dot on the huge map of her country—she knew that. It was not necessary to travel to find out. Had she not been at the top of her class in geography? In her country alone lived some sixty, eighty, a hundred million people—she could not remember the number—it changed yearly. When the country was new millions of buffalo walked up and down on the plains. She was a she-calf among the buffalo but she had found lodgment in a town, in a house made of boards and painted yellow, but the field below the house was dry now and long grass grew there. However, tiny pools remained and frogs lived in them and croaked loudly while crickets sang in the dry grass. Her life was sacred—the house in which she lived, the room in which she sat, became a church, a temple, a tower. The lie she had told had started a new force within her and the new temple, on which she was to live, was now being built.

Thoughts like giant clouds, seen in a dim night sky, floated through her mind. Tears came to her eyes and her throat seemed to be swelling. She put her head down on the window sill and convulsive sobs shook her.

That was, she knew, because she had been brave enough and quick-witted enough to tell the lie, to reestablish the romance of existence within herself. The foundation stone for the temple had been laid.

May did not think anything out clearly, did not try to do that. She felt—she knew her own truth. Words heard, read in books in school, in other books loaned her by the school-teachers, words said casually, without feeling—by thin-lipped, flat-breasted young women who were teachers at the Sunday school, words that had seemed as nothing to her when said, now made a great sound in her mind. They were repeated to her in stately measure by some force, seemingly outside herself and were like the steady rhythmical tread of an army marching on earth roads. No, they were like rain on the roof over her head, on the roof of the house that was herself. All her life she had lived in a house and the rains had come unheeded—and the words she had heard and now remembered were like rain drops falling on roofs. There was a subtle perfume remaining. "The stone which the builders refused is become the headstone of the corner."

As the thoughts marched through May's mind her small shoulders shook with sobs, but she was happy—strangely happy and something within herself was singing. The singing was a song that was always alive somewhere in the world, it was the song of life, the song that crickets sang, the song the frogs croaked hoarsely. It ran away out of her room, out of the darkness into the night, into days, into far lands—it was the old song, the sweet song.

May kept thinking about buildings and builders. "The stone which the builders refused is become the headstone of the corner." Someone had said that and others had felt what she now felt—they had had the feeling she could not put into words and they had tried putting it into words. She was not alone in the world. It was not a strange path she walked in life, but many had walked it, many were walking it now. Even as she sat in the window, thinking so strangely, many men and women in many places and many lands sat at other windows having the same thoughts. In a world, where many men and women had killed the thing within themselves, the path of the rejected was the true path and how many had walked the path! The trees along the way were marked. Signs had been hung up by those who wanted to show others the way. "The stone which the builders refused is become the headstone of the corner."

Lillian had said, "men are no good," and it was clear Lillian had also killed the thing within herself, had let it be killed. She had let some Jerome Hadley kill it, and then she had grown slowly and steadily more and more angry at life, had come to hate life, had thrown it away. And the thing had happened to her mother, too. That was the reason for her life of silence—death walking about. "The dead rise up to strike the dead."

The story May had told to Maud Welliver was not a lie—it was the living truth. He had tried to kill and had come near succeeding. May had walked in the valley of the shadow of death. She knew that now. Her own sister, Lillian, had come to her when she walked with Death and wanted Life. "If you are going to go on the turf I'll get you in with men who have money," Lillian had said. She had got no closer to understanding than that.

May decided that after all she would not try to be Maud Welliver's friend. She would see her and talk to her but, for the present, she would keep herself to herself. The living thing within her had been wounded and needed time to recover. Of all the feelings, the strong emotion, that swept through her on that evening, cleansing her internally, as she had been trying by splashing in the tub in the woodshed to cleanse herself externally, one impulse got itself definitely expressed. "I'll go it alone, that's what I'll do," she murmured between sobs as she sat by the window with her head in her hands, and heard the sweet song of the insects, singing of life in the darkness of the fields.

CHAPTER IV

"THERE WAS A man here. For weeks he lay sick to the point of death, in our house, and all the time I did not dare sleep. Night and day I was on the watch. How often at night I have crept down across this very field, in the middle of the night, in the darkness looking for the black, trying to discover if he was still on the trail."

It was early summer and May sat talking with Maud Welliver by a tree in the field back of the Edgley's kitchen door—building steadily her tower of romance. Two or three times each week, since that first talk by the blacksmith shop, Maud had managed to get to the Edgley house unobserved by her aunt. In her passionate devotion to the little dark-skinned woman, who had lived through so many and such romantic adventures in life, she was ready to risk anything, even to the wrath of her father's iron-jawed housekeeper.

To the Edgley house she came always at night, and the necessity of that was understood by May and perhaps better understood by Lillian Edgley. On the next day, after the meeting by the blacksmith shop, Maud's father had spoken his mind concerning the Edgleys. The Welliver family sat at supper in the evening. "Maud," John Welliver began, looking sternly at his daughter, "I don't want you should have anything to do with that Edgley family that lives on this street." The railroad man cursed the ill luck that had led him to take a house on the same street where such cattle lived. One of his brother employees on the road, he said, had told him the story of the Edgleys. "They are such an outfit," he declared wrathfully. "God only knows why they are allowed to stay here. They should be tarred and feathered and run out of town. Why, to live on the same street with them is like living in the midst of cattle."

The railroad man looked hard at his daughter. To him she was a young woman and a virgin, and by these tokens walked a dangerous trail through life. On dark streets, adventurous men lay in wait for all such women and they employed other women, of the Edgley stripe, to decoy innocent virgins into their hands. There was much he would have liked to say to his daughter but not much he could say. Among themselves men could speak openly of such women as the Edgley sisters. They were a thing—well. To tell the truth—during young manhood almost every man went to see such women, went with other men into a house inhabited by such women. To go to such a place one needed to have been drinking a little. It happened. Several young men were together and went from place to place drinking. "Let's go down the line," one of them said. The men went straggling off along a street, two by two. Little was said and they were all a little ashamed of their mission. Then they came to a house, always on a dark foul street, and one of the young men, a bold fellow, knocked at the door. A fat woman, with a hard face, came to let them in and they went into a room and stood about, looking foolish. "O, girls,—company," the fat woman shouted and several women came and stood about. The women looked bored and tired.

John Welliver had himself been to such places. Well, that was when he was a young workman. Later a man met a good woman and married her, tried to forget the other women, did forget them. In spite of all the things said, most men after marriage went straight. They had a living to make and children growing up and there was no time for any such nonsense. Among his fellow workmen, the railroad man often spoke of the kind of women he believed the three Edgley women to be. "It's my notion," he said, "that it's better to have such places in order that good women may be let alone, but they ought to be off by themselves somewhere. A good woman never ought to see or know about such cattle."

In the presence of his daughter and of his sister, the housekeeper, now that the subject of the Edgleys had been broached the railroad man was embarrassed. He kept his eye on the plate before him and stole a shy look at his daughter's face. How white and pure it looked. "I wish I had kept my mouth shut," he thought—but a sense of the necessity of the occasion led him on. "My Maud might be led to take up with the Edgley women, knowing nothing," he thought. "Well," he said, "there are three women in that family and they are all alike. There is one, who works at the hotel—where she meets traveling men—and the oldest one doesn't work at all. And there is another, too, the youngest that everyone thought was going to turn out all right because she stood high in school and is said to be smart. Everyone thought she would be different but she isn't, you see. Why, right before everyone, in a berry field, where she was at work, she went into a wood with a man."

"I know about it and I've told Maud," the railroad man's sister said sharply. "We don't need to talk about it no more."

Maud Welliver had listened with flushed cheeks to her father's words, and even as he talked had made up her mind she would see May again and soon. Since coming to Bidwell she had not left the house at night, but now she felt suddenly quite strong and well. When the supper was finished and darkness came on she got up from her chair on the porch and spoke to her aunt, at work inside the house. "I feel better than I have for months, aunty," she said, "and I'm going for a little walk. You know the doctor said I was to walk all I could and I can't walk during the day on account of the heat. I'll just go uptown a little while."

Maud went cautiously along the sidewalk toward the business section of town and then crossed over and returning on the opposite side, stole along, walking on the grass at the edge of lawns. What an adventure! She felt like one being admitted into some strange world filled with romance. For her May Edgley's tales had become golden apples of existence, to taste which she would risk anything. "What a person!" she thought as she crept forward in the darkness, lifting and putting down her feet on the grass like a kitten compelled to walk in water. She thought of May Edgley's adventure in the wood with Jerome Hadley. How stupid her father had been, how stupid everyone in the town of Bidwell! "It must be so with men and women everywhere," she thought vaguely. "They go on thinking they know what's happening, and they know nothing." She thought of May Edgley, small and a woman, alone in the forest with a man—a dark determined man, intent upon murder. The man held in his hand a little package containing a white powder. A few grains of it in a cup of coffee and a human life would go out. A man who walked and talked and went about the streets of Bidwell with other men would become a white lifeless bit of clay. Maud had been at several times in her life close to the door of death. She imagined a scene. There was a rich man's home with soft carpets, woven of priceless stuffs, brought from the Orient. One walking on the carpets made no sound. The feet sank softly into the velvety stuff and soft-voiced servants moved about. A man entered and sat at breakfast. The movies had not at that time come to Bidwell but Maud had read many popular novels and several times, at Fort Wayne, had been to the theatre.

There was a woman in the rich man's house—his guilty wife. She was slender and willowy. Ah, there was something serpentine about her. In Maud's imagination she lay on a silken couch beside the table, at which the man now sat down to eat his breakfast. A wood fire burned in the fireplace. The woman's hand stole forward and a tiny pinch of the white powder went into the coffee cup; then she raised a white hand and stroked the man's cheek. She closed her eyes and lay back on the silken couch. The dastardly deed was done and the woman did not care. She was not even curious as to how death would come. She yawned and waited.

The man drank his coffee and arising moved about the room and then a sudden pallor came upon his cheeks. It was quite noticeable as he was a ruddy-cheeked man with soft grey hair—a strong commanding figure of a man, a leader among men. Maud pictured him as the president of a great railroad system. She had never seen a railroad president but her father had often spoken of the president of the Nickel Plate and had described him as a big fine looking fellow.

What a thing is passion, so terrible, so strange. It takes such unimaginable turns. The woman on the silken couch, the willowy serpentine woman, had turned from her husband, from the commander of men, from the strong man, the powerful one who swept all before him, and had given her illicit but powerfully fascinating love to a railroad mail clerk.

Maud had seen Jerome Hadley. When the Wellivers had first come to Bidwell she, with her aunt and father, had been driven about town with a real-estate man and his wife. They were looking for a house in which to live and as they drove about the real-estate man's wife, who sat on the back seat of a surrey with Maud and her aunt, had pointed to Jerome Hadley, walking past in the street, and had told in a whisper the story of his going into the wood with May Edgley.

Maud was half sick on that day and had not listened. The railroad journey from Fort Wayne to Bidwell had given her a headache.

However, she had looked at Jerome. He had sloping shoulders, pale grey eyes and sandy hair, and when he walked he toed out badly and his trousers were baggy. And for that man the woman on the silken couch, the railroad president's wife, was ready to commit murder. What an unexplainable, what a strange thing is love! The windings and twistings of its pathway through life cannot be followed by the human mind.

The scene being enacted in Maud Welliver's mind played itself out. The strong man in the richly furnished room put his hand to his throat and staggered. He reeled from side to side and clutched at the backs of chairs. The noiseless servants had all gone out of the room. The woman half arose from the couch as the man fell to the floor and in falling struck his head on the corner of a table so that his blood ran out upon the silken carpets. The woman smiled sardonically. It was terrible. She cared not the least in the world and a slow cruel smile came and remained fixed on her face. Then there was the sound of running feet. The servants were coming, they were running, running desperately. The woman lay back on the couch and yawned again. "I had better scream and then faint," she thought and she did the two things, did them with the air of a tired actor rehearsing a well known part for a play. It was all for love, for a strange and mysterious thing called passion. She did it for Jerome Hadley's sake, that she might be free to walk with him the illicit paths of love.

Maud Welliver tiptoed cautiously forward on the lawns on the further side of Duane Street in Bidwell, looking across at the dark house where she had come to live. In Fort Wayne she had known nothing like this. What a terrible thing might have happened in Bidwell but for May Edgley! The scene in the rich man's home faded and was replaced by another. She saw May standing in the forest with Jerome Hadley. How he had changed! He stood alert, intent, determined, holding the poison package in his hand and he was threatening, threatening and pleading. In the other hand he held money, a great package of bills. He thrust the bills forward and pleaded with May Edgley and then grew angry and threatened again.

Before him stood the small, white-faced woman, frightened now, but terribly determined also. The word "never" was upon her lips. And now the man threw the money away into the bushes and sprang forward. His hand was at the woman's throat, the murderous hand of the infuriated mail clerk. It pressed hard. May fell to the ground.

Jerome Hadley did not quite dare let the woman die. Too many people had seen the two go into the wood together. He stood over her until she had a little recovered and then the threatening and pleading began again, but all the time the little woman stood firm, shaking her head and saying the brave word "never." "Kill me if you will," she said, "but I'll take no part in this murder. My reputation is gone and I am an outlaw among men and women but I'll take no part in this murder, and if you go on with it I will betray you."

The September evening when May uttered the startling sentences, regarding a strange man and a mysterious black, set down at the head of this section of the story of her adventures, was warm and clear. Brightly the stars shone in the sky and in the field back of the Eldgley's kitchen door all the little ponds had become dry. Since that first evening when she had met May a great change had taken place in Maud. May had led her up to the ramparts of the tower of romance and as often as possible now the two sat together under a tree in the field or on the floor by the open window in May's room. To the field they went through the kitchen door, along the creek where the elders and willows grew and over stones in the bed of the creek itself, to a wire fence. How alone and how far away from the life of the town they were in the field at night! Buggies and the few automobiles then owned in Bidwell passed on distant roads, and over the town, soft lights played on the sky and soft lights seemed to play over the spirits of the two women. On a distant street, that led down to the town waterworks, a group of young men went tramping along on a board sidewalk. They were singing a song. "Listen, May," Maud said. The voices died away and another sound came. Jerry Haden, a cripple who walked with a crutch and who delivered evening papers, went along quickly, his crutch making a sharp clicking sound on the sidewalks. What a hurry he was in. "Click! click!" went the crutch.

It was a time and place for the growth of romance. A desire to reach out to life, to command life grew within Maud. One evening she, alone and unaided, mounted the tower of romance and told May of how a young man in Fort Wayne had wanted to marry her. "He was the son of the president of a railroad company," she said. The matter was of no importance and she only spoke of it to show what men were like. For a long time he came to the house almost every evening and when he did not come he sent flowers and candy. Maud had cared nothing for him. There was a certain air he had that wearied her. He seemed to think himself in some way of better blood than the Wellivers. The idea was absurd. Maud's father knew his father and knew that he had once been no more than a section hand on the railroad. His pretensions wearied Maud and she finally sent him away.

Maud told May, on several evenings of the imaginary young man whom, because of his pride of blood, she had cast adrift, and on the September evening wanted to speak of something else. For two or three evenings she had been on the point of saying what was in her mind but could not bring the matter to her lips. It trembled within her like a wild bird caught and held in her hand, as, in the dim light, she looked at May. "She won't do it. I'll never get her to do it," she thought.

In Fort Wayne, before she came to Bidwell, and when she had just graduated from the high school Maud had for a time walked upon the border line of love, had stood for a moment in the very pathway of Cupid's darts. Near the house where the Wellivers then lived there was a grocery run by an alert erect little man of forty-five, whose wife had died. Maud often went to the store to buy supplies for the Welliver home and one evening she arrived just as the grocer, a man named Hunt, was locking the store for the night. He unlocked the door and let her in. "You won't mind if I don't light the lights again," he said. He explained that the grocerymen of Fort Wayne had made an agreement among themselves that they would sell no goods after seven in the evening. "If I light the lights and people see us in here they will be coming in and wanting to be waited on," he explained.

Maud stood in the uncertain light by a counter while the grocer wrapped her packages. At the back of the store there was a lamp fastened to a bracket on the wall and burning dimly and the soft yellow light fell on her hair and on her white smiling face as the grocer fumbled in the darkness back of the counter and from time to time looked up at her. How beautiful her long pale face in that light! He was stirred and delayed the matter of getting the packages wrapped. "My wife and I were not very happy together but I was happy when I lived alone with my mother," he thought. He let Maud out at the door, locked it and went along beside her carrying the packages. "I'm going your way," he said vaguely. He began to speak of his boyhood in a town in Ohio and told of how he had married at the age of twenty-three and had come to Fort Wayne where his wife's father owned the store that was now his own. He spoke to Maud as to one who knew most of the details of his life. "Well, my wife and her father are both dead and I own the place— I've come out all right," he said. "I wonder why I left my mother. I thought more of her than anyone else in the world but I got married and went away and left her, went away and left her, to live alone until she died," he said. They came to a corner and he put the packages into Maud's arms. "You got me started thinking of mother. You're like her," he said suddenly and then hurried away.

Maud had got into the habit of going to the store, just at closing time in the evening and when she did not come the grocer was upset. He closed the store and, walking to a nearby corner, stood under an awning before a hardware store, also closed for the night, and looked down along the street where Maud lived. Then he took a heavy silver watch from his pocket and looked at it. "Huh!" he exclaimed and went off along another street to his boarding house, stopping several times in the first block to look back.

It was early June and the Wellivers had lived in Bidwell, for four months and, during the last year of her life at Fort Wayne Maud had been so continually ill that she had seldom seen the grocer, but now a letter had come from him. The letter came from the city of Cleveland. "I am here at a convention of the K of Ps," he wrote, "and I have met a man here who is a widower like myself. We are in the same room at the hotel. I want to stop to see you on the way home and would like to bring my friend along. Can't you get another girl and we'll all spend an evening together. If you can do it, you get a surrey and meet us at the seven-fifty train next Friday evening. I'll pay for the surrey of course and we'll go off somewhere to the country. I've got something very important I want to say to you. You write me here and let me know if it's all right."

Maud sat in the field beside May and thought of the letter. An answer must be sent at once. In fancy she saw the little bright-eyed grocer standing before May, the hero of the passage in the wood with Jerome Hadley, the woman who lived the romance of which she herself dreamed. At the postoffice during the afternoon she had heard two young men talking of a dance to be given at a place called the Dewdrop. It was to be held on Friday evening, and a bold impulse had led her to go to a livery stable and make inquiry about the place. It was twenty miles away and on the shores of Sandusky Bay. "We will go there," she had thought, and had engaged the surrey and horses and now she was face to face with May and the thought of the little grocer and his companion frightened her. Freeman Hunt the widower had a bald head and a grey mustache. What would his friend be like? Fear made Maud's body tremble and when she tried to speak, to tell May of her plan, the words would not come. "She'll never do it. I'll never get her to do it," she thought again.

"There was a man here. For weeks he lay sick to the point of death in our house and all the time I did not dare sleep."

May Edgley was building high her tower of romance. Having several times listened, as Maud told of the imaginary son of the railroad president who had been determined to marry her, she had set about making a romantic lover of her own. Books she had read, the remembrance of childhood tales of love and romantic adventure poured in upon her mind. "There was a man here. He was just twenty-four but what a life he had led," she said absentmindedly. She appeared to be lost in thought and for a long time was silent. Then she got suddenly to her feet and ran to where two large maple trees stood on a little hill in the midst of the field. Maud also got to her feet and her body shook with a new fear. The grocer was forgotten. May returned and again sat on the grass. "I thought I saw someone snooping there behind that tree," she said. "You see I have to be careful. A man's life depends on my being careful."

Warning Maud that whatever happened she was not to tell the secret, now for the first time to be told to another, May launched into her tale. On a dark night, when it was raining and when the trees shook in the wind, she had got out of bed in the Edgley house and had opened her window to behold the storm. She could not imagine what had led her to do it. It was something she had never done before. To tell the truth a voice outside herself seemed to be calling her, commanding her. Well, she had thrown up the window and had stood looking out. How the wind screamed and shrieked! Furies seemed abroad in the night. The house itself trembled on its foundations and great trees bent almost to the ground. Now and then there was a flash of lightning and she could see the whole outdoors as plain as day—"I could even see the leaves on the tree." May had thought the world must be coming to an end but for some strange reason she was not in the least afraid. It was impossible to explain the feeling she had on that night. Well, she couldn't sleep. Something, outside there, in the darkness, seemed to be calling, calling to her. "All of this happened more than two years ago, when I was just a young girl in school," she explained.

On that night when the storm raged May had seen, during one of the flashes of lightning, a man running desperately across the very field, where now she and Maud sat so quietly. Even from where she stood by the window in the upstairs room she could see that he was white and that his face was drawn and tired from long running. Behind him, perhaps a dozen strides behind, was another man, a giant black, with a club in his hand. In a moment May knew, she knew everything, knowledge came into her mind and illuminated it as the lightning had illuminated the scene in the field. The giant black with the club was about to kill the other man, the white man in the field. In a moment she knew she would see a murder done. The fleeing man could not escape. At every stride the black gained. There came a second flash of lightning and then the white man stumbled and fell. May threw up her hands and screamed. She had always been ashamed of the fact but why deny it—she fainted.

What a night that had turned out to be! Even to speak of it made May shudder, even yet. Her father had heard her scream and came running to her room. She recovered—she sat up—in a few quick words she told her father what she had seen.

Well, you see, her father and she had got out of the house somehow. They were both in their night dresses and in the woodshed back of the house her father had fumbled about and had got hold of an axe. It was the only weapon of any kind he could lay his hands on about the place.

And there they were, in the darkness. No more flashes of lightning came and it began to rain. It poured. The rain came in torrents and the wind blew so that the trees seemed to be shouting to each other, calling to each other like friends lost in some dark pit.

There was plenty of shouting after that but neither May nor her father was afraid. They were perhaps too excited for fear to take hold of them. May didn't know exactly how she felt. No words could describe how she felt.

Followed by her father she ran, down the little hill back of the kitchen, got across the creek, stumbled and fell several times, picked herself up and ran on again. They came to the fence at the edge of the field. Well, they got over somehow. It was strange how the field, across which they had both walked so many times in the daytime (as a child May had always played there and she thought she knew every blade of grass, every little pond, and hillock)—it was strange how it had changed. It was exactly as though she and her father had run out upon a wide treeless plain. They ran, it seemed for hours and hours, and still they were in the field. Later when May thought of the experiences of that night she understood how men came to write fairy tales. Why, the ground in the field might have been made of rubber that stretched out as they ran.

They could see no trees, no buildings—nothing. For a time she and her father kept close together, running desperately, into nothingness, into a wall of darkness.

Then her father got lost from her, was swallowed up in the darkness.

What a roaring of voices went on. Trees somewhere, away off in the distance, were shouting to each other. The very blades of grass seemed to be talking—in excited whispers, you understand.

It was terrible! Now and then May could hear her father's voice. He just swore. "Gol darn you," he shouted over and over. The words were grunted forth.

Then there was another and terrible voice—it must have been the voice of the black, intent upon murder. May could not understand what he said. He, of course, just shouted words in some strange foreign language—a gibberish of words.

Then May stopped running. She was too exhausted to run any more and sat down on the ground at the edge of one of the little ponds. Her hair had all fallen about her face. Well, she wasn't afraid. The thing that had happened was too big to be afraid of. It was like being in the presence of God and one couldn't be afraid. How could one? A blade of grass isn't afraid in the presence of the sun, coming up. That's the way May felt—little you see—a tiny thing in the vast night—nothing.

How wet she was! Her clothes clung to her. All about the voices went on and on and the storm raged. She sat with her feet in a puddle of water and things seemed to fly past her, dark figures running, screaming, swearing, saying strange words. She herself did not doubt—when she thought of it all after it was over—that the giant black and her father had both run past her a dozen times, had passed so close to her that she might have put out her hand and touched them.

How long did she sit there in the darkness? That was something she never knew and her father was like her about it too. Later he couldn't have said, for the life of him, how long he ran about in the darkness, trying to strike something with the axe. Once he ran against a tree. Well, he drew back and sank the axe into the tree. Sometime—in the daytime—May would show Maud the tree with the great gash in it. Her father sank the axe so deeply into the body of the tree that he had work getting it out again and even in the midst of his excitement he had to laugh to think of what a silly fool he had been.

And there was May sitting with her feet in the puddle, the hair clinging to her bare shoulders, her head in her hands, trying to think, trying perhaps to catch some meaningful word in the strange roar of voices. Well, what was she thinking about? She didn't know.

And then a hand touched her, a white strong firm hand. It just crept up out of the darkness, seemed to come out of the very ground under her. There was one thing sure—although she lived to be a thousand years old, May would never know why she didn't scream, faint away, get up and run madly, butting her head against things.

"Love is a strange thing," she told Maud Welliver, as the two sat in the field that warm clear starlit evening. Her voice trembled. "I knew a man had come to whom I would be faithful unto death," she explained.

That was the beginning of the strangest and most exciting time in May's whole life. Never had she thought she would tell anyone in the world about it, at least not until the time came for her marriage, and when all the dangers that still faced the man she loved had passed like a cloud.

On that terrible night, and while the storm still raged, the hand that had crept so strangely and unexpectedly into hers had at once quieted and reassured her. It was too dark to see the face and the body of the man back of the hand, but for some reason she knew at once that he was beautiful and good. She loved the man at once and completely, that was the truth. Later he had told her that his own experience was the same. For him also there came a great peace of the spirit, after his hand found hers in the midst of that roaring darkness.

They got out of that field and into the Edgley house somehow, crawled along together and when they got to the house they did not light a lamp or anything but sat on the floor of May's room hand in hand, talking in low quiet tones. After a long time, perhaps an hour, May's father came home. He had got out of the field and had wandered on a country road and as he went along he heard stealthy footsteps behind him. That was the black following the wrong man and it's a wonder he didn't kill John Edgley. What happened was that the drayman began to run and got into a grove of trees and there lost his pursuer. Then he took off his shoes and managed to find his way home barefooted. The black's having followed the wrong man turned out to be a good thing. The man up in May's room was free, for the first time in more than two years, he was free.

It had turned out that the man was quite badly injured, the black having, in his excitement, aimed a blow at his head that would have done for him had it struck fair. However, the blow glanced off and only bruised his head and made it bleed and as he sat in the darkness on the floor in May's room with his hand in hers, telling her his story, the blood kept dropping thump, thump, on the floor. May had thought, at the time, it was water falling from her hair. It just went to show what a man he was, afraid of nothing, enduring everything without a murmur. Later he was sick with a fever for weeks and May never left his room, but gradually nursed him back to health and strength, and no one in Bidwell had ever known of his presence in the house. Later he left town at night, on a dark night when, to save yourself, you couldn't see your hand before your face.

As to the man's story—it had never been told to anyone and if May told it to Maud Welliver it was because she had to have at least one friend who knew all. Even her father, who had risked his life, did not know.

May put her hands over her face and leaned forward and for a long time she was silent. In the grass the insects kept singing and on a distant street Maud could hear the footsteps of people walking. What a world she had come into when she left Fort Wayne and came to Bidwell! Indiana was not like Ohio! The very air was different. She breathed deeply and looked about into the soft darkness. Had she been alone she could not have stood being in a place where such wonderful things as had just been described to her could happen. How quiet it was in the field now. She put out a hand softly and touched May's dress and tried to think but her own thoughts were vague, they swam away into a strange world. To go to a theatre, to read books, to hear of the commonplace adventures of other people— how dull and uneventful her life had been before she knew May. Once her father had been in a wreck on the railroad and by a miracle had escaped uninjured and, when company came to the Welliver house, he always told of the wreck, how the cars were piled up and how he, walking over the tops of cars in the darkness of a rainy night was pitched off and went flying, head over heels, only by a pure miracle to land on his feet in dense bushes, uninjured, only badly shaken up. Maud had thought the tale exciting, she had been stupid

enough to think it exciting. What contempt she now had for such
weak commonplace adventures. What a vast change knowing May
Edgley had made in her life!

"You won't tell. You promise on your life you won't tell." May's
hand gripped Maud's and the two women sat in silence, intent, shaken
with some vast emotion that seemed to run over the dry grass in the
field, through the branches of distant trees, and that seemed to effect
even the stars in the sky. To Maud the stars appeared about to speak.
They came down close out of the sky. "Be cautious," they seemed
to be saying. Had she lived in old times, in Judea, and had she been
permitted to go into the room where Jesus sat at the last supper with
his disciples, she could not have felt more completely humble and
thankful that she, of all the people in the world had been permitted
to be where she was at the moment.

"He was a prince in his own country," May said suddenly breaking
the silence that had become so intense that in another moment Maud
thought she would have screamed. "He lived, Oh, far away. In his
own country the father, a king, had decided to marry the prince to
the princess of a neighboring kingdom, and on the same day his
sister was to marry the brother of his betrothed. Neither he nor
his sister had ever seen the man and woman they were to marry.
Princes and princesses don't, you know. That is the way such things
are arranged when princes and princesses are concerned.

"He thought nothing about it, was all ready for the marriage, and
then one night something came into his head and he had an almost
overpowering desire to see the woman, who was to be his wife, and
the man who was to be his sister's husband. Well, he went at night
and crept up the side of a great wall to the window of a tower, and
through the window saw the man and woman. How ugly they
were—horrible! He shuddered. For a time he thought he would let
go his hold on the stone face of the wall and be dashed to bits on the
rocks beneath. He was ready to die with horror—didn't care much.

"And then he thought of his sister, the beautiful princess. Whatever
happened she had to be saved from such a marriage.

"And so home the prince went and confronted his father and there
was a terrible scene, the father swearing the marriage would have to
be consummated. The neighboring king was powerful and his kingdom was of vast extent and the marriage would make the son, born
of the marriage, the most powerful king in the whole world. The
prince and the king stood in the castle and looked at each other.
Neither of them would give in an inch.

"There was one thing of which the prince was sure—if he did not marry his sister would not have to. If he went away there would be a quarrel between the two old kings. He was sure of that.

"First though he gave the king, his father, his chance. 'I won't do it,' he declared and he stuck to his word. The king was furious. 'I'll disinherit you,' he cried, and then he ordered his son to go out of his presence and not to come back until he had made up his mind to go ahead with the marriage.

"What the king did not expect was that he would be taken at his word. For what the young man, the prince, did, you see, was to just walk out of the castle and right on out into the world.

"Poor man, his hands were then as soft as a woman's," May explained. "You see in all his former life he had never even lifted his hand to do a thing. When he dressed he didn't even button his own clothes. A prince never did.

"And so the prince ran away and managed, after unbelievable hardships, to make his way to a seaport, where he got a place as sailor on a ship just leaving for foreign parts. The captain of the ship did not know, and the other sailors did not know that he was a king's son, nor did they know that a great outcry was going up and horsemen riding madly over the whole country, trying to find the lost prince.

"So he got away and was a sailor and in the castle his father was so furious he would not speak to anyone. He shut himself up in a room of the castle and just swore and swore.

"And then one day he called to him a giant black, one who had been his slave since he was born, and was the strongest, the fleetest of foot and the smartest man too, of all the king's servants. 'Go over land and sea,' shouted the king. 'Go into all strange far away lands and amongst all peoples. Do not let me ever see your face again until you have found my son and have brought him back to marry the woman I have decided shall be his wife. If you find him and he will not come strike him down if you must, but do not kill him. Stun him and bring him to me. Do not let me see your face again until you have done my bidding.' He threw a handful of gold at the black's feet. That was to pay the fares on railroads and buy his meals at hotels," May explained.

"And all the time the king's son was sailing on and on, over unknown seas. He passed icebergs, islands and continents, and saw great whales and at night heard the growling of wild beasts on strange shores.

"He wasn't afraid, not he. And all the time he kept getting stronger and his hands got harder, and he could do more work and do it quicker than almost any man on the ship. Almost every day the captain called him aside. 'Well,' he said, 'you are my bravest and best sailor. How shall I reward you?'

"But the young prince wanted no reward. He was so glad to escape from that horrible king's daughter. How homely she was. Why her teeth stuck out of her mouth like tusks and she was all covered with wrinkles and haggard.

"And the ship sailed and sailed, and it hit a hidden rock, sticking up in the bottom of the ocean, and was split right in two. All but the prince were drowned.

"He swam and swam and came at last to an island that had a mountain on it, and no one lived there, and the mountain was filled with gold. After a long time a passing ship took him off but he told no one of the golden mountain. He sailed and sailed and came to America, and started out to get money to buy a ship and go get the gold and go back to his own country, rich enough so he could marry almost anyone he chose. He had worked and worked and saved money, and then the giant black got on his trail. He tried to escape, time after time he tried to escape. He had been trying that time May found him half-dead in the field.

"The way that came about was that he was on a train passing through Bidwell at night and it was the nine-fifty, that didn't stop but only threw off a mail sack. He was on that train and the black was on it, too, and, as the train went flying through Bidwell in the terrible storm, the prince opened a door and jumped and the black jumped after him. They ran and ran.

"By a miracle neither of them was hurt by the leap from the train, and then they had got into the field where May had seen them.

"I can't think what kept me awake on that night," May said again. She arose and walked toward the Edgley house. "We are betrothed. He has gone to earn money to buy a ship and get the gold. Then he will come for me," she said in a matter of fact tone.

The two women went to the wire fence, crawled over and got into the Edgley back yard. It was nearly midnight and Maud Welliver had never before been out so late. In the Welliver house her aunt and father sat waiting for her, frightened and nervous. "If she doesn't come soon I'll get the police to look for her. I'm afraid something dreadful has happened."

Maud did not, however, think of her father or of the reception that awaited her in the Welliver house. Other and more sombre thoughts occupied her mind. She had come on that evening to the Edgley house, intending to ask May to go with her on the excursion to the Dewdrop with the two grocers, and that was now an impossibility. One who was loved by a prince, who was secretly betrothed to a prince, would never let herself be seen in the company of a grocer, and, beside May, Maud knew no other woman in Bidwell she felt she could ask to go on the trip, on which she did not feel she could go alone. The whole thing would have to be given up. With a catch in her throat she realized what the trip had meant to her. In Fort Wayne, in the presence of the grocer Hunt, she had felt as she had never felt in the presence of another man. He was old, yes, but there was something in his eyes when he looked at her that made her feel strange inside. He had written that he had something to say to her. Now it could never be said.

In the darkness the two women passed around the Edgley house and came to the front gate, and then Maud gave way to the grief struggling for expression within. May was astonished and tried to comfort her. "What's the matter? What's the matter?" she asked anxiously. Stepping through the gate she put an arm about Maud Welliver's shoulders and for a long time the two figures rocked back and forth in the darkness, and then May managed to get her to come to the Edgley front porch and sit beside her. Maud told the story of the proposed trip and of what it had meant to her—spoke of it as a thing of the past, as a hopeless dream that had faded. "I wouldn't dare ask you to go," she said.

It was ten minutes later when Maud got up to go home and May was silent, absorbed in her own thoughts. The tale of the prince was forgotten and she thought only of the town, of what it had done to her, what it would do again when the chance offered. The two grocers were both, however, from another place and knew nothing of her. She thought of the long ride to the shore of Sandusky Bay. Maud had conveyed to her some notion of what the trip meant to her. May's mind raced. "I could not be alone with a man. I wouldn't dare," she thought. Maud had said they would go in a surrey and there was something, that could be used now, in the story she had told about the prince. She could insist that, because of the prince, Maud was not to leave her alone with another man, with the strange grocer, not for a moment.

May arose and stood irresolutely by the front door of the Edgley house and watched Maud go through the gate. How her shoulders drooped. "Oh, well, I'll go. You fix it up. Don't you tell anyone in the world, but I'll go," she said and then, before Maud Welliver could recover from her surprise, and from the glad thrill that ran through her body, May had opened the door and had disappeared into the Edgley house.

CHAPTER V

THE DEWDROP, WHERE the dance Maud and May were to attend was to be held was, in May Edgley's day and no doubt is now, a dreary enough place. An east and west trunk line here came down almost to the water's edge, touching and then swinging off inland again, and on a narrow strip of land between the tracks and the bay several huge ice houses had been built. To the west of the ice houses were four other buildings, buildings less huge but equally stark and unsightly. The shore of the bay, turned beyond the ice houses, leaving the four latter buildings standing at some distance from the railroad, and during ten months of the year they were uninhabited and stared with curtainless windows—that looked like great dead eyes—out over the water.

The buildings had been erected by an ice company, with headquarters at Cleveland, for the housing of its workmen during the ice-cutting season, and the upper floors, reached by outside stairways, had rickety balconies running about the four sides. The balconies served as entry ways to small sleeping rooms each provided with a bunk built against the inner wall and filled with straw.

Still further west was the village of Dewdrop itself, a place of some eight or ten small unpainted frame houses, inhabited by men who combined fishing with small farming, and on the shore before each house a small sailing craft was drawn, during the winter months, far up on the sand out of the reach of storms.

All summer long the Dewdrop remained a quiet sleepy place and, far away, over the water, smoke from factory chimneys in the growing industrial city of Sandusky, at the foot of the bay, could be seen—a cloud of smoke that drifted slowly across the horizon and was torn and tossed by a wind. On summer days, on the long beaches a few fishermen launched their boats and went to visit the nets while their children played in the sand at the water's edge. Inland the farming country—black land, partially covered at certain seasons of the year with stagnant water—was not very prosperous and the road leading down to the Dewdrop from the towns of Fremont, Bellevue, Clyde, Tiffin, and Bidwell was often impassable.

On June days, however, in May Edgley's time, parties came down along the road to the beach and there was the screaming of town children, the laughter of women and the gruff voices of men. They stayed for a day and an evening and went, leaving upon the beach many empty tin cans, rusty cooking utensils and bits of paper that lay rotting at the base of trees and among the bushes back from the shore.

The hot months of July and August came and brought a little life. The summer crew came to take the ice out of the ice houses and load it into cars. They came in the morning and departed in the evening, and, as they were quiet workmen with families of their own, did nothing to disturb the quiet of the place. At the noon hour they sat in the shade of one of the ice houses and ate their luncheons while they discussed such problems as whether it was better for a workman to pay rent or to own his own house, going into debt and paying on the installment plan.

Night came and an adventurous girl, daughter of one of the fishermen, went to walk on the beach. Thanks to wind and rain the beach kept itself always quite clean. Great tree stumps and logs had been carried up on to the sand by winter storms but the wind and water had mellowed these and touched them with delightful color. On moonlight nights the old roots, clinging to the tree trunks, were like gaunt arms reached up to the sky, and on stormy nights these moved back and forth in the wind and sent a thrill of terror through the breast of the girl. She pressed her body against the wall of one of the ice houses and listened. Far away, over the water, were the massed lights of the great town of Sandusky and over her shoulder the few feeble lights of her own fishing town. A group of tramps had dropped off a freight train that afternoon and were making a night of it about the empty workingmen's lodging houses. They had jerked doors off their hinges and were throwing them down from the balconies above and soon a great fire would be lit and all night the fishing families would be disturbed by oaths and shouts. The adventurous girl ran swiftly along the beach but was seen by one of the road adventurers. The fire had been lighted and he took a burning stick in his hand and hurled it over her head. "Run little rabbit," he called as the burning stick, after making a long arch through the air, fell with a hiss into the water.

That was a prelude to the coming of winter and the time of terror. In the hard month of January, when the whole bay was covered with thick ice, a fat man in a heavy fur overcoat, got off a train, that stopped beside the ice houses, and from a car at the front of the train a great multitude of boxes, kegs and crates were pitched into the deep snow at the track side. The world of the cities was coming to break the winter silence of the Dewdrop and the fur coated man and his helpers had come to set the stage for the drama. Hundreds of thousands of tons of ice were to be cut and stored in sawdust in the great ice houses and for weeks, the quiet secluded spot would be astir with life. The silence would be torn by cries, oaths, bits of drunken song—fights would be started and blood would flow.

The fat man waded through the snow to the four empty houses and began to look about. From the little cluster of native houses thin columns of smoke went up into the winter sky. He spoke to one of his helpers. "Who lives in those shacks?" he asked. He himself had much money invested at the Dewdrop but visited the place but once each year and then stayed but a few days. He walked through the big dining room and along the upper galleries where the ice cutters slept, swearing softly. During the year much of his property had been destroyed. Windows had been broken and doors torn from their hinges and he took pencil and paper from his pocket and began to figure. "We'll have to spend all of three hundred dollars this year," he meditated. The thoughts of the money, thus thrown away, brought a flush to his cheeks and he looked again along the shore towards the tiny houses. Almost every year he decided he would go to the houses and do what he called "raising the devil." If doors were torn from hinges and windows smashed these people must have done it. No one else lived at the Dewdrop. "Well I suppose they are a rough gang and I'd better let them alone," he concluded, "I'll send a couple of carpenters down tomorrow and have them do just what has to be done. It's better to keep the ice cutters filled up with beer than to waste money giving them luxurious quarters."

The fat man went away and other men came. Fires were lighted in the kitchens of the great boarding-houses, carpenters nailed doors back on hinges and replaced broken windows and the Dewdrop was ready again for its season of feverish activity.

The fisher folk hid themselves completely away. On the day when the first of the ice cutters arrived one of them spoke to his assembled family. He looked at his daughter, a somewhat comely girl of fifteen, who could sail a boat through the roughest storm that ever swept down the bay. "I want you to keep out of sight," he said. One winter night a fire had broken out in the dining room of the smallest of the houses where the ice cutters boarded and the fishermen with their wives had gone to help put it out. That was an event they could never forget. As the men worked, carrying buckets of water from a hole cut in the ice of the bay, a group of young roughs, from Cleveland, tried to drag their wives into another of the houses. Screams and cries arose on the winter air and the men ran to the defense of their women. A battle began, some of the ice cutters fighting on the side of the fishermen, some on the side of the young roughs, but the fishermen never knew they had helpers in the struggle. Out of a mass of swearing, laughing men they had managed to drag their women and escape to their own houses and the thoughts of what might have happened, had they been unsuccessful, had brought the fear of man upon them. "I want you to keep out of sight," the fisherman said to his assembled family, but as he said it he looked at his daughter. He imagined her dragged into the upper galleries of the boarding-houses and handed about among the city men—something like that had come near happening to her mother. He stared hard at his daughter and she was frightened by the look in his eyes. "You," he began again, "now you—well you keep yourself out of sight. Those men are looking for just such girls as you." The fisherman went out of the room and his daughter stood by a window. Sometimes, on Sundays, during the ice-cutting time, the men who had not gone to spend the day in the city walked in the afternoon along the beach past the houses of the fishermen and, more than once, she had peeked out at them from behind a curtain. Sometimes they stopped before one of the houses and shouted and a wit among them exercised his powers. "Hey there, house," he shouted, "is there any woman in there wants a louse for a lover." The wit leaped upon the shoulders of one of his companions and with his teeth snatched the cap off his head. Turning towards the house he made an elaborate bow. "I'm only a little louse but I'm cold. Let me crawl into your nest," he shouted.

There were six young men from Bidwell who went to the dance given at the Dewdrop on the June evening when May went there with Maud and the two widowed grocers, homeward bound from the K. of P. convention at Cleveland. The dance was held in one of the large rooms, on the first floor of one of the boarding-houses, one of the rooms used as a dining and drinking place by the ice cutters in the months of January and February. A group of farmers' sons gave the dance and Rat Gould, a one-eyed fiddler from Clyde, came with two other fiddlers, to furnish the music. The dance was open to all who paid fifty cents at the door, and women paid nothing. Rat Gould had announced it at other dances given at Clyde, Bellevue, Castalia and on the floors of newly built barns. There was an idea. At all dances, where Rat had officiated, for several weeks previously, the announcement had been made. "There will be a dance at the Dewdrop two weeks from next Friday night," he had cried out in a shrill voice. "A prize will be given. The best dressed lady gets a new calico dress."

Three of the young men from Bidwell who came to the dance, were railroad employees, brakemen on freight trains. They, like John Welliver, worked for the Nickel Plate and their names were Sid Gould, Herman Sanford and Will Smith. With them, to the dance, went Harry Kingsley, Michael Tompkins and Cal Mosher, all known in Bidwell as young sports. Cal Mosher tended bar at the Crescent Saloon near the Nickel Plate station in Bidwell and Michael Tompkins and Harry Kingsley were house painters.

The going of the six young men to the dance was unpremeditated. They had met at the Crescent Saloon early on that June evening and there was a good deal of drinking. There had been a ball game between the baseball teams of Clyde and Bidwell during the week before, and that was talked over, and, thinking and speaking of the defeat of the Bidwell team, all six of the young men grew angry. "Let's go over to Clyde," Cal Mosher said. The young men went to a livery stable and hired a team and surrey and set out, taking with them a plentiful supply of whiskey in bottles. It was decided they would make a night of it. As they drove along Turner's Pike, between Bidwell and Clyde they stopped before farmhouses. "Hey, go to bed you rubes. Get the cows milked and go on to bed," they shouted. Michael Tompkins, called Mike, was the wit of the party and he decided upon a stroke to win applause. At one of the farmhouses he went to the door and told the woman who came to answer his knock that a friend of hers wanted to speak to her in the road and the woman, a plump red-cheeked farmer's wife, came boldly out and stood in the road beside the surrey. Mike crept up behind her and throwing his arms about her neck pulled her quickly backward. The woman screamed with fright as Mike kissed her on the cheek and, jumping into the surrey, Mike joined in the laughter of his companions. "Tell your husband your lover has been here," he shouted at the woman, now fleeing toward the house. Cal Mosher slapped him on the back. "You got a nerve, Mike," he said filled with admiration. He slapped his knees with his hands. "She'll have something to talk about for ten years, eh? She won't get over talking about that kiss Mike gave her for ten years."

At Clyde, the Bidwell young men went into Charley Shuter's saloon and there got into trouble. Sid Gould was pitcher for the Bidwell team and during the game at Clyde, during the week before, had been hurt by a swiftly pitched ball that struck him on the side of the head as he stood at bat. He had been unable to continue pitching, and the man who took his place was unskillful and the game was lost, and now, standing at the bar in Charley Shuter's saloon, Sid remembered his injury and began to talk in a loud voice, challenging another group of young men at another end of the bar. Charley Shuter's bartender became alarmed. "Here, now, don't you go starting nothing. Don't you go trying to start nothing in this place," he growled.

Sid turned to his friends. "Well, the cowardly pup, he beaned me," he said. "Well, I had the team, this town thinks so much of, eating out of my hand. For five innings they never got a smell of a hit. Then what did they do, eh? They fixed it up with their cowardly pitcher to bean me—that's what they did."

One of the young men of Clyde, loafing the evening away in the saloon, was an outfielder on the Clyde ball team and as Sid talked he went out at the front door. From store to store and from saloon to saloon he ran hurriedly, whispering, sending messengers out in all directions. He was a tall blue-eyed soft-voiced man but he had now become intensely excited. A dozen other young men gathered about him and the crowd started for Shuter's saloon but when they had got there the young men from Bidwell had come out to the sidewalk, had unhitched their horses from the railing before the saloon door and were preparing to depart. "Yah, you," bawled the blue-eyed outfielder. "Don't tell lies and then sneak out of town. Stand up and take your medicine."

The fight at Clyde was short and sharp and when it had lasted three minutes, and when Sid Gould had lost two teeth and two of his companions had acquired bleeding heads, they managed to struggle

into the surrey and start the horses. The blue-eyed outfielder, white
with wrath and disappointment, sprang on the steps. "Come back,
you cheap skates," he cried. The surrey rattled off over the cobble-
stones and several Clyde young men ran in the road behind. Sid
Gould drew back his arm and caught the outfielder a swinging blow
on the nose and the blow knocked him out of the surrey to the road
so that a wheel ran over his legs. Leaning out, and mad now with
joy, Sid issued a challenge. "Come over to Bidwell, one at a time,
and I'll clean up your whole town alone. All I want is to get at you
fellows one or two at a time," he challenged.

In the road north of Clyde, Cal Mosher, who was driving, stopped
the horses and there was a discussion as to whether the journey
should be continued on to the town of Fremont, in search of new
and perhaps more enticing adventures, or whether it would be better to
go back to Bidwell and mend broken teeth, cut lips and blackened
eyes. Sid Gould, the most badly injured member of the party, settled
the matter. "There's a dance down at the Dewdrop tonight. Let's
go down there and stir up the farmers. This night is just started for
me," he said, and the heads of the horses were turned northward.
On the back seat Will Smith and Harry Kingsley fell into a troubled
sleep, Herman Sanford and Michael Tompkins attempted a song and
Cal Mosher talked to Sid. "We'll get up another game with that
bunch from Clyde," he said. "Now you listen and I'll tell you how
to work it. You pitch the game, see. Well, you fan every man
that faces you for eight innings. That will show them up, show what
mutts they are. Then, when it comes to the ninth inning, you start
to bean 'em. You can lay out three or four of that gang before the
game ends in a scrap, and when that time comes we'll have our own
gang on hand."

At the Dewdrop, when the six young men from Bidwell arrived at
about eleven o'clock, the dance was in full swing. The doors and
windows to the dining room of one of the big frame boarding-houses
had been thrown open and the floor carefully swept, and over
the windows and doorways green branches of trees had been
hung. The night was fine—with a moon—and, on a white beach,
twenty feet away, the waters of the bay made a faint murmuring
sound. At one end of the dance hall and on a little raised platform
sat Rat Gould with his brother Will, a small grey-haired man who
played a base viol larger than himself. Two other men, fiddlers like
Rat himself filled out the orchestra. Nearly every dance announced

was a square dance and Rat did the "calling off," his shrill voice rising above the shuffle of feet and the low continuous hum of conversations. "Swing your pardners round and round. Bow your heads down to the ground. Kick your heels and let her fly. The night is fine and the moon's on high," he sang.

In a corner of the big room with her escort, the grocer, from the town of Muncie in Indiana, sat May Edgley. He was a rather heavy and fleshy man of forty-five, whose wife had died during the year before, and for the first time since that event he was with a woman and the thought had excited him. There was a round bald spot on the top of his head and blushes kept running up his cheeks, into his hair and out upon the bald spot, like waves upon a beach. May had put on a white dress, bought for the ceremony of graduation from the Bidwell high school and, the owner being out of town, had borrowed from Lillian,—unknown to her—a huge white hat, decorated with a long ostrich feather, of the variety known as a willow plume.

She had never before been to a dance and her escort had not danced since boyhood but at Maud Welliver's suggestion they had tried to take part in a square dance. "It's easy," Maud had said. "All you got to do is to watch and do what everyone else is doing."

The attempt turned out a failure, and all the other dancers giggled and laughed at the fat man from Muncie as he rolled and capered about. He ran in the wrong direction, grabbed other men's partners, whirled them about and even got into the wrong set. A madness of embarrassment seized him and he rushed for May, as one hurries into the house at the coming of a sudden storm, and taking her by the arm started to get off the floor, out of sight of the laughing people—but Rat Gould shouted at him. "Come back, fat man," he shrieked and the grocer, not knowing what else to do, started to whirl May about. She also laughed and protested but before she could make him understand that she did not want to dance any more his feet flew out from under him and he sat down, pulling May down to sit upon his round paunch.

For May that evening was terrible and the time spent at the dance hung fire like a long unused and rusty old gun. It seemed to her that every passing minute was heavily freighted with possibilities of evil for herself. In the surrey, coming out from Bidwell, she had remained silent, filled with vague fears and Maud Welliver was also silent. In a way she wished May had not come. Alone with Grover Hunt on such a night, she felt she might have had something to say, but all the time, in her mind floated vague visions of May—alone in the wood with Jerome Hadley, May struggling for life there, in the darkness of the field on that other night—and grasping the hand of a prince. Grover Hunt's hand took hold of hers and he also became silent with embarrassment. When they had got to the Dewdrop, and when they had danced in two square dances, Maud went to May. "Mr. Hunt and I are going to take a little walk together," she said. "We won't be gone long." Through a window May saw the two figures go off along the beach in the moonlight.

The man who had brought May to the dance was named Wilder, and he also wanted May to go walk with him, into the moonlight outside, but could not bring himself to the point of asking so bold a favor. He lit a cigar and held it outside the window, taking occasional puffs and blowing the smoke into the outer air and told May of the K. of R convention at Cleveland, of a ride the delegates had taken in automobiles and of a dinner given in their honor by the business men of Cleveland. "It was one of the largest affairs ever held in the city," he said. The Mayor had come and there was present a United States Senator. Well, there was one man there. He was a fat fellow who could say such funny things that everyone in the room rocked with laughter. He was the master of ceremonies and all evening kept telling the funniest stories. As for the Muncie grocer, he had been unable to eat. Well, he laughed until his sides ached. Grocer Wilder tried to reproduce one of the tales told by the Cleveland funny man. "There were two farmers," he began, "they went to the city of Philadelphia, to a church convention, and at the same time and in the same city a convention of brewers was being held. The two farmers got into the wrong place."

May's escort stopped talking and growing suddenly red, leaned out at the window and puffed hard at his cigar. "Well, I can't remember," he declared. It had come into his mind that the story he had started to tell was one a man could not tell to a woman. "Gee, I nearly put me foot into it! I came near making a break," he thought.

May looked from her escort to the men and women dancing on the floor. In her eyes fear lurked. "I wonder if anyone here knows me, I wonder if anyone knows about me and Jerome Hadley," she thought. Fear, like a little hungry mouse, gnawed at May's soul. Two red-cheeked country girls sitting on a nearby bench put their heads together and whispered "Oh, I don't believe it," one of them shouted and they both gave way to a spasm of giggles. May turned to look at them and something gripped at her heart. A young farm hand, with a shiny red face and with a white handkerchief tied about his neck, beckoned to another young man and the two went outside into the moonlight. They also whispered and laughed. One of them turned to look back at May's white face and then they lit cigars and walked away. May could no longer hear the voice of grocer Wilder telling of his adventures at the convention at Cleveland. "They know me, I'm sure they know me. They have heard that story. Something dreadful will happen to me before the night is over," she thought.

May had always wanted to be in some such place as the one to which she had now come, some place where many strange people had congregated and where she could move freely about among strange people. Before the Jerome Hadley incident, and the giving up of the idea of becoming a schoolteacher she had thought a great deal of what she would do when she became a teacher. Everything had been carefully planned. She would get a place as teacher in some town or in the country, far from Bidwell and from the Edgleys and there she would live her own life and make her own way. There would be no handicap of birth and she could stand upon her own feet. Well, that would be a chance. Her natural smartness would at last count for something real and in the new place she would go about to dances and to other social gatherings. Being the school-teacher, and in a way responsible for the future of their children, people would be glad to invite her into their houses, and all she wanted was a chance, the opportunity to step unknown into the presence of people who had never been to Bidwell and had never heard of the Edgleys.

Then she would show what she could do! She would go—well, to a dance or to a house where many people had congregated to have a good time. She would move about, saying things, laughing, keeping everyone on tiptoes. What things her quick mind would make up to say! Words would become little sharp swords with which she played. How many pictures her mind had made of herself in the midst of such an assemblage. It was not her fault if she found herself the centre toward which all eyes looked and, in spite of the fact that she was the outstanding figure in any assemblage of people among whom she went, she would always remain modest. After all, she would not say things that would hurt people. Indeed she would not do that! Such a thing would not be necessary. It would all be very lovely. Several people would be talking and up she would come and for a moment she would listen, to catch the drift of what was being said, and then her own word would be said. Well it would startle people. She would have a new, a novel, a startling but attractive point of view on any subject that was brought up. Her mind was extraordinarily quick. It would attend to things.

With her fancy thus filled with the thoughts of the possibilities of herself as a glowing social figure May turned toward her escort who, puzzled by her apparent indifference, was striving manfully to remember the funny things the Cleveland man had said at the dinner given for the K. of Ps. Many of the man's stories could not be repeated to a lady—it had been what is called a stag dinner—but others could be. Of the ones that could be told anywhere—they were called parlor stories—he remembered one and launched into it. May pitied him. He forgot the point, could not remember where the story began and ended. "Well," he began, "there was a man and woman on a train. It was on a train on the B. and O. No, I think the man said it was on the Lake Shore and Michigan Southern. Perhaps they were riding on a train on the Pennsylvania Railroad. I have forgotten what the woman said to the man. It was about a dog another woman was trying to conceal in a basket. They do not allow dogs in passenger cars on railroads, you know. Something very funny happened. I thought I would die laughing when the man told about it."

"If I had that story to tell I could make something out of it," May thought. She imagined herself telling the story of the man and the woman and the dog. How she would decorate it, add little touches. That fat man in Cleveland might have been funny but had she been intrusted with the telling of the story, she was sure he would have been outdone. Her mind began to recast the story and then the fear, that had all evening been lurking within, came back and she forgot the man, the woman and the dog on the train. Again her eyes searched the faces in the room and when a new man or woman came in she trembled. "Suppose Jerome Hadley were to come here tonight," she thought and the thought made her ill. It was a thing that might happen. Jerome was a young man and a bachelor and he no doubt went about to places, to dances and to shows at the Bidwell Opera House, and he might now, at any moment, come into the very room in which she was sitting and walk directly to her. In the berry field he had been bold and had not cared what he said and, if he came to the dance, he would walk directly to her and might even take her by the arm. "I want you," he would say. "Come outside with me."

May tried to think what she would do if such a thing happened. Would she struggle and refuse to go, thus attracting the attention of everyone in the room, or would she go quietly and make her struggle with the man outside alone in the darkness? Her mind ran into a tangle of thoughts. It was true that Jerome Hadley had done something quite terrible to her, had tried to kill something within her, but after all she had surrendered to him. She had lain with the man—filled with fear, trembling to be sure—but the thing had been done. In a strange sort of way she belonged to Jerome Hadley and suppose he were to come and demand again that she submit. Could she refuse? Had she become, and in spite of herself, the property of the man?

With her head a whirlpool of thought May stared, half wildly, about. If in her own room in the Edgley house, and when she had hidden herself away by the willows by the creek, she had built herself a tower of romance in which she could live and from the windows of which she could look down upon life, striving to understand it, to understand people, the tower was now being destroyed. Hands were tearing at it, strong, determined hands. She had felt them as she sat in the surrey with Maud and the two grocers, outbound from Bidwell. Then as now she wondered why she had consented to come to the dance. Well, she had come because not to come would bring a disappointment to Maud Welliver, the only woman who had come in any way close to herself, and now she was at the dance and Maud had gone away, outdoors into darkness. She had gone away with a man and it had been understood that would not happen. There was the matter of the prince, her lover. It had been understood that, because of the prince, Maud would not leave her alone with another man, and she had left, had gone outdoors with a grocer and had left another grocer sitting beside May.

Hands were tearing at her tower of romance, the tower she had built so slowly and painfully, the tower in which she had found the prince, the tower in which she had found a way to live and to be happy in spite of the ugliness of actuality. Dust arose from the walls. An army of men and women, male and female Jerome Hadleys, were charging down upon it. There would be rape and murder and how could she, left alone, withstand them. The prince had gone away. He was now far, far away, and the invaders would clamor over the walls. They would throw her down from the walls. The beautiful hangings in the tower, the rich silken gowns, the stones from strange lands, all the treasures of the tower would be destroyed.

May had worked herself into a state of mind that made her want to scream. In the room the dance went on, the shrill voice of Rat Gould called off and the fiddles made dance music to which heavy feet scraped over rough boards. By her side sat Grocer Wilder, still talking of the K. of P. convention at Cleveland and May felt that, in coming to the dance, she had raised a knife that in a moment would be plunged into her own breast. She arose to go out of the room, out into the night, out of the sight of people—but for a moment stood uncertain, looking vaguely about. Then she sat heavily down. Grocer Wilder also arose and his face grew red. "I've made a break," he thought. He wondered what he had said that had offended May. "Maybe she didn't want me to smoke," he told himself and threw the end of his cigar out through a window. The moment reminded him of many moments of his married life. It was like having his wife back, this feeling of having offended a woman, without knowing in just what the offense lay.

And then, through a door at the front, the six Bidwell young men came into the room. They had stopped outside for a final drink out of the bottles carried in their hip pockets and, the appetite for drink being satisfied, another appetite had come into the ascendency. They wanted women.

Sid Gould, accompanied by Cal Mosher, led the way into the dance hall. His face had become badly swollen during the drive north from Clyde and he walked uncertainly.

He walked directly toward May, who turned her face to the wall and tried to hide herself. She looked like a rabbit, cornered by dogs, and when she turned on her seat and half knelt, trying to hide her face, the rim of Lillian Edgley's white dress hat struck against the wall and the hat fell to the floor. Trembling with excitement she turned and picked it up. Her face was chalky white.

Sid Gould was well known in the Edgley household. One summer evening, in the year before May's mother's death, he had got into a row with the Edgleys. Being a little under the influence of drink and wanting a woman he shouted at Kate Edgley, walking through the streets of Bidwell with a traveling man, and a fight had been started in which the traveling man blackened Sid's eyes. Later he was taken into the mayor's office and fined and the whole affair had given the Edgley men and women a good deal of satisfaction and had been discussed endlessly at the table. Old John Edgley and the sons had sworn they also would beat the ball player. "Just let me catch him alone somewhere, so I don't get stuck for no fine, and I'll pound the head off'n him," they declared.

In the dance hall, and when his eyes alighted upon the figure of May Edgley, Sid Gould remembered his beating at the hands of the traveling man and the ten dollar fine he had been compelled to pay for fighting on the street. "Well, look here," he cried turning to his companions, now straggling into the room, "here's one of the Edgley chickens, a long ways from the home coop."

"There she is—that little chicken over there by the wall." Sid laughed and leaning over slapped his knees with his hands. The twisted swollen face made the laugh a grotesque, something horrible. Sid's companions gathered about him. "There she is," he said, again pointing a wavering forefinger. "It's the youngest of that Edgley gang, the one that's just gone on the turf, the one that was so blamed smart in school. Jerome Hadley says she's all right, and I say she's mine. I saw her first."

In the hall all became quiet and many eyes were turned toward the laughing man and the shrinking trembling woman by the wall. May tried to stand erect, to be defiant, but her knees shook so that she sat quickly down on the bench. Grover Wilder, now utterly confused, touched her on the arm, intending to ask for an explanation of her strange behavior, but at the touch of his finger she again sprang to her feet. She was like some little automatic toy that goes stiffly through certain movements when you touch some hidden spring. "What's the matter, what's the matter?" Grocer Wilder asked wildly.

Sid Gould walked to where May stood and took hold of her arm and she went meekly when he led her toward the door, walking demurely beside him. He was amazed, having expected a struggle. "Well," he thought, "I got into trouble over that Kate Edgley but this one is different. She knows how to behave. I'll have a good time with this kid." He remembered the trial and the ten dollars he had been compelled to pay for his first attempt to get into the good graces of one of the Edgley women. "I'll get the worth of my money now and I won't pay this one a cent," he thought. He turned to his companions still straggling at his heels. "Get out," he cried. "Get your own women. I saw this one first. You go get one of your own."

Sid and May had got outside and nearly to the beach before strength came back into May's body and mind. She walked beside Sid on the white sand and toward the beach. "Don't be afraid little kid. I won't hurt you," he said. May laughed nervously and he loosened the grip of his hand on her arm.

And then, with a cry of joy she sprang away from him and leaning quickly down grasped one of the pieces of driftwood with which the sand was strewn. The stick whistled through the air and descended upon Sid's head, knocking him to his knees. "You, you!" he stuttered and then cried out. "Hey, rubes!" he called and two of his companions, who had been standing at the door of the dance hall, ran toward him. Swinging the stick about her head May ran past them and in her nervous fright struck Sid again. In her mind the thing that was happening was in some odd way connected with the affair in the wood with Jerome. It was the same affair. Sid Gould and Jerome were one man, they stood for the same thing, were the same thing. They were something strange and terrible she had to meet, with which she had to struggle. The thing they represented had defeated her once, had got the best of her. She had surrendered to it, had opened the gates that led into the tower of romance, that was herself, that walled in her own secret and precious life. Something terribly crude, without understanding had happened then—it must not, could not happen again! She had been a child and had understood nothing but now she did understand. There was a thing within herself that must not be touched by unclean hands. A terrible fear of people swept over her. There was Maud Welliver, whom she had tried to take as a friend, and Lillian who had tried to be a sister to her, had wanted to help her achieve life. As for Maud— she knew nothing, she was a child—and Lillian was crude, she understood nothing.

May's mind put all men in a class with Jerome Hadley. There was something men wanted from women, that Jerome had wanted and now this other man, Sid Gould. They were all, like the Edgleys— Lillian and Kate and the two boys—people who went after the thing they wanted brutally, directly. That was not May's way and she decided she wanted nothing more to do with such people. "I'll never go back to Bidwell," she kept saying over and over as she ran in the uncertain light along the beach.

Sid Gould's companions, having run out of the dance hall, could not understand that he had been knocked over by the slight girl he had led into the darkness, and when they heard his curses and groans and saw him reeling about, quite overcome by the second blow May had aimed at his head—combined with the liquor within— they imagined some man had come to May's rescue. When they ran forward and saw May with the stick in her hand and swinging it wildly about they paid little attention to her but began at once looking for her companion. Two of them followed May as she ran along the beach and the others returned to the dance hall. A group of young farmers came crowding to the door and Cal Mosher hit one of them a swinging blow with his fist. "Get out of the way," he cried, "we're going to clean up this place."

May ran like a frightened rabbit along the beach, stopping occasionally to listen. From the dance hall came an uproar and oaths and cries broke the silence of the night. At her heels two men ran, lumbering along slowly. The drink within had taken effect and one of them fell. As she ran May came presently into the place of huge stumps and logs, thrown up by the storms of winter, and saw Maud Welliver standing at the edge of the water with the grocer Hunt—who had his arm about Maud's waist. The frightened woman ran so close to them that she might have touched Maud's dress but they were unconscious of her presence and, as for May, she was in an odd way afraid of them also. She was afraid of everything human. "It all comes to something ugly and terrible," she thought frantically.

May ran for nearly two miles, along the beach, among the tree stumps, the roots of which stuck up into the air like arms raised in supplication to the moon. Perhaps the dry withered old tree arms, sticking up thus, kept her physical fear alive, as it is not likely Sid Gould's drunken companions followed her far. She ran clinging to Lillian Edgley's hat—she had borrowed without permission—and that, I presume, seemed a thing of beauty to her. Something conscientious and fine in her made her cling desperately to the hat and she had held it in her left hand and safely out of harm's way, even in the moment when she was belaboring Sid Gould with the stick of driftwood.

And now she ran, still clinging to the hat, and was afraid with a fear that was no longer physical. The new fear that swept in upon her comprehended something more than the grotesque masses of tree roots, that now appeared to dance madly in the moonlight, something more than Sid Gould, Cal Mosher and Jerome Hadley—that had become a fear of life itself, of all she had ever known of life, all she had ever been permitted to see of life—that fear was now heavy upon her.

Little May Edgley did not want to live any more. "Death is a kind and comforting thing to those who are through with life," an old farm horse had seemed to say to a boy, who, a few days later, ran in terror from the sight of May Edgley's dead body to lean trembling on the old horse's manger.

What actually happened on that terrible night when May ran so madly was that she came in her flight to where a creek runs down into the bay. There are good fishing places off the mouth of the creek. At the creek's mouth the water spreads itself out, so that the small stream looks, from a distance, like a strong river, but one coming along the beach—running along the beach, in the moonlight, let us say—from the west would run almost to the eastern bank in the shallow water, that came only to the shoe tops.

One would run thus, in the shallow water, and the clear white beach—east of the creek's mouth—would seem but a few steps away, and then one would be plunged suddenly down into the narrow deep current, sweeping under the eastern bank, the current that carried the main body of the water of the stream.

And May Edgley plunged in there, still clinging to Lillian's white hat—the white willow plume bobbing up and down in the swift current—and was swept into the bay. Her body, caught by an eddy was carried in and lodged among the submerged tree roots, where it stayed, lodged, until the farmer and his hired man accidentally found it and laid it tenderly on the boards beside the farmer's barn.

The little hard fist clung to the hat, the white grotesque hat that Lil Edgley was in the habit of putting on when she wanted to look her best—when she wanted, I presume, to be beautiful.

May may have thought the hat was beautiful. She may have thought of it as the most beautiful thing she had ever seen in the actuality of her life.

Of that one cannot speak too definitely, and I only know that, if the hat ever had been beautiful, it had lost its beauty when, a few days later, it fell under the eyes of a boy who saw the bedraggled remains of it, clutched in the drowned woman's hand.

An Ohio Pagan

CHAPTER I

TOM EDWARDS WAS a Welshman, born in Northern Ohio, and a descendant of that Thomas Edwards, the Welsh poet, who was called, in his own time and country, Twn O'r Nant—which in our own tongue means "Tom of the dingle or vale."

The first Thomas Edwards was a gigantic figure in the history of the spiritual life of the Welsh. Not only did he write many stirring interludes concerning life, death, earth, fire and water but as a man he was a true brother to the elements and to all the passions of his sturdy and musical race. He sang beautifully but he also played stoutly and beautifully the part of a man. There is a wonderful tale, told in Wales and written into a book by the poet himself, of how he, with a team of horses, once moved a great ship out of the land into the sea, after three hundred Welshmen had failed at the task. Also he taught Welsh woodsmen the secret of the crane and pulley for lifting great logs in the forests, and once he fought to the point of death the bully of the countryside, a man known over a great part of Wales as The Cruel Fighter. Tom Edwards, the descendant of this man was born in Ohio near my own native town of Bidwell. His name was not Edwards, but as his father was dead when he was born, his mother gave him the old poet's name out of pride in having such blood in her veins. Then when the boy was six his mother died also and the man for whom both his mother and father had worked, a sporting farmer named Harry Whitehead, took the boy into his own house to live.

They were gigantic people, the Whiteheads. Harry himself weighed two hundred and seventy pounds and his wife twenty pounds more. About the time he took young Tom to live with him the farmer became interested in the racing of horses, moved off his farms, of which he had three, and came to live in our town.

In the town of Bidwell there was an old frame building, that had once been a factory for the making of barrel staves but that had stood for years vacant, staring with windowless eyes into the streets, and Harry bought it at a low price and transformed it into a splendid stable with a board floor and two long rows of box stalls. At a sale of blooded horses held in the city of Cleveland he bought twenty young colts, all of the trotting strain, and set up as a trainer of race horses.

Among the colts thus brought to our town was one great black fellow named Bucephalus. Harry got the name from John Telfer, our town poetry lover. "It was the name of the mighty horse of a mighty man," Telfer said, and that satisfied Harry.

Young Tom was told off to be the special guardian and caretaker of Bucephalus, and the black stallion, who had in him the mighty blood of the Tennessee Patchens, quickly became the pride of the stables. He was in his nature a great ugly-tempered beast, as given to whims and notions as an opera star, and from the very first began to make trouble. Within a year no one but Harry Whitehead himself and the boy Tom dared go into his stall. The methods of the two people with the great horse were entirely different but equally effective. Once big Harry turned the stallion loose on the floor of the stable, closed all the doors, and with a cruel long whip in his hand, went in to conquer or to be conquered. He came out victorious and ever after the horse behaved when he was about.

The boy's method was different. He loved Bucephalus and the wicked animal loved him. Tom slept on a cot in the barn and day or night, even when there were mares about, walked into Bucephalus' box-stall without fear. When the stallion was in a temper he sometimes turned at the boy's entrance and with a snort sent his iron-shod heels banging against the sides of the stall, but Tom laughed and putting a simple rope halter over the horse's head led him forth to be cleaned or hitched to a cart for his morning's jog on our town's half-mile race track. A sight it was to see the boy with the blood of Twn O'r Nant in his veins leading by the nose Bucephalus of the royal blood of the Patchens.

When he was six years old the horse Bucephalus went forth to race and conquer at the great spring race meeting at Columbus, Ohio. He won two heats of the trotting free-for-all—the great race of the meeting—with heavy Harry in the sulky and then faltered. A gelding named "Light o' the Orient" beat him in the next heat. Tom, then a lad of sixteen, was put into the sulky and the two of them, horse and boy, fought out a royal battle with the gelding and a little bay mare, that hadn't been heard from before but that suddenly developed a whirlwind burst of speed.

The big stallion and the slender boy won. From amid a mob of cursing, shouting, whip-slashing men a black horse shot out and a pale boy, leaning far forward, called and murmured to him. "Go on, boy! Go boy! Go boy!" the lad's voice had called over and over all through the race. Bucephalus got a record of 2.06¼ and Tom Edwards became a newspaper hero. His picture was in the Cleveland *Leader* and the Cincinnati *Enquirer*, and when he came back to Bidwell we other boys fairly wept in our envy of him.

Then it was however that Tom Edwards fell down from his high place. There he was, a tall boy, almost of man's stature and, except for a few months during the winters when he lived on the Whitehead farms, and between his sixth and thirteenth years, when he had attended a country school and had learned to read and write and do sums, he was without education. And now, during that very fall of the year of his triumph at Columbus, the Bidwell truant officer, a thin man with white hair, who was also superintendent of the Baptist Sunday School, came one afternoon to the Whitehead stables and told him that if he did not begin going to school both he and his employer would get into serious trouble.

Harry Whitehead was furious and so was Tom. There he was, a great tall slender fellow who had been with race horses to the fairs all over Northern Ohio and Indiana, during that very fall, and who had just come home from the journey during which he had driven the winner in the free-for-all trot at a Grand Circuit meeting and had given Bucephalus a mark of 2.06 ¼.

Was such a fellow to go sit in a schoolroom, with a silly school book in his hand, reading of the affairs of the men who dealt in butter, eggs, potatoes and apples, and whose unnecessarily complicated business life the children were asked to unravel,—was such a fellow to go sit in a room, under the eyes of a woman teacher, and in the company of boys half his age and with none of his wide experience of life?

It was a hard thought and Tom took it hard. The law was all right, Harry Whitehead said, and was intended to keep no-account kids off the streets but what it had to do with himself Tom couldn't make out. When the truant officer had gone and Tom was left alone in the stable with his employer the man and boy stood for a long time glumly staring at each other. It was all right to be educated but Tom felt he had book education enough. He could read, write and do sums, and what other book-training did a horseman need? As for books, they were all right for rainy evenings when there were no men sitting by the stable door and talking of horses and races. And also when one went to the races in a strange town and arrived, perhaps on Sunday, and the races did not begin until the following Wednesday—it was all right then to have a book in the chest with the horse blankets. When the weather was fine and the work was all done on a fine fall afternoon, and the other swipes, both niggers and whites, had gone off to town, one could take a book out under a tree and read of life in far away places that was as strange and almost as fascinating as one's own life. Tom had read *Robinson Crusoe*, *Uncle Tom's Cabin* and *Tales from the Bible*, all of which he had found in the Whitehead house and Jacob Friedman, the school superintendent at Bidwell, who had a fancy for horses, had loaned him other books that he intended reading during the coming winter. They were in his chest—one called *Gulliver's Travels* and the other *Moll Flanders*.

And now the law said he must give up being a horseman and go every day to a school and do little foolish sums, he who had already proven himself a man. What other schoolboy knew what he did about life? Had he not seen and spoken to several of the greatest men of this world, men who had driven horses to beat world records, and did they not respect him? When he became a driver of race horses such men as Pop Geers, Walter Cox, John Splan, Murphy and the others would not ask him what books he had read, or how many feet make a rod and how many rods in a mile. In the race at Columbus, where he had won his spurs as a driver, he had already proven that life had given him the kind of education he needed. The driver of the gelding "Light o' the Orient" had tried to bluff him in that third heat and had not succeeded. He was a big man with a black mustache and had lost one eye so that he looked fierce and ugly, and when the two horses were fighting it out, neck and neck, up the back stretch, and when Tom was tooling Bucephalus smoothly and surely to the front, the older man turned in his sulky to glare at him. "You damned little whipper-snapper," he yelled, "I'll knock you out of your sulky if you don't take back."

He had yelled that at Tom and then had struck at the boy with the butt of his whip—not intending actually to hit him perhaps but just missing the boy's head, and Tom had kept his eyes steadily on his own horse, had held him smoothly in his stride and at the upper turn, at just the right moment, had begun to pull out in front.

Later he hadn't even told Harry Whitehead of the incident, and that fact too, he felt vaguely, had something to do with his qualifications as a man.

And now they were going to put him into a school with the kids. He was at work on the stable floor, rubbing the legs of a trim-looking colt, and Bucephalus was in his stall waiting to be taken to a late fall meeting at Indianapolis on the following Monday, when the blow fell. Harry Whitehead walked back and forth swearing at the two men who were loafing in chairs at the stable door. "Do you call that law, eh, robbing a kid of the chance Tom's got?" he asked, shaking a riding whip under their noses. "I never see such a law. What I say is Dod blast such a law."

Tom took the colt back to its place and went into Bucephalus' box-stall. The stallion was in one of his gentle moods and turned to have his nose rubbed, but Tom went and buried his face against the great black neck and for a long time stood thus, trembling. He had thought perhaps Harry would let him drive Bucephalus in all his races another season and now that was all to come to an end and he was to be pitched back into childhood, to be made just a kid in school. "I won't do it," he decided suddenly and a dogged light came into his eyes. His future as a driver of race horses might have to be sacrificed but that didn't matter so much as the humiliation of this other, and he decided he would say nothing to Harry Whitehead or his wife but would make his own move.

"I'll get out of here. Before they get me into that school I'll skip out of town," he told himself as his hand crept up and fondled the soft nose of Bucephalus, the son royal of the Patchens.

Tom left Bidwell during the night, going east on a freight train, and no one there ever saw him again. During that winter he lived in the city of Cleveland, where he got work driving a milk wagon in a district where factory workers lived.

Then spring came again and with it the memory of other springs—of thunder-showers rolling over fields of wheat, just appearing, green and vivid, out of the black ground—of the sweet smell of new plowed fields, and most of all the smell and sound of animals about barns at the Whitehead farms north of Bidwell. How sharply he remembered those days on the farms and the days later when he lived in Bidwell, slept in the stables and went each morning to jog race horses and young colts round and round the half-mile race track at the fair grounds at Bidwell.

That was a life! Round and round the track they went, young colthood and young manhood together, not thinking but carrying life very keenly within themselves and feeling tremendously. The colt's legs were to be hardened and their wind made sound and for the boy long hours were to be spent in a kind of dream world, and life lived in the company of something fine, courageous, filled with a terrible, waiting surge of life. At the fair ground, away at the town's edge, tall grass grew in the enclosure inside the track and there were trees from which came the voices of squirrels, chattering and scolding, accompanied by the call of nesting birds and, down below on the ground, by the song of bees visiting early blossoms and of insects hidden away in the grass.

How different the life of the city streets in the springtime! To Tom it was in a way fetid and foul. For months he had been living in a boarding house with some six, and often eight or ten, other young fellows, in narrow rooms above a foul street. The young fellows were unmarried and made good wages, and on the winter evenings and on Sundays they dressed in good clothes and went forth, to return later, half drunk, to sit for long hours boasting and talking loudly in the rooms. Because he was shy, often lonely and sometimes startled and frightened by what he saw and heard in the city, the others would have nothing to do with Tom. They felt a kind of contempt for him, looked upon him as a "rube" and in the late afternoon when his work was done he often went for long walks alone in grim streets of workingmen's houses, breathing the smoke-laden air and listening to the roar and clatter of machinery in great factories. At other times and immediately after the evening meal he went off to his room and to bed, half sick with fear and with some strange nameless dread of the life about him.

And so in the early summer of his seventeenth year Tom left the city and going back into his own Northern Ohio lake country found work with a man named John Bottsford who owned a threshing outfit and worked among the farmers of Erie County, Ohio. The slender boy, who had urged Bucephalus to his greatest victory and had driven him the fastest mile of his career, had become a tall strong fellow with heavy features, brown eyes, and big nerveless hands—but in spite of his apparent heaviness there was something tremendously alive in him. He now drove a team of plodding grey farm horses and it was his job to keep the threshing engine supplied with water and fuel and to haul the threshed grain out of the fields and into farmers' barns.

The thresherman Bottsford was a broad-shouldered, powerful old man of sixty and had, besides Tom, three grown sons in his employ. He had been a farmer, working on rented land, all his life and had saved some money, with which he had bought the threshing outfit, and all day the five men worked like driven slaves and at night slept in the hay in the farmers' barns. It was rainy that season in the lake country and at the beginning of the time of threshing things did not go very well for Bottsford.

The old thresherman was worried. The threshing venture had taken all of his money and he had a dread of going into debt and, as he was a deeply religious man, at night when he thought the others asleep, he crawled out of the hayloft and went down onto the barn floor to pray.

Something happened to Tom and for the first time in his life he began to think about life and its meaning. He was in the country, that he loved, in the yellow sunwashed fields, far from the dreaded noises and dirt of city life, and here was a man, of his own type, in some deep way a brother to himself, who was continuously crying out to some power outside himself, some power that was in the sun, in the clouds, in the roaring thunder that accompanied the summer rains—that was in these things and that at the same time controlled all these things.

The young threshing apprentice was impressed. Throughout the rainy days, when no work could be done, he wandered about and waited for night, and then, when they all had gone into the barn loft and the others prepared to sleep, he stayed awake to think and listen. He thought of God and of the possibilities of God's part in the affairs of men. The thresherman's youngest son, a fat jolly fellow, lay beside him and, for a time after they had crawled into the hay, the two boys whispered and laughed together. The fat boy's skin was sensitive and the dry broken ends of grass stalks crept down under his clothes and tickled him. He giggled and twisted about, wriggling and kicking and Tom looked at him and laughed also. The thoughts of God went out of his mind.

In the barn all became quiet and when it rained a low drumming sound went on overhead. Tom could hear the horses and cattle, down below, moving about. The smells were all delicious smells. The smell of the cows in particular awoke something heady in him. It was as though he had been drinking strong wine. Every part of his body seemed alive. The two older boys, who like their father had serious natures, lay with their feet buried in the hay. They lay very still and a warm musty smell arose from their clothes, that were full of the sweat of toil. Presently the bearded old thresherman, who slept off by himself, arose cautiously and walked across the hay in his stockinged feet. He went down a ladder to the floor below, and Tom listened eagerly. The fat boy snored but he was quite sure that the older boys were awake like himself. Every sound from below was magnified. He heard a horse stamp on the barn floor and a cow rub her horns against a feed box. The old thresherman prayed fervently, calling on the name of Jesus to help him out of his difficulty. Tom could not hear all his words but some of them came to him quite clearly and one group of words ran like a refrain through the thresherman's prayer. "Gentle Jesus," he cried, "send the good days. Let the good days come quickly. Look out over the land. Send us the fair warm days."

Came the warm fair days and Tom wondered. Late every morning, after the sun had marched far up into the sky and after the machines were set by a great pile of wheat bundles he drove his tank wagon off to be filled at some distant creek or at a pond. Sometimes he was compelled to drive two or three miles to the lake. Dust gathered in the roads and the horses plodded along. He passed through a grove of trees and went down a lane and into a small valley where there was a spring and he thought of the old man's words, uttered in the silence and the darkness of the barns. He made himself a figure of Jesus as a young god walking about over the land. The young god went through the lanes and through the shaded covered places. The feet of the horses came down with a thump in the dust of the road and there was an echoing thump far away in the wood. Tom leaned forward and listened and his checks became a little pale. He was no longer the growing man but had become again the fine and sensitive boy who had driven Bucephalus through a mob of angry, determined men to victory. For the first time the blood of the old poet Twn O'r Nat awoke in him.

The water boy for the threshing crew rode the horse Pegasus down through the lanes back of the farm houses in Erie County, Ohio, to the creeks where the threshing tanks must be filled. Beside him on the soft earth in the forest walked the young god Jesus. At the creek Pegasus, born of the springs of Ocean, stamped on the ground. The plodding farm horses stopped. With a dazed look in his eyes

Tom Edwards arose from the wagon seat and prepared his hose and pump for filling the tank. The god Jesus walked away over the land, and with a wave of his hand summoned the smiling days.

A light came into Tom Edwards' eyes and grace seemed to come also into his heavy maturing body. New impulses came to him. As the threshing crew went about, over the roads and through the villages from farm to farm, women and young girls looked at the young man and smiled. Sometimes as he came from the fields to a farmer's barn, with a load of wheat in bags on his wagon, the daughter of the farmer stepped out of the farm house and stood looking at him. Tom looked at the woman and hunger crept into his heart and, in the evenings while the thresherman and his sons sat on the ground by the barns and talked of their affairs, he walked nervously about. Making a motion to the fat boy, who was not really interested in the talk of his father and brothers, the two younger men went to walk in the nearby fields and on the roads. Sometimes they stumbled along a country road in the dusk of the evening and came into the lighted streets of a town. Under the store-lights young girls walked about. The two boys stood in the shadows by a building and watched and later, as they went homeward in the darkness, the fat boy expressed what they both felt. They passed through a dark place where the road wound through a wood. In silence the frogs croaked, and birds roosting in the trees were disturbed by their presence and fluttered about. The fat boy wore heavy overalls and his fat legs rubbed against each other. The rough cloth made a queer creaking sound. He spoke passionately. "I would like to hold a woman, tight, tight, tight," he said.

One Sunday the thresherman took his entire crew with him to a church. They had been working near a village called Castalia, but did not go into the town but to a small white frame church that stood amid trees and by a stream at the side of a road, a mile north of the village. They went on Tom's water wagon, from which they had lifted the tank and placed boards for seats. The boy drove the horses.

Many teams were tied in the shade under the trees in a little grove near the church, and strange men—farmers and their sons—stood about in little groups and talked of the season's crops. Although it was hot, a breeze played among the leaves of the trees under which they stood, and back of the church and the grove the stream ran over stones and made a persistent soft murmuring noise that arose above the hum of voices.

In the church Tom sat beside the fat boy who stared at the country girls as they came in and who, after the sermon began, went to sleep while Tom listened eagerly to the sermon. The minister, an old man with a beard and a strong sturdy body, looked, he thought not unlike his employer Bottsford the thresherman.

The minister in the country church talked of that time when Mary Magdalene, the woman who had been taken in adultery, was being stoned by the crowd of men who had forgotten their own sins and when, in the tale the minister told, Jesus approached and rescued the woman Tom's heart thumped with excitement. Then later the minister talked of how Jesus was tempted by the devil, as he stood on a high place in the mountain, but the boy did not listen. He leaned forward and looked out through a window across fields and the minister's words came to him but in broken sentences. Tom took what was said concerning the temptation on the mountain to mean that Mary had followed Jesus and had offered her body to him, and that afternoon, when he had returned with the others to the farm where they were to begin threshing on the next morning, he called the fat boy aside and asked his opinion.

The two boys walked across a field of wheat-stubble and sat down on a log in a grove of trees. It had never occurred to Tom that a man could be tempted by a woman. It had always seemed to him that it must be the other way, that women must always be tempted by men. "I thought men always asked," he said, "and now it seems that women sometimes do the asking. That would be a fine thing if it could happen to us. Don't you think so?"

The two boys arose and walked under the trees and dark shadows began to form on the ground underfoot. Tom burst into words and continually asked questions and the fat boy, who had been often to church and for whom the figure of Jesus had lost most of its reality, felt a little embarrassed. He did not think the subject should be thus freely discussed and when Tom's mind kept playing with the notion of Jesus, pursued and tempted by a woman, he grunted his disapproval. "Do you think he really refused?" Tom asked over and over. The fat boy tried to explain. "He had twelve disciples," he said. "It couldn't have happened. They were always about. Well, you see, she wouldn't ever have had no chance. Wherever he went they went with him. They were men he was teaching to preach. One of them later betrayed him to soldiers who killed him."

Tom wondered. "How did that come about? How could a man like that be betrayed?" he asked. "By a kiss," the fat boy replied.

On the evening of the day when Tom Edwards—for the first and last time in his life—went into a church, there was a light shower, the only one that fell upon John Bottsford's threshing crew during the last three months the Welsh boy was with them and the shower in no way interfered with their work. The shower came up suddenly and a few minutes was gone. As it was Sunday and as there was no work the men had all gathered in the barn and were looking out through the open barn doors. Two or three men from the farm house came and sat with them on boxes and barrels on the barn floor and, as is customary with country people, very little was said. The men took knives out of their pockets and finding little sticks among the rubbish on the barn floor began to whittle, while the old thresherman went restlessly about with his hands in his trouser pockets. Tom who sat near the door, where an occasional drop of rain was blown against his check, alternately looked from his employer to the open country where the rain played over the fields. One of the farmers remarked that a rainy time had come on and that there would be no good threshing weather for several days and, while the thresherman did not answer, Tom saw his lips move and his grey beard bob up and down. He thought the thresherman was protesting but did not want to protest in words.

As they had gone about the country many rains had passed to the north, south and east of the threshing crew and on some days the clouds hung over them all day, but no rain fell and when they had got to a new place they were told it had rained there three days before. Sometimes when they left a farm Tom stood up on the seat of his water wagon and looked back. He looked across fields to where they had been at work and then looked up into the sky. "The rain may come now. The threshing is done and the wheat is all in the barn. The rain can now do no harm to our labor," he thought.

On the Sunday evening when he sat with the men on the floor of the barn Tom was sure that the shower that had now come would be but a passing affair. He thought his employer must be very close to Jesus, who controlled the affairs of the heavens, and that a long rain would not come because the thresherman did not want it. He fell into a deep reverie and John Bottsford came and stood close beside him. The thresherman put his hand against the door jamb and looked out and Tom could still see the grey beard moving. The man was praying and was so close to himself that his trouser leg touched Tom's hand. Into the boy's mind came the remembrance of how

John Bottsford had prayed at night on the barn floor. On that very morning he had prayed. It was just as daylight came and the boy was awakened because, as he crept across the hay to descend the ladder, the old man's foot had touched his hand.

As always Tom had been excited and wanted to hear every word said in the older man's prayers. He lay tense, listening to every sound that came up from below. A faint glow of light came into the hayloft, through a crack in the side of the barn, a rooster crowed and some pigs, housed in a pen near the barn, grunted loudly. They had heard the thresherman moving about and wanted to be fed and their grunting, and the occasional restless movement of a horse or a cow in the stable below, prevented Tom's hearing very distinctly. He, however, made out that his employer was thanking Jesus for the fine-weather that had attended them and was protesting that he did not want to be selfish in asking it to continue. "Jesus," he said, "send, if you wish, a little shower on this day when, because of our love for you, we do not work in the fields. Let it be fine tomorrow but today, after we have come back from the house of worship, let a shower freshen the land."

As Tom sat on a box near the door of the barn and saw how aptly the words of his employer had been answered by Jesus he knew that the rain would not last. The man for whom he worked seemed to him so close to the throne of God that he raised the hand, that had been touched by John Bottsford's trouser leg to his lips and secretly kissed it—and when he looked again out over the fields the clouds were being blown away by a wind and the evening sun was coming out. It seemed to him that the young and beautiful god Jesus must be right at hand, within hearing of his voice. "He is," Tom told himself, "standing behind a tree in the orchard." The rain stopped and he went silently out of the barn, towards a small apple orchard that lay beside the farm house, but when he came to a fence and was about to climb over he stopped. "If Jesus is there he will not want me to find him," he thought. As he turned again toward the barn he could see, across a field, a low grass-covered hill. He decided that Jesus was not after all in the orchard. The long slanting rays of the evening sun fell on the crest of the hill and touched with light the grass stalks, heavy with drops of rain and for a moment the hill was crowned as with a crown of jewels. A million tiny drops of water, reflecting the light, made the hilltop sparkle as though set with gems. "Jesus is there," muttered the boy. "He lies on his belly in the grass. He is looking at me over the edge of the hill."

CHAPTER II

John Bottsford went with his threshing crew to work for a large farmer named Barton near the town of Sandusky. The threshing season was drawing near an end and the days remained clear, cool and beautiful. The country into which he now came made a deep impression on Tom's mind and he never forgot the thoughts and experiences that came to him during the last weeks of that summer on the Barton farms.

The traction engine, puffing forth smoke and attracting the excited attention of dogs and children as it rumbled along and pulled the heavy red grain separator, had trailed slowly over miles of road and had come down almost to Lake Erie. Tom, with the fat Bottsford boy sitting beside him on the water wagon, followed the rumbling puffing engine, and when they came to the new place, where they were to stay for several days, he could see, from the wagon seat, the smoke of the factories in the town of Sandusky rising into the clear morning air.

The man for whom John Bottsford was threshing owned three farms, one on an island in the bay, where he lived, and two on the mainland, and the larger of the mainland farms had great stacks of wheat standing in a field near the barns. The farm was in a wide basin of land, very fertile, through which a creek flowed northward into Sandusky Bay and, besides the stacks of wheat in the basin, other stacks had been made in the upland fields beyond the creek, where a country of low hills began. From these latter fields the waters of the bay could be seen glistening in the bright fall sunlight and steamers went from Sandusky to a pleasure resort called Cedar Point. When the wind blew from the north or west and when the threshing machinery had been stopped at the noon hour the men, resting with their backs against a straw-stack, could hear a band playing on one of the steamers.

Fall came on early that year and the leaves on the trees in the forests that grew along the roads that ran down through the low creek bottom lands began to turn yellow and red. In the afternoons when Tom went to the creek for water he walked beside his horses and the dry leaves crackled and snapped underfoot.

As the season had been a prosperous one Bottsford decided that his youngest son should attend school in town during the fall and winter. He had bought himself a machine for cutting firewood and with his two older sons intended to take up that work. "The

logs will have to be hauled out of the wood lots to where we set up
the saws," he said to Tom. "You can come with us if you wish."

The thresherman began to talk to Tom of the value of learning.
"You'd better go to some town yourself this winter. It would be
better for you to get into a school," he said sharply. He grew excited
and walked up and down beside the water wagon, on the seat of
which Tom sat listening and said that God had given men both minds
and bodies and it was wicked to let either decay because of neglect.
"I have watched you," he said. "You don't talk very much but you
do plenty of thinking, I guess. Go into the schools. Find out what
the books have to say. You don't have to believe when they say
things that are lies."

The Bottsford family lived in a rented house facing a stone road
near the town of Bellevue, and the fat boy was to go to that town—
a distance of some eighteen miles from where the men were at
work—afoot, and on the evening before he set out he and Tom
went out of the barns intending to have a last walk and talk together
on the roads.

They went along in the dusk of the fall evening, each thinking his
own thoughts, and coming to a bridge that led over the creek in the
valley sat on the bridge rail. Tom had little to say but his companion
wanted to talk about women and, when darkness came on, the
embarrassment he felt regarding the subject went quite away and
he talked boldly and freely. He said that in the town of Bellevue,
where he was to live and attend school during the coming winter,
he would be sure to get in with a woman. "I'm not going to be
cheated out of that chance," he declared. He explained that as his
father would be away from home when he moved into town he
would be free to pick his own place to board.

The fat boy's imagination became inflamed and he told Tom his
plans. "I won't try to get in with any young girl," he declared shrewdly.
"That only gets a fellow in a fix. He might have to marry her. I'll
go live in a house with a widow, that's what I'll do. And in the
evening the two of us will be there alone. We'll begin to talk and
I'll keep touching her with my hands. That will get her excited."

The fat boy jumped to his feet and walked back and forth on the
bridge. He was nervous and a little ashamed and wanted to justify
what he had said. The thing for which he hungered had he thought
become a possibility—an act half achieved. Coming to stand before
Tom he put a hand on his shoulder. "I'll go into her room at night,"
he declared. "I'll not tell her I'm coming, but will creep in when

she is asleep. Then I'll get down on my knees by her bed and I'll kiss her, hard, hard. I'll hold her tight, so she can't get away and I'll kiss her mouth till she wants what I want. Then I'll stay in her house all winter. No one will know. Even if she won't have me I'll only have to move, I'm sure to be safe. No one will believe what she says, if she tells on me. I'm not going to be like a boy any more, I'll tell you what—I'm as big as a man and I'm going to do like men do, that's what I am."

The two young men went back to the barn where they were to sleep on the hay. The rich farmer for whom they were now at work had a large house and provided beds for the thresherman and his two older sons but the two younger men slept in the barn loft and on the night before had lain under one blanket. After the talk by the bridge however, Tom did not feel very comfortable and that stout exponent of manhood, the younger Bottsford, was also embarrassed. In the road the young man, whose name was Paul, walked a little ahead of his companion and when they got to the barn each sought a separate place in the loft. Each wanted to have thoughts into which he did not want the presence of the other to intrude.

For the first time Tom's body burned with eager desire for a female. He lay where he could see out through a crack, in the side of the barn, and at first his thoughts were all about animals. He had brought a horse blanket up from the stable below and crawling under it lay on his side with his eyes close to the crack and thought about the love-making of horses and cattle. Things he had seen in the stables when he worked for Whitehead, the racing man, came back to his mind and a queer animal hunger ran through him so that his legs stiffened. He rolled restlessly about on the hay and for some reason, he did not understand, his lust took the form of anger and he hated the fat boy. He thought he would like to crawl over the hay and pound his companion's face with his fists. Although he had not seen Paul Bottsford's face, when he talked of the widow, he had sensed in him a flavor of triumph. "He thinks he has got the better of me," young Edwards thought.

He rolled again to the crack and stared out into the night. There was a new moon and the fields were dimly outlined and clumps of trees, along the road that led into the town of Sandusky, looked like black clouds that had settled down over the land. For some reason the sight of the land, lying dim and quiet under the moon, took all of his anger away and he began to think, not of Paul Bottsford, with hot eager lust in his eyes, creeping into the room of the widow at

Bellevue, but of the god Jesus, going up into a mountain with his woman, Mary.

His companion's notion of going into a room where a woman lay sleeping and taking her, as it were unawares, now seemed to him entirely mean and the hot jealous feeling that had turned into anger and hatred went entirely away. He tried to think what the god, who had brought the beautiful days for the threshing, would do with a woman.

Tom's body still burned with desire and his mind wanted to think lascivious thoughts. The moon that had been hidden behind clouds emerged and a wind began to blow. It was still early evening and in the town of Sandusky pleasure seekers were taking the boat to the resort over the bay and the wind brought to Tom's ears the sound of music, blown over the waters of the bay and down the creek basin. In a grove near the barn the wind swayed gently the branches of young trees and black shadows ran here and there on the ground.

The younger Bottsford had gone to sleep in a distant part of the barn loft, and now began to snore loudly. The tenseness went out of Tom's legs and he prepared to sleep but before sleeping he muttered, half timidly, certain words, that were half a prayer, half an appeal to some spirit of the night. "Jesus, bring me a woman," he whispered.

Outside the barn, in the fields, the wind, becoming a little stronger, picked up bits of straw and blew them about among the hard up-standing stubble and there was a low gentle whispering sound as though the gods were answering his appeal.

Tom went to sleep with his arm under his head and with his eye close to the crack that gave him a view of the moonlit fields, and in his dream the cry from within repeated itself over and over. The mysterious god Jesus had heard and answered the needs of his employer John Bottsford and his own need would, he was quite sure, be understood and attended to. "Bring me a woman. I need her. Jesus, bring me a woman," he kept whispering into the night, as consciousness left him and he slipped away into dreams.

After the youngest of the Bottsfords had departed a change took place in the nature of Tom's work. The threshing crew had got now into a country of large farms where the wheat had all been brought in from the fields and stacked near the barns and where there was always plenty of water near at hand. Everything was simplified. The separator was pulled in close by the barn door and the threshed grain was carried directly to the bins from the separator. As it was not a part of Tom's work to feed the bundles of grain into the whirling teeth of the separator—this work being done by John Bottsford's two elder sons—there was little for the crew's teamster to do. Sometimes John Bottsford, who was the engineer, departed, going to make arrangements for the next stop, and was gone for a half day, and at such times Tom, who had picked up some knowledge of the art, ran the engine.

On other days however there was nothing at all for him to do and his mind, unoccupied for long hours, began to play him tricks. In the morning, after his team had been fed and cleaned until the grey coats of the old farm horses shone like racers, he went out of the barn and into an orchard. Filling his pockets with ripe apples he went to a fence and leaned over. In a field young colts played about. As he held the apples and called softly they came timidly forward, stopping in alarm and then running a little forward, until one of them, bolder than the others, ate one of the apples out of his hand.

All through those bright warm clear fall days a restless feeling, it seemed to Tom, ran through everything in nature. In the clumps of woodland still standing on the farms flaming red spread itself out along the limbs of trees and there was one grove of young maple trees, near a barn, that was like a troop of girls, young girls who had walked together down a sloping field, to stop in alarm at seeing the men at work in the barnyard. Tom stood looking at the trees. A slight breeze made them sway gently from side to side. Two horses standing among the trees drew near each other. One nipped the other's neck. They rubbed their heads together.

The crew stopped at another large farm and it was to be their last stop for the season. "When we have finished this job we'll go home and get our own fall work done," Bottsford said. Saturday evening came and the thresherman and his sons took the horses and drove away, going to their own home for the Sunday, and leaving Tom alone. "We'll be back early, on Monday morning," the thresherman said as they drove away. Sunday alone among the strange farm people brought a sharp experience to Tom and when it had passed he decided he would not wait for the end of the threshing season but a few days off now—but would quit his job and go into the city and surrender to the schools. He remembered his employer's words, "Find out what the books have to say. You don't have to believe, when they say things that are lies."

As he walked in lanes, across meadows and upon the hillsides of the farm, also on the shores of Sandusky Bay, that Sunday morning

Tom thought almost constantly of his friend the fat fellow, young
Paul Bottsford, who had gone to spend the fall and winter at
Bellevue, and wondered what his life there might be like. He had
himself lived in such a town, in Bidwell, but had rarely left Harry
Whitehead's stable. What went on in such a town? What happened
at night in the houses of the towns? He remembered Paul's plan
for getting into a house alone with a widow and how he was to
creep into her room at night, holding her tightly in his arms until
she wanted what he wanted. "I wonder if he will have the nerve.
Gee, I wonder if he will have the nerve," he muttered.

For a long time, ever since Paul had gone away and he had no
one with whom he could talk, things had taken on a new aspect in
Tom's mind. The rustle of dry leaves underfoot, as he walked in a
forest—the playing of shadows over the open face of a field—the
murmuring song of insects in the dry grass beside the fences in
the lanes—and at night the hushed contented sounds made by the
animals in the barns, were no longer so sweet to him. For him no
more did the young god Jesus walk beside him, just out of sight
behind low hills, or down the dry beds of streams. Something within
himself, that had been sleeping was now awakening. When he returned
from walking in the fields on the fall evenings and, thinking of Paul
Bottsford alone in the house with the widow at Bellevue, half wish-
ing he were in the same position, he felt ashamed in the presence
of the gentle old thresherman, and afterward did not lie awake listening to the older man's prayers. The men who had come from nearby
farms to help with the threshing laughed and shouted to each other
as they pitched the straw into great stacks or carried the filled bags
of grain to the bins, and they had wives and daughters who had come
with them and who were now at work in the farmhouse kitchen,
from which also laughter came. Girls and women kept coming out
at the kitchen door into the barnyard, tall awkward girls, plump
red-cheeked girls, women with worn thin faces and sagging breasts.
All men and women seemed made for each other.

They all laughed and talked together, understood one another.
Only he was alone. He only had no one to whom he could feel warm
and close, to whom he could draw close.

On the Sunday when the Bottsfords had all gone away Tom came
in from walking all morning in the fields and ate his dinner with
many other people in a big farmhouse dining room. In preparation
for the threshing days ahead, and the feeding of many people, several
women had come to spend the day and to help in preparing food.

The farmer's daughter, who was married and lived in Sandusky, came with her husband, and three other women, neighbors, came from farms in the neighborhood. Tom did not look at them but ate his dinner in silence and as soon as he could manage got out of the house and went to the barns. Going into a long shed he sat on the tongue of a wagon, that from long disuse was covered with dust. Swallows flew back and forth among the rafters overhead and, in an upper corner of the shed where they evidently had a nest, wasps buzzed in the semi-darkness.

The daughter of the farmer, who had come from town, came from the house with a babe in her arms. It was nursing time, and she wanted to escape from the crowded house and, without having seen Tom, she sat on a box near the shed door and opened her dress. Embarrassed and at the same time fascinated by the sight of a woman's breasts, seen through cracks of the wagon box, Tom drew his legs up and his head down and remained concealed until the woman had gone back to the house. Then he went again to the fields and did not go back to the house for the evening meal.

As he walked on that Sunday afternoon the grandson of the Welsh poet experienced many new sensations. In a way he came to understand that the things Paul had talked of doing and that had, but a short time before, filled him with disgust were now possible to himself also. In the past when he had thought about women there had always been something healthy and animal-like in his lusts but now they took a new form. The passion that could not find expression through his body went up into his mind and he began to see visions. Women became to him something different than anything else in nature, more desirable than anything else in nature, and at the same time everything in nature became woman. The trees, in the apple orchard by the barn, were like the arms of women. The apples on the trees were round like the breasts of women. They were the breasts of women—and when he had got on to a low hill the contour of the fences that marked the confines of the fields fell into the forms of women's bodies. Even the clouds in the sky did the same thing.

He walked down along a lane to a stream and crossed the stream by a wooden bridge. Then he climbed another hill, the highest place in all that part of the country, and there the fever that possessed him became more active. An odd lassitude crept over him and he lay down in the grass on the hilltop and closed his eyes. For a long time he remained in a hushed, half-sleeping, dreamless state and then opened his eyes again.

Again the forms of women floated before him. To his left the bay was ruffled by a gentle breeze and far over towards the city of Sandusky two sailboats were apparently engaged in a race. The masts of the boats were fully dressed but on the great stretch of water they seemed to stand still. The bay itself, in Tom's eyes, had taken on the form and shape of a woman's head and body and the two sailboats were the woman's eyes looking at him.

The bay was a woman with her head lying where lay the city of Sandusky. Smoke arose from the stacks of steamers docked at the city's wharves and the smoke formed itself into masses of black hair. Through the farm, where he had come to thresh, ran a stream. It swept down past the foot of the hill on which he lay. The stream was the arm of the woman. Her hand was thrust into the land and the lower part of her body was lost—far down to the north, where the bay became a part of Lake Erie—but her other arm could be seen. It was outlined in the further shore of the bay. Her other arm was drawn up and her hand was pressing against her face. Her form was distorted by pain but at the same time the giant woman smiled at the boy on the hill. There was something in the smile that was like the smile that had come unconsciously to the lips of the woman who had nursed her child in the shed.

Turning his face away from the bay Tom looked at the sky. A great white cloud that lay along the southern horizon formed itself into the giant head of a man. Tom watched as the cloud crept slowly across the sky. There was something noble and quieting about the giant's face and his hair, pure white and as thick as wheat in a rich field in June, added to its nobility. Only the face appeared. Below the shoulders there was just a white shapeless mass of clouds.

And then this formless mass began also to change. The face of a giant woman appeared. It pressed upward toward the face of the man. Two arms formed themselves on the man's shoulders and pressed the woman closely. The two faces merged. Something seemed to snap in Tom's brain.

He sat upright and looked neither at the bay nor at the sky. Evening was coming on and soft shadows began to play over the land. Below him lay the farm with its barns and houses and in the field, below the hill on which he was lying, there were two smaller hills that became at once in his eyes the two full breasts of a woman. Two white sheep appeared and stood nibbling the grass on the woman's breasts. They were like babes being suckled. The trees in the orchards near the barns were the woman's hair. An arm of the stream that ran down to the bay, the stream he had crossed on the wooden bridge when he came to the hill, cut across a meadow beyond the two low hills. It widened into a pond and the pond made a mouth for the woman. Her eyes were two black hollows—low spots in a field where hogs had rooted the grass away, looking for roots. Black puddles of water lay in the hollows and they seemed eyes shining invitingly up at him.

This woman also smiled and her smile was now an invitation. Tom got to his feet and hurried away down the hill and going stealthily past the barns and the house got into a road. All night he walked under the stars thinking new thoughts. "I am obsessed with this idea of having a woman. I'd better go to the city and go to school and see if I can make myself fit to have a woman of my own," he thought. "I won't sleep tonight but will wait until tomorrow when Bottsford comes back and then I'll quit and go into the city." He walked, trying to make plans. Even a good man like John Bottsford, had a woman for himself. Could he do that?

The thought was exciting. At the moment it seemed to him that he had only to go into the city, and go to the schools for a time, to become beautiful and to have beautiful women love him. In his half ecstatic state he forgot the winter months he had spent in the city of Cleveland, and forgot also the grim streets, the long rows of dark prison-like factories and the loneliness of his life in the city. For the moment and as he walked in the dusty roads under the moon, he thought of American towns and cities as places for beautifully satisfying adventures, for all such fellows as himself.

I'm a Fool

It was a hard jolt for me, one of the most bitterest I ever had to face. And it all came about through my own foolishness, too. Even yet sometimes, when I think of it, I want to cry or swear or kick myself. Perhaps, even now, after all this time, there will be a kind of satisfaction in making myself look cheap by telling of it.

It began at three o'clock one October afternoon as I sat in the grand stand at the fall trotting and pacing meet at Sandusky, Ohio.

To tell the truth, I felt a little foolish that I should be sitting in the grand stand at all. During the summer before I had left my home town with Harry Whitehead and, with a nigger named Burt, had taken a job as swipe with one of the two horses Harry was campaigning through the fall race meets that year. Mother cried and my sister Mildred, who wanted to get a job as a school teacher in our town that fall, stormed and scolded about the house all during the week before I left. They both thought it something disgraceful that one of our family should take a place as a swipe with race horses. I've an idea Mildred thought my taking the place would stand in the way of her getting the job she'd been working so long for.

But after all I had to work, and there was no other work to be got. A big lumbering fellow of nineteen couldn't just hang around the house and I had got too big to mow people's lawns and sell newspapers. Little chaps who could get next to people's sympathies by their sizes were always getting jobs away from me. There was one fellow who kept saying to everyone who wanted a lawn mowed or a cistern cleaned, that he was saving money to work his way through college, and I used to lay awake nights thinking up ways to injure him without being found out. I kept thinking of wagons running over him and bricks falling on his head as he walked along the street. But never mind him.

I got the place with Harry and I liked Burt fine. We got along splendid together. He was a big nigger with a lazy sprawling body and soft, kind eyes, and when it came to a fight he could hit like Jack Johnson. He had Bucephalus, a big black pacing stallion that could do 2.09 or 2.10, if he had to, and I had a little gelding named Doctor Fritz that never lost a race all fall when Harry wanted him to win.

We set out from home late in July in a box car with the two horses and after that, until late November, we kept moving along to the race meets and the fairs. It was a peachy time for me, I'll say that. Sometimes now I think that boys who are raised regular in houses, and never have a fine nigger like Burt for best friend, and go to high schools and college, and never steal anything, or get drunk a little, or learn to swear from fellows who know how, or come walking up in front of a grand stand in their shirt sleeves and with dirty horsey pants on when the races are going on and the grand stand is full of people all dressed up—What's the use of talking about it? Such fellows don't know nothing at all. They've never had no opportunity.

But I did. Burt taught me how to rub down a horse and put the bandages on after a race and steam a horse out and a lot of valuable things for any man to know. He could wrap a bandage on a horse's leg so smooth that if it had been the same color you would think it was his skin, and I guess he'd have been a big driver, too, and got to the top like Murphy and Walter Cox and the others if he hadn't been black.

Gee whizz, it was fun. You got to a county seat town, maybe say on a Saturday or Sunday, and the fair began the next Tuesday and lasted until Friday afternoon. Doctor Fritz would be, say in the 2.25 trot on Tuesday afternoon and on Thursday afternoon Bucephalus would knock 'em cold in the "free-for-all" pace. It left you a lot of time to hang around and listen to horse talk, and see Burt knock some yap cold that got too gay, and you'd find out about horses and men and pick up a lot of stuff you could use all the rest of your life, if you had some sense and salted down what you heard and felt and saw.

And then at the end of the week when the race meet was over, and Harry had run home to tend up to his livery stable business, you and Burt hitched the two horses to carts and drove slow and steady across country, to the place for the next meeting, so as to not over-heat the horses, etc., etc., you know.

Gee whizz, Gosh amighty, the nice hickorynut and beechnut and oaks and other kinds of trees along the roads, all brown and red, and the good smells, and Burt singing a song that was called Deep River, and the country girls at the windows of houses and everything. You can stick your colleges up your nose for all me. I guess I know where I got my education.

Why, one of those little burgs of towns you come to on the way, say now on a Saturday afternoon, and Burt says, "let's lay up here." And you did.

And you took the horses to a livery stable and fed them, and you got your good clothes out of a box and put them on.

And the town was full of farmers gaping, because they could see you were race horse people, and the kids maybe never see a nigger before and was afraid and run away when the two of us walked down their main street.

And that was before prohibition and all that foolishness, and so you went into a saloon, the two of you, and all the yaps come and stood around, and there was always someone pretended he was horsey and knew things and spoke up and began asking questions, and all you did was to lie and lie all you could about what horses you had, and I said I owned them, and then some fellow said "will you have a drink of whiskey" and Burt knocked his eye out the way he could say, off-hand like, "Oh well, all right, I'm agreeable to a little nip. I'll split a quart with you." Gee whizz.

But that isn't what I want to tell my story about. We got home late in November and I promised mother I'd quit the race horses for good. There's a lot of things you've got to promise a mother because she don't know any better.

And so, there not being any work in our town any more than when I left there to go to the races, I went off to Sandusky and got a pretty good place taking care of horses for a man who owned a teaming and delivery and storage and coal and real estate business there. It was a pretty good place with good eats, and a day off each week, and sleeping on a cot in a big barn, and mostly just shovelling in hay and oats to a lot of big good-enough skates of horses, that couldn't have trotted a race with a toad. I wasn't dissatisfied and I could send money home.

And then, as I started to tell you, the fall races come to Sandusky and I got the day off and I went. I left the job at noon and had on my good clothes and my new brown derby hat, I'd just bought the Saturday before, and a stand-up collar.

First of all I went down-town and walked about with the dudes. I've always thought to myself, "put up a good front" and so I did it. I had forty dollars in my pocket and so I went into the West House, a big hotel, and walked up to the cigar stand. "Give me three twenty-five cent cigars," I said. There was a lot of horsemen and strangers and dressed-up people from other towns standing around in the lobby and in the bar, and I mingled amongst them. In the bar there was a fellow with a cane and a Windsor tie on, that it made me sick to look at him. I like a man to be a man and dress up, but not to go put on that kind of airs. So I pushed him aside, kind of rough, and had me a drink of whiskey. And then he looked at me, as though he thought maybe he'd get gay, but he changed his mind and didn't say anything. And then I had another drink of whiskey, just to show him something, and went out and had a hack out to the races, all to myself, and when I got there I bought myself the best seat I could get up in the grand stand, but didn't go in for any of these boxes. That's putting on too many airs.

And so there I was, sitting up in the grand stand as gay as you please and looking down on the swipes coming out with their horses, and with their dirty horsey pants on and the horse blankets swung over their shoulders, same as I had been doing all the year before. I liked one thing about the same as the other, sitting up there and feeling grand and being down there and looking up at the yaps and feeling grander and more important, too. One thing's about as good as another, if you take it just right. I've often said that.

Well, right in front of me, in the grand stand that day, there was a fellow with a couple of girls and they was about my age. The young fellow was a nice guy all right. He was the kind maybe that goes to college and then comes to be a lawyer or maybe a newspaper editor or something like that, but he wasn't stuck on himself. There are some of that kind are all right and he was one of the ones.

He had his sister with him and another girl and the sister looked around over his shoulder, accidental at first, not intending to start anything—she wasn't that kind—and her eyes and mine happened to meet.

You know how it is. Gee, she was a peach! She had on a soft dress, kind of a blue stuff and it looked carelessly made, but was well sewed and made and everything. I knew that much. I blushed when she looked right at me and so did she. She was the nicest girl I've ever seen in my life. She wasn't stuck on herself and she could talk proper grammar without being like a school teacher or something like that. What I mean is, she was O. K. I think maybe her father was well-to-do, but not rich to make her chesty because she was his daughter, as some are. Maybe he owned a drug store or a drygoods store in their home town, or something like that. She never told me and I never asked.

My own people are all O. K. too, when you come to that. My grandfather was Welsh and over in the old country, in Wales he was—But never mind that.

The first heat of the first race come off and the young fellow setting there with the two girls left them and went down to make a bet. I knew what he was up to, but he didn't talk big and noisy and let everyone around know he was a sport, as some do. He wasn't that kind. Well, he come back and I heard him tell the two girls what horse he'd bet on, and when the heat was trotted they all half got to their feet and acted in the excited, sweaty way people do when they've got money down on a race, and the horse they bet on is up there pretty close at the end, and they think maybe he'll come on with a rush, but he never does because he hasn't got the old juice in him, come right down to it.

And then, pretty soon, the horses came out for the 2.18 pace and there was a horse in it I knew. He was a horse Bob French had in his string but Bob didn't own him. He was a horse owned by a Mr. Mathers down at Marietta, Ohio.

This Mr. Mathers had a lot of money and owned some coal mines or something, and he had a swell place out in the country, and he was stuck on race horses, but was a Presbyterian or something, and I think more than likely his wife was one, too, maybe a stiffer one than himself. So he never raced his horses hisself, and the story round the Ohio race tracks was that when one of his horses got ready to go to the races he turned him over to Bob French and pretended to his wife he was sold.

So Bob had the horses and he did pretty much as he pleased and you can't blame Bob, at least, I never did. Sometimes he was out to win and sometimes he wasn't. I never cared much about that when I was swiping a horse. What I did want to know was that my horse had the speed and could go out in front, if you wanted him to.

And, as I'm telling you, there was Bob in this race with one of Mr. Mathers' horses, was named "About Ben Ahem" or something like that, and was fast as a streak. He was a gelding and had a mark of 2.21, but could step in .08 or .09.

Because when Burt and I were out, as I've told you, the year before, there was a nigger, Burt knew, worked for Mr. Mathers and we went out there one day when we didn't have no race on at the Marietta Fair and our boss Harry was gone home.

And so everyone was gone to the fair but just this one nigger and he took us all through Mr. Mathers' swell house and he and Burt tapped a bottle of wine Mr. Mathers had hid in his bedroom, back in a closet, without his wife knowing, and he showed us this Ahem horse. Burt was always stuck on being a driver but didn't have much chance to get to the top, being a nigger, and he and the other nigger gulped that whole bottle of wine and Burt got a little lit up.

So the nigger let Burt take this About Ben Ahem and step him a mile in a track Mr. Mathers had all to himself, right there on the farm. And Mr. Mathers had one child, a daughter, kinda sick and not very good looking, and she came home and we had to hustle and get About Ben Ahem stuck back in the barn.

I'm only telling you to get everything straight. At Sandusky, that afternoon I was at the fair, this young fellow with the two girls was fussed, being with the girls and losing his bet. You know how a fellow is that way. One of them was his girl and the other his sister. I had figured that out.

"Gee whizz," I says to myself, "I'm going to give him the dope."

He was mighty nice when I touched him on the shoulder. He and the girls were nice to me right from the start and clear to the end. I'm not blaming them.

And so he leaned back and I give him the dope on About Ben Ahem. "Don't bet a cent on this first heat because he'll go like an oxen hitched to a plow, but when the first heat is over go right down and lay on your pile." That's what I told him.

Well, I never saw a fellow treat any one sweller. There was a fat man sitting beside the little girl, that had looked at me twice by this time, and I at her, and both blushing, and what did he do but have the nerve to turn and ask the fat man to get up and change places with me so I could set with his crowd.

Gee whizz, craps amighty. There I was. What a chump I was to go and get gay up there in the West House bar, and just because that dude was standing there with a cane and that kind of a necktie on, to go and get all balled up and drink that whiskey, just to show off.

Of course she would know, me setting right beside her and letting her smell of my breath. I could have kicked myself right down out of that grand stand and all around that race track and made a faster record than most of the skates of horses they had there that year.

Because that girl wasn't any mutt of a girl. What wouldn't I have give right then for a stick of chewing gum to chew, or a lozenger, or some liquorice, or most anything. I was glad I had those twenty-five cent cigars in my pocket and right away I give that fellow one and lit one myself. Then that fat man got up and we changed places and there I was, plunked right down beside her.

They introduced themselves and the fellow's best girl, he had with him, was named Miss Elinor Woodbury, and her father was a manufacturer of barrels from a place called Tiffin, Ohio. And the fellow himself was named Wilbur Wessen and his sister was Miss Lucy Wessen.

I suppose it was their having such swell names got me off my trolley. A fellow, just because he has been a swipe with a race horse, and works taking care of horses for a man in the teaming, delivery, and storage business, isn't any better or worse than any one else. I've often thought that, and said it too.

But you know how a fellow is. There's something in that kind of nice clothes, and the kind of nice eyes she had, and the way she had looked at me, awhile before, over her brother's shoulder, and me looking back at her, and both of us blushing.

I couldn't show her up for a boob, could I?

I made a fool of myself, that's what I did. I said my name was Walter Mathers from Marietta, Ohio, and then I told all three of them the smashingest lie you ever heard. What I said was that my father owned the horse About Ben Ahem and that he had let him out to this Bob French for racing purposes, because our family was proud and had never gone into racing that way, in our own name, I mean. Then I had got started and they were all leaning over and listening, and Miss Lucy Wessen's eyes were shining, and I went the whole hog.

I told about our place down at Marietta, and about the big stables and the grand brick house we had on a hill, up above the Ohio River, but I knew enough not to do it in no bragging way. What I did was to start things and then let them drag the rest out of me. I acted just as reluctant to tell as I could. Our family hasn't got any barrel factory, and, since I've known us, we've always been pretty poor, but not asking anything of any one at that, and my grandfather, over in Wales—but never mind that.

We set there talking like we had known each other for years and years, and I went and told them that my father had been expecting maybe this Bob French wasn't on the square, and had sent me up to Sandusky on the sly to find out what I could.

And I bluffed it through I had found out all about the 2.18 pace, in which About Ben Ahem was to start.

I said he would lose the first heat by pacing like a lame cow and then he would come back and skin 'em alive after that. And to back up what I said I took thirty dollars out of my pocket and handed it to Mr. Wilbur Wessen and asked him, would he mind, after the first heat, to go down and place it on About Ben Ahem for whatever odds he could get. What I said was that I didn't want Bob French to see me and none of the swipes.

Sure enough the first heat come off and About Ben Ahem went off his stride, up the back stretch, and looked like a wooden horse or a sick one, and come in to be last. Then this Wilbur Wessen went down to the betting place under the grand stand and there I was with the two girls, and when that Miss Woodbury was looking the other way once, Lucy Wessen kinda, with her shoulder you know, kinda touched me. Not just tucking down, I don't mean. You know how a woman can do. They get close, but not getting gay either. You know what they do. Gee whizz.

And then they give me a jolt. What they had done, when I didn't know, was to get together, and they had decided Wilbur Wessen would bet fifty dollars, and the two girls had gone and put in ten dollars each, of their own money, too. I was sick then, but I was sicker later.

About the gelding, About Ben Ahem, and their winning their money, I wasn't worried a lot about that. It come out O.K. Ahem stepped the next three heats like a bushel of spoiled eggs going to market before they could be found out, and Wilbur Wessen had got nine to two for the money. There was something else eating at me.

Because Wilbur come back, after he had bet the money, and after that he spent most of his time talking to that Miss Woodbury, and Lucy Wessen and I was left alone together like on a desert island. Gee, if I'd only been on the square or if there had been any way of getting myself on the square. There ain't any Walter Mathers, like

I said to her and them, and there hasn't ever been one, but if there was, I bet I'd go to Marietta, Ohio, and shoot him to-morrow.

There I was, big boob that I am. Pretty soon the race was over, and Wilbur had gone down and collected our money, and we had a hack down-town, and he stood us a swell supper at the West House, and a bottle of champagne beside.

And I was with that girl and she wasn't saying much, and I wasn't saying much either. One thing I know. She wasn't stuck on me because of the lie about my father being rich and all that. There's a way you know. . . . Craps amighty. There's a kind of girl, you see just once in your life, and if you don't get busy and make hay, then you're gone for good and all, and might as well go jump off a bridge. They give you a look from inside of them somewhere, and it ain't no vamping, and what it means is—you want that girl to be your wife, and you want nice things around her like flowers and swell clothes, and you want her to have the kids you're going to have, and you want good music played and no rag time. Gee whizz.

There's a place over near Sandusky, across a kind of bay, and it's called Cedar Point. And after we had supper we went over to it in a launch, all by ourselves. Wilbur and Miss Lucy and that Miss Woodbury had to catch a ten o'clock train back to Tiffin, Ohio, because, when you're out with girls like that you can't get careless and miss any trains and stay out all night, like you can with some kinds of Janes.

And Wilbur blowed himself to the launch and it cost him fifteen cold plunks, but I wouldn't never have knew if I hadn't listened. He wasn't no tin horn kind of a sport.

Over at the Cedar Point place, we didn't stay around where there was a gang of common kind of cattle at all.

There was big dance halls and dining places for yaps, and there was a beach you could walk along and get where it was dark, and we went there.

She didn't talk hardly at all and neither did I, and I was thinking how glad I was my mother was all right, and always made us kids learn to eat with a fork at table, and not swill soup, and not be noisy and rough like a gang you see around a race track that way.

Then Wilbur and his girl went away up the beach and Lucy and I sat down in a dark place, where there was some roots of old trees the water had washed up, and after that the time, till we had to go back in the launch and they had to catch their trains, wasn't nothing at all. It went like winking your eye.

Here's how it was. The place we were setting in was dark, like I said, and there was the roots from that old stump sticking up like arms, and there was a watery smell, and the night was like—as if you could put your hand out and feel it—so warm and soft and dark and sweet like an orange.

I most cried and I most swore and I most jumped up and danced, I was so mad and happy and sad.

When Wilbur come back from being alone with his girl, and she saw him coming, Lucy she says, "we got to go to the train now," and she was most crying too, but she never knew nothing I knew, and she couldn't be so all busted up. And then, before Wilbur and Miss Woodbury got up to where we was, she put her face up and kissed me quick and put her head up against me and she was all quivering and—Gee whizz.

Sometimes I hope I have cancer and die. I guess you know what I mean. We went in the launch across the bay to the train like that, and it was dark, too. She whispered and said it was like she and I could get out of the boat and walk on the water, and it sounded foolish, but I knew what she meant.

And then quick we were right at the depot, and there was a big gang of yaps, the kind that goes to the fairs, and crowded and milling around like cattle, and how could I tell her? "It won't be long because you'll write and I'll write to you." That's all she said.

I got a chance like a hay barn afire. A swell chance I got.

And maybe she would write me, down at Marietta that way, and the letter would come back, and stamped on the front of it by the U.S.A. "there ain't any such guy," or something like that, whatever they stamp on a letter that way.

And me trying to pass myself off for a bigbug and a swell—to her, as decent a little body as God ever made. Craps amighty—a swell chance I got!

And then the train come in, and she got on it, and Wilbur Wessen he come and shook hands with me, and that Miss Woodbury was nice too and bowed to me, and I at her, and the train went and I busted out and cried like a kid.

Gee, I could have run after that train and made Dan Patch look like a freight train after a wreck but, socks amighty, what was the use? Did you ever see such a fool?

I'll bet you what—if I had an arm broke right now or a train had run over my foot—I wouldn't go to no doctor at all. I'd go set down and let her hurt and hurt—that's what I'd do.

I'll bet you what—if I hadn't a drunk that booze I'd a never been such a boob as to go tell such a lie—that couldn't never be made straight to a lady like her.

I wish I had that fellow right here that had on a Windsor tie and carried a cane. I'd smash him for fair. Gosh darn his eyes. He's a big fool—that's what he is.

And if I'm not another you just go find me one and I'll quit working and be a bum and give him my job. I don't care nothing for working, and earning money, and saving it for no such boob as myself.

The Man's Story

DURING HIS TRIAL for murder and later, after he had been cleared through the confession of that queer little bald chap with the nervous hands, I watched him, fascinated by his continued effort to make something understood.

He was persistently interested in something, having nothing to do with the charge that he had murdered the woman. The matter of whether or not, and by due process of law, he was to be convicted of murder and hanged by the neck until he was dead didn't seem to interest him. The law was something outside his life and he declined to have anything to do with the killing as one might decline a cigarette. "I thank you, I am not smoking at present. I made a bet with a fellow that I could go along without smoking cigarettes for a month."

That is the sort of thing I mean. It was puzzling. Really, had he been guilty and trying to save his neck he couldn't have taken a better line. You see, at first, everyone thought he had done the killing; we were all convinced of it, and then, just because of that magnificent air of indifference, everyone began wanting to save him. When news came of the confession of the crazy little stage-hand everyone broke out into cheers.

He was clear of the law after that but his manner in no way changed. There was, somewhere, a man or a woman who would understand just what he understood and it was important to find that person and talk things over. There was a time, during the trial and immediately afterward, when I saw a good deal of him, and I had this sharp sense of him, feeling about in the darkness trying to find something like a needle or a pin lost on the floor. Well, he was like an old man who cannot find his glasses. He feels in all his pockets and looks helplessly about.

There was a question in my own mind too, in everyone's mind— "Can a man be wholly casual and brutal, in every outward way, at a moment when the one nearest and dearest to him is dying, and at the same time, and with quite another part of himself, be altogether tender and sensitive?"

Anyway it's a story, and once in a while a man likes to tell a story straight out, without putting in any newspaper jargon about beautiful heiresses, cold-blooded murderers and all that sort of tommyrot.

As I picked the story up the sense of it was something like this—

The man's name was Wilson,—Edgar Wilson—and he had come to Chicago from some place to the westward, perhaps from the mountains. He might once have been a sheep herder or something of the sort in the far west, as he had the peculiar abstract air, acquired only by being a good deal alone. About himself and his past he told a good many conflicting stories and so, after being with him for a time, one instinctively discarded the past.

"The devil—it doesn't matter—the man can't tell the truth in that direction.—Let it go," one said to oneself. What was known was that he had come to Chicago from a town in Kansas and that he had run away from the Kansas town with another man's wife.

As to her story, I knew little enough of it. She had been at one time, I imagine, a rather handsome thing, in a big strong upstanding sort of way, but her life, until she met Wilson, had been rather messy. In those dead flat Kansas towns lives have a way of getting ugly and messy without anything very definite having happened to make them so. One can't imagine the reasons—Let it go. It just is so and one can't at all believe the writers of Western tales about the life out there.

To be a little more definite about this particular woman—in her young girlhood her father had got into trouble. He had been some sort of a small official, a travelling agent or something of the sort for an express company, and got arrested in connection with the disappearance of some money. And then, when he was in jail and before his trial, he shot and killed himself. The girl's mother was already dead.

Within a year or two she married a man, an honest enough fellow but from all accounts rather uninteresting. He was a drug clerk and a frugal man and after a short time managed to buy a drug store of his own.

The woman, as I have said, had been strong and well-built but now grew thin and nervous. Still she carried herself well with a sort of air, as it were, and there was something about her that appealed strongly to men. Several men of the seedy little town were smitten by her and wrote her letters, trying to get her to creep out with them at night. You know how such things are done. The letters were unsigned. "You go to such and such a place on Friday evening. If you are willing to talk things over with me carry a book in your hand."

Then the woman made a mistake and told her husband about the receipt of one of the letters and he grew angry and tramped off to the trysting place at night with a shotgun in his hand. When no one appeared he came home and fussed about. He said little mean tentative things. "You must have looked—in a certain way—at the man when he passed you on the street. A man don't grow so bold with a married woman unless an opening has been given him."

The man talked and talked after that, and life in the house must have been gay. She grew habitually silent, and when she was silent the house was silent. They had no children.

Then the man Edgar Wilson came along, going eastward, and stopped over in the town for two or three days. He had at that time a little money and stayed at a small workingmen's boarding-house, near the railroad station. One day he saw the woman walking in the street and followed her to her home and the neighbors saw them standing and talking together for an hour by the front gate and on the next day he came again.

That time they talked for two hours and then she went into the house; got a few belongings and walked to the railroad station with him. They took a train for Chicago and lived there together, apparently very happy, until she died—in a way I am about to try to tell you about. They of course could not be married and during the three years they lived in Chicago he did nothing toward earning their common living. As he had a very small amount of money when they came, barely enough to get them here from the Kansas town, they were miserably poor.

They lived, when I knew about them, over on the North side, in that section of old three- and four-story brick residences that were once the homes of what we call our nice people, but that had afterward gone to the bad. The section is having a kind of rebirth now but for a good many years it rather went to seed. There were these old residences, made into boarding-houses, and with unbelievably dirty lace curtains at the windows, and now and then an utterly disreputable old tumble-down frame house—in one of which Wilson lived with his woman.

The place is a sight! Someone owns it, I suppose, who is shrewd enough to know that in a big city like Chicago no section gets neglected always. Such a fellow must have said to himself, "Well, I'll let the place go. The ground on which the house stands will some day be very valuable but the house is worth nothing. I'll let it go at a low rental and do nothing to fix it up. Perhaps I will get enough out of it to pay my taxes until prices come up."

And so the house had stood there unpainted for years and the windows were out of line and the shingles nearly all off the roof. The second floor was reached by an outside stairway with a handrail that had become just the peculiar grey greasy black that wood can become in a soft-coal-burning city like Chicago or Pittsburgh. One's hand became black when the railing was touched; and the rooms above were altogether cold and cheerless.

At the front there was a large room with a fireplace, from which many bricks had fallen, and back of that were two small sleeping rooms.

Wilson and his woman lived in the place, at the time when the thing happened I am to tell you about, and as they had taken it in May I presume they did not too much mind the cold barrenness of the large front room in which they lived. There was a sagging wooden bed with a leg broken off—the woman had tried to repair it with sticks from a packing box—a kitchen table, that was also used by Wilson as a writing desk, and two or three cheap kitchen chairs.

The woman had managed to get a place as wardrobe woman in a theatre in Randolph Street and they lived on her earnings. It was said she had got the job because some man connected with the theatre, or a company playing there, had a passion for her but one can always pick up stories of that sort about any woman who works about the theatre—from the scrubwoman to the star.

Anyway she worked there and had a reputation in the theatre of being quiet and efficient.

As for Wilson, he wrote poetry of a sort I've never seen before, although, like most newspaper men, I've taken a turn at verse making myself now and then—both of the rhymed kind and the newfangled vers libre sort. I rather go in for the classical stuff myself.

About Wilson's verse—it was Greek to me. Well now, to get right down to hardpan in this matter, it was and it wasn't.

The stuff made me feel just a little bit woozy when I took a whole sheaf of it and sat alone in my room reading it at night. It was all about walls, and deep wells, and great bowls with young trees standing erect in them—and trying to find their way to the light and air over the rim of the bowl.

Queer crazy stuff, every line of it, but fascinating too—in a way. One got into a new world with new values, which after all is I suppose what poetry is all about. There was the world of fact—we all know or think we know—the world of flat buildings and middle-western farms with wire fences about the fields and fordson tractors running up and down, and towns with high schools and advertising billboards, and everything that makes up life—or that we think makes up life.

There was this world, we all walk about in, and then there was this other world, that I have come to think of as Wilson's world—a dim place to me at least—of far-away near places—things taking new and strange shapes, the insides of people coming out, the eyes seeing new things, the fingers feeling new and strange things.

It was a place of walls mainly. I got hold of the whole lot of Wilson's verse by a piece of luck. It happened that I was the first newspaper man who got into the place on the night when the woman's body was found, and there was all his stuff, carefully written out in a sort of child's copy book, and two or three stupid policemen standing about. I just shoved the book under my coat, when they weren't looking, and later, during Wilson's trial, we published some of the more intelligible ones in the paper. It made pretty good newspaper stuff—the poet who killed his mistress,

> "He did not wear his purple coat,
>   For blood and wine are red"—

and all that. Chicago loved it.

To get back to the poetry itself for a moment. I just wanted to explain that all through the book there ran this notion, that men had erected walls about themselves and that all men were perhaps destined to stand forever behind the walls—on which they constantly beat with their fists, or with whatever tools they could get hold of. Wanted to break through to something, you understand. One couldn't quite make out whether there was just one great wall or many little individual walls. Sometimes Wilson put it one way, sometimes another. Men had themselves built the walls and now stood behind them, knowing dimly that beyond the walls there was warmth, light, air, beauty, life in fact—while at the same time, and because of a kind of madness in themselves, the walls were constantly being built higher and stronger.

The notion gives you the fantods a little, doesn't it? Anyway it does me.

And then there was that notion about deep wells, men everywhere constantly digging and digging themselves down deeper and deeper into deep wells. They not wanting to do it, you understand, and no one wanting them to do it, but all the time the thing going on just the same, that is to say the wells getting constantly deeper and deeper, and the voices growing dimmer and dimmer in the distance—and again the light and the warmth of life going away and going away, because of a kind of blind refusal of people to try to understand each other, I suppose.

It was all very strange to me—Wilson's poetry, I mean—when I came to it. Here is one of his things. It is not directly concerned with the walls, the bowl or the deep well theme, as you will see, but it is one we ran in the paper during the trial and a lot of folks rather liked it—as I'll admit I do myself. Maybe putting it in here will give a kind of point to my story, by giving you some sense of the strangeness of the man who is the story's hero. In the book it was called merely "Number Ninety-seven," and it went as follows:

> The firm grip of my fingers on the thin paper of this cigarette is a sign that I am very quiet now. Sometimes it is not so. When I am unquiet I am weak but when I am quiet, as I am now, I am very strong.

> Just now I went along one of the streets of my city and in at a door and came up here, where I am now, lying on a bed and looking out at a window. Very suddenly and completely the knowledge has come to me that I could grip the sides of tall buildings as freely and as easily as I now grip this cigarette. I could hold the building between my fingers, put it to my lips and blow smoke through it. I could blow confusion away. I could blow a thousand people out through the roof of one tall building into the sky, into the unknown. Building after building I could consume, as I consume the cigarettes in this box. I could throw the burning ends of cities over my shoulder and out through a window.

It is not often I get in the state I am now in—so quiet and sure of myself. When the feeling comes over me there is a directness and simplicity in me that makes me love myself. To myself at such times I say strong sweet words.

I am on a couch by this window and I could ask a woman to come here to lie with me, or a man either for that matter.

I could take a row of houses standing on a street, tip them over, empty the people out of them, squeeze and compress all the people into one person and love that person.

Do you see this hand? Suppose it held a knife that could cut down through all the falseness in you. Suppose it could cut down through the sides of buildings and houses where thousands of people now lie asleep.

It would be something worth thinking about if the fingers of this hand gripped a knife that could cut and rip through all the ugly husks in which millions of lives are enclosed.

Well, there is the idea you see, a kind of power that could be tender too. I will quote you just one more of his things, a more gentle one. It is called in the book, "Number Eighty-three."

I am a tree that grows beside the wall. I have been thrusting up and up. My body is covered with scars. My body is old but still I thrust upward, creeping toward the top of the wall.

It is my desire to drop blossoms and fruit over the wall.

I would moisten dry lips.

I would drop blossoms on the heads of children, over the top of the wall.

I would caress with falling blossoms the bodies of those who live on the further side of the wall.

My branches are creeping upward and new sap comes into me out of the dark ground under the wall.

My fruit shall not be my fruit until it drops from my arms, into the arms of the others, over the top of the wall.

And now as to the life led by the man and woman in the large upper room in that old frame house. By a stroke of luck I have recently got rather a line on that by a discovery I have made.

After they had moved into the house—it was only last spring—the theatre in which the woman was employed was dark for a long time and they were more than usually hard up, so the woman tried to pick up a little extra money—to help pay the rent I suppose—by sub-letting the two little back rooms of that place of theirs.

Various people lived in the dark tiny holes, just how I can't make out as there was no furniture. Still there are places in Chicago called "flops" where one may sleep on the floor for five or ten cents and they are more patronized than respectable people know anything about.

What I did discover was a little woman—she wasn't so young but she was hunchbacked and small and it is hard not to think of her as a girl—who once lived in one of the rooms for several weeks. She had a job as ironer in a small hand-laundry in the neighborhood and someone had given her a cheap folding cot. She was a curiously sentimental creature, with the kind of hurt eyes deformed people often have, and I have a fancy she had herself a romantic attachment of a sort for the man Wilson. Anyway I managed to find out a lot from her.

After the other woman's death and after Wilson had been cleared on the murder charge, by the confession of the stage hand, I used to go over to the house where he had lived, sometimes in the late afternoon after our paper had been put to bed for the day. Ours is an afternoon paper and after two o'clock most of us are free.

I found the hunchback girl standing in front of the house one day and began talking with her. She was a gold mine.

There was that look in her eyes I've told you of, the hurt sensitive look. I just spoke to her and we began talking of Wilson. She had lived in one of the rooms at the back. She told me of that at once.

On some days she found herself unable to work at the laundry because her strength suddenly gave out and so, on such days, she stayed in the room, lying on the cot. Blinding headaches came that lasted for hours during which she was almost entirely unconscious of everything going on about her. Then afterward she was quite conscious but for a long time very weak. She wasn't one who is destined to live very long I suppose and I presume she didn't much care.

Anyway, there she was in the room, in that weak state after the times of illness, and she grew curious about the two people in the front room, so she used to get off her cot and go softly in her stockinged feet to the door between the rooms and peek through the keyhole. She had to kneel on the dusty floor to do it.

The life in the room fascinated her from the beginning. Sometimes the man was in there alone, sitting at the kitchen table and writing the stuff he afterward put into the book I collared, and from which I have quoted; sometimes the woman was with him, and again sometimes he was in there alone but wasn't writing. Then he was always walking and walking up and down.

When both people were in the room, and when the man was writing, the woman seldom moved but sat in a chair by one of the windows with her hands crossed. He would write a few lines and then walk up and down talking to himself or to her. When he spoke she did not answer except with her eyes, the crippled girl said. What I gathered of all this from her talk with me, and what is the product of my own imaginings, I confess I do not quite know.

Anyway what I got and what I am trying, in my own way, to transmit to you is a sense of a kind of strangeness in the relationship of the two. It wasn't just a domestic household, a little down on its luck, by any means. He was trying to do something very difficult— with his poetry I presume—and she in her own way was trying to help him.

And of course, as I have no doubt you have gathered from what I have quoted of Wilson's verse, the matter had something to do with the relationships between people—not necessarily between the particular man and woman who happened to be there in that room, but between all peoples.

The fellow had some half-mystic conception of all such things, and before he found his own woman had been going aimlessly about the world looking for a mate. Then he had found the woman in the Kansas town and—he at least thought—things had cleared, for him.

Well, he had the notion that no one in the world could think or feel anything alone, and that people only got into trouble and walled themselves in by trying it, or something of the sort. There was a discord. Things were jangled. Someone, it seems, had to strike a pitch that all voices could take up before the real song of life could begin. Mind you I'm not putting forth any notions of my own. What I am trying to do is to give you a sense of something I got from having read Wilson's stuff, from having known him a little, and from having seen something of the effect of his personality upon others.

He felt, quite definitely, that no one in the world could feel or even think alone. And then there was the notion, that if one tried to think with the mind without taking the body into account, one got all balled-up. True conscious life built itself up like a pyramid. First the body and mind of a beloved one must come into one's thinking and feeling and then, in some mystic way, the bodies and minds of all the other people in the world must come in, must come sweeping in like a great wind—or something of the sort.

Is all this a little tangled up to you, who read my story of Wilson? It may not be. It may be that your minds are more clear than my own and that what I take to be so difficult will be very simple to you.

However, I have to bring up to you just what I can find, after diving down into this sea of motives and impulses—I admit I don't rightly understand.

The hunchback girl felt (or is it my own fancy coloring what she said?)—it doesn't really matter. The thing to get at is what the man Edgar Wilson felt.

He felt, I fancy, that in the field of poetry he had something to express that could never be expressed until he had found a woman who could, in a peculiar and absolute way, give herself in the world of the flesh—and that then there was to be a marriage out of which beauty would come for all people. He had to find the woman who had that power, and the power had to be untainted by self-interest, I fancy. A profound egotist, you see—and he thought he had found what he needed in the wife of the Kansas druggist.

He had found her and had done something to her. What it was I can't quite make out, except that she was absolutely and wholly happy with him, in a strangely inexpressive sort of way.

Trying to speak of him and his influence on others is rather like trying to walk on a tightrope stretched between two tall buildings above a crowded street. A cry from below, a laugh, the honk of an automobile horn, and down one goes into nothingness. One simply becomes ridiculous.

He wanted, it seems, to condense the flesh and the spirit of himself and his woman into his poems. You will remember that in one of the things of his I have quoted he speaks of condensing, of squeezing all the people of a city into one person and of loving that person.

One might think of him as a powerful person, almost hideously powerful. You will see, as you read, how he has got me in his power and is making me serve his purpose.

And he had caught and was holding the woman in his grip. He had wanted her—quite absolutely, and had taken her—as all men, perhaps, want to do with their women, and don't quite dare. Perhaps too she was in her own way greedy and he was making actual love to her always day and night, when they were together and when they were apart.

I'll admit I am confused about the whole matter myself. I am trying to express something I have felt, not in myself, nor in the words that came to me from the lips of the hunchback girl whom, you will remember, I left kneeling on the floor in that back room and peeking through a keyhole.

There she was, you see, the hunchback, and in the room before her were the man and woman and the hunchback girl also had fallen under the power of the man Wilson. She also was in love with him—there can be no doubt of that. The room in which she knelt was dark and dusty. There must have been a thick accumulation of dust on the floor.

What she said—or if she did not say the words what she made me feel was that the man Wilson worked in the room, or walked up and down in there before his woman, and that, while he did that, his woman sat in the chair, and that there was in her face, in her eyes, a look—

He was all the time making love to her, and his making love to her in just that abstract way, was a kind of love-making with all people, and that was possible because the woman was as purely physical as he was something else. If all this is meaningless to you, at least it wasn't to the hunchback girl—who certainly was uneducated and never would have set herself up as having any special powers of understanding. She knelt in the dust, listening, and looking in at the keyhole, and in the end she came to feel that the man, in whose presence she had never been and whose person had never in any way touched her person, had made love to her also.

She had felt that and it had gratified her entire nature. One might say it had satisfied her. She was what she was and it had made life worth living for her.

Minor things happened in the room and one may speak of them.

For example, there was a day in June, a dark warm rainy day. The hunchback girl was in her room, kneeling on the floor, and Wilson and his woman were in their room.

Wilson's woman had been doing a family washing, and as it could not be dried outdoors she had stretched ropes across the room and had hung the clothes inside.

When the clothes were all hung Wilson came from walking outside in the rain and going to the desk sat down and began to write.

He wrote for a few minutes and then got up and went about the room, and in walking a wet garment brushed against his face.

He kept right on walking and talking to the woman but as he walked and talked he gathered all the clothes in his arms and going to the little landing at the head of the stairs outside, threw them down into the muddy yard below. He did that and the woman sat without moving or saying anything until he had gone back to his desk, then she went down the stairs, got the clothes and washed them again—and it was only after she had done that and when she was again hanging them in the room above that he appeared to know what he had done.

While the clothes were being rewashed he went for another walk and when she heard his footsteps on the stairs the hunchback girl ran to the keyhole. As she knelt there, and as he came into the room, she could look directly into his face. "He was like a puzzled child for a moment and then, although he said nothing, the tears began to run down his cheeks," she said. That happened and then the woman, who was at the moment re-hanging the clothes, turned and saw him. She had her arm filled with clothes but dropped them on the floor and ran to him. She half knelt, the hunchback girl said, and putting her arms about his body and looking up into his face pleaded with him. "Don't. Don't be hurt. Believe me I know everything. Please don't be hurt," was what she said.

And now as to the story of the woman's death. It happened in the fall of that year.

In the place where she was sometimes employed—that is to say in the theatre—there was this other man, the little half-crazed stage-hand who shot her.

He had fallen in love with her and, like the men in the Kansas town from which she came, had written her several silly notes of which she said nothing to Wilson. The letters weren't very nice and some of them, the most unpleasant ones, were by some twist of the fellow's mind, signed with Wilson's name. Two of them were afterwards found on her person and were brought in as evidence against Wilson during his trial.

And so the woman worked in the theatre and the summer had passed and on an evening in the fall there was to be a dress rehearsal at the theatre and the woman went there, taking Wilson with her. It was a fall day, such as we sometimes have in Chicago, cold and wet and with a heavy fog lying over the city.

The dress rehearsal did not come off. The star was ill, or something of the sort happened, and Wilson and his woman sat about, in the cold empty theatre, for an hour or two and then the woman was told she could go for the night.

She and Wilson walked across the city, stopping to get something to eat at a small restaurant. He was in one of the abstract silent moods common to him. No doubt he was thinking of the things he wanted to express in the poetry I have tried to tell you about. He went along, not seeing the woman beside him, not seeing the people drifting up to them and passing them in the streets. He went along in that way and she—

She was no doubt then as she always was in his presence—silent and satisfied with the fact that she was with him. There was nothing he could think or feel that did not take her into account. The very blood flowing up through his body was her blood too. He had made her feel that, and she was silent and satisfied as he went along, his body walking beside her but his fancy groping its way through the land of high walls and deep wells.

They had walked from the restaurant, in the Loop District, over a bridge to the North Side, and still no words passed between them.

When they had almost reached their own place the stagehand, the small man with the nervous hands who had written the notes, appeared out of the fog, as though out of nowhere, and shot the woman.

That was all there was to it. It was as simple as that.

They were walking, as I have described them, when a head flashed up before the woman in the midst of the fog, a hand shot out, there was the quick abrupt sound of a pistol shot and then the absurd little stage-hand, he with the wrinkled impotent little old woman's face—then he turned and ran away.

All that happened, just as I have written it and it made no impression at all on the mind of Wilson. He walked along as though nothing had happened and the woman, after half falling, gathered herself together and managed to continue walking beside him, still saying nothing.

They went thus, for perhaps two blocks, and had reached the foot of the outer stairs that led up to their place when a policeman came running, and the woman told him a lie. She told him some story about a struggle between two drunken men, and after a moment of talk the policeman went away, sent away by the woman in a direction opposite to the one taken by the fleeing stage-hand.

They were in the darkness and the fog now and the woman took her man's arm while they climbed the stairs. He was as yet—as far as I will ever be able to explain logically—unaware of the shot, and of the fact that she was dying, although he had seen and heard everything. What the doctors said, who were put on the case afterwards, was that a cord or muscle, or something of the sort that controls the action of the heart, had been practically severed by the shot.

She was dead and alive at the same time, I should say.

Anyway the two people marched up the stairs, and into the room above, and then a really dramatic and lovely thing happened. One wishes that the scene, with just all its connotations, could be played out on a stage instead of having to be put down in words.

The two came into the room, the one dead but not ready to acknowledge death without a flash of something individual and lovely, that is to say, the one dead while still alive and the other alive but at the moment dead to what was going on.

The room into which they went was dark but, with the sure instinct of an animal, the woman walked across the room to the fireplace, while the man stopped and stood some ten feet from the door—thinking and thinking in his peculiarly abstract way. The fireplace was filled with an accumulation of waste matter, cigarette ends—the man was a hard smoker—bits of paper on which he had scribbled—the rubbishy accumulation that gathers about all such fellows as Wilson. There was all of this quickly combustible material, stuffed into the fireplace, on this—the first cold evening of the fall.

And so the woman went to it, and found a match somewhere in the darkness, and touched the pile off.

There is a picture that will remain with me always—just that—the barren room and the blind unseeing man standing there, and the woman kneeling and making a little flare of beauty at the last. Little flames leaped up. Lights crept and danced over the walls. Below, on the floor of the room, there was a deep well of darkness in which the man, blind with his own purpose, was standing.

The pile of burning papers must have made, for a moment, quite a glare of light in the room and the woman stood for a moment, beside the fireplace, just outside the glare of light.

And then, pale and wavering, she walked across the light, as across a lighted stage, going softly and silently toward him. Had she also something to say? No one will ever know. What happened was that she said nothing.

She walked across to him and, at the moment she reached him, fell down on the floor and died at his feet, and at the same moment the little fire of papers died. If she struggled before she died, there on the floor, she struggled in silence. There was no sound. She had fallen and lay between him and the door that led out to the stairway and to the street.

It was then Wilson became altogether inhuman—too much so for my understanding.

The fire had died and the woman he had loved had died.

And there he stood looking into nothingness, thinking—God knows—perhaps of nothingness.

He stood a minute, five minutes, perhaps ten. He was a man who, before he found the woman, had been sunk far down into a deep sea of doubt and questionings. Before he found the woman no expression had ever come from him. He had perhaps just wandered from place to place, looking at people's faces, wondering about people, wanting to come close to others and not knowing how. The woman had been able to lift him up to the surface of the sea of life for a time, and with her he had floated on the surface of the sea, under the sky, in the sunlight. The woman's warm body—given to him in love—had been as a boat in which he had floated on the surface of the sea, and now the boat had been wrecked and he was sinking again, back into the sea.

All of this had happened and he did not know—that is to say he did not know, and at the same time he did know.

He was a poet, I presume, and perhaps at the moment a new poem was forming itself in his mind.

At any rate he stood for a time, as I have said, and then he must have had a feeling that he should make some move, that he should if possible save himself from some disaster about to overtake him.

He had an impulse to go to the door, and by way of the stairway, to go down stairs and into the street—but the body of the woman was between him and the door.

What he did and what, when he later told of it, sounded so terribly cruel to others, was to treat the woman's dead body as one might treat a fallen tree in the darkness in a forest. First he tried to push the body aside with his foot and then as that seemed impossible, he stepped awkwardly over it.

He stepped directly on the woman's arm. The discolored mark where his heel landed was afterward found on the body.

He almost fell, and then his body righted itself and he went walking, marched down the rickety stairs and went walking in the streets.

By chance the night had cleared. It had grown colder and a cold wind had driven the fog away. He walked along, very nonchalantly, for several blocks. He walked along as calmly as you, the reader, might walk, after having had lunch with a friend.

As a matter of fact he even stopped to make a purchase at a store. I remember that the place was called "The Whip." He went in, bought himself a package of cigarettes, lighted one and stood a moment, apparently listening to a conversation going on among several idlers in the place.

And then he strolled again, going along smoking the cigarette and thinking of his poem no doubt. Then he came to a moving picture theatre.

That perhaps touched him off. He also was an old fireplace, stuffed with old thoughts, scraps of unwritten poems—God knows what rubbish! Often he had gone at night to the theatre, where the woman was employed, to walk home with her, and now the people were coming out of a small moving-picture house. They had been in there seeing a play called "The Light of the World."

Wilson walked into the midst of the crowd, lost himself in the crowd, smoking his cigarette, and then he took off his hat, looked anxiously about for a moment, and suddenly began shouting in a loud voice.

He stood there, shouting and trying to tell the story of what had happened in a loud voice, and with the uncertain air of one trying to remember a dream. He did that for a moment and then, after running a little way along the pavement, stopped and began his story again. It was only after he had gone thus, in short rushes, back along the street to the house and up the rickety stairway to where the woman was lying—the crowd following curiously at his heels—that a policeman came up and arrested him.

He seemed excited at first but was quiet afterwards and he laughed at the notion of insanity, when the lawyer who had been retained for him, tried to set up the plea in court.

As I have said his action, during his trial, was confusing to us all, as he seemed wholly uninterested in the murder and in his own fate. After the confession of the man who had fired the shot he seemed to feel no resentment toward him either. There was something he wanted, having nothing to do with what had happened.

There he had been, you see, before he found the woman, wandering about in the world, digging himself deeper and deeper into the deep wells he talked about in his poetry, building the wall between himself and all us others constantly higher and higher.

He knew what he was doing but he could not stop. That's what he kept talking about, pleading with people about. The man had come up out of the sea of doubt, had grasped for a time the hand of the woman, and with her hand in his had floated for a time upon the surface of life—but now he felt himself again sinking down into the sea.

His talking and talking, stopping people in the street and talking, going into people's houses and talking, was I presume but an effort, he was always afterward making, not to sink back forever into the sea, it was the struggle of a drowning man I dare say.

At any rate I have told you the man's story—have been compelled to try to tell you his story. There was a kind of power in him, and the power has been exerted over me as it was exerted over the woman from Kansas and the unknown hunchback girl, kneeling on the floor in the dust and peering through a keyhole.

Ever since the woman died we have all been trying and trying to drag the man Wilson back out of the sea of doubt and dumbness into which we feel him sinking deeper and deeper—and to no avail.

It may be I have been impelled to tell his story in the hope that by writing of him I may myself understand. Is there not a possibility that with understanding would come also the strength to thrust an arm down into the sea and drag the man Wilson back to the surface again?